THE LIGHT AT THE
END OF THE WORMHOLE

A novel

The Infinite Charter Series:

The Light at the End of the Wormhole (2014)

The Gallery of God's Wrath (2015)

The Dark Side of the Sun (TBA)

Copyright © 2014 Brandon M. Stephens
Cover art courtesy of 99designs

Published by Wordsmith Wonderland

ISBN-13: 9780990746904
ISBN-10: 0990746909

Dedicated to God, Mom, Dad, Sis, sis, and countless others
who have offered words, sights, and sounds of
encouragement, support, and inspiration.
Thank you.

— 01 —

The Light cast no shadows as it thrashed against the confines of its glass prison. Sometimes it settled, as if exhausted, only to begin again seconds later. With no mouth to scream or eyes to weep, color and intensity were its only means of expression. Its struggle for freedom painted the walls every shade imaginable.

In the beginning, the Light was called "quintessence," the fifth element; the human element. That is what the language of the Infinite Charter said, deep within its miles of text. The Light was formless, yet took many shapes, and shaped many things. It had been there all along, residing in the heart of every man, woman, and child, yet its discovery changed the world.

Clyde Evans had seen hundreds of lightkeepers, perhaps thousands. A decade of hunting the Reapers who filled them taught him not to stare into the device, especially when it was "occupied." A single glance fostered sympathy and Hunters weren't allowed to sympathize.

If Clyde stared long enough, he might forget this was currency, plain and simple. Light existed only to be sold for Solaran blessings. It was a unit of exchange, nothing more and nothing less. It had no feelings. It didn't care that it was being sucked out of people's bodies, stored in keepers, and exchanged for warp drives and terraformers. One must not humanize this human element. The shifting colors were just random quantum anomalies.

At least that's what he'd been told. That's what he believed. That's what the Infinite Charter *told him* to believe... and one must never question the Charter.

Then again, the Infinite Charter said a lot of things, most of which Clyde couldn't be bothered to remember because they didn't pertain to his job... which is ironic because enforcing the Charter *is* his job. He exists to correct those who think the Charter is just a piece of paper. It is an institution, a way of life.

Clyde's current target, Brock Mason, was in dire need of correction. Standing nearly seven feet tall, Mason was a hulking wall of genetically-engineered muscle, but he hadn't always been that way. In the years since he'd gone rogue, he grew from a brittle twig to a battle tank. Somewhere in his grief-stricken mind he got the idea that he would "make them pay" and began to physically alter himself to fit this new modus operandi.

Mason went off the grid for five years and came back *different*. Bigger and angrier, mostly. As usual, Clyde received a thorough dossier when he was ordered to knock the treads off this behemoth, but sitting face to face with him put it all into harsh perspective. Height and weight are mere numbers, but death is a very real thing and Mason had already killed five Hunters. Everyone who went after him just *disappeared*.

Clyde wouldn't mind disappearing. *But I'll do that on my own terms, thanks.*

Something didn't feel right. As he watched Brock Mason drum his thick fingers on the tabletop, leaving fat prints in the dust, Clyde just knew the man was mulling over how many ways he could rip a Hunter in half. The Solaran Galactic Registry had no shortage of Hunters to throw at the problem. He would not be missed.

They also had no shortage of Reapers, which made Clyde wonder why they wanted Mason captured *alive*. They were both expendable, worthless shells filled with valuable Light.

"Did you come alone?" Mason asked, snapping Clyde out of his reverie. Rule number one: never let the other guy begin the negotiations.

Clyde nodded to the window, where heavy raindrops from a sky the color of cold steel thumped the panes so hard he could scarcely hear the police cruisers idling outside, or the splash of officers' boots in the alley three stories below as they took positions around the exits and rusting fire escapes. The building was surrounded.

Rule number two: never rendezvous with a killer alone.

"I don't mean *them*," Mason corrected. "Nevermind the humans, I don't need humans. Are there more like *us* out there?" He donned a smile that could scare the scales off a snake. "I'm building an army. I need gifted people."

Fortunately, Clyde was no snake. "Scions constitute less than one percent of the total population and you're in no position to be so picky," he said with a friendly smile. "Anyway, if you want to convince someone to join your cause, I'm all you've got... but I'm here to deliver the terms of your surrender, not join whatever flavor of the week revolution you're starting. Trust me, Brock, these things never end well for people like you."

Mason leaned back, having seemingly lost interest. His rusty, cushionless chair groaned under the strain. His clenched fist rested protectively near the lightkeeper.

"Did you know, in the early days, we used to do it by hand?" Mason said. "We didn't need keepers. A Scion would just lay hands on someone and *pull* the Light out of 'em, like stealing the glow from a lightbulb. Every Scion was trained to do it. The ability to manipulate Light is in our blood. Only the chosen few can wield that power." He grinned. "But I guess that was too barbaric, too visceral, so they gave us lightkeepers. Makes it seem less brutal when you've got a shiny piece of tech in your hands, don't it?"

Clyde shrugged. "Cool story. It'd be cooler if it were true. Now, let's talk about your surrender..."

"It *is* true," Mason said proudly. "They created the first Scions to give them what they need. *We* enforce their new world order. The whole thing crumbles if *we* choose to resist! Light belongs to humans. I won't bottle it and deliver it to the Solarans anymore." He drilled a finger into the tabletop, punctuating every syllable: "You've got a decision to make, Hunter. You either walk outta here a free man, like me, or you don't walk out at all. Choose."

"I see," Clyde said with a slow nod. "Look, Mason, here's what's going to happen. You're gonna turn yourself *and* that Light in for processing. A few weeks or months from now, you'll be back on duty and glad you're not dead or worse. That's the closest you'll ever get to freedom. Frankly, you ought to be thankful the Registry even wants you back."

"Not gonna happen," Mason said, his voice low, deep, and subtly threatening, like the growl of a lion when an inferior predator nears its kill. His enormous palm slid over the lightkeeper, smothering its glow.

"What's done is done," Clyde reasoned. "Holding on to her Light won't bring her back, Brock. You can't give it back once taken. They never should've given you that assignment. They should've found some other Reaper, someone who wasn't as close to her, and-"

"It was a loyalty test," Mason said. "Why else would they ask me to purge her? Not just harvest a little, oh no, they told me to take it *all*... and I was stupid enough, loyal enough, to do it."

The look of pure hatred in Mason's eyes as he recounted his last order would've been enough to make a lesser man turn back.

But the weight of duty – or was it loyalty – pinned Clyde to his seat and kept him at the negotiation table.

The word "Hunter" had never sat right with Clyde Evans. He preferred to think of himself as a shepherd, bringing lost sheep back into to the fold. This is not what he was told. This is what he told himself, to make the job a little easier, to make himself feel like the good guy. It worked, most of the time. At the end of the day, he usually felt good about what he was forced to do.

Unfortunately, it was barely noon. The end of the day was still a long way off.

"No one else gets reaped," Mason said after a long, dark pause, "Even if I have to kill every Reaper with my bare hands. Every Hunter, too, if that's what it takes."

"That would take bigger hands than yours."

"No, just lots of small ones," Mason said as his grip tightened around the lightkeeper, like an iron vise. "I gave you a choice, Hunter. What's it gonna be?"

"No, *I* gave *you* a choice. The Registry wants you back and they're willing to strike this whole thing from the books if you just come in peacefully," Clyde said, being the good shepherd. "Trust me, there's no happy ending for a Reaper who won't reap. Don't throw your life away, Brock."

"Still trying to talk me down, eh? They trained you well, dog. You won't bite what you were told to fetch."

"We know you've been planning to bomb a dozen Light collection centers all across the eastern seaboard," Clyde said. "She wouldn't want that, Brock."

"Watch it," Brock said, pulling the lightkeeper in closer. "Don't talk about my wife like she ain't here. I'm warning you, keep her name out your mouth, Hunter."

"Whatever's in that keeper isn't your wife," Clyde said flatly. "It's Solaran property, the same as you and I. Anne Mason is *dead. Dead.* The sooner you accept that, the sooner we can-"

The first warning was the last.

Clyde instantly found himself at the other end of the room, slumped against the wall, lying in the pile of splintered wood and twisted metal that had once been their negotiating table. Through the stinging smoke, he could vaguely see Mason standing, with the flickering lightkeeper in his hands.

Much later, Clyde realized there'd been an explosion. In the heat of the moment, he thought he'd been sucker punched by a freight train and tossed across the room. But when Mason's eyes locked on him, one thought ricocheted through the Hunter's mind:

He's going to do it again.

Driven by raw instinct, Clyde scrambled away on his hands and knees as a second explosion ripped a hole in the wall where he'd been. The blast lifted and ragdolled him through an open doorway and into another room of the tiny apartment. He thumped his head against a rusty bed frame and lay dazed for a moment. As the debris from the second blast settled, he heard heavy footsteps fleeing the scene, followed by another explosion in a distant room of the abandoned tenement. His target was getting away.

Clyde had half a mind to stay there and accept defeat, but he'd failed too many missions as it was. Too many more and they would send Hunters after him. That and the panicked cops barking in his earpiece drove him onward. Clyde tapped his communicator and told them he was still alive and to hold their positions, while he dealt with the situation. This was a battle between Scions.

Mason was gone and the lightkeeper with him. Clyde muttered curses under his breath as he staggered through the destroyed room, crossing the rubble where their friendly chat had literally blown up in his face. The window had been blasted from its frame and driving rain poured through the gaping hole.

With the ability to manipulate Light came the ability to manipulate the laws of physics. The same substance that allowed a starship to defy gravity and surpass the speed of light, allowed men like Brock Mason to blow stuff up on command. Every Scion had a special gift. Some were dangerous, some merely strange, but all were closely watched and regulated. The Registry existed to keep such people under control.

Clyde knew Mason's gift was fire-based. Fire was nothing more than a rampant chemical reaction and starting them was one of the most common gifts. He knew the man could accelerate molecular activity to the point of ignition, but never expected Mason had evolved to the point of being able to detonate objects with such force and speed. There was nothing about it in his dossier and the Registry *never* overlooked such things. Most Scions stabilized in their mid-twenties. By then, the Registry had run them through the ringer and thoroughly documented everything they could do. But Mason was thirty-five. The old dog had learned a new trick...

Clyde reached the hall and drew his sidearm. He checked the magazine and power cell, shoved them into the receiver, and thumbed the settings down to "stun." The gun's aperture narrowed to a pinpoint, to fire electrically-charged needles, rather than bullets. Armed, Clyde headed after the man, who already had a thirty second lead.

The abandoned apartment block was a victim of the urban decay consuming the Eastern Sprawl. District 19 lay somewhere on the inland edge of former New York State, but only nostalgists and historians called the states by their names anymore. With nearly two-thirds of the mainland covered in heavy urban sprawl, where NYC was knocking on St. Louis's door, the old words lost meaning.

Thanks to Solaran intervention, shortages of food, healthcare, construction materials, and energy became things of the past.

Cities spread like a virus right up until people started moving off-world, leaving behind vast concrete jungles owned by absentee landlords and corporations that had folded decades ago, giving rebels like Mason plenty of places to hide.

Clyde carefully made his way down the darkened hall. He could feel Mason was near. Not near enough to be an immediate threat, but still in the building, on the same level. That put three stories between him and the ground floor, three stories to catch this guy before he gets outside and starts murdering cops.

Clyde turned at the sound of footsteps and his senses flared. He sensed a Scion's gift activating nearby, but no one was there. A half second later, whatever he'd sensed was gone. A ghost. He found fresh shoeprints in the dust, too small to be Mason's, but the trail ended as abruptly as it'd began. Someone or something else was in the building.

Another blast shuddered the walls. *Below me*, Clyde thought and quickly moved toward the stairs, gun in hand. He thumbed the safety off as he stepped into the dark stairwell and began to make his way down. Rain beat against a high, narrow window, lined with iron bars. Over the rhythmic patter of the drops, he heard a man yelling.

Mason called out in a rage as another explosion rocked the building. Clyde gripped the railing and stooped to watch Mason from the shadows of the stairwell. The giant was crouching awkwardly in the middle of the hall amidst a pile of pulverized drywall and rebar. He appeared to be favoring one leg as he looked around in bewilderment, searching for the target of his latest detonation. Clearly, he'd missed his mark.

"Hunter couldn't handle me himself, could he?" Mason barked at a smoking hole in the wall. "Had to bring a friend, huh? Come out and face me! Where are you!? I'll level the whole damn building if I have to!"

Clyde felt something again. There was someone near, armed with a gift. He was sure of it now, but the sensation came and went erratically, blinking in and out of existence. In all his years as a Hunter, he'd never experienced such a thing. His ability to detect the presence of other Scions was unique. He could sense when a gift was being used, but never before had his senses been confounded in such a way.

None of that mattered right now. Mason was chasing a ghost and Clyde couldn't let the distraction go to waste. If Mason carried on like this, he might actually bring the building down, intentionally or otherwise. Clyde stepped out of the stairwell, weapon raised. Mason was still down, clearly injured, and Clyde resolved to keep him that way.

"It's over, Brock. Stay down, eyes on the floor," the Hunter warned as he approached. Mason's gaze darted to meet him and his gift flared in retaliation... but nothing happened. No explosion. Not even a spark. The look in his eyes spoke of pure rage and an unadulterated desire to incinerate Clyde Evans, but nothing happened.

"It's over," Clyde said again.

As he moved closer, he noticed the nine inch hunting knife embedded in Mason's left thigh and the slashes on his forearms. Clyde lowered his weapon as Mason's pants leg grew redder by the second.

"What did you do to me? Why won't my power work?" Mason growled, just as Clyde turned his attention to the shadows all around them, searching for the phantom assailant who'd wounded his target.

"I certainly didn't do *that*," the Hunter said, with a nod to the knife. "But I'm blocking your gift. That's what *my* gift does. You slipped a few by me, but you won't be doing it again, Brock. Like I said, 'it's over.'"

The large man begrudgingly lowered himself to the floor in surrender, while Clyde swept through the nearest rooms, searching for the rogue attacker. But he found no one, only more shoeprints in the dust, all of which ended abruptly as if the intruder had learned to fly… or vanished entirely.

"If you can block gifts, you should've joined us," Mason groaned. "We'd be untouchable if we had someone like you. Scions are the only weapon the Solarans have. Take that away from them and the whole system-"

"Quiet. I'm saving your life. Whatever you're trying to do, it's not gonna work. Give it up before you get yourself and a lot of innocent people killed," Clyde said as he returned to Mason's side and crouched before him, ignoring the eerie sensation that they were being watched. "Paramedics are on the way. Apply pressure to the wound and don't remove the knife or you'll bleed out… not that I need to tell you that." He winced at the thick blade buried hilt-deep in the man's thigh. "Whoever did this, he sure got you good."

"*She*," Brock corrected and the fury in his eyes made it very clear no one was going to touch the knife until he was dead or heavily sedated.

Clyde backed away. "If the Registry wants you as badly as they seem, they'll spare no expense in fixing you up," he said, as reassurance. "You'll live to reap another day."

"Never," the man hissed between his teeth. "I ain't going back. I'll pull this knife out and-"

"You're going back." Clyde spoke solemnly as he stood over his target and found the lightkeeper, half-buried in soot and ash, yet still shining brightly. He knelt to pick it up and the device's lock responded to his touch – the touch of a Scion; the touch of one who serves the Solaran regime. "You're going back… but she doesn't have to. If you want to save her, there's only one thing I can do for you."

With a decisive twist of the handle, he released the lightkeeper's contents. The Light spilled out, flooding the hall with a thousand luminous hues, as diverse as humanity itself. It flowed around and between the two men, like wind through a forest, before expanding outward.

The Light cast no shadows. Its brightness was such that it was both painful to behold and impossible to look away from. Like blood in water, it grew fainter as it dispersed, until at last, it was gone, and darkness returned.

12   B. Stephens

– 02 –

Clyde pushed his way into the District 19 precinct headquarters, a windowless, ten story dagger of smooth stone and steel, home to about fifty Scions, their handlers, and another two dozen or so visiting operatives, all carefully micromanaged by the Solaran Registry.

When not getting blown up, Clyde spends most of his time in his tiny square office, which doubles as Registry-controlled housing. He lives and works in the same place, because his work is his life.

From this appointed space, his only view of the outside world is a wall-to-wall monitor, which only shows what he is permitted to see, usually a clear blue sky or a bustling cityscape. Clyde's frequent petitions to have it display what's actually outside have been frequently denied.

Like most Registry installations, D19's HQ is designed to be a paragon of order, the aesthetic equivalent of a hospital clean room. The blinding lights, the purity of the décor, and the monolithic weight of the black marble desk guarding the entryway had always made him feel like an errant dust bunny wandering into a place that had just been swept *very* thoroughly. Today, he felt it more than ever, because he knew he'd dropped the ball on the Mason case.

Clyde passed through the silvery metal arches of the Light scanners, which read his unique aura in half a nanosecond and confirmed he "belonged." As if that weren't enough, he also knew at least one of the two Scions at the guards' station was a mind reader. Clyde could feel the man's gift performing the mental equivalent of a pat down on his brain. At least it wasn't a full cavity search.

Meanwhile, the second guard just sat there, menacingly placid. Clyde had no idea what that guy's gift was, but he imagined it was something to hurt people who *didn't* belong. After his dance with Brock Mason the previous day, Clyde was hurting enough already, so he made his way toward the elevators. To his surprise, the man spoke:

"While you were away, you received a call, via an encrypted channel," the guard said to Clyde's back. "It was the same person. Twice."

Clyde half-turned. "What for?"

"That's above my security clearance."

"Then it's above mine, too."

"Obviously not," the guard said. His tone made it quite clear that this was never intended to be a two-way conversation. "I was told to notify you he will call again. You have been notified. Move along, Mr. Evans."

Well, that settled the matter. Clyde continued to his office, where he promptly shut the door, and sank deep into his high-backed chair. Years of working from the same room, behind the same desk, trapped between the same four walls, had molded the seat to his ass in a very special way. After the thrashing he'd taken, he just wanted to sit there and do nothing for the rest of the day, possibly for the rest of his life.

But he had three other active cases, and more waiting in the queue, *and* a shady caller who might ring again at any moment.

Now that Mason was in custody, that was one job he could strike off the list, but there were always more.

The call indicator flashed just as Clyde was beginning to like the relative solitude of his room. The timing was too perfect to be a coincidence. A flashing hologram display hovering an inch above the surface of his desktop displayed a line of scrambled digits, where there should be a name and number or digital address. Some of the characters weren't even digits, but strange symbols.

Clyde's hand hovered over the 'answer' button on the user interface. Against his better judgment, he pressed it. The video feed activated by default, but when the caller's image flickered to life, there was only a wall of static and a scrolling marquee of error codes.

"Hello," Clyde said hesitantly, unsure if the audio was functioning.

"This is the office of Clyde Evans, yes?" said a male voice, slightly deep. The words were slow, deliberate, and enunciated with utter precision, as if by machine.

"Yes, I'm him. To whom am I speaking?"

"I am interested in hiring you, Mr. Evans. Are you available for work?"

Strange thing to say to a Registry-owned Scion, but Clyde played along: "Only when it's permitted. Whatever you need done, I'd have to clear it with my handler," he said. "And to whom am I speaking?" he asked again.

"Please, allow me to rephrase my line of inquiry," the stranger recanted. "I have connections high inside the Registry. *Very* high. It is permitted, Mr. Evans. That is not the question. The question is, 'are you interested?'"

"That's all well and good, but *who are you*, sir?"

There was a brief pause, during which Clyde could hear movement; a slight shuffling, clicking, and the muffled groan of something mechanical. Due to the dry tone, he was beginning to suspect the caller might be speaking through a synthesizer or translator, but the ambient noise was proof of a physical entity on the other end. Clyde could hear each shift in posture.

"Hear me out. I have need of you and I suspect you have need of me," the caller said. "You have a singular talent, Mr. Evans, but I would not have called if I did not feel we have something to offer one another. Though your ranking is low, your potential is high, and I have need of your unique gift."

Clyde leaned back, caught slightly off-guard by this. What did this man know of his record or his gift? Neither was public knowledge.

"As I said, I have relevant connections within the Registry," the stranger continued.

"If you know my record, you'll know I've failed more missions than not," Clyde said. "The people I hunt tend to get away. I'm only a level three."

"Yes, but your gift is much stronger than that." There was more subtle movement on the other end; a whirring of servos, the creaking of a chair. "You are where you are now because of your lackluster performance, not a lack of potential. This may come as a surprise, but you are up for administrative review, Mr. Evans… and possible termination."

Clyde sat up straight. "My handler would've given me a heads up if things were that bad. If this is a joke, it's not funny. Who is this?"

"Your handler doesn't know about your situation yet and once she does, it will be too late. You know how this goes, Mr. Evans. Before the week's end, you will be summoned before a council of your peers, where you will be deemed unfit for duty. Your name will be added to the pool and a Hunter or Reaper will be ordered to harvest your Light for the glory of the Solaran empire. By the time you are notified through the typical channels, these events will already be in motion."

"And what does that make you, an atypical channel?" Clyde said. "People on the inside don't call it an 'empire.' I've only heard that word from rebels and malcontents. Are you threatening me? I haven't done anything to deserve-"

"That is precisely the problem: you have not *done* anything. Your gift is an exceptional one, Mr. Evans, but the Registry is an organization which demands your all... and you've been holding back. I know why. I know *why* you sometimes let your targets slip away. I know *why* you released the Light."

"The keeper malfunctioned," Clyde said quickly.

"Yes, of course it did. You are not alone, Mr. Evans. There are others like you, who secretly despise this system, but continue to play their part. It need not be this way. I think you would be more comfortable working for me."

"I'm going to hang up unless you identify yourself," Clyde said, his finger hovering over the button to let the man know he wasn't kidding. "Something tells me you're not an outsider. I almost want to believe you. Is this a test? Is my loyalty being questioned?"

"I do not question that which I know the answer to."

Clyde firmly depressed the button.

"That won't change anything," the caller said, miraculously still there.

Clyde mashed the button twice more and began searching for a way to cut the power.

"Are you going to let me finish, Mr. Evans?"

"Are you going to let me stop you?"

"I cannot, in good conscience."

Clyde groaned. He couldn't end the call. He hoped someone, somewhere was recording this, but his gut told him this guy was ten steps ahead of him on all fronts. He even considered leaving the room, but where could he go?

"What do you want from me?" Clyde asked wearily.

"I have moved beyond the stage of merely wanting your assistance, Mr. Evans. I *need* you." The stranger shifted positions again, electric motors whirring with each movement. "I am not here to blackmail or threaten you, but I want you to know the lay of the land before you embark on the path I have set forth for you."

"Well, what do you need from me?" Clyde said.

"We need one another," The Stranger corrected. "Just like you and every other Scion, Mr. Mason is Registry property – Solaran property. You damaged that property. I'm sure they'll deduct his medical bills and all other damages from your pay, which means the bounty from your latest capture will be rather... underwhelming."

"Thanks, but I'm well aware of their billing practices," Clyde said flatly.

"I have deposited one hundred thousand credits into your personal account, to let you know how much I value our future partnership," the stranger said.

A hundred thousand was a lot for a lowly level three, who lived in Registry-appointed housing, ate Registry-appointed food and was paid in crumbs. If he actually believed what the caller was saying, Clyde would've been on the edge of his seat.

He was not.

However, he sank deeper into its cushions as his mind turned over the details of what was happening. This caller couldn't possibly have known about the Mason case – or *any* fresh case – unless he truly was connected. Clyde hadn't even submitted his official report on it yet. He had, however, delivered Brock Mason to a holding facility the day before. Perhaps Mason had given a statement and the details were somehow leaked.

"You're thinking. That's good," the stranger said pleasantly.

"I'm not thinking about the money," Clyde said.

"I know. You're better than that. That is why I want you to work for me, Mr. Evans. You are a very special Hunter and there is a very special Scion I need found. If you do this, I will personally have you promoted straight to level ten. You will become my personal Scion. If you never want to hunt again, you won't have to."

Clyde took a deep breath and clasped his hands behind his head, feeling awfully lost and numb for reasons he couldn't quite explain.

"So, you're a handler?" he asked.

"Something like that," the caller replied.

"Who's the target?"

"Have you ever heard of the Chronomancer?"

Despite the boulder of uncertainty sinking into the pit of his stomach, Clyde could not help but smirk. In fact, he nearly laughed. He believed in a great many things and had encountered Scions with all kinds of incredible gifts, but the Chronomancer was a step too far.

"The Chronomancer is a myth," Clyde said, "Something they tell young upstarts to make them think they're capable of anything." Despite the subject matter, his tone was very serious for a man who'd nearly burst into laughter a moment ago. "I don't believe any man − Scion or otherwise − can travel through *time*. The Chronomancer is a joke. If that's who you want me to track down, I may as well roll over now and forfeit my Light to the next Reaper I see. Even if he is real, how the hell could I-"

"*She* is very real," the stranger said, unfazed. "Her name is Clarice Eisenholm and I have witnessed her ability with my own eyes. She once worked for me."

"So she's seen your face? Did you scare her away?"

"Perhaps. That is for you to decide," the stranger said, neither amused nor offended. "Her gift began as spatial teleportation and later evolved to temporal relocation: time travel. She has been on the run from the Registry for most of her life. Acquiring her trust was not easy. Reacquiring it may be impossible. But finding and protecting her? That is well within the realm of possibility."

"I'm listening," Clyde said.

"I hired Miss Eisenholm to perform a very specific task for me and commissioned a spacecraft to help her carry it out," the caller explained. "She vanished before completing her assignment. I thought we'd built a rapport, but such is the risk of working with one as unstable as Miss Eisenholm. I want her back, Mr. Evans. It is of the utmost importance."

"I can see that," Clyde said, lightly tapping his fingers on the edge of the desk as he thought over what was said... *and* what wasn't.

"She abandoned the task she agreed to undertake," the stranger repeated. "I must know *why*. The offense itself is forgivable, but I need Claire Eisenholm returned to me. This requires *you*, Mr. Evans. Anyone else and she'll-"

"Vanish," Clyde said. "I understand. Since I can block her gift, I'm the only one who can catch her."

"Precisely. And I want her unharmed. I am not her enemy, nor is this an act of retaliation or punishment. I just want to have a word with her; I need to know why she fled and what she saw. It is of the utmost importance."

Every time they ordered him to haul someone in, it was 'of the utmost importance.' It was always for freedom, or justice, or the greater good. At the end of the day, when the hunt reached its inevitable end, Clyde found only three types of people: the scared, the angry, and the weary. It was always the same.

The more he thought about it, the more he realized 'scared, angry, and weary' accurately described how he felt at this very moment.

"What if she knows I'm coming?" he asked.

"She'll run. Running is what she's best at. Catching runners is what you're best at. Don't worry about her hopping across the timeline. Miss Eisenholm is in the late stages of blacklight. She will not exert herself. In a way, you could say she is already cornered."

Clyde frowned. Blacklight poisoning... the bane of all high-level Scions. The condition began when one's gift was pushed too far. Most called it a disease of the soul, not of the body. The person would begin to waste away, all their color faded until they were white as snow, while their internal organs turned to black sludge. It could be fatal if the Scion continued using his or her gift.

Some pious-minded individuals liked to think of it as God's way of keeping man in his place. The secular view was that blacklight was a failsafe implemented by the Solarans to keep Scions in check. The Solarans created the first Scions. Naturally, they must have made a control mechanism, right? To Clyde, it was a little of both. Even the most powerful Scions knew they could only push so hard. They could only bend the rules of this world so far before something had to give. Their powers, no matter how great, had a limit, an impassable wall.

Clyde should've guessed someone powerful enough to bend time would suffer from blacklight. It worked in his favor: Claire would be easy to spot in a crowd and, like the stranger said, she would think twice about using her gift.

"I have faith in you," the stranger added, when Clyde had nothing to say and far too much to think about. "I will give you everything you need. All of my connections will be at your disposal, along with a massive expense account. I have already assembled a team to assist you in this hunt, and a ship."

His eyes widened. "A *what*?"

"Needless to say, this job will take you off-world," the stranger clarified. "Miss Eisenholm's mission took her far from Earth. Her ship, the *Darkstar Abyssal*, is at your disposal. I suspect she will want her ship back; think of it as bait, if you will. I know you have never left Earth before, but there is a first time for everything, Mr. Evans. District 19 is no longer your prison."

Clyde ran a hand through his hair, feeling the lump on his skull where he'd brained himself on a rusty bedframe. At least he could feel again, even if all he felt was sharp pain. Maybe this was all a dream. Maybe he's concussed in a hospital somewhere.

"I have uploaded a boarding pass to your inbox," the stranger said. "You will fly out west to meet your crew and see the vessel you will call home for the next few weeks, months, however long it takes to catch our wayward traveler. My representative will meet you there to discuss the details. He will be my face and serve as your handler for the duration of this assignment.

"Should you decide not to take the job, so be it. You don't belong to me, Mr. Evans. Every man is born free, should live free, and die free. I would never press a man into service against his will… but I strongly advise you to come and see what I am offering."

Clyde said nothing for a long moment before finally confessing, "I'll be there."

"Perfect. That is all I ask." The line went dead.

− 03 −

Terraforming was one of the Solarans' greatest gifts to mankind. In few places was that more evident than District 455, formerly Las Vegas, Nevada. From the narrow viewport of a hypersonic jetliner, Clyde gazed down on the cityscape as his flight banked for a landing. The desert city had been converted into a fertile oasis, a zone of expansive grasslands stretching for nearly twenty miles in all directions. There were homes with gardens greener than anything he'd ever seen back home.

A mile-high obelisk of what appeared to be smooth metal stood in the city center, like a spike through its heart. No man knew for sure what Solaran 'steel' truly was, though terraformers, warp drives, and even lightkeepers were all made of the same *stuff*. Rumor had it that the Solarans knew how to turn Light into physical matter.

Whatever the case, terraformers were massive and cost a lot of Light. Nations often saved for years just to buy *one* and the Light tax climbed a little higher every time a new planet was claimed. Colonization was a costly enterprise.

The Vegas spire was a gift, given to the United States shortly after First Contact as a gesture of good will. This was around the time the Solarans irrigated 80% of the Saharan Desert, accelerated the growth of the shrinking Amazon rainforest, and de-irradiated the Zone of Exclusion around Chernobyl, among other things. They made a very strong argument for why humankind was better off with them. The Infinite Charter was a *good* thing. They made damn sure no one forgot that.

This particular spire did not do anything fancy. It only condensed water from dry air to irrigate the Mojave. In the absence of water, it could transmute "unneeded" elements into hydrogen and oxygen and literally make water, out of whatever was available. It did this of its own accord, with no human intervention. Like all spires, no one went in. No one came out. It had no doors or windows; no vents, seams, or crevices. The terraforming spires are, like their creators, a mystery. Their inner workings are completely self-contained and distanced from human eyes and human understanding.

This spire sat dead center in the bustling Las Vegas Strip, where a million people passed by it each day, just like any other skyscraper. But not a single soul knew what lurked under its glassy, silver façade, or how it worked. They only knew that it *did*. For them, that was enough.

Because it was a good thing.

* * *

"My son is your biggest fan. He's seen every one of your matches," the woman said as she set down her luggage and extended a pad and stylus to the man she'd been accosting for nearly two minutes... which is a rather long time to bother a total stranger in a busy airport terminal.

"You must have me confused with someone else," the man said for the millionth time. "I'm not him."

He looked down on her through the lenses of his heavily-tinted sunglasses, beneath a dark ball cap. His lanky, broad-shouldered build and tailored suit gave him the refined look of a

Secret Service agent, but the feel of a seedy nightclub bouncer. Behind the shades, he had the type of face that could be handsome had it not been used as a punching bag all his life.

"Don't be that way," his adoring fan said. "I know it's you. It's a shame what happened last year, but everybody knows the fights are rigged anyway. You're the *real* champion." She thrust the datapad and stylus toward him once more, but the man looked down at them as if she were offering something dead and rotten. "C'mon, my son would never let me say I saw Gino Ainsworth in person and didn't get his autograph."

Behind the shades, he rolled his eyes. "Go. Away."

"Gino 'The White Knight' Ainsworth. The Ultimate Defense. The Unbreakable Man. You're him," the woman said, noting the slight smirk that was bleeding through the man's stony face. But the expression quickly vanished when he realized her flattery had actually gotten through to him. His features became like granite again.

"I'm not him," Gino grunted and waved her off. "Get lost woman before I tell security I'm being harassed." An officer stood paces away, eyeing them both.

The woman's smile immediately inverted as she shoved the writing utensils into her purse before picking up her luggage. "Fine," she huffed, "I'll tell my son you're an *ass*. Gino Ainsworth… Hmph, some role model you turned out to be. How *rude*."

Role model? The man nearly laughed. He punched people's faces in for a living. In what universe did that make him a role model?

The moment she was out of sight, Gino checked the time on his platinum watch. Clyde Evans's flight was due thirty seconds ago and he was getting sick of waiting. Picking people up from the airport was so beneath him. He had better things to do than play wingman to a lowly level three Hunter. He only tolerated this because it would get him back in the Arena, where he belonged. This entire ordeal was only a minor setback, a pothole on the road to fame and glory.

As people began to pour out of the terminal, he scanned the entryway, searching for any sign of Evans. A short while later, Gino caught sight of someone matching his description loitering by the baggage claim. He seemed smaller than expected, average in every way and utterly unimpressive. Cargo pants, a white button-up shirt, and a gray jacket. His hair was dark brown, slightly on the messy side, and his face absolutely forgettable. To Gino, he was a nobody, a loser. Then again, most potholes weren't particularly memorable.

Never one to hesitate, Gino Ainsworth approached him and got straight to the point. "Are you Clyde Evans?" he asked, his voice deep and demanding.

The man stopped and looked up. After searching Gino's face for a moment, he replied, "Yes," as he offered his hand and a friendly smile. Gino stared at it in disgust, as if Clyde had shoved a slab of roadkill at him. "Are you the client or his representative?" the Hunter asked.

"Neither. The chauffeur," Gino said sourly as he gave the offered hand a half-hearted shake, if only so Evans would put it away. "Our employer refuses to show his face here or anywhere else. His representative is waiting with the ship an hour away. Get your bags and let's go."

"I expected as much," Evans said as he collected his suitcases from the carousel. He paused and gave Gino another strange look before adding, "I don't think I got your name…"

The words came like a left hook out of the blue. Gino stuffed his ball cap into his jacket and removed his shades, so he could give Evans a hard stare. "'Cuz I didn't give it. You *really* don't know who I am?"

"Should I?" Clyde asked, studying his face for a moment longer, but still coming up empty-handed.

"Gino Ainsworth. Three-time Arena champion of Class B," the fighter declared as he returned the shades to his face and lifted one of the three suitcases, while Clyde gathered the other two. "You know damn well who I am. Quit playing around."

"I don't follow the Arena," Clyde said as they walked together. "I'm not much of a sports fan."

"It's not a 'sport,' it's a spectacle," was Gino's gravelly reply. "You put two Scions in a ring, have them pummel each other to near-death, and fools will shell out hard-earned credits to see it. Then they have a healer patch us up and we do it all over again at another venue."

"Sounds like fun... if you're into that sort of thing."

"Don't patronize me. I've filled stadiums in every corner of the galaxy. Keep up," Gino demanded, even though Clyde was right beside him, walking at the same pace, despite carrying twice the luggage. "Our ship's at an airfield, where you'll meet the rest of the team. I ain't the client, I ain't his rep, and I ain't your *friend*. I don't know much about the guy who brought us together, but I've heard things. Most people call him 'The Stranger.' He has no name and never shows his face, but his word and his money are good, so don't screw this up."

"What've you got riding on this?" Evans asked.

"A lot... but you're the so-called 'team leader' around here, which means I have a lot riding on *you*. I don't even know the details of the mission. All I know is you're doing some detective work, searching for a missing person who could be anywhere from here to Farside and I'm supposed to run block for you."

"Run block?" Evans said with a sly smile. "Ohhh, you're the muscle? I see." He was enjoying this more than he should. "As far as I know, the mission is a basic bounty hunt. 'Detective work' sounds about right. We're looking for a rogue Scion, a woman The Stranger and The Registry want found."

"No, *you're* looking for her. That's not my job," Ainsworth said as they exited the terminal and entered an underground parking deck. "Finding the girl is on you. Don't bother me unless you need someone's head knocked around."

The two men exited the airport's automatic doors and it was like stepping from a freezer into an oven as the humid Nevada heat hit them, even in the underground parking deck.

"I'm supposed to take orders from you, but I'd prefer you keep those orders to a bare minimum," Gino added. "Understand?"

"You said there's a team. Who else will I be working with?" Clyde asked as they walked the rows of automobiles.

"Our employer assembled very thorough dossiers on each of us. Too thorough, if you ask me," Gino muttered. "There's a copy in the car, for you to check out on the way. The rest of us have read them already."

"So you already know plenty about me?" Clyde mused. "That's all well and good, but files don't tell the full story. In my experience, they're often… lacking."

Gino's only reply was a grunt. They reached the car, a silver sedan, very foreign and very expensive. After the long drive, it still had a thin film of desert dust on its otherwise pristine finish. The two men paused at the trunk, where Evans set down his suitcases and turned to Gino.

"Tell me straight, what's *your* opinion of the team?" he asked. "Have you met them? You seem like a man who cherishes his opinions, so let's have it."

"'A man who cherishes his opinions?'" Gino muttered as he tried to figure out if that was supposed to be a carefully-crafted insult or a thinly-veiled compliment. Or both?

Ignoring the question for a moment, he swiped the digital key over the trunk sensor and the lid popped open. "It's a six-man team, including you. The ship is a pile of junk, but it's roomy enough and looks like it *might* fly, if we're lucky. We have a pilot, a mechanic, and a doctor; standard crew for starhopping without a clue," Gino summarized. "You, me, and the tech specialist makes six."

"Okay, those are facts, but what's your *opinion*?" Clyde said as he lifted two suitcases into the trunk. Gino violently shoved the third in before turning to face him.

"My opinion doesn't matter… but if I had to single one out, it'd be the techie. I don't like her. I don't like *any* of them, but she stands out as the worst." He paused to brush some nonexistent dust from his suit lapel. "I'm the only one with a real pedigree, Evans, and I'm not interested in being on this trip a minute longer than necessary. The sooner you find your man – or woman, girl, *whatever* – the sooner I can be done with this farce. There's no room for incompetence. As team leader, you have the right to terminate anyone you deem unnecessary or prohibitive to the mission. I suggest you make use of that option."

"You mean terminate their *contract*."

"Of course. Did you think I meant something else?" Gino shut the trunk and turned away, tucking his sunglasses into his coat pocket as he went. "That's my cherished opinion. Take it or leave it. I'm here to ensure the mission goes smoothly. It's *my* job to make sure no one, friend or foe, hinders our progress. Understood?"

* * *

The *Darkstar Abyssal* waited at a private airstrip an hour south of the city, while a car sped through the Mojave, traveling twenty MPH over the posted limit of 130, with Vegas greenery shrinking in its rearview mirrors. After some initial grumbling about America's stubborn refusal to convert to the metric system, Gino fell peaceably silent. In the passenger seat, Clyde held the lives of his would-be crewmates in his hands.

Either The Stranger was as well-connected as he claimed to be, or he'd stumbled upon a top notch information broker. The dossiers were disturbingly accurate. Clyde found a list of every report on every suspect he'd apprehended in his ten-year career... as well as many he hadn't. He found medical records, footage of his training, and more. The file couldn't be more detailed if God Himself had written it.

Seeing his life laid bare made him realize the predicament he was in. Every intentional mistake, every minor act of rebellion; they knew what he was doing. And he was not alone. A brief perusal of the other five profiles was enough to reveal he was the only Hunter on the team, but not the only one to be flagged by the Registry.

Gino Ainsworth was a 28-year old disgraced gladiator and, as much as Clyde hated to admit it, truly did have the best 'pedigree.' Despite feigning otherwise, Clyde had heard of this "White Knight" before. He'd even seen a match or two. Gino's stage name described the crystal armor he wore, a product of his gift. He could conjure it at a moment's notice and was nearly indestructible in it, hence his level eight ranking... which was dropped to six when he was ousted from the Arena months ago, due to some controversial remarks about the Solarans.

The team doctor, George Jenner, possessed a level five gift – healing – which was average at best, but backed up by a proper medical degree and twenty years of experience. When a person develops a gift, that person becomes Solaran property. The Solarans do not *educate* their property; they *train* them, indoctrinate them, and put their skills to use. The fact that Jenner had received an education struck Clyde as odd. He was either a late bloomer or had kept his powers hidden through medical school.

Unfortunately, his gift was eventually discovered and he was forced into service, like all Scions. The file wasn't entirely clear on what George Jenner had done to get on the Registry's bad side. As far as Clyde could see, his only crime was not leaving an assignment when he was told. Alien worlds carried alien pathogens; on a newly-established colony, a healer is worth his weight in gold. Apparently, Jenner got too attached to one of the backwater colonies he was sent to protect and paid the price when he refused to walk away.

With a sigh, Clyde moved on to the next file. The pilot and mechanic were a pair. Neither was a Scion, just two seemingly ordinary guys recruited by The Stranger because they are good at what they do. Isaac Gibbs was a 34-year old former freighter captain whose career was largely unremarkable, other than the fact that he'd been in and around spacecraft since adolescence and had seen virtually every inch of known space.

In short, he seemed like a man who knew the ins and outs of interstellar travel, which meant he knew how to get things when and where they needed to be. Perhaps that was why his ship was impounded for smuggling contraband between Luna and P-154, an offense that could've resulted in major prison time had the charges not been mysteriously dropped.

Gibbs's pilot and longtime accomplice, Jayce Magnusson, 31, had also gotten a full pardon. The two men's files were dripping with The Stranger's influence. It wasn't explicitly stated, but Clyde could clearly see they'd been rescued from rotting in a cell, or worse.

A pattern was forming. Was the entire team composed of people saved from the chopping block? This 'Stranger' was going around scooping up what the Solarans throw away. But why?

Clyde took a break from reading to peer out the sedan's tinted windows, where he found stark desert as far as the eye could see. Obscure rock formations loomed in the distance, like castles in a giant's sandbox.

If someone wants to hide a spaceship, this is the place to do it, he thought. There was something clandestine about it all. He was working for the Registry, in a sense, but leading a crew who'd all gotten on the Registry's bad side at some point in their life.

Only one file remained: the tech specialist. Ellica Niehaus, was a computer programmer from P-93 and an unregistered Scion – a "sleeper" – which meant she'd eluded the Registry for all twenty-three years of her life, until now. Clyde was more than impressed. He knew the amount of information the Registry had at its disposal and how tirelessly they hunted for new blood. Keeping a gift hidden was no simple feat.

Neihaus hailed from the Platforms, the 300-plus orbital colonies encircling the Earth, which ranged from small private space stations, to massive city-sized superstructures with half a million residents. Clyde had no idea where Platform 93 fell on that spectrum, but platformers were known as tech-savvy, counterculture urbanites. The Plats were Earth cities on speed, where life moved lightning-quick. Clyde had met very few of them in his lifetime, but the ones he knew always talked fast, thought fast, and seemed rather... sketchy. His handler called them "shifty-eyed hustlers" and "good-for-nothing space gypsies." Then again, his handler's opinion of him wasn't exactly glamorous either.

Ellica Niehaus fit the bill perfectly. She had been arrested three times: first at age twelve for 'digital trespassing,' a legal gray area which was basically a slap on the wrist for hacking. Her file made it clear she didn't stop there, though that was the last time she was caught. Her next run-in with the law was a minor drug charge and the third was public indecency for "performing lewd acts" on a subway train. The police report did not elaborate.

But Ellica Niehaus knew how to hide and how to find people. A few months ago, the Registry discovered she had a gift, which meant they would be coming after her to make this 'space gypsy' into one of their own. Needless to say, she didn't want that. Less than forty-eight Earth hours after she realized she was a wanted woman, Niehaus tracked down The Stranger. She was the only member of the team who wasn't recruited. She *chose* this assignment. She was living proof that The Stranger wasn't impossible to find.

Armed with a possible contingency plan, Clyde shut off the datapad and returned his eyes to the long road ahead, content that he could now see more than one way out of it.

– 04 –

Serenity Acres Aircraft Graveyard lay miles from the highway, at the end of a long dirt road. The silver sedan followed a narrow path through cacti as tall as men and boulders the size of houses, kicking up a fishtail of dust in its wake. Upon reaching the edge of a circular valley, its destination came into panoramic view.

Serenity Acres was the final resting place for hundreds of aircraft, some predating First Contact. There were old commercial jets, gutted like enormous whales and laid out to rot in the sand and sun. There was even the occasional propeller craft, antiques that could fetch a small fortune had they been preserved. Instead, they came here to die.

As the car descended into the valley, Clyde's gaze scanned the window from his place in the passenger seat. He knew almost nothing about aviation, but even he could see very little of the inventory was spacecraft and even fewer were spaceworthy.

"Our ship's *here*?" he asked as Gino guided the car along a cliffside road overlooking the bowl-shaped valley, which was bisected by a cracked runway and looked eerily similar to an impact crater.

"Over there," Gino said, pointing to a cluster of hangars and a crude control tower at the far end as they descended into the valley.

Shoddy fill-ins and patched asphalt gave Serenity Acres an ancient feel, like an old, forgotten place, left to age disgracefully, protected only by a chain-link fence, topped with barbed wire. The open gate dangled on broken hinges, caked with rust.

The scale of the vessels became more apparent as they drove deeper inside, past the jetliners, whose wings had been sheared off and carted away to another section of the facility, where they were lined up like monolithic tombstones. There was order amidst the chaos. Beyond the wings was a section with nothing but old turbine engines, some half-buried in the sand and some raised on stands and scaffolding, to be transplanted into aircraft. But no such transplants were taking place and likely never would. The entire site was devoid of life or activity.

After they crossed the runway, Clyde found the dirt road flanked on both sides by rows of enormous metallic spheres, each covered by camouflaged tarps, flapping in the dry desert breeze. They were the hearts of starships, the crown jewels of Solaran technology. Faster-than-light travel was among the first gifts the Solarans offered to mankind in exchange for Light, and remained one of the most coveted. Each spherical core was capable of warping spacetime, enabling an object to effortlessly exceed the speed of light, a feat which should be impossible.

Tampering with, studying, storing, or dismantling *one* of them could merit a death sentence. Serenity Acres had dozens lying around, unattended and undocumented.

"Was the *Darkstar Abyssal* built here?" Clyde asked, Gino did not reply. "I thought warp cores could only be installed at The Forge, under Solaran supervision."

"Ask someone who gives a damn," Gino growled as he parked outside a hangar, beside a darkly-tinted black sedan of the same make and model as theirs. "We're here. Everyone's waiting," he added as he shut off the car and stepped out.

Clyde disembarked to find the dust hard-packed, like concrete beneath the gumsoles of his shoes. The massive hangar doors were opened just enough for a person to slip through, but not enough to see what was happening inside, though he could hear the sounds of work: power tools, ratchets and the occasional hammer. A control tower loomed on the opposite side of the hangar, casting a long shadow.

Gino headed straight inside. Clyde was left behind before he could decide whether to grab his luggage or enter without it. But the sound of a car door opening proved he was not as alone as he thought.

A man in a white longcoat emerged from the black sedan. His corporate casual attire sharply contrasted the deserted scrapyard's rusty overtones. Only his black tie and dark shades broke the sea of white.

But his appearance isn't what struck Clyde as odd. The oppressive sensation that accompanied the man's presence set off alarms in the Hunter's head.

He's using a gift, Clyde thought and was instantly on guard. He could feel the subtle undercurrent of something trying to creep into his head. Telepathy? Mind control? It made his eyeballs tingle and his skin crawl.

"Good day, Mr. Evans," the man said with a disarming smile and a slight accent. British? Something European? Clyde couldn't place it. It defied definition.

From his coat pocket, the man fished a silver badge which dangled from a chain like an old-fashioned timepiece, glinting in the harsh Nevada sun.

A Scion's crest was one of the smallest examples of Solaran technology: a perpetual motion machine. Its dodecagonal frame – twelve sides, representing the twelve members of the Solaran High Council – held a series of concentric rings, infinitely whirring around and around, with no conceivable power source.

Each ring was inscribed with the Registry's insignia and numbered according to rank. This one had ten rings, the highest rank possible.

"My name is Andrew Leitner. I'll be your handler for the duration of this assignment," the man said as he pocketed the badge and offered his gloved hand instead.

Clyde remained impassive as he firmly grasped the man's hand. "So, you're The Stranger's representative?" he asked as they broke contact.

"Sometimes I *am* The Stranger," the man said with a faint grin and a social slickness Clyde found off-putting. "But, generally, I'm just *a* stranger. That is my unique gift, Mr. Evans. You will remember this conversation. You will remember speaking with a man. You will remember my words and, if you're lucky, might even vaguely recall my face. But, once we part ways, you wouldn't know me if you were looking right at me. I am, and always will be, a stranger to you."

"Nice trick," Clyde said, unimpressed. Another illusionist. He'd seen them before, though never quite like this. He'd decoded such spells before and could do so again, if he wanted.

"It is a surprisingly useful gift in my line of work." Leitner added, spreading his hands before him. "But enough about me. You have an interesting talent as well. It is said that a Scion's gift is a manifestation of his personality. I think you're a man who likes to pick things apart and figure them out on the most fundamental level. You learn what makes them tick and then make the ticking... stop. The inverse of a watchmaker. Who better to catch a rogue time traveler?"

"And what does your gift say about you?" Clyde replied. "You like to be the man behind the curtain. I suppose it's no wonder you represent The Stranger."

"I am just a messenger," Leitner said. "Walk with me for a moment, Mr. Evans. There are a few things I'd like to discuss in private, before you meet the others."

"This isn't private enough?" Clyde asked as he followed, half-expecting a tumbleweed to blow across their path at any moment.

Leitner nodded skyward. "No. Neihaus is in the control tower, probably reading our lips."

Clyde glanced up. "She can see us from there?"

"The girl has eyes like a hawk. And I think she took a sniper rifle with her as well, purely for the scope, of course. There's a small arsenal aboard the ship. I recommend you familiarize yourself with it as well… but that's not the point. Point is, we are being watched."

"Why is there a 'small arsenal' on my ship?"

Andrew Leitner didn't answer right away. He waited until they were on the other side of the hanger, shielding them from the prying eyes allegedly in the high tower. Even still, he lowered his voice when he continued:

"There are *other* things aboard that ship as well, which my client would like to remain confidential. That's what I wish to discuss, before you proceed."

Clyde nodded in understanding.

"The *Darkstar Abyssal* was the Chronomancer's ship, a very special ship, commissioned specifically for her," the man explained. "It has two unique pieces of Solaran technology on board, which you will not find anywhere else in the galaxy. She'll want it back and I suspect she'll come for it… but she's not the only one. The Registry wants the *Darkstar* as well."

"We *are* the Registry. What are you saying?"

"It's complicated," Leitner replied. "There are many layers to this, Clyde. At the top you have the Solaran High Council. Their word is absolute, but there are a dozen of them, each with his own agenda. The left hand doesn't always know what the right is doing. Sometimes..." he brought his palms together, tightly clasped, "sometimes one hand knows what the other is up to and will try to put a stop to it. Why is there an armory on your ship? Why do you have an ex-champion as your bodyguard? To be the *strongest* hand, that's why."

"I had no idea the Registry was such a mess. We're supposed to be a symbol of order."

"Oh, we are. There is order beneath the chaos, my friend," Leitner said, momentarily removing his shades to reveal a mischievous glint in his steely gray eyes. Or blue. Or brown. "Your orders come straight from the top. You are well within your rights to defend this ship at all costs, Mr. Evans. The same goes for Claire Eisenholm. Your orders to capture her override *any* and *all* prior warrants or bounties on her head or yours. Man's laws no longer apply to you. As your handler, I want you to fully understand the authority you wield. Do not hold back in your pursuit of her. Are we clear?"

"Diplomatic immunity?" Clyde said. "Only Hunter Elites have that kind of authority. You're sending me out there with a huge target on my back: I'm in a wanted ship, searching for a wanted woman. With all due respect, how is this going to get me *off* the Registry's shitlist?"

"It won't," Leitner said as he returned his sunglasses to his face and looked skyward. "But you'll earn a powerful friend *and* your freedom."

"What's so special about the *Darkstar*?" Clyde asked. "Better yet, what was it built to do, that you'd defend it so fiercely and that a time traveler would want it so badly?"

"Well... I was going to tell you, but it seems we've run out of time," Leitner said, with a sly smirk. "Can't talk about it now. Shall we discuss the weather instead?" A twinge of irritation creased the corners of Clyde's brows. "Better yet," Leitner said with a knowing look, "let's ask Miss Neihaus about the weather, since she's eavesdropping on us from around that corner. Come out, Ell, I know you're there."

Ellica's presence was announced by an annoyed sigh before she stepped out from her hiding place. A heavy black rifle hung from her narrow shoulders by a strap. The weapon was longer than she was tall, with a barrel as thick as a man's arm and a massive scope powerful enough to target ants on the moon. It didn't help that she was barely an inch over four-eleven and rail thin, wearing a black miniskirt perched low on her hips, and a gray tank top. Her spindly legs were wrapped in striped tights, and she had absolutely no curves to speak of, but strode up to them like she ruled every man in the universe.

Clyde's first thought was that she couldn't possibly be the full twenty-three years her file claimed; more like seventeen or eighteen, at best. More than anything, it was her childish face and the sprinkling of freckles that did it. With her boyishly short bright red hair and choice of attire, he found it impossible to believe this was anything but a rogue teenager fulfilling her adolescent daydreams of playing with the adults.

"How's the weather?" Leitner asked again, obviously toying with her.

"Hot," she said, rolling her eyes.

"As astute as ever, I see." The man returned his attention to Clyde. "Mr. Evans, as you can see, this is your tech specialist, Miss Ellica Neihaus. Ell, this is Clyde Evans, your new boss."

She peered up into his eyes expectantly and he found hers were a very striking blue... but there was something not quite right about them. They didn't seem to be contact lenses, but they clearly weren't natural either. Clyde couldn't pinpoint what was amiss and stared into them for far longer than he should have.

She did not look away. In fact, she made a point of capturing his gaze in a manner he found far too suggestive. "'Sup. Ya like 'em?" she said with a wink. "It's 'Ell,' by the way. Just Ell, none of that 'Miss Neihaus' shit."

"Well, it's a pleasure to meet you... Ell," Clyde said in a level tone, going for the polar opposite of whatever wavelength she was on. She quickly shoved out her hand for a shake, proving she was capable of a modicum of formality. Clyde accepted it firmly before looking to Leitner once more, but the man brushed him off.

"Miss Neihaus is just too clever for us," Leitner mused as he moved aside, preparing to leave. "So sharp, this girl. It's a wonder she doesn't cut herself."

"You first, Flipass," Ell retorted sharply, but the man merely chuckled.

"Don't mistake the jabs for animosity," he said to Clyde. "Ell has more than proven her right to be here and I have the utmost respect for her skills... but computer hackers aren't known for keeping confidential things confidential. We'll continue our discussion after the briefing, Mr. Evans. See you soon."

With a slight bow, the man departed toward the hangar entrance, leaving Clyde and Ell alone. He was hardly gone ten seconds before she turned to Clyde and said, "Who was that douchebag? I don't like him. He's slippery."

On that, they could agree. Clyde opened his mouth to reply, but froze when he couldn't seem to bring a name to the forefront. "Why'd you call him 'Flipass?'"

Ell shrugged. "Couldn't remember his name. It's a word from back home. A word for rats, snitches, bitches, traitors. You know, people ya can't trust. Flipasses will flip on ya in a sec," she snapped her fingers, "and when they do, it's *your* ass on the line."

She brightened as her gaze zeroed in on Clyde. "I don't trust that guy, but you seem legit. Wanna shoot some stuff?" she said, caressing the gun like a stiff, dead snake. "I *love* this thing. You soulda seen it, I was puttin' holes the size of stripper tits in one of those planes waaaay over there and it was sooo fucking loud."

Clyde's only reply was a blank stare, not because of *what* she said, but *how* she said it. Her speech ramped up, until anything longer than five or six words came out blindingly quick. She was a verbal machine gun. From the capital to the final punctuation, she went lightspeed and his brain didn't stand a chance of keeping up.

He didn't snap out of it until she grabbed his arm and said, "C'mon, lemme show you," as she tried to haul him away to her improvised shooting range.

Instantly awakened from his daze, Clyde planted his feet and refused to be moved, which was easy enough with a girl a third his size. She tried to pull him toward the control tower, but he ended up dragging her toward the hangar instead, reasoning that they had work to do and no time for fooling around, especially with guns.

"And watch your mouth," he added, as the cherry on top.

"Fine, be like that," Ell conceded after pawing at him like a feral cat. With a disappointed sigh, she followed him toward the entrance, where the other man had gone. "Once we're done with the meet'n'greet, I got somethin' I wanna show you, *in private*. Tell Flipass two can play that game."

"Something pertaining to the mission, I hope."

"Yeah. It's real important. Swing by my room – I mean, my *'office'* – when you got a min, 'kay? I got some intel that might blow your mind."

* * *

When she was younger and the world was still a mystery to her, Ell would watch the transports come and go over P-93's spaceport. She was used to spacecraft, the way they looked, the way they sounded, the way they moved as their pilots maneuvered them into and out of the docks. On the Platforms, where vessels the size of skyscrapers glided by the windows of her tiny apartment every day, space travel was a fact of life.

Because of this, she didn't doubt for a moment that the *Darkstar Abyssal* was spaceworthy. She had seen far worse specimens take flight. Petty wars, piracy, and hooliganism in the outer colonies brought spacecraft limping into P-93's docks shot full of holes, trailing coolant and fuel, with their engines flickering like dying candles. Machines were surprisingly resilient creatures, so the *Darkstar*'s condition didn't really faze her.

But she suspected Clyde wouldn't see things that way. He was a space virgin. The stars and how people reached them were still a mystery to him. He probably didn't even know the difference between an intrastellar shuttle and an extrasolar warp rabbit.

The *ESV Darkstar Abyssal* looked vaguely like a fat bird roosting on a shipping crate, with firecrackers strapped to its ass and rapiers for wings. In an age when the flying brick was all the rage, the *Darkstar*'s designers had made a feeble attempt at having her appear sleek and aerodynamic, like the earthbound aircraft of ages long gone. But it looked like they'd given up halfway.

She was stylish and graceful at the bow, but grew progressively bloated and clunky astern. The cockpit and nose section were smooth, like the neck of a plump penguin. But she flared out at midship, where her tandem drive cores were housed. Past that, she was all engines and plumbing. Four enormous thrusters were clustered at the stern, with gaping intakes for scavenging stardust to extend her already enormous range. These could be closed for reentry, along with the slender wings tucked against her fuselage, like folded switchblades.

The *Darkstar Abyssal* was a little over 115 tonnes dry and nearly doubled that when its fuel tanks were filled to capacity. But, thanks to the dual gravity drives, its takeoff weight was limited only by how much could be crammed into storage space. She was built for hauling and that fact was most apparent in the cargo bay, which was essentially a long box grafted onto the underside of the fuselage. A ramp at the front allowed cargo to be driven in or out, while the rear had an elevator.

None of this was out of the ordinary for Ell, who had seen ships of similar design. What really made the *Darkstar* stand out was its condition. It wasn't battle-scarred or falling apart at the seams, but its hull had a patina of reddish-brown rust, making the entire ship appear dirty, old, and worn. It looked as if someone had gone over every inch of it with sandpaper, hosed it down with saltwater, and then left it to endure the elements for a thousand years, ensuring it would never shine again. Inside, she was state of the art, but *outside* she looked like a salvaged rustbucket, riveted and tacked together, and fit right in with the rest of the derelict hulks at Serenity Acres, decaying in the desert sun.

"The girl sabotaged her," Ell explained when Clyde stopped to 'admire' this unique feature of the ship. He did not look pleased.

"Flew her through an electrical storm somewhere in deep space. Fried everything. Gibbs has been rewiring her for, like, a week," Ell went on to say. "I just got here two days ago and set about reinstalling the avionics suite. That's 350 petabytes of software to install and recalibrate, by the way. I been workin' my ass off," she said proudly.

"You programmed a starship all by yourself?"

"Instruction manuals. You should try 'em sometime."

Clyde said nothing for a while. He stood, not even blinking. Ell could live with being ignored, but when people got quiet and didn't do *anything* it drove her crazy. She thrived on motion, action, noise, activity. Without that, she got fidgety. Long spans of peaceful silence literally gave her withdrawals.

"Sabotaged?" Clyde said, finally turning to Ell. "Are you sure? Why would she sabotage a ship she wants so badly?" He had the pensive look of a man who was working on the world's greatest jigsaw puzzle, but missing half of the pieces.

"Is any of the data salvageable?" he said, when Ell's only response was a shrug. "I wanna know where this ship's been, how it got there, and what it did. I have a feeling our client did something to spook Claire Eisenholm. If he doesn't fess up, we'll have to sort it out ourselves."

Ell delightedly rubbed her mischievous little paws together. "Diggin' up dirt? This, I like. The files are corrupted to all hell, but I'll get right on it, cap'n."

His reply was merely a slight nod, as his attention had already returned to the ship. Clyde stood with his hands in his pockets, taking in every rivet and panel, probably wondering what story they told. She could see he liked this game. *Mysteries. Is that what you're into?* Ell thought. *You gonna dream about Claire Eisenholm every night?*

Ell looped an arm around his shoulder while his attention was diverted and crept a little closer. When he didn't attempt to wriggle free of her right away, she smiled and nestled into the warmth of human contact. "What's the matter?" she purred in his ear, but the moment was over before it began. Clyde shrugged her off before she could get comfortable and headed up the cargo ramp, leaving her behind. Ell giggled and followed him aboard.

"Nothing's wrong. I'm accustomed to not having much information to go on," Clyde said, oblivious to her flirting. "Being out of the loop comes with the territory. But I always find my way back into it."

"Ooh, I'm lookin' forward to it," Ell remarked, not really hearing anything he said. She shifted the rifle's position. The gun was remarkably light, but the strap was starting to dig into her shoulder. With a quick two-step, she overtook Clyde and half-turned, strolling backwards while facing him, with her hands clasped coyly behind her back. "I can give you the tour. Where should we start, my room or yours?"

Clyde abruptly stopped.

His expression was difficult to read, but the fact that he wore no expression at all was proof positive that he was about to shut her down, hard. Ell waited expectantly but, to her disappointment, (or relief,) Isaac Gibbs came clomping down the metal stairs and into the cargo bay. He was heard long before he was seen.

Gibbs was average height, but nearly as wide as he was tall, a rotund, sweaty man who lumbered everywhere he went. He was already balding in his mid-thirties. The dark hair that should be atop his head had migrated down into a scruffy beard. To Ell, he looked like he belonged in a coal mine or chopping wood someplace, not fixing spacecraft. The greasy, bear of man strode right up to them with a hearty smile and outstretched arms, and a tool belt that rattled with every step.

"Already, Ell? Can't the man breathe for a moment 'fore you sink yer claws into him?" he said and rumbled with laughter before tugging off one of his gloves and offering a clean hand to Clyde. "Ike Gibbs, sir. Flight engineer. A pleasure to have ya aboard."

"Clyde Evans. It's a pleasure to *be* aboard," her beau-to-be replied, while Ell stood by, ignored. "I hear you've had your work cut out for you, Mr. Gibbs. Will she fly?"

"Will she fly? 'Will she fly,' he asks. Can you believe this guy?" the man said, giving Clyde a heavy slap on the shoulder and another of those unrestrained, guttural laughs he was known for.

Ell took a step back, feeling utterly forgotten. Not that she minded. Ike was too touchy-feely. He liked to shake hands, bump fists, slap friends on the back, and wasn't opposed to the occasional bear hug or two. Ell had wandering hands too, but there was a *limit*, especially from a man who smelled of mechanical fluids and burnt wiring.

"She'll fly alright," Gibbs said, gesturing to the cargo bay around them, as if the amount of empty storage space was indicative of a vessel's true potential. Coming from a background in smuggling Solaran tech, there was likely a very good reason he felt that way.

"I'll show you around later, but what's-his-face has called a briefing in the comm room. Right this way," Gibbs said, leading Clyde toward the stairs, with Ell trailing behind. Halfway up, he chuckled to himself and turned to them, over his shoulder. "She'll fly, pal. She'll fly far and fast and right up the asses of anyone who thinks they can stop us. It's what she was built to do... I think."

"You *think*?" Clyde said curiously.

Gibbs merely shrugged. "They don't tell us much o' nothin' these days. Honestly, I don't know what this ship was built to do. All I know is what she *can* do."

"And what's that?" Ell asked.

"Damn near anything."

– 05 –

Within minutes of setting foot on the *Darkstar Abyssal*, Clyde found himself seated around a conference table with six other people, three of whom he didn't know at all, and three he didn't know as well as he'd like.

After ascending the steps from the cargo bay, he passed through a thick pressurized door into a central corridor, which ran the length of the ship. Another door led aft and was marked with enough caution labels to make Clyde uneasy. Somewhere back there was the main reactor, the dual drive cores, and a maze of plumbing and heat exchangers, which served the thrusters.

Gibbs led Clyde and Ell forward, past the dormitories, warning him to mind his step. Some of the wall panels lay open with bundles of wires scattered across the floor. "She's a work in progress," Gibbs assured them.

The others were already waiting when he reached the communications room, a round chamber at the heart of the ship, with a circular console covered in touchscreens, surrounded by swiveling office chairs on rails.

The console projected a slowly-turning sphere, which Clyde immediately identified as Earth. Yellow lines indicated the orbits of the Platforms and various satellites. The amount of traffic up there clouded the display, making Earth look like an unraveling ball of yellow yarn.

Two of the paths orbited much further than the others, halfway between the Earth and Luna. From them, straight red lines shot off into deep space, like railway tracks to the cosmos.

Warp gates, Clyde realized. They were highways into deep space. These orbiting stations were massive Solaran devices devices capable of propelling ships that lacked FTL capabilities to distant stars. The *Darkstar Abyssal* could do that without the aid of warp gates, but not every ship could. Others had to rely on the heavily-regulated gates, sit in line, undergo inspections and searches, and pay hefty fees to travel between stars.

Clyde took a seat, following the example set by the two men already there. One was the bespectacled doctor, George Jenner, a heavyset man in a frayed sport coat, who regarded him with a slight nod.

Beside the doctor was the pilot, Jayce Magnusson, a well-built man with a square jaw and a strong upper body. His file said he'd flown experimental craft for a military contractor before teaming up with Gibbs. He sat half-reclining and regarded Clyde with a brief, "Afternoon, captain," in a lazy accent Clyde couldn't pin down.

"Afternoon, gentlemen," Clyde said as he linked his hands in his lap and finally noticed Gino posted in the corner, alone, with his arms folded and a surly look on his face. "Care to join us, Mr. Ainsworth?"

"I can hear just fine from here," the fighter muttered. At least he'd shown up.

Gibbs dropped into his seat with a world weary grunt and made himself at home. Ell flopped into one as well and draped the rifle across her lap before putting her feet up on the console and twiddling her thumbs while she reclined.

She's far too comfortable in a miniskirt, Clyde thought, but this was a briefing room, not etiquette school. With everyone gathered at the round table, the meeting began.

"Welcome," The Stranger's representative said expansively. For a man who didn't want to be remembered, he had a flair for the theatrical. "It is nice to finally have you all in one place... especially you, Mr. Evans. Hang on just a sec..." He caught Clyde's eye before returning his attention to the touchscreens before him. Immediately, another speaker took charge of the briefing.

"I trust you enjoyed your flight?" The Stranger said, through the ship's PA system.

No image accompanied the voice, but there was no mistaking who it was. The Stranger's no frills tone wasn't easily forgotten. There was nothing specifically out of the ordinary about his manner of speaking, but it stuck in a way no other voice could. It crept into Clyde's skull and made its presence known, such that no introduction was necessary, and applying a name or face to it would somehow diminish who and what he was.

"Let us waste no time," The Stranger added. "Mr. Leitner, please proceed."

"Yes, of course. Andrew Leitner, at your service, for those of you who don't remember," the man said, briefly flashing his ten-ringed badge again. "There isn't much to be said, so I'll try to keep this briefing *brief*. I suppose the best place to begin is with the target herself."

"Do you have a dossier on her?" Clyde asked.

"Not exactly. I'll forward a file with pics and what we know, but conventional records have very little to say about Claire Eisenholm. All we have to go on is the personal knowledge my client and I gleaned while working with her," Leitner said. "She was born six years ago but, biologically, she's about twenty-seven or twenty-eight. Her gift only allows her to travel *backwards*, so she has repeated a few years. Do-overs, basically. Claire has lived the same six years over and over again, due to going back in time a few months here, a year there, so forth and so on." He gestured vaguely. "Claire doesn't discuss her past much, but from what little time I spent with her, I gathered she's done a lot of repeating, a lot of *running*… and not just from the Registry. She has lived a difficult life."

"Trouble at home?" Ell said.

"That just about sums it up, yes," Leitner said sadly. "Product of a bad childhood, I think… but let's not speculate too much. The important thing to take away is that extensive time travel pushes her gift beyond its natural limits and she already has very severe blacklight."

"What exactly *is* blacklight?" the pilot, Jayce Magnusson, asked. "I've heard of it before, but how sick is she? What if she dies before we find her?"

"It varies slightly from person to person," Doctor Jenner said. "The most visible symptom is the loss of color. The skin, eyes, hair, it all fades to white, even scars and birthmarks. There is internal damage as well. Organ failure usually follows, with effects similar to necrosis. The blood turns thick and black and that's what usually kills the victim. A heart can't pump sludge. It's not a pleasant way to go. It's… unnatural."

"Everything about Scions is unnatural," Magnusson muttered. "No offense, of course."

"None taken," Clyde said quickly. "Blacklight is a dynamic ailment: it either gets *better* or *worse*. It's never static. If she stops using her gift, she'll recover and be able to use it again, which means we're on a timetable." He looked to Leitner. "How bad is Claire's case, in particular?"

The Stranger spoke instead: "I saw her last. She was as white as the lights above your heads and she had spider marks on her chest and face."

"Black veins... that's a sign she's in the late stages," Clyde mused. "But what did she do to get that way? I'll need to know more about her mission if I'm to figure out why she abandoned it."

"I'm sorry, but Miss Eisenholm's assignment is highly classified," The Stranger said.

Clyde looked to the rep, his handler.

"I am not at liberty to say, nor was I there when she vanished," Leitner said.

A collective sigh washed over the room.

"These are questions you should direct to Miss Eisenholm, once you find her," The Stranger said sharply. "I do not know when, where, or how she contracted blacklight. All I know is she appeared with it quite suddenly and was hysterical."

"Blacklight has neurological side effects as well," Dr. Jenner added.

"Let us not be *too* quick to write her off as insane," The Stranger said. "She left for a *reason* − a sane reason. She has had plenty of time to clear her head since then. *Find* her. An explanation is due."

"Teleportation is a funny thing," Leitner said calmly. "Anytime she appears, we don't know if she's coming from a few feet away, miles away, or *years* away. It's easy for you to blame my client for Miss Eisenholm's state, but I think a far more rational interpretation is that the Claire he saw was returning from a future where she saw something very traumatic... something involving my client and the mission she was asked to carry out."

"The mission you aren't telling us about," Ell quipped.

"The simplest explanation," Clyde said to The Stranger, "is that her mission went to Hell in a handbasket and she traveled back in time to abort it, which is precisely why we need to know *what* that mission was."

Andrew Leitner merely smiled. "You don't *need* that information. But at least you understand why my client wants to get to the bottom of this. This girl is faulting him for an offense he has not yet committed."

"And *will not* commit, if only I knew what it is," The Stranger declared. "I want to repair my working relationship with Miss Eisenholm. At the very least, I wish to know what damaged it in the first place."

"She spared the ship," Clyde said, trying a different approach. "You said the *Darkstar Abyssal* was an important part of her assignment. Claire and the ship are lock and key to one another, right? If the mission spooked her so badly, why spare the one thing which made it all possible in the first place? If she wanted to abort the mission, she should've destroyed this ship... yet you seem convinced she'll come looking for it."

"That's a good point," Gibbs said, scratching his beard.

"And what became of her crew?" Clyde asked.

With a few strokes of his hand, Leitner zoomed the nav map out from Earth to a view of the entire Sol System. Then it backed out even further, to a map of the entire galaxy. A purple line pointed far off from Sol into Farside, the lawless outer rim of the Milky Way. Beyond that was the Abyss, the dark void between galaxies, where travel was forbidden by the Charter.

"The *Darkstar Abyssal* was found adrift in a decaying Earth orbit approximately one month ago. There were no souls aboard," Leitner explained as a blinking dot appeared, indicating where the *Darkstar* had been discovered and retrieved.

"We think she flew it through a powerful electrical disturbance, probably somewhere in *this* region," Gibbs explained, gesturing to a point on the galactic hologram.

It meant nothing to Clyde, who had no idea what any of the stars or systems were, only that they were very, very, *very* far away, even for a ship like the *Darkstar*. "Have we ruled out the possibility of an accident?" he asked.

Gibbs nodded. "Unlike most ships her size, the *Darkstar* is extrasolar: she can generate her own warp field and plot her own jumps. Most freighters in her weight class need a warp gate for that. They don't have the means to go hyper-relativistic on their own. Point is, she's built for crossin' the galaxy unassisted. The ship's computer woulda thrown up all kinds of warnings if Eisenholm tried to plot a warp jump through an electrical storm or an asteroid field or a planet or…"

"He's trying to say it was intentional," Jayce Magnusson cut in. "Flying through an electrical disturbance of that magnitude will wipe every computer clean. The ship would survive, physically, but there would be no way to tell where it's been or who was on board. All the records are fried. And she aimed it *juuuust* right, to drop it into a somewhat stable orbit. That was no accident."

"The scorch marks on the hull are what happens when you accelerate a ship to a couple thousand times the speed of light and fly it through space dust and debris without a proper physics envelope to protect it. The *Darkstar* had no power, but the cores retained enough charge to decelerate the ship and drop it into orbit 'fore they died too." Gibbs sat back and folded his arms across his chest. "She was either clever or lucky. She saved this ship for a reason, I'd say. Coulda just plotted a collision course with the nearest planet if she wanted to *destroy* it… but she didn't. She just *purged* it, to cover her tracks, I think."

"Before plotting that fateful jump, Miss Eisenholm teleported herself and the crew away, leaving the ship unmanned for a brief period," The Stranger explained. "I know not why they departed. I'm not entirely sure if they consented to this or if she whisked them away against their will. She already had blacklight at this point. After taking them away, she returned alone a short time later, plotted the jump to Earth, and vanished again, leaving the *Darkstar* to its fate. The rest is as Mr. Gibbs described. My people recovered the ship from Eath orbit, transported it here, and began repairs."

"And you know this... how?" Clyde asked.

"I was watching, in real time, as it happened," The Stranger said. "Much like I am watching you now. I witnessed the *Darkstar Abyssal*'s final moments."

"And you still ain't got a clue why she suddenly bailed on you?" Ell said. "No idea at all?"

The voice said nothing in reply.

"C'mon, there's something you're not telling us," Clyde said when the silence lingered far too long. "How can you expect me to do this if you're not willing to put everything on the table? *What* was her mission?"

"Her mission was research of an exploratory nature. This is a research vessel," The Stranger said flatly. "It never reached its destination, though I suspect Miss Eisenholm did. I *must* know what she saw there! That is *all* I will say at this time."

"Just focus on getting her back," Leitner demanded.

"What if he *can't*?" Gino said. "What if Evans fails? Does anyone here honestly think a lowly level three Hunter can find the Chronomancer?"

Clyde cast him a sideways glance.

"He's the only one who can control her. If he cannot do it, it cannot be done," The Stranger replied. "And you *will* support him in this endeavor, Mr. Ainsworth."

"I'll find her. You needn't worry about that," Clyde said. There was no sense drawing this out. The Stranger and his parrot were running them in circles with no intention of telling them any more than what was absolutely needed. "Where do we start? Do you have any leads? Can you at least tell us that much or should I fly blindly into space and see what bites?"

"Yes, we have a lead," Leitner said, working the holo display as if he were the director of an orchestra. The navmap collapsed back down to Earth level, with the various lines orbiting the planet. It then zoomed in on a ring-shaped space station: a platform.

"Neither Eisenholm nor her crew have been heard from since their disappearance," the man explained, "but we have some of our best people keeping their eyes and ears open for any sign of them. What you see here is Platform 222, population 450,000. One week ago, a gentleman by the name of Desmond Williams was identified on a surveillance camera there. He was Claire's flight engineer, the man who designed all non-Solaran aspects of the ship you're currently aboard. He is also the first and *only* member of her crew to turn up."

"Perfect," Ell said. "So, you bagged him, right? He's in custody and we'll just go pick him up. Case closed."

"No," The Stranger said. "On the chance he is waiting for a crewmate or accomplice, I have chosen not to disturb him. But we've watched him closely, in the hopes that he may draw others out, perhaps even Eisenholm herself. He has been loitering on P-222, as if waiting to be discovered. What happens next is up to you, Mr. Evans."

"We can use him to lure the girl out and end this," Gino said. "He's perfect bait."

"She has run from the Registry for years," Dr. Jenner replied quietly. "I can't see her walking into such an obvious trap. She must be smarter than that."

"We'll see," Clyde said. He agreed with the doc, but wasn't willing to rule out Gino's idea yet. "I'd like to get a look at this guy first. Let's see who we're dealing with, why he showed up when and where he did, and if he's alone." He looked around at the others. "Does that sound good?" A murmur of approval swept over the room and he turned to Leitner again. "I guess that means we're headed to P-222. Do you have any other intel on this guy?"

"You have a researcher for that," The Stranger said.

Ell beamed. Clyde shrugged.

"Now that you have a destination, I think this meeting is adjourned," Leitner said, "unless there are any additional questions… other than the ones you've already asked."

After a short pause, when no one spoke, Clyde replied, "Before we get on with this, I have one final question for our client: what's in this for you? Other than getting Eisenholm back and continuing your 'research' what do you stand to gain?"

"Nothing," The Stranger said. "I have fundamental differences with the Registry. An enemy of theirs is potentially a friend of mine. That is no secret. Those who know me, know I am a friend to Scions in need. *Your* friend, Mr. Evans. And Claire's friend."

"That remains to be seen."

"Understandable," The Stranger said. "You aren't the first to run afoul of the Registry and you aren't the first I've offered assistance to. They have a history of eating their own. I am a seeker of truth, Mr. Evans. I question all things and when the answer is not to my liking, I take action. I am currently at a crossroads regarding what action to take regarding the Registry and *our* role in its continued operation. Let me say this: how they respond to you and Miss Eisenholm will weigh *heavily* upon my final decision."

"So why keep so many secrets from your own people?" Clyde asked but the line had already gone dead.

"Meeting adjourned," Leitner said while gesturing for all to rise. As he took his leave, he tapped Clyde on the shoulder and whispered into his ear: "Slight change of plans, friend. We won't be continuing our discussion after all. Get to P-222. Find Desmond Williams. He'll tell you whatever you want to know about this ship. But remember: that information is for your ears only."

The ship? Clyde couldn't care less about the damn ship. He quickly stood and cornered Leitner before the man could slip away. "Why not give us a straight answer!?" he demanded, while keeping his voice conspiratorially low. "All this secrecy and mystery… your 'client' acts too much like a Solaran. Is that what you meant when you said my orders come from the top?"

"What *is* a Solaran? Would you know one if it looked you in the eyes? Would you hate them less if they walked among us, instead of ruling from on high?" Leitner smiled his slippery smile. "Don't waste my time or yours with foolish questions. If you really are curious, Eisenholm has your answers. Find her. Ask her. Until you do, we've nothing to discuss, and I have other matters to attend to."

A minute later, he was gone and Clyde couldn't remember the man's face, his smug smirk, or the unadulterated condescension in his tone.

But he remembered not liking him *at all.*

– 06 –

"A car, a spaceship, and a locker full of things that go boom," Gino said as he stepped out of the vehicle and tossed the keys to Clyde. "What other toys did we get?"

"That might be the first positive thing I've heard outta you all day," Isaac Gibbs chuckled.

Clyde had to admit the car was a nice touch. The Stranger offered little in the way of information, but provided plenty of material support. A car, a ship, an armory, a crew, and an enormous expense account; it was almost too good to be true.

"If everybody's settled, it's time we lifted off," Clyde said as he finally collected his bags from the trunk.

Gibbs pressed a button on the wall and the cargo ramp began to rise with a heavy electric hum, sealing them off from the sand-swept scrapyard beyond the hangar doors. Clyde took one last breath of Earth air. In a few minutes, they would all be inhaling whatever the *Darkstar*'s atmospheric generators churned out. The next time the door opened, they would be on P-222, breathing whatever passed for air up there.

It won't be so different, Clyde told himself, but he had only known one planet all his life... and was now leaving it behind.

Gino shared no such sentiments: "It's just a rock," he said, when he noticed the wistful look in Clyde's eyes. "If you've seen one, you've seen 'em all."

"Yeah... but it's *my* rock."

"I like that kind of thinkin.' Most folks these days don't give Earth the respect she deserves. All hail the homeworld!" Gibbs chanted as he gave Clyde a heavy slap on the back. "Anyway, you'll adjust in due time. Need a hand with yer bags, cap'n?"

"Thanks, but I'll manage. And I can do without the 'captain,' if you don't mind. Let me earn the title," Clyde said as he began to turn toward the stairs, but he stopped short and stared at the car, as if pondering something. "Shouldn't we tie it down? What if we hit turbulence?"

Gibbs roared with laughter and Gino slowly shook his head in pity.

"You *really* haven't been up before, have ya?" Gibbs said, still chuckling. "This ain't an airplane. She's in her own little physics bubble, isolated from outside forces. You won't feel a thing. No matter how rough the ride gets, that car ain't goin' nowhere, cap'n."

Contorting the laws of physics within a limited area allowed a ship to go from zero to over a thousand times the speed of light in the blink of an eye without turning the crew or the ship itself to jelly. Clyde had heard of such things, but never given it much thought.

Like any space newbie, he soon made the mistake of asking, "How?"

"It's Solaran tech," Gibbs replied humorlessly. "Nobody knows *how*. And if you get caught tryin' to find out... it doesn't end well. Men *die* for that information."

"You speak from personal experience?" Gino said.

"Nah. Jay and I got caught tradin' Soltech. We just buy and sell it. We don't reverse engineer it, but I know guys who've tried. Yer brain's gotta be more than a little sideways to even attempt that sort of thing. It changes you."

"Are you saying that knowing how it works would drive a person insane?" Clyde asked.

"I'm just sayin' it takes a different kind of mind. An inhuman mind."

"I don't buy that. Eventually, someone will figure it out," Clyde said. "We'll figure out a way to travel to the stars or terraform or defy gravity without relying on... space magic. Someday we won't have to pay tribute to *them*. We'll learn to do things ourselves."

"I like your old-fashioned spirit," Gibbs said with a grin. "You don't sound like any Hunter I ever met... not that I've met many."

"That's because he's an idiot," Gino said as he turned to trudge up the stairs. "We got a raw deal. The Infinite Charter was tipped in the Solarans' favor from the start. Nearly two hundred years later, people are still driving themselves nuts trying to make it right. Nothing's gonna change, so stop talking about it. Makes me sick every time I hear that crap, especially from a damned Hunter."

* * *

The *ESV Darkstar Abyssal* slowly rolled out of the enormous hangar that had been her home for the past month. A swirling blue glow emanated from her idling thrusters. The tandem drives rose to a steady whine as they began the process of wrapping the ship in an invisible envelope of altered physics, priming her for liftoff. The gravity inside the vessel was a comfortable 1g, but outside was slowly dropping toward zero, shrugging off the pull of the Earth. The only visible effect was a slight lift as the landing gear unweighted.

Isaac Gibbs made his way to the cockpit, following the long corridor which ran the length of the ship. After passing through the comm room and two heavy bulkheads, he reached the flight deck, where Jayce Magnusson was already at the controls.

"Will our *captain* be joining us on the bridge?" Jay said as he performed a final check of the gauges while guiding the ship out of the hangar.

"He's in his cabin gettin' settled in and reading up on our mystery girl," Gibbs said as he settled into the co-chair. "His way of keepin' his head in the game, I suppose."

"I get the impression he'd rather worry about the game than space," Magnusson replied.

"And why shouldn't he? Flyin' the ship is our job. Findin' the girl is his," Gibbs said. "Leave huntin' to the Hunter and this'll be over before it began."

"One can only hope."

"Hope's good. Can never have too much hope, I say," Gibbs replied without lifting his eyes from the readouts.

The engines were steady. The coolant flow was slightly above normal, which was always a good sign. Fuel levels were low, but they weren't traveling far and would top off at P-222. On a full tank, she could go to Farside and back.

"She's a hell of a ship," Gibbs said, taking it all in. "Built for runnin' deep. Wish we had a bird like this when we were makin' drops, Jay. They never woulda caught us."

The other man shook his head. "If we'd gotten caught in this thing, we'd be dead. She's too dirty, even for us."

Gibbs frowned. Magnusson was referring to the mass accelerator cannon which ran the length of the ship. He was talking about a class of weapons outlawed by every developed nation in the world nearly a century ago. The type of weapon no sane man would dare use, because if he missed he could punch a hole in a small moon.

They found the weapon buried deep in the *Darkstar*'s substructure. The Stranger insisted they focus their repairs only on the ship's damaged electronics, but some things were hard to miss once the wrenches started turning.

"If anybody asks, we're a research vessel and that railgun is used for launching data probes," Gibbs said, giving Magnusson a sharp look. "But no one's gonna ask, 'cuz no one's gonna know it's there. Ya hear me?"

"Does the Hunter know?"

"Probably. He ought to. I bet The Stranger told him behind our backs." Gibbs paused for a long while before continuing. "Either way, it's well-hidden. Someone would have to tear this ship apart to find that thing. *We* barely knew what it was, and we've wrenched on hundreds of ships. Stop worrying; this bird's got diplomatic immunity. No one can touch us and it's not like *we* put it there."

"Still raises the question of why it's there in the first place. Exploratory mission? Hell no, not with a gun that big," Magnusson whispered. "And there's the matter of the flight computer. This thing's got IFF codes for every major military in the galaxy. Who's he trying to sneak by in this bucket?"

Gibbs chuckled. "If they think we're friendlies, we won't have to launch any 'probes' at 'em," he mused. "Just enjoy the ride, Jay. Be glad we're back in the saddle."

Magnusson still wasn't convinced, but he let the subject drop. "All I'm saying is, research vessels don't carry weapons of mass destruction in their bellies, nor do they try to fly under the radar the way this thing is built to. And the cameras," he said in a sharp whisper.

"What cameras?" Gibbs asked.

"That's my point! The Stranger said he witnessed Eisenholm's freak out, right? How? We rewired the whole damn ship; did *you* see any hidden cams anywhere, cuz' I sure as hell didn't. Unless she had her breakdown in front of an open communcations channel, the only way he could've witnessed it is if he was *on this ship* when it happened."

At this, Gibbs began to scratch his grizzled chin. "Leave that to the detective, Jay," he grumbled in surrender. "Clyde will sort out what's what. He don't know jack shit about space travel, but I think he's a sharp kid."

"I think you trust this Hunter too much," Magnusson said, refocusing on the flight. "I mean, he seems like an alright guy, but he's still Registry." He sighed and adjusted the trim on the ship's controls. "Anyway, we have a job to do. I just wanted to get that off my chest, man. This whole thing doesn't feel right. You know what I mean?"

"I do," Gibbs said emptily. "But it's over our heads now." He picked up the intercom and, in his best announcer voice, informed their passengers that they would be taking off soon. "Last call for anyone gettin' off," Gibbs bellowed. "Next stop: Platform 222. ETA: one hour. Thank you and have a nice day."

His message was still echoing through the halls as the *Darkstar* began to rise. She was a few meters off the ground before the landing gear folded away. Thin wings fanned out like porcupine quills, six on each side, nearly grazing the sand in her shadow.

Magnusson eased forward on the throttle, while gently pulling back on the yoke. The drive cores hummed to life, rising to a crescendo as the nose pointed skyward. There was a slight shudder in his seat as the engines reached full throttle and she pushed off, trailing a cone of ionized blue plasma in her wake. The wing blades cut sharp contrails as she rolled over and rocketed into the upper atmosphere.

* * *

Clyde knocked three times on Ell's door.

"It's open," she said from within, her voice muffled by the airtight seals. After swiping his hand over the touchpad, the door slid aside and he entered.

The lights were dim, metal shades drawn down over narrow windows. Ell's room was slightly smaller than his, but she had clearly made herself at home. It looked the way he felt a technophile's lair should. The bed was covered in datapads, hard drives, and laptop computers. Her bags and half a dozen metal cases were piled in a corner. Other than the various electronics and the clothes on her back, she hadn't unpacked a thing.

The obscenely large sniper rifle was propped against a wall in one corner and wouldn't be returning to the armory any time soon. She'd claimed it as her personal plaything and Clyde was, more or less, fine with that.

A bottle of expensive champagne stood on the nightstand, still corked and wrapped in a sleeve which kept it cryogenically chilled to just above freezing. Clyde wasn't sure if he was fine with that, but the door shut behind him.

Ell reclined at a small desk with her feet up, as always, while pecking away at a computer. But there was no keyboard or screen. Her fingers typed on air, while mesh gloves recorded each keystroke, and she spared him only the briefest glance. In the dim lighting, her blue eyes seemed to glow like headlamps.

"Ocular implants," Clyde said, as it all became clear. "I knew something seemed a little odd when you first looked at me. You have false eyes."

She confirmed his suspicions with a grin and another quick glance over her shoulder. "Most people figure that out in ten seconds. Ten minutes for the slow ones. You: two hours."

"I had other things to think about than your hi-tech eyes," Clyde said as he cleared away some of the clutter and took a seat on the hard bed.

Ell turned around to face him and rested her chin in her gloved hands.

"Why'd you do it?" he asked. "The eyes, I mean. Bad accident? Birth defect?"

"Why? Why not?" she said with a shrug. "Somethin's gotta be *wrong* with my eyes for me to wanna change 'em? Few years ago, I did a job for a surgeon on P-78. He was under investigation for trafficking illegal mods, human upgrades and stuff, and wanted somebody to cover his tracks 'fore the feds got wise. He offered to pay in cash or gimme any upgrade I wanted." She smirked. "I went for the upgrade. Simple as that."

"You let a backalley surgeon carve out your eyeballs and replace them with... those?"

"I had him replace my eyeballs with high-definition imaging matrices grafted onto my optic nerves," she replied. "I've got built-in night vision, far sight, I can even project video feeds directly into my head, or save everything I see on this." She gestured to a little black choker sitting on the desk. "It's got a microprocessor and close-range wireless interface to a tiny chip at the base of my neck that can pick up and save everything I see, video or stills, 3d or 2d."

"So you have photographic memory?"

"Yup. Everything short of seein' through walls. That woulda cost extra," she laughed. "And the best part: it's not Solaran. Ya know why I like computers? 'Cuz *we* invented 'em. Pure human tech and they keep getting better."

"Yeah... technology sure is fascinating," Clyde said dryly. Frankly, he found it rather creepy, but her enthusiasm was contagious. If she liked having robot eyeballs, more power to her, but he wouldn't be lining up for a pair of his own anytime soon.

"Anyway, you said you wanted to see me about something," Clyde added. "This *is* a professional inquiry, right, not a social call?" His gaze involuntarily flickered to the champagne.

"I wish it was both... but it ain't," Ell said with the utmost seriousness. She grabbed one of the larger datapads from the pile and switched it on, speaking as she navigated through a few touchscreens: "Ever since I heard about who we'd be tracking, all I could think is that there's no way in hell we'd catch this chick. I mean, time travel? C'mon..."

"I take it you've heard of the Chronomancer before?"

"Who hasn't? Figured she was boogeyman-type stuff. An urban legend. People like her don't get caught. I'm a hacker, Clyde. I make my living sellin' information and bein' in everybody's business, but even I know some folks are ghosts. Some ya just can't see or catch."

"Anyone can be caught," Clyde said.

The statement plunked into their conversation like an iceberg in the Caribbean. Ell paused, looked him squarely in the eyes, and waited for the blockage to melt.

"Yeah. Sure. You go on believing that." She navigated more touchscreens and passed through three layers of password protection with her fingers typing on air. "Reducing people to little points of data is what I do. I'm the one who put together the dossiers. I'm a natural at it. It's my best trick... well, that and this thing I do with my tongue. Maybe I'll show you sometime."

"No thanks."

"Damn. Well, anyway, I got sick of comin' up blank in my search for Chronomancer dirt, so I started diggin' up stuff on *you* and came across something interesting. You'll wanna see this."

Clyde leaned in as she angled the datapad toward him and activated a video. The screen filled with a windowless concrete room, presumably filmed from a security camera mounted in the upper corner. He immediately recognized it as an interrogation chamber inside one of District 19's Registry sub-HQs. There was a steel table in the center, where a large man was seated in a metal chair, with his hands cuffed. Clyde squinted at the screen, though he was already quite sure who it was.

"That's Brock Mason."

"He's in Registry custody, thanks to you," Ell said, "but peep this." She raised the volume as Mason answered a question asked via loudspeaker. The interrogator was not physically present.

That's not standard procedure, Clyde thought.

"...I was tryin' to hit the girl," Mason said. His words slurred as if fighting sedation. "I lost the Hunter, but he had backup."

"Hunter Evans was sent alone," the interrogator said in a deadpan voice. "Need I remind you you're under oath and this inquiry is being recorded, Mr. Mason? Are you sure you encountered another Scion that day?"

Mason emitted what sounded like a low growl or perhaps a weary groan. "I *saw* her. The bitch appeared outta nowhere. Evans was *not* alone!"

"Are you sure, Mr. Mason? You were under severe mental duress." Mason silently rolled his thick neck and angrily drummed a finger on the table, but the interrogator pressed on: "Describe this *other* Scion, Mr. Mason."

"She was barely two meters away. I know what I saw. A girl. Might've been twenty-something. A head shorter than me. She had glasses and was dressed all in black." He muttered something inaudible before raising his voice once more. "Had a knife in her hand. That's why I tried to blast her. Self defense. She..." he hesitated for a moment and his eyes gazed down at the table. He was thinking, choosing his next words carefully. "She must've been high level."

When Mason didn't go on, the interrogator nudged him with another question: "What makes you believe this person was a 'high level' Scion?"

"She had blacklight," Mason said calmly. "Skin as white as these walls. Her hair and eyes, too. I thought she might be blind or something, but she could def see me. And there were these... these jagged black lines creepin' up her neck. I thought it was a bad tattoo, but... nah, had to be blacklight. Lowbies don't get blacklight, only the ones strong enough to hit their limit. That's how I *know* she's gotta be top tier."

Clyde realized Mason was figuring this out as he went. The man had looked Claire Eisenholm squarely in the eyes and was only now realizing that he had come face-to-face with a notorious level ten Scion... a Scion he believed had been sent to kill him.

Nothing happened for a while. Clyde thought the volume had cut out, when in fact there was simply no one speaking. Mason sat contemplating the bare tabletop and his shackled wrists. Clyde looked to Ell, but she gestured for him to watch the video a little longer. Nearly a full minute passed before the interrogator spoke:

"Mr. Mason, would you be able to spot this person in a crowd or lineup?"

"She's a fucking snowman. What do *you* think?" Mason snapped.

"Would you be able to refrain from violence if you encountered this person again?"

"Not if the bitch comes at me with a knife." Mason shrugged his massive shoulders and calmed slightly. "Maybe. I was a nice guy once, you know." His deep chuckle sounded like a growl.

"Would you be willing to serve the Registry once more, in a different capacity?"

"Would you be willing to take these shackles off?"

After another long pause, the door behind him opened and two men entered, wearing the black and silver colors of the

Registry. They lifted Mason from his seat and led him out into the hall. The huge man was heavily drugged. Between the truth serum and sedatives, he put up little resistance. His shackled feet shuffled unsteadily as they herded him out.

A fraction of a second before the door shut, Ell froze the video and zoomed in on the narrow crack. She performed some manipulations to enhance the resolution, sharpening the lines and illuminating the shadows to bring out hidden details. "That's not even the best part. Do you see what I see?" she asked, pointing.

Whatever it was, Clyde could only see a few inches of it, but a few inches was all it took. What he saw in the video was a tall, thin, bipedal creature standing in the hall, wearing a mechanical suit of synthetic black mesh and silvery Solaran metal.

Very few people had ever interacted directly with a Solaran. If they had faces, they never showed them. It is anyone's guess what lurks behind the opaque mask of a Solaran suit. Were they insectoid or avian or reptilian or eerily similar to humans? Were they machines? For all Clyde knew, Solarans could be sentient pond slime, packed into a suit to give them form and speech and mobility. They could be *anything*.

They didn't set foot on Earth for nothing. The last time all twelve Solarans had visited the planet was nearly two hundred years ago, when the Infinite Charter was written and the first Scions, the Original Six, were given gifts. After that day, everything changed.

Clyde could count on one hand the number of times a Solaran had addressed the public in his lifetime... but here was one *personally* ushering Brock Mason into the hall, all because he'd seen a pale girl in an abandoned apartment in New York. The video was as chilling as it was puzzling.

"How'd you come across this?" he asked Ell.

"I was looking for information on you. Even with your gift, I wanted to know why The Stranger was so sure *you*, of all people, could find this chick." She shut off the datapad and offered it to him. "Now I know: she already came to you once and she might come again. When were you gonna tell us you ran into the Chronomancer before?"

"I was waiting for the right moment," Clyde said, accepting the datapad. "But *how* did you get this?" he asked again.

"I hacked into their database. Duh."

"*Don't* do that again. Ever."

"It's not that hard. I just-"

He locked eyes with her and the seriousness she saw there immediately shut her mouth. "Ell, I'm not kidding with you. Digging up info on people is one thing. Snooping on Solarans is an entirely different beast. Some things you just don't fuck with. Are we clear?"

She slowly nodded.

Clyde tucked the datapad into his jacket and continued in a calmer tone. He hadn't expected her to be culled so easily.

"You seem pretty thorough in what you do, so I presume you read my mission report while you were in there. I didn't include the sighting in my report because, frankly, I didn't *see* anything. I only sensed her. The Chronomancer was the last thing on my mind until The Stranger called. That's when I realized I might've come across something major."

Ell was silent for a moment, before finally asking, "So, now what? We just wait for her to show up again?"

"Claire's blacklight is pretty bad," he said, after thinking for a moment. "She probably knows her limits, but I felt her teleport half a dozen times that day. She's putting her health on the line every time she does it... so *why*? There must be a reason she intervened, I just haven't figured it out yet."

When Ell didn't respond, he went on: "Running is Claire's natural defense mechanism. But if she's so unstable, why'd she rescue her crew? She teleported them away to safety, then came *back* to sabotage the ship. That's not the work of a hysterical madwoman. She knew what she was doing."

Ell smiled. "You're sayin' she's got an agenda? She's not just a girl on the run. She's a girl on a mission."

Clyde nodded. "Yeah... and if that video is any indicator, there's a Solaran trying to stop her."

"Are you gonna tell the others? About your brush with the Chronomancer, I mean.

"I'll clue them in," Clyde said, "but there's something I'd like you to do for me first. You're my tech specialist. Can you check this ship from bow to stern? I want a report on the location of every camera, microphone, and any other listening or control devices on this thing. Check the car in the cargo bay, too. Debug the whole ship."

"You think we're being watched?"

"I *know* we're being watched. The only question is, 'how closely?' I don't trust The Stranger and I don't care if he knows it. If his story's true, he *watched* Eisenholm go off the deep end and didn't lift a finger to help. Whatever happened between them, I don't like it," Clyde said flatly. "If there's even *one* room on this ship that's actually private, I'd like to know about it. And if there isn't, I want you to make one. Think you can do that before we reach Platform 222?"

"You trust me to do that?"

He stared into those creepy blue eyes, glowing in the low light. "Trust has to start somewhere. Thanks for the heads up about Mason," Clyde said as he stood and placed a hand on her shoulder. "I don't want you going anywhere near the Registry's servers again... but this is still good intel, so thanks, Ell."

She smiled and gave a mock salute. "I'll get right on it, cap'n! Keep me busy. You know I get frisky when I've got nothin' to do."

"Ummm... right... we wouldn't want that, would we?" Clyde mused as he backed away toward the door. "I appreciate it, Ell. Hopefully, we'll get some answers at 222. Then I'll decide where I stand on our boss and what this has to do with the Solarans."

– 07 –

Platform 222 was a massive steel wheel, twenty miles across, hanging in geosynchronous orbit 55,000 miles above Europe. Nightfall on the eastern hemisphere shrouded the continent in darkness, speckled with city lights, as the *Darkstar Abyssal* drifted into the line of ships queued outside of P-222's port.

On the flight deck, Clyde leaned over Magnusson's shoulder to get a better view. "It's bigger than I thought," he remarked as he observed the enormous space station.

"Yeah, she's one of the larger platforms," Gibbs commented as he tapped codes into a transponder. "Not the biggest, though. Not by a long shot."

Far ahead, ships at the front of the line were guided into airlocks. The *Darkstar Abyssal* waited half a dozen ships back, behind a rather large freighter, which obscured Clyde's view of the proceedings.

Seconds later, a man's voice came through the ship's receiver and verified the identification codes Gibbs had transmitted when they joined the queue. An exchange of flight jargon followed, most of which went right over Clyde's head. He didn't fully tune in until it came time to pay the docking fees. Once the red tape was behind them, the traffic controller concluded with, "*ESV Darkstar Abyssal* you are cleared for docking in Bay E4b. Thank you and please enjoy your stay."

The station's rotation created the illusion of gravity. Within the pressurized torus was a cityscape with the tops of its buildings pointing inward. Four spokes radiated from the central hub, where ships entered. Once inside, the outer doors would be sealed, the airlock would pressurize, and doors leading into the spokes would open.

Magnusson guided the *Darkstar* in. They shared the airlock with five other ships, most of which were shuttles, space yachts, or transports smaller than their own. The *Darkstar*'s slender wings folded back, though there was more than enough room inside to comfortably accommodate all the vessels.

Then they waited.

This is taking too long, Clyde thought. He'd watched a dozen or so ships pass through the lock while they sat in line. Everything moved like clockwork until it was the *Darkstar*'s turn, then it all ground to a halt.

"What's going on?" he asked, looking to Magnusson, but the pilot only shrugged.

"Our ID's and passenger manifest checked out," Gibbs said, rubbing his bushy chin. "If somethin' was fishy, they'd have called us on it then. Maybe somebody's sleepin' on the job. Idiots in the control room..."

Right on cue, the flight controller sent out a general message to the waiting ships: "Sorry for the delay, ladies and gentlemen. We have one more vessel incoming."

A ship emerged from near the back of the queue and approached the airlock, bypassing the line of waiting ships. Its hull was black and silver, sleek as an arrow, with a nose like an eagle's hooked beak, riding twin cones of blue thrust. Her wings folded back and tucked away as she banked hard into the airlock and nested between an aging transport and an expensive mid-sized yacht.

The *Darkstar Abyssal* floated near the back of the airlock, lurking in the shadows, but as the late arrival turned and cut its engines, Clyde caught a glimpse of the name on its side, in bold silver print: *ISV Noble Valiant*. The twelve-pointed star of the Registry was emblazoned on her hull like a badge of honor.

"A Registry cruiser," Gibbs muttered as his eyes narrowed on the newcomer. "Sons of bitches can't wait in line like the rest of us?"

"Actually, that's an interceptor," Magnusson corrected.

"Should we be worried?" Clyde said. He already was.

"I doubt it," Magnusson replied as the airlock began to close, sealing them inside with the bird of prey. "Probably has a crew of no more than a dozen, at best. Interceptors are built for running fast and hard, but we have the advantage of range. We have a larger fuel capacity and warp capabilities, too."

"The Registry's interceptors can't go hyper-relativistic," Gibbs added as the airlock shut. "I heard it's 'cuz they wanna keep their Scions on a short leash, so they make 'em use the warp gates. I guess The Stranger didn't get the memo."

A loud, droning hiss began as the bay quickly filled with atmospheric gasses, matching pressure with the interior of P-222.

"Okay, so the ship's not a major threat," Clyde said, "but who's aboard it? A dozen Hunter Elites *is* a problem. If they get to our guy first..."

"Sounds like it's a race, then," Gibbs added.

"In that case, I'll land as quickly as possible, so we can hit the ground before they do," Magnusson said.

The pressure equalized and four doors opened, each leading to a spoke of the station. Magnusson guided the *Darkstar* forward, casually slipping by the other traffic, including the

Noble Valiant, before laying into the throttle a little harder and pulling away.

Inside Platform 222, spacecraft landed on vertically-stacked decks, alphabetized A-Z, inside the columnar spokes. The *Darkstar* was assigned to deck 'E', nearly all the way at ground level. They flew past ships of all shapes, sizes, and purposes. Her rusty hull looked very out of place racing through the glitzy docks of Platform 222, but the ugly duckling flew like a swan. There was no shortage of grace as she nosed up, decelerated, and extended her landing gear. They were at the landing zone in under a minute.

"Nice flying, Mr. Magnusson," Clyde said as the *Darkstar* rotated into position above its landing pad. "Once you've set her down, meet me in the communications room so we can get down to business."

* * *

There was an overwhelming sense of déjà vu as Gino Ainsworth entered the comm room and found everyone exactly as they'd been during the previous briefing. Evans seemed to be slipping into his role as 'captain' quite nicely. He stood at the front of the room with his hands clasped behind his back, like a general in the situation room.

The others sat around the center console, awaiting his orders... except Niehaus, who was speaking with Evans in lowered voices. They exchanged a few whispered words before she smiled, handed him a datapad, and took her seat.

Gino's eyes narrowed upon him. Females and business didn't mix... if Neihaus could even be considered 'female.' To him, she was the equivalent of a small rodent. Gino planted himself in a seat next to her, but said nothing as the captain began.

"Alright, I'll try to make this quick," Evans said as he tapped upon the console. "I want our stay on P-222 to be as short and sweet as possible, with an emphasis on sweet. In, out, and *gone* before trouble catches us."

"Are you anticipating trouble?" Doctor Jenner queried.

"No," Evans replied, "but isn't that when trouble always comes? The plan is to find and extract Desmond Williams, ASAP."

Gino's brows rose. "You mean kidnap him? Snag him and bag him?"

"I mean take him with us… preferably with his consent. The Registry is more interested in the Chronomancer than expected. Since Williams is the only lead, they'll want him. Whoever reaches him first gets a leg up on the hunt. We can't afford to miss this opportunity."

"So what are we waiting for?" Gino asked, spreading his hands. "Instead of talking about it, let's go get him. I thought you were a *Hunter*."

Ell shot him a spiteful glare and Gino returned the favor. If looks could kill, they were eviscerating one another with their eyes.

"I think Williams will be glad to come with us once he learns a Registry interceptor just landed and is parked three levels above our heads," Evans said, unfazed by the open hostility. "He either comes with us − friends of his former employer − or he goes with *them*, the enemy."

"What if he doesn't want to go with either?" Gibbs asked. He gestured to Gino. "Do we bag him and gag him, like this fine gentleman suggested?"

Clyde chuckled, thinking it was a joke. It wasn't. "I'll cross that bridge when we get to it. 'Til then, let's keep the talk of kidnapping to a minimum, okay."

A Hunter who didn't want to talk about snatching unsuspecting victims? Gino found the thought laughable, but resolved to bridle his cynicism a little longer.

Evans manipulated the touchscreens until a mug shot of a thin-faced black male came into view. He had a shrewd, almost wolfish air about him, with devious eyes and a scruffy goatee. Gino immediately didn't like him. Then again, he didn't like most people.

"This is Desmond Williams," Evans explained. "The Stranger's intel places him at a nightclub on 19th Street and Main, not too far from here. He has entered this club at about the same time, every other day, for the past week, beginning five days ago. According to The Stranger's data, he spends two thousand credits a night there, then leaves."

"Maybe he'll buy us a few rounds," Ell teased.

"Showing his face like that... is he *trying* to get caught?" Dr. Jenner asked.

"Possibly. We know Eisenholm purposefully sent the *Darkstar* back to Earth and now Williams shows up in a blatantly obvious fashion. He's sending a message. I'd like to know to whom and what he's trying to say. If he sticks to the same pattern, he should appear tomorrow evening – that's P-222 time, of course. Niehaus and I will scope out the club and plant surveillance measures. I want eyes all over that place, so we'll know if Williams or some other person of interest shows up. Mr. Ainsworth, you're coming with us, just in case."

Though Gino was glad to finally have something to do, his frown did not wane. "Whatever you say... captain."

Clyde carried on without missing a beat: "Gibbs, Magnusson, I want you to prep the ship. Get her refueled and ready to take off at a moment's notice. You have full access to the expense account, so buy whatever you need to get her operating at 110%. And if you can learn anything about that interceptor – who's on board, what they're doing here, *anything* – I'll appreciate it. Doctor, I want you to hold down the fort while we're away. We won't be gone long, but you can never know in a place like this. That interceptor over our heads bothers me. Any questions?"

"Boxers or briefs?" Ell said.

Clyde sighed. "Meeting adjourned. Let's get moving. Gino, Ell, meet me in the cargo bay in ten minutes," he said as he headed toward the door.

"How about five?" Gino muttered under his breath as he exited the room.

− 08 −

City 222 was an old dark pleasure town, bathed in hazy twilight, with narrow alleys, tight buildings, and streets lined with neon signage. Streetlamps gave the illusion of illumination, without actually lighting anything. It was cheap and expensive at the same time. Bright, alive, and bustling with activity, yet hard and soulless. A contradiction, an urban mirage; it was the sort of city where a man's eyes could play tricks on his wallet.

Clyde immediately didn't like it. He'd done his homework, but the reality of Platform 222 was far worse than the forcasts of its travel brochures. It had a distinct odor. Even on the landing pads, far above the city proper, the air was heavy with the scent of sweat, sex, and something he couldn't quite place. Something primal. It sucker punched him the moment the cargo ramp dropped.

Video billboards and holograms streamed advertisements for casinos, clubs, and chemical delights, bombarding him from all directions. Clyde walked to the edge of the deck and peered over the railing. They were nearly a quarter-mile up. Over a dozen vertigo-inducing decks were stacked beneath them, like dinner plates in a giant's cabinet, each holding a ship, sometimes two.

The *Noble Valiant* waited somewhere above his head, likely hunting the same quarry. Clyde breathed in deep, acclimating himself to the heady atmosphere, before turning on his heels and walking back to the ship to gather his companions. There was no time to waste.

Minutes later, after a long ride on the cargo elevator, they were prowling the streets. Clyde took the wheel, Ell rode shotgun, and Gino had the backseat all to himself, to brood in solitude. It was night time in P-222. It was *always* night time in P-222. A false sky speckled with lights cast a faint orange glow on the city, but darkness prevailed.

The vehicle's computer automatically synched with the platform's network to display the local time, 3:15 a.m., but strange people in clingy, luminescent attire, with hair of all colors and styles, still clogged the sidewalks. The women wore more accessories than clothing. Their heels were higher than their skirts were long, and they swaggered down the walkways like stilted gazelles, latched onto men who were draped in gold, platinum, and the latest designer brands, their identities shrouded in a cloud of consumerism.

Clyde thought the oddities were confined to one district, but he drove for blocks and found it was all the same. Parties. Clubs. Brothels. Motels. Drug dens. Clubs. Motels. It repeated, ad nauseum, all dark shameless shades of the same vices. He couldn't spit without hitting a strip club.

Someone touched him. He flinched when he found Ell wrist-deep in his coat pocket.

"*Excuse* me?" Clyde said as he yanked her hand free of his pocket. "Can I help you, ma'am? Looking for something?"

"Geez, sorry," she said, cowed. "I just wanted to see your badge." The device's plain steel chain dangled from his pocket. "I never seen one up close."

"Yes you have," Gino said from the backseat. "That guy... what's-his-face..."

"Flipass doesn't count," Ell quipped. "I ain't seen *Clyde's* badge."

"You could've asked," he said as he fished the device from his pocket and forked it over.

"She's a platformer. They've no regard for personal space or property," Gino sneered. "We should be grateful it's housebroken."

Ell flashed him her middle finger in the rearview mirror, but, a half-second later, she was silently studying the three-ringed badge with juvenile fascination.

The traffic light turned green and the car began to move again, gliding under the dim streetlights on spokeless rims, with intermittent electrical arcs illuminating its fender wells.

"Personal insults aside, you should've asked," Clyde said again. "I don't mind letting you see it."

"Yeah, yeah, I know," she droned as she turned the device upside down and held it at eye level. She suddenly whipped around to face Gino. "Hey, where's yours? Bet it's got more rings. I wanna see it."

"He's an Arena fighter. That's a different branch. Only official Reapers, Hunters, and other operatives get badges," Clyde explained.

"Oh." A very disappointed Ell sat back and returned the item. "Well, whatever. Thanks anyway."

"Ironic, isn't it?" Gino said. "If you like their toys so much, why not become a Hunter? If you weren't hiding your gift they'd have snatched you up and given you a shiny badge of your own. They'll take anyone, even an ingrate like you."

"What *is* your gift anyway?" Clyde asked.

"She omitted that minor detail from the files."

"'Cuz it's none o' your business," Ell fired back. "And just 'cuz I think the badge looks cool, don't mean I wanna sell my soul to get one. It's slavery. I could just as easily score one off the black market... or *borrow* Clyde's."

"I wouldn't miss it," he said with a shrug.

"Does the gun come with it?" Ell jabbed a finger at the sidearm on his hip. "They train you to use that thing?"

"Yes, but it's coded to me," Clyde said. "Actually, Gino and I probably received very similar training. Why not ask him? You two should get to know each other."

Gino snorted.

Ell turned to face him. "I bet Clyde could kick your ass, if he wanted to."

"He's welcome to try anytime," Gino remarked. "I could've been a Hunter, you know, but someone decided I was better suited for the Arena. The difference between us is I put on a better show. Once they learn you have a gift, it's anyone's guess where they'll assign you. But they'll always find a use for you... if you let them."

"See, you admit it's slavery!" Ell said with finality, and settled cozily into her seat as if she'd won an argument no one else was participating in.

"I looked up one of your matches earlier," Clyde said to Gino. "Impressive. I think say they made the right choice. A man who can generate crystal body armor can rake in quite a crowd. Gino 'The White Knight' Ainsworth. It has a nice ring to it..."

"I *despise* that name," Gino replied. "The Arena is corrupted by imbeciles like you who think it's *all* about 'putting on a good show.' To hell with them. When I step into the ring, every ounce of my being is dedicated to destroying who or whatever stands before me."

"Ooooh, he's so *intense*," Ell teased. "You look so pretty, strutting around in your shiny armor. Can you conjure a crystal purse for me? Or a diamond ring? How about some glass slippers?"

Gino muttered something unintelligible.

"He's still mad they kicked him out," Ell said. "Ya know, in the *actual* feudal system − not the storybook version − a knight is nothin' but a slave who'll die for his master. You're their bitch. Now you know what happens when you don't play by their rules, *bitch*."

"Screw their rules," Gino said, "and screw you, too."

Ell threw up her hands. "Fuck the whole system, I say. I chose to opt out. I live by my own rules."

"Opt out? You mean *hide*," Gino said, "like a coward."

"Well, maybe if you'd kept your head down and ran your mouth a little less, you'd still be in the limelight, champ." Ell laughed. "Oops. I meant *former* champ."

Clyde cruised past the nightclub they were searching for. He found parking half a block away, pulled in, and shut off the car. But neither Ell nor Gino seemed to notice.

She wasn't done: "I'm so sick of your attitude," Ell said. "You're a pampered prince who spits on the throne and declares himself leader of the free world. You think you're the first person to speak out? You think you're the first to fly a middle finger at the Solarans? You ain't half as anti-establishment as you think you are."

"The Registry may have decided the course of my life, but they won't decide how I carry it out," Gino said. "I may fight in their Arena, but I do it *my way*. I'm no one's bitch."

"But you *are*," Ell laughed. "You're their poster boy! You can't have it both ways."

"This isn't about me and my life," Gino said. "I'm fairly sure we were talking about your lack of etiquette. In what universe is it okay to stick your hand in someone's pocket? Evans may put up with you, but try that on anyone else and see how it goes."

"Quit tryin' to change the subject," Ell said. "I just warm up to people a li'l faster than you, that's all. Try mouthin' off like that to anyone else and see what happens, jackass. You'll get fucked up so fast-"

"Yeah, I've noticed how quickly you 'warm up' to people. You're the resident expert on fucking up, down, and every other position imaginable. Slut."

Clyde sighed. *Here we go...*

"Oh, *this* again!?" Ell snapped around to give her accuser a piece of her mind. "Fucking hypocrite! What the hell is your problem, anyway? A girl tries out a couple guys and she's a slut, but when a *man* does it, he's-"

"Gay. A man who sleeps with a couple of guys is pretty damn gay," Gino barked, "and *still* a slut, if ya ask me."

Ell pounced so fast, Clyde almost didn't catch her. He narrowly managed to hook an arm around her waist and yank her back into the front seat. A fraction of a second later and she would've made it into the backseat and set about clawing Gino's face off. In that instant, he realized how little he knew about these people. She was like a wild animal and Gino was as unrepentant and caustic as ever, hurling obscenities at her, even as she raged.

"That's enough," Clyde said, in a calm, even tone. He looked Ell in the eyes, unblinking. "We're here and you have a job to do. Can you do what we came to do?"

"I'm fine. Lemme go," she hissed. "Just tell your boy to watch his fuckin' mouth."

"He will," Clyde said as he cautiously released her.

"I'm no one's 'boy.' Keep your animal in check," Gino muttered as he exited the vehicle and stood apart, with his nose to the proverbial sky. "Let's get this over with."

* * *

"That's a hell of a ship you've got," one of the two technicians commented as he hauled a heavy fueling hose away from the cargo bay's rear doors. He wore a reflective yellow vest over his baggy orange jumpsuit. Another technician, dressed the same, came behind him and hefted the hose onto his shoulders.

"I ain't never seen a ship that small drink so much," the second man said. "Had we known, we'd have brought a bigger fueling truck."

"Or two," the other tech said. "No prob. We'll be back in a few minutes to finish the job." He tipped his hat as they began coiling the hose onto the back of the fueling rig.

"Thanks," Gibbs said as he stood by, observing. He had offered to give a hand, but the men declined, citing company policy, insurance liabilities and such.

A minute later, the hoses were loaded and the truck drove away and onto the cargo lift. With a sigh, Isaac Gibbs returned to the *Darkstar*'s bay, where Magnusson stood waiting.

"Did they say anything?" the pilot asked.

"Haven't heard a word," Gibbs replied. "I hung 'round the fueling depot for 'bout an hour, flappin' my gums, but nobody's heard a word about that *Noble Valiant*. I figured gossip would spread quick in a place like this."

"Yeah... a ship like that ought to make a buzz," Magnusson added.

"Right. She's new, sexy, probably fast as hell. Flashy, too," Gibbs said as he fished a cigarette from his pocket. "I figured the techs ought to know somethin.' She still runs on fuel, don't she? She still needs her reactor flushed and seeded the same as everybody else, right? But, nope, nobody's been near her... or nobody wants to talk."

His many years in space had caused him to lay off smoking, but the feel of a cigarette between his lips was something Gibbs had never given up. When the old itch came back, he couldn't resist. "I don't like it," he said as he stuck the useless thing into his mouth.

"They just landed, same as us. Give it time," Magnusson replied. He paused thoughtfully, before nodding to something in the distance. "Hmmm... looks like our boys are back. That was quick." Gibbs followed his lead and spotted a fueling truck emerging from the elevator. "I'll be inside if you need me," Magnusson said before turning away and heading up the stairs into the *Darkstar*'s living quarters, leaving Gibbs to deal with the last of the refueling effort.

The tanker pulled alongside the spacecraft and a man in an orange jumpsuit climbed down. He was tall, thin, with long, straight blonde hair hanging just past his shoulders. Gibbs nearly mistook him for a woman. His first thought was that this fellow seemed awfully soft for a technician. His thoughts of why the first two men hadn't returned came much later.

"Are you Clyde Evans, the registered captain of this vessel?" the man asked as he approached. He had narrow blue eyes behind thin, silver-framed glasses. His sharp gaze briefly flitted to the unlit cigarette before quickly snapping up to meet Gibbs's eyes.

"'Fraid not. Isaac Gibbs, lead flight engineer."

"Ah, yes. My mistake. Well, Mr. Gibbs, if you would be so kind as to direct me to this vessel's fueling port, we may begin," the technician said. "The previous crew was called away to service a vessel on pad D5c. My name is Lee. I will be your serviceman for the duration of this procedure."

"Right this way, Mr. Lee. It's inside," Gibbs said. The technician gathered the large hose from the back of his truck and began uncoiling it. Gibbs moved to help and Lee gladly accepted the assistance.

Together, the two men carried the large hose into the ship's cargo bay and plugged the nozzle into a port near the rear exit.

Lee locked it in place and, using a datapad clipped to his belt, entered the requested amount and mixture of fuel. The tanker's pump churned to life and began delivering the goods.

"Five minutes, sir," Lee said while they waited for the truck to finish pumping the mixture of cesium and deuterium fuel into the *Darkstar*'s reserve tanks. His eyes slowly took in the cargo bay, studying every rivet and panel. "I must say, this is an impressive ship, Mr. Gibbs. From the exterior, I believed it to be a Class 3 tug, but it is clearly a cargo vessel, as evidenced by the extensive amount of storage space in her bay."

"Close. She's based on a tug, I think," Gibbs said.

"With such great fuel reserves, I am sure her range is astounding." Lee adjusted his spectacles. "Far greater than any tugboat. May I ask where you acquired such a vessel?"

"That'd be a question for her owner. I just wrench on her," Gibbs said, with much good humor. He tossed his cigarette aside and ground it out, as if it were lit. "She ain't half as astounding as that silver interceptor in bay H, though. Did you see that thing?"

"The *Noble Valiant*, you mean? Yes. I had the pleasure of refueling her shortly before being called here," Lee said. "She is one of the Registry's latest models; fast, efficient, *deadly*, and even more beautiful up close. The future of spaceflight is truly amazing, Mr. Gibbs, and we have the Solarans to thank for all of it. Is it true this vessel has two drive cores?"

"Where'd you hear that?" Gibbs said. He prepared to nudge the conversation back toward the *Valiant*, but was cut short by the bespectacled technician.

"How do you meet your energy and coolant needs? Dual cores in a ship this size is very impressive, Mr. Gibbs."

"We find a way," Gibbs said with a nervous chuckle.

Lee laughed as well, but the sound was dull, hollow, and awkward, just like his smile. "I understand completely, Mr.

Gibbs. I am an engineer as well. An electrical engineer, to be precise. My colleagues regard me as something of a wizard when it comes to moving electrons." He nodded slowly, as if affirming his own statement. "Men like you and I can do amazing things – *shocking* things – when we reach the height of our ingenuity. Some might say it is like magic. I disagree, but they are entitled to their opinions… however incorrect they may be."

Gibbs merely nodded, absent-mindedly. After the pun, he tuned the man out.

A brief silence settled between them, which was finally shattered by a beep from the technician's datapad. The refueling was complete. "Perfect," Lee said as he uncoupled the nozzle and removed the hose. "Absolutely perfect. Well, it looks like you're all set, Mr. Gibbs."

"Good, good." He helped Lee tote the equipment back to the waiting tanker. Not until the man was climbing into the driver's cab did Gibbs ask, "Any clue what that ship's here for? The *Valiant*, I mean. A ship like that don't come 'round for nothing.'"

Lee dismissed his concerns at once. "Oh, you know how the Registry can be," he said with another of his awkward, stiff laughs. "They always come around for reasons none can fathom. They're always so secretive, so *sneaky*." He grinned. "Sadly, I haven't the slightest clue what the reason might be, Mr. Gibbs. I am sorry." He climbed into the cab, shut the door, and started the engine.

Gibbs waved and turned away, only to hear Lee's voice one last time.

"I was, however, greeted by two Scions when I went to service their vessel," Lee said from the open window of his truck. "Level tens, both. Serious business, that. I would be frightened if men such as those were hot upon *my* trail. I thank the gods that they are not."

The Silq Serpent was a massive nightclub, three stories tall, perched on the corner of 19th Street and Main. Red neon lights outlined the building's edges. A hologram of a crimson anaconda coiling around a martini glass adorned the entryway, looming over the long line of guests waiting to enter. Every few seconds it dipped its fangs into the drink, took a sip, and spewed holographic flames into the night sky.

Despite Ell's insistence that he use his authority to bypass the crowds, Clyde decided to keep a low profile and wait in line like everyone else. Ten minutes later, they reached the entrance. To his surprise, the bouncer thought nothing of the gun on his hip. They were allowed inside without having to flash his badge at all. The man didn't even check Ell's backpack.

He wondered if this might be why Desmond Williams chose this club. Nothing was screened.

Once inside, only red neon and flickering LEDs guided the trio as they ventured deeper. The music was so loud, they could feel the bass in their bones. The press of bodies became thick long before they reached the dance floor, where people moved rhythmically, like a giant wave rolling to the beat. There were two levels of neon-lined balconies overlooking the main floor. Holographic flames danced on the ceiling, as if the entire roof were a blazing inferno.

They got straight down to business, despite Ell insisting they sample the circular bar at the center of the room. "Research," she called it. "Necessary research."

"I'll get you something before we leave!" Clyde said as she set down her bag near the first security camera. By yelling into one another's ears, they were just barely able to communicate over the pounding noise.

Ell drew a roll of black tape from her bag of tricks, tore off a small strip, and began wrapping it around a loose wire dangling from beneath the camera housing.

"How is this supposed to help us!?" Gino said. He was far closer than she liked *and* he was yelling, but Ell resisted the urge to punch him in the nose.

"It's not regular tape, dumbass!" she replied. "It's a nanomaterial that reads electrical impulses and datastreams." She didn't care if he heard.

He and Clyde both yelled "WHAAAT!?" half a dozen times as she tried to explain how this piece of surveillance tech worked, until she gave up.

The tape would pick up any data flowing through the conduit – data from the club's security cameras. "And *this*," she said, drawing out a tiny pin, "is the transmitter. Sends it all back to the *Darkstar* to be analyzed."

She stuck the metal pin through the taped section of wire. After giving the pinhead a slight twist, the device was primed and ready to start recording.

Gino didn't catch a word of her explanation. He looked to Clyde, who merely shrugged. Ell zipped up her bag, slung it over her shoulder, and they moved on.

"That covers the door!" Clyde said, close enough for them both to hear. "Let's get some on level two and another in VIP on level three!" Ell nodded and the trio moved toward the stairs. It was slightly quieter on the second level, but not by much.

"I don't like clubs," Gino remarked, looking around warily as she began tapping into another security feed. This one had an excellent view of the main floor and half of the tables on the second level.

"What the hell *do* you like?" Ell fired back.

"Peace and quiet."

"Well, you do a fine job of wrecking both," she snapped.

Gino folded his arms and summoned just enough self-control to avoid a repeat of what had happened in the car.

Ell finished the second camera and closed her bag. "C'mon," she said as she walked away. Clyde began to follow, but Gino caught him by the shoulder.

"I think I'll go take a look around," he said and quickly moved away toward the stairs before anyone could say otherwise.

"Well, this is going great..." Clyde murmured to himself before catching up with Ell, who was far better at weaving through crowds. This was, after all, her natural habitat. Thankfully, the clusters of people thinned out around the perimeter, where the security cameras were located. By the time he reached her, she was already wrapping another wire.

"Don't do that. I lost sight of you for a second," he said.

"Whatever, Dad, I don't need to be babysat. I got a Taser in the bag," she said. "What's with you, anyway? You act like everybody's out to get us."

"Doesn't take everybody. Just one," Clyde said. He leaned on the padded velvet walls and folded his arms across his chest. "Gino went to take a look around."

"Well, damn, I was hopin' he'd jumped over the railing. That'd be worth drinkin' to."

"Ease up. He's not so bad," Clyde said. "Claire likes him, for some reason." When Ell looked to him in muted disbelief, he added, "It was in the info The Stranger sent. Apparently Claire's a *huge* fan of the Arena... especially our White Knight. She's a Gino Ainsworth groupie."

"And she's bat-shit crazy," Ell said as she grabbed the box of transmitter nodes. "Ya know what *really* pisses me off? The way he just doesn't give a damn. He talks at me like I'm nothin.' Last guy underestimated me like that got his balls bashed in with a baseball bat. I've come too far to be looked down on by some fucking has-been."

Professional pride? Clyde certainly hadn't expected that from Ell, of all people. Then again, she had a rather impressive skill set, despite her less than glamorous background. A certain amount of respect was due… and Gino hadn't given *any*.

"Well…" Clyde thought for a moment. "He just needs a purpose, is all. He's a fighter spoiling for a fight. Stop giving him one and he'll lay off."

"Sounds like a bully to me," Ell said as she finished her work and bagged the gear. "If he likes fightin' so much, maybe a bat to the nuts is exactly what he needs. Beat some of that testosterone outta him."

"Yeah, because being assaulted usually makes a person *less* hostile," Clyde said. Ell took the sarcasm well and actually smiled a little, but the effect was minimal. "He's slightly maladjusted, but if you two don't kill one another, I think you'll get along fine… eventually."

"Whatever. Let's finish this and go."

He guided her to the stairs leading up to the VIP area on level three. A rather large bouncer blocked the entryway and looked down on Clyde like a boot hovering over an ant.

"Goin' somewhere?" the wall of meat asked. His eyes checked their wrists, which were not adorned with the fluorescent red bracelets seen on the other VIP guests.

"Clyde Evans. Registry agent," he said, flashing the almighty badge. "I'm here on official business." The bouncer seemed momentarily at a loss for words and looked to Ell. "She's my research assistant," Clyde said. "We suspect a fugitive may be in the area and we require access to your surveillance equipment. Perhaps I should speak to your manager…"

The bouncer shook his head and stepped aside, gesturing for them to enter. No man in his right mind would dare argue with a Scion.

The Silq Serpent was an expensive club in an already expensive city. Nowhere was that more apparent than in the VIP section, where plush couches lined the walls. There were only a few guests and they were far calmer than the gyrating, undulating masses of bodies on the main floor, or the not-quite-drunk-but-quickly-getting-there bodies on the second floor.

"You're a hell of a liar," Ell said as she began working on another camera, this one overlooking the entire VIP area. She stood in the couch to reach it, which earned her a scolding glance from Clyde. "Seriously? You know how many people make out on this thing any given night? A few shoeprints won't make a diff."

"Manners, Ell." Clyde moved the segment of lounge furniture aside, so she could work without trampling the upholstery. "And I wasn't lying. You *are* my research assistant. It's true."

"The best lies are."

Clyde took a seat on the couch to wait. There was a neon-lit bar at the opposite end of the VIP section, where a plastic woman in a skimpy uniform was serving drinks. She played her part well and kept the customers coming back. There was another gorilla-like bouncer lumbering around the edges of the room. He repeatedly cast glances in Clyde's direction.

Ell suddenly flopped down into his lap. "All done!" she exclaimed. "Now what? Wanna hit the bar... or jus' chill here and wait for somethin' to *come up*?"

"Now we put everything back where we found it and *leave*," Clyde said as he dumped her off and tried to catch his breath. She stared up at him with an impish grin while toying with the oversized pillows. He did not like that look or the things it suggested...

"Ya know, this job would be sooo much better if it was just the two of us," Ell said, in what was probably supposed to be a seductive tone. Unfortunately, she had the voice of a whinnying horse.

"No, it wouldn't." Clyde shoved the couch into place with her still on it. "We should find Gino. He's been gone a while." Just as he turned, he spotted the man in question approaching from the stairs, with a drink in hand. Soon, he was in their midst and Ell's mood instantly soured.

"Glad you could join us, Mr. Ainsworth," Clyde said with a smile. "How'd you get past the bouncer?"

"I'm Gino Ainsworth and this is VIP. Do the math," he said before shoving the drink at Ell. "Take it." She experimentally took a sip and winced. "I figured you wouldn't want something girly," Gino grumbled in a droll tone. "That's the strongest they've got… and it's a hundred creds a cup, so don't waste it."

"You figured right," she purred before bravely downing the whole thing in a matter of seconds. "Apology accepted. Now gimme another."

"Apology? The drink was to shut you up."

Not again, Clyde thought. "We should get back to the ship." He quickly grabbed Ell by the arm and tugged her to her feet. "Let's go."

"Awww, you're no fun."

"We aren't here for fun," Clyde said. "C'mon, both of you. We shouldn't hang around here until Williams shows up. We have almost 24 hours before his next scheduled appearance. Try not to spend it all in one place."

"I want to go check out that interceptor," Gino said adamantly. "We have eyes on the club, but no eyes on that ship. As the team bodyguard, I think I should-"

"No," Clyde said. "No one goes anywhere near that ship. We watch and we wait. That's all."

– 09 –

With the lights dimmed and a blanket draped over his shoulders, Clyde fought a losing battle with his own eyelids. The starships drifting by his window were a welcome distraction, but he hadn't slept since leaving District 19 and it showed.

A long, champagne-colored space yacht drifted by, with its three engines flashing bright white, and he was instantly able to distinguish the make and model. It was a Japanese-built GSX3100, though he couldn't tell if it was the new fourth-gen model introduced in late 2119 or the recently-discontinued mk-III.

His studies were paying off. He read *So You've Bought a Spaceship: Interstellar Travel for Dummies*, from cover-to-digital-cover hours ago. After that, he read, *Shoot the Moon*, the autobiography of Commander James F. Grayson, the most decorated man in the Earth Coalition Space Force. Numerous internet forums recommended it as mandatory reading for anyone with even a passing interest in ship-to-ship combat, as if Grayson were a modern day Sun Tzu.

Now Clyde was nodding off with his nose buried in *They Can Still Hear You Scream*, the memoirs of a notorious space pirate who'd allegedly hijacked, raided, looted, and scuttled 647 spacecraft. The man wrote *Scream* while wasting away in a cell on Mimas, where he will undoubtedly spend the rest of his days. For a book about thievery and murder, Clyde found it surprisingly dull. Then again, few things were more interesting than the insides of his eyelids at the moment.

Maybe a quick nap wouldn't hurt...

Clyde suddenly whipped around in his seat and found himself nose to navel with Gibbs's grimy t-shirt. "Ain't mean to startle ya," the portly engineer said. "I tried to call, but you weren't answerin,' so I let myself in. Ell just picked up yer guy on one of her cameras. He's in the club. It's showtime, cap'n."

Realization came slowly, but when the dots connected Clyde tossed away his reading material and checked his watch. "He's early," he said as he snatched his holster, weapon, and badge from the nightstand, thrust his arms into his long coat and charged toward the door. "Where are Gino and Ell?"

The latter question answered itself. Clyde covered the hall in about a dozen long strides and found Ell at the gun locker, near the stairs to the cargo bay, selecting a sidearm.

"You're not bringing that," Clyde said, just as Gibbs caught up. A single glance was enough to dissuade her and Ell remorsefully returned the weapon to its resting place. "Where's Gino? We gotta go."

"Dunno," Ell replied with an innocent shrug, "but he said he'd be back in time."

"Well he's not." Clyde whipped out his communicator.

"Don't bother," Ell said. "The whole station's comms have been down for half an hour. Some of these older platforms run on a unified network, where exploiting one vunerability can cause the whole system to-"

"Thanks, Ell, but, honestly, I don't care," Clyde said as he shoved the useless device back into his pocket and pinched his eyes in frustration. "Sorry. Unless you can fix it in ten seconds flat, we gotta move."

"Nobody expected Williams to show up two hours ahead of schedule," Gibbs commented.

"Maybe someone did, just not us," Clyde said. "Either way, we gotta go. We can't miss this window. Ell, you're coming with me. Gibbs, if Gino shows up, tell him to stay put. Ship's yours 'til we get back. Full lockdown." Gibbs nodded as Clyde led Ell toward the stairs. "Where's Williams? You've got eyes on him, right?"

"VIP section. He showed up five minutes ago and bought rounds for the whole place."

"He's making a scene, probably trying to draw us out. There's no telling what's going through this guy's head," Clyde said as they hurried down the steps and into the cargo bay. He mashed the button to lower the ramp. "You're driving."

"Afraid you'll fall asleep at the wheel, cap'n?" she said, noting the shadows under his eyes and his dodgy gaze.

"That's the least of my worries."

* * *

Desmond Williams was no stranger to difficult decisions. The past few weeks had been filled with them. But those days were almost over. He just had to make one final choice. After this, he'd be set.

"We can't rush these things, ladies," he said as he lay back on the plush velvet couches and weighed his options. He held a bottle of expensive brandy in one hand while his other palmed a generous portion of Ava's bare flesh. She showed more skin than clothing and had an ass to die for. Meanwhile, Lana had the most immaculate breasts he'd seen all week. And Janice... well, Janice had a pretty face, and not much else, but he really enjoyed her company for some reason.

It was amazing what a few counterfeit credit cards could do. He was burning through creds by the thousands and people were flocking to him like flies to shit. The joke was on them: he hadn't a penny to his name. Not that it mattered on Platform 222, where image was everything and his fake money could buy him a handful of Lana's fake tits and Ava's ass cheeks.

With the sharp gaze of a seasoned grifter, Desmond studied the swirling crowds. VIP was filling quickly. He told the bouncer to let them in − *all* of them − and put it on his tab. In retrospect, that wasn't such a good idea. How was he supposed to spot a Hunter in this crowd?

The thought was gone as quickly as it'd come. Ava slid into his lap and began working her unique brand of magic. Lana stroked his neck and whispered something into his ear. Whatever non-carnal thoughts he had evaporated like piss on summer pavement.

Desmond waved a hand to call the female bartender over. "Drinks! We need more drinks, right away." She eagerly abandoned her post to collect another five hundred credit tip.

As she slid out from behind the bar, Desmond thought he spotted something near the edge of his vision. Something white. So white and impossibly colorless it stood out clear as day in the darkened nightclub, filled with audacious red and orange flames. But when he looked again, it was gone, and the bartender was standing in front of him, awaiting his demands and her payment.

Desmond didn't miss a beat. "I'll have two more bottles of... whatever this is," he said holding up the brandy. "And some shotglasses for my three lovely..." he stopped short. There it was again! Dammit! Desmond abruptly stood. "Put it on my tab," he said, giving the barwoman a tap on the shoulder and a brisk smile before gliding past her.

Janice caught him by the wrist just as he was about to walk away. She batted her long lashes and said, in a voice that could steal the sugar from a glass of sweet tea, "Where are you going? We're just getting started."

"Gotta take a piss," Desmond lied and pulled away. "Be back in a sec. Don't go *nowhere*." The three ladies giggled collectively, like a trio of tipsy hyenas.

Soon he was weaving through the crowd, looking left and right and left again, searching for the chronic apparition, the ghost haunting him. *Where are you?*

"You asshole!" she screeched.

He wheeled around at the sound of her voice and found himself face-to-face with a pair of clear, milk-white eyes, behind thick black-framed glasses. He would've sworn she was blind if she wasn't staring right through him.

"Claire... fancy seein' you here," Desmond said with a wily grin. "Not the person I was hopin' for, but this is progress, I suppose."

Claire Eisenholm was breathing heavily. She looked as if she was about to give him an earful, but had to pause to gather herself first. A maze of thin black lines crept up her neck. They seemed to move subtly with each labored breath, tentacles threatening to strangle the life out of her. She hadn't thinned, as far as he could tell, but the veins on her neck and face stood out, giving her a strained, emaciated look. She was paler than when he'd seen her last, and *that* was a feat unto itself.

"You look like shit," Desmond said, when she didn't spit back an insult quickly enough for his liking. He smiled devilishly. "Bird shit."

"Go to Hell," the pasty-faced apparition hissed, barely above a whisper. She aimed a trembling finger at his face. "You're a dead man, Desmond. Three days from now, you're gonna *die* on a Registry interceptor. I hope you're proud of yourself, you fucking idiot. After all I went through to protect you..."

"Oh, you can see the *future* now? Cute," Desmond said. "Well, if that's how it's gonna go down, let me enjoy my last days. I've got three things I wanna do before I die and they're all sittin' right over there, sweetheart. See ya."

He gave her a mock salute before turning to leave, but she caught him by the shoulder and spun him to face her. Her touch was cold.

"You're a selfish son of a bitch," she said. "They'll break you. You'll snitch in a heartbeat and they're gonna milk you for all you're worth."

Desmond slapped her hand off of him. Claire swayed uneasily, as if she might fall, but he steadied her by gripping her shoulders and peering into her blank eyes. "*I'm* selfish?" he said incredulously. "After what you did to us, *I'm* the selfish one!? You dropped us on a dead planet, told us to disappear, and for *what*!? We had a good thing going and you blew it, Claire. It took me a month to get off that damn planet!"

He paused, staring into those wild eyes which seemed to be watching something far, far, beyond him. He was mere centimeters from her face, but her gaze was lightyears away. She had been that way long before the blacklight. He knew, from the moment he first saw her, on a windswept airfield in Nevada, that Claire Eisenholm wasn't all there. She was damaged goods and everything she touched ended up as broken as she was. He didn't need to psychoanalyze her to figure that out.

"W-Where are the others?" she said, her gaze momentarily finding a focal point. "I... I saved them, didn't I? I... I thought..."

"Fuck the others," Desmond said. "Far as I know, no one else made it. They're dead or worse, all because *you* lost your nerve... or your mind... probably *both*."

"I told you *why*. *He* can't be trusted. *He's* one of *them*," she raved.

Desmond laughed. "Right, you *did* tell me that, babe. Must've missed it between the screaming and the ranting, and the psycho-bitch babble. Get help, Claire. Something's eatin' you up inside and it ain't me, 'them,' or The Stranger. And stop jumping rope with the timeline. White's not a good look on you."

She wore a mask of absolute fury. She would be red in the face if she were capable of it. Behind her thick glasses, the colorless eyes brimmed with unbridled rage... and then they softened. Her lips quivered and gray tears began to well up in the corners of her eyes.

Desmond sighed. "You've got to be kidding me..."

"You'll see," she said through the sobs. "You'll *all* see! I'm going to finish what I started. He'll pay for this. I'll make them pay."

"Claire, don't-" She vanished as suddenly as she'd appeared. There was no cloud of smoke or flash of light. Just a slight 'pff' as the air collapsed on the spot where a person had once been. "She's gonna kill herself if she keeps that up," Desmond murmured to himself and thought no more of her.

But, as much as he hated and pitied her, he wasn't so foolish as to disregard a warning from a time traveler, even one as cracked as Claire Eisenholm. Without another word, he shoved through the crowd as casually as if nothing had happened. He didn't want to die, especially not in the hands of the Registry. He'd survived too much to end up there.

He made his way to the stairs and headed down. Goodbye Ava's ass. Goodbye Lana's tits. Goodbye Janice's... umm... charming personality?

He strolled out the front door of the Silq Serpent with his face low, buried in the collar of his jacket. People were streaming in. Lots of people. He hated this feeling almost as much as he hated Claire for making him feel it again. The feeling of being hunted. The feeling that nowhere was safe. The feeling that he had to lie, cheat, and steal just to live another day.

Well, that last feeling was one he'd grown quite fond of, but those *other* feelings, he hated.

He moved against the flow of human traffic, trying to keep his eyes down, while also watching for anything remotely Registry-like. An armed man in dark pants and a jacket caught his gaze. There was recognition on the man's face... and a Scion's badge around his neck.

Desmond broke into a run and the man gave chase, calling his name in the streets. The Hunter had a gun on his hip. There was a twiggy little redhead with him. She proved to be a faster runner than them both and was gaining ground quickly. Desmond got half a block before the nippy Chihuahua caught up, pounced on him, and they both went down hard. He rolled across the pavement and right back onto his feet while the girl was still getting up. The Hunter was right behind them and closing fast.

Fuck this, Desmond thought. He whipped back around, snatched the girl up and locked his arm around her neck, holding her as a human shield, while his other hand went for the pistol tucked in his waistband.

He pressed the warm steel to her head and ordered the Hunter to stay back, or else.

* * *

"What is *that*?" Doctor Jenner said as he entered the comm room and found Gibbs and Magnusson. The latter was pecking at a datapad, while an enormous hologram of a planet dominated the room. It wasn't Earth.

A slight grin spread across Gibb's face. "That would be Numira," he said, "the last planet this ship saw 'fore she got fried... *if* Jay knows what he's talkin' about."

Doctor Jenner stepped into the room and inspected the large planet and streams of text hovering beside it. If the data was correct, it appeared to be a very dense gas giant, possibly even a waterworld in the habitable zone of a distant star.

"It's just a hunch," Jayce Magnusson said, without looking up from his calculations. "It's been a while since I've done this sort of thing manually, but, if my math is right, this is where Claire ditched her crew before sending the *Darkstar* back to Earth."

Jenner rubbed his chin thoughtfully. "On a waterworld? That's... interesting."

"*If* my math is right," Magnusson repeated. "I could be wrong."

With a hearty laugh, Gibbs came forth and threw his arm over Magnusson's shoulder, nearly toppling the man. "His math is *always* right," he said to the doctor. "He's my best navigator *and* a helluva pilot. I ain't never seen him miss his mark before."

"I don't know about that, but it does look like I might be onto something. Take a look at this, doc," Magnusson said as he set aside the datapad and turned his attention to the nav map. He zoomed the image out, away from the planet. Other than the star it orbited, Numira was the only celestial body in its system.

"That's a magnetar," he said, pointing to the star. "A neutron star with a magnetic field strong enough to-"

"Strong enough to sabotage a ship's electronics," Jenner concluded. Slowly, he smiled. "I see. You really might be onto something here, Mr. Magnusson."

"I think she flew right through it, or very close," Magnusson said. "At full warp, the *Darkstar* could phase through before the heat and pressure penetrate the physics envelope. But the magnetic field... that's the real killer. It's much bigger than the star and most drives aren't calibrated to deal with magnetic forces."

"What do you know about the planet itself?" Jenner asked. "And why didn't The Stranger just tell us aboutthis place, instead of dodging the issue?"

"Aye, that's the big question," Gibbs said. "It's on the outer edge of Farside, technically beyond the boundary. The Infinite Charter forbids travel out there."

"So, the *Darkstar* was there illegally?" the doctor said. "This gets better by the minute…"

"Claire and her crew were on Registry business," Jay said. "'Illegal' doesn't apply. If you wanna test a special ship in secret, Farside is the perfect proving ground. All those uninhabited planets to use as target practice…"

"What are you trying to say?" Jenner asked.

Jayce Magnusson shrugged. "Nevermind. I'll figure out what's afoot soon enough. My next step is to check the-"

He was cut short by a steady beeping from the console, the ship's equivalent of a screeching doorbell.

"I guess Gino's back," Gibbs grumbled, irritated by the noise. "Too soon to be Clyde and Ell. We'll fill them in on this when they get back," he said of the looming planet before switching the holo image over to the external camera feed, so they could identify the visitor.

It wasn't Gino.

Dr. Jenner squinted at the display and adjusted his glasses. "Who is that?"

"No friend of mine," Magnusson said.

A thin-faced man with long blonde hair and silver-framed glasses stared into the camera with narrow blue eyes and a placid expression. The bureaucratic, buttoned-up air about him, made it clear he'd wait all day if he had to.

"I know him," Gibbs muttered with disdain. "It's Lee, the fuel tech from yesterday."

"What's he doing here again?"

"Hell if I know." Gibbs pressed the intercom and put on his most welcoming tone: "Afternoon, friend. What can I do ya for?"

"Is that you, Mr. Gibbs?" the technician said with a pleasant smile. "I apologize for the disturbance. The docking authority sent me to clear up some minor discrepancies in your ship's records. May I come in?"

"I'm sure we could come down to the office and clear that up, right?"

"Well, yes... but it would be much more expedient if you just let me in," Lee said cooly. "Is Mr. Evans present? I have some forms for him to sign as well." He held up a silver briefcase for them to see.

Gibbs looked to Magnusson, who mouthed the words 'no way.' He then looked to Jenner, who slowly shook his head. The jury had spoken.

"I think I'd rather handle that at the docking office," Gibbs said again with a smile. "We're in the middle of somethin' here. I'll be down there in... mmm... how does an hour or so sound? Or you could just message the necessary forms to us."

Lee's shoulders sank. "But, Mr. Gibbs, I insist."

"As do I," the portly engineer replied.

Lee sighed. "Well... so be it..."

A blinding flash followed. When the stars in their eyes cleared and the three men looked again, the image was static. No more Lee. The ship's lights flickered, followed by the sound of electrical arcing and the loud pop of overloading fuses somewhere in the bowels of the vessel.

Operating on pure instinct and adrenaline, Gibbs immediately ran from the room, making a beeline for the hall. Magnusson, with his longer stride, overtook him. They both had the same idea: get to the weapons locker, ASAP.

"I'll take care of it," Jayce Magnusson said. "You and doc get to the cockpit and-"

They both turned into the main corridor and skidded to a stop. Lee was standing there with a blank look on his face. In his right hand was a metal case. In his left was a submachine gun and it wasn't one of theirs. A thin stream of smoke wafted from his long white overcoat, as if he's just stepped out of a smoker. The wall outlet beside him was blackened and smoldering.

The man slicked back his frizzed blonde hair with the barrel of his gun and locked eyes with the two men, neither of whom could take their eyes off the silver badge around his neck, with its ten rings spinning wildly.

"Hello, Mr. Gibbs. And you must be Mr. Magnusson. I apologize for the deception," he said with a pleasant smile and a slight nod of his head. Had the circumstances been different, he could've been a friendly neighbor, asking to borrow some sugar.

Gibbs began to slowly back away, but Magnusson stood his ground. The weapons were at the far end of the hall, past the Scion. So damn close…

"My name is Saimon Hawke. Hunter Elite. That's level ten, for those of you who do not know or cannot count," the intruder said. "I am here to take possession of Clyde Evans and the vessel known as the *Darkstar Abyssal*. Your cooperation, while not required, would be greatly appreciated."

* * *

Things went from bad to worse in the blink of an eye. Desmond Williams had Ell as a human shield. He pressed a gun to her temple and every person on the street suddenly froze to watch the spectacle. An agonizing second of nothingness ticked by before those who wanted to flee fled. Meanwhile, those who wanted to watch continued to stare, and those who wanted to film whipped out their phones and cameras.

I hate this city, Clyde thought as he stood, frozen.

The thought that his target might be armed hadn't even occurred to him until Shit's Creek overflowed its banks. But his instincts were still sharp, or sharp enough. His hand reflexively went for the weapon at his side, but he hesitated with his fingers an inch from the holster.

He had a clear shot – the man shouldn't have chosen a hostage a foot shorter than him and scrawny to boot. He was a grown man hiding behind a sapling. If Ell wasn't squirming so much, Clyde could've fed him a bullet.

But he couldn't bring himself to take advantage of Williams's minor lapse in common sense, if that's truly what it was. If he shot the man, he lost potential information. Jenner could patch him up back at the ship, but that's not how he wanted to kick things off with someone who might be their *only* link to the Chronomancer. Clyde needed him alive and he suspected Desmond Williams knew that.

"Your move, cowboy. You can start by backin' the fuck up," Desmond said with a straight face. Ell tried to bash him in the mouth with the back of her head, but he tightened his grip on her. Despite her constant struggling, his eyes never left Clyde's. There was desperation in his gaze, but the man wasn't crazy or careless. It was as if the desperation sharpened him, as if he was used to teetering on the edge.

"You don't wanna do this," Clyde said, slowly raising his empty hands, palms open. "There's nowhere for you to go, Desmond. Just let the girl go and-"

Desmond swiftly shook his head. "Not gonna happen. There's a whole galaxy of places to go." He finally broke eye contact, but only for a millisecond. He was looking for a way out and stalling for time until he could find one.

"No one's here to hurt you," Clyde said. "I just wanna talk."

"You're gonna have to sweeten the deal, cowboy. I ain't talkin' to the Registry."

"Good. I'm not Registry. Not exactly. My name is Clyde Evans. I work for your old boss. You know the one." Clyde smiled, in what he hoped came across as a gesture of friendship. They had something in common. Whether that would be a benefit or a liability remained to be seen.

Either way, it got a response. Desmond gave him a very questioning look.

"Dammit, Clyde, shoot this motherfucker!" Ell said and the situation exploded.

She stomped her heel into the man's foot and Desmond responded by shoving her to the ground. In that brief second, Clyde drew his weapon and aimed it at the man's dome, but it only took an instant for Desmond to take Ell down and press a knee into her spine to keep her there. He put his gun to the back of her head, execution style.

It was a classic police takedown, possibly military, and completely changed Clyde's perception of who and what he was dealing with. Desmond Williams had combat training.

"He wants you back, Desmond," Clyde said, with a slight tremor in his voice. "He wants Claire back, too, but I need help tracking her down. Let's talk about this…"

"Toss away your gun and we will."

"You first," Clyde said.

"How 'bout the same damn time!" Ell said.

"You don't know when to shut up, do you?" Desmond sneered and pistol-whipped her.

"We can wait for the cops," Clyde said calmly. The sound of sirens was rising in the distance, drawing closer. He paused, letting the ambient street sounds speak for themselves, letting it clamp down on Desmond like a noose. "I have a badge. All you have is a hostage. This won't look good on you, Williams. Let her go."

Desmond murmured something under his breath. He looked to the left again, and then to the right. There was no way he was escaping with Ell and if he tried to get away without her, Clyde wouldn't hesitate to put two rounds in his kneecaps. He was far beyond the stage of playing nicely.

"Fine... you win." The man stuffed the pistol back into his waistband and pulled his shirt down over it before standing and offering a hand to the girl he'd threatened to kill a moment ago. "Sorry 'bout that," he said with a grin.

Ell immediately snatched his gun and quickly backed away, joining Clyde. "Clever girl," Desmond mused, "but you might need *these*." He shook his sleeve and the bullets tumbled to the ground.

Clyde didn't sense a gift and The Stranger said nothing about Desmond being a Scion. It was just good old-fashioned slight of hand.

"You shoulda shot him," Ell scolded as she deposited the empty gun in her backpack.

"I still might," Clyde said.

"I hope you have a fast ship," Desmond said. "There's a Registry interceptor somewhere on this station. A little birdie told me they're looking for me."

"I do," Clyde said. "You're coming with us. The *Darkstar* can lose them."

Desmond's brows rose. For the first time, he looked genuinely surprised and wasn't afraid to show it. He studied Clyde's face for a moment, probably seeking any signs of deception, but if Clyde was lying, it certainly wasn't written there.

"You're bullshitting me," Desmond said, testing the waters. "The *Darkstar* is here, right now? I'll believe it when I see it. Claire swore she was gonna-"

"She tried, but only succeeded in trashing the electronics," Clyde said as he holstered his gun. "I think we both have a lot to discuss, Mr. Williams. Are you coming with us or not?"

The sirens were getting dreadfully close now. Clyde looked back as a black car rounded the corner half a block away, with a flashing red light in its window.

"We should go," Desmond said, clearly getting antsy.

"Too late," Clyde said and clamped his hand down on Desmond's wrist. "I'll talk to them and explain everything. It's no big deal."

Despite his calm tone, he also had a bad feeling about this. He had the authority to get out of this situation, but if the locals wanted to make a big deal out of it, Clyde and company could get tied up in red tape. If that happened, it was only a matter of time before word reached the two level ten Scions sitting pretty in their shiny ship, the *Noble Valiant*.

But there was another option. The street was far from deserted. Any one of a hundred people could be the gun-waving maniac who took a girl hostage a minute ago. *We weren't even here*, Clyde thought, mentally rewriting history. He glanced toward his own vehicle, waiting less than thirty feet away. They could be gone before anyone was the wiser.

"Change of plans. Start walking," Clyde said and nudged Desmond toward the sedan. Far behind them, he heard the police car's tires screech to a halt and a door open and close.

"We're running?" Ell said, excitedly. "Running from the police?"

"No, we're *walking*. And I didn't see any police. Neither did you," Clyde said without glancing back. "Running would be fleeing the scene. *Walk*. Act natural."

* * *

Isaac Gibbs slowly backed away into the comm room, leaving Jayce Magnusson in the hall, face to face with the enemy. Magnusson was a head taller than the blonde-haired, steely-eyed intruder, but he knew he'd die in a fight. Physicality would not save him. All he had was his mind and he wasn't sure if he even had the advantage in that department. No Hunter reached level ten by being an idiot. This man could probably kill them all with both hands tied.

Which fuse had blown? How much voltage? Maybe he could seal the man in one part of the ship. Maybe he could isolate the power surges to buy some time. Nowhere was safe until they figured out how to lock this guy down.

"What do you want?" Magnusson said calmly.

"Is Mr. Evans here?" Saimon Hawke asked.

The sound of his voice infuriated Magnusson. He wanted to throw the first punch and let the chips fall where they may, but he was a wall between this killer and the other two men. Hawke had a killer's eyes, a liar's smile, and a sadist's trigger finger.

Doctor Jenner stood frozen in fear. "Move," Gibbs grunted as he shoved the doctor aside, so he could reach the center console. He began furiously punching keys on the touchpads, probably trying to do exactly what Magnusson had contemplated a moment ago: isolate the power grid and prevent Hawke from zipping through the wiring... if that was, indeed, what Hawke had done. Damn Scions and their tricks. So unpredictable.

But the Hunter raised his gun. "Step away from the console, Mr. Gibbs. I don't like complications. This is your first and only warning." Gibbs froze, but did not stand down. "So be it. You were warned."

Hawke set down his case and pressed his hand to the wall. The sound of sizzling wires followed. Gibbs screamed as he was thrown from the console by God-only-knows how much voltage and left convulsing in a corner, foaming at the mouth.

Magnusson didn't think. He sprang. "Son of a bitch!" he cried out as he charged at the Hunter, but a full-auto burst from the submachine gun laid him down quick. He veered to the side, slammed into the wall, and slumped down, leaving a red stain.

Whose blood is that? Mine? No... can't be... He couldn't even tell where he'd been hit. Pain blossomed all over his body. Jayce Magnusson gripped his bleeding side as he slumped to the floor and fought to think of something other than pain and death.

He bit his lip hard and muttered a string of expletives as the Hunter gingerly stepped over him, headed for the comm room, where Gibbs and Jenner were. Through the open door, Magnusson could see Gibbs's head, where he lay on the floor, showing no signs of getting up anytime soon. His wide eyes were red and glassy. Every few seconds, he involuntarily twitched.

Hawke stopped and knelt over Gibbs's body. To him, it was like watching a cockroach breathe its last after hitting it with a blast of insect spray. Magnusson tried to drag himself to his feet, but his body's only response was another burst of pain, as if he'd been struck by a second volley of lead. He couldn't move.

"I take it Mr. Evans *isn't* here?" Hawke said as he aimed his gun at Isaac Gibbs's prone body. There was only one man left who could stop him.

George Jenner tackled the Hunter, sending them both tumbling into the hall. What he lacked in fighting prowess, he made up for in sheer willpower and a refusal to quit. Hawke's grip on the submachine gun never faltered, even as they struggled. A burst of stray bullets flashed into the comm room before he broke free of the doctor's grip.

Gibbs's body jerked one final time.

Doctor Jenner threw a sloppy punch, which the Hunter easily deflected and followed by delivering a solid counterpunch to the doctor's chest. The blow might not have amounted to much, but it was laced with electricity. A flash of white-hot lightning left Jenner weak in the knees. Never one to do things halfway, Hawke squeezed the trigger on him as well, perforating the doctor's body with a dozen rounds. The man staggered back and hit the wall, but didn't fall, even as his shirt began to well up with blood.

Saimon Hawke was amused. "Ah, yes, you must be the healer, right?" he said curiously. "I was given special instructions regarding you. You have debts to be settled, doctor. Hang on just a moment..."

The pure, unbridled fear in Jenner's eyes and the strain on his face was difficult to watch. More than anything, Magnusson noticed there was no pain there. The man was still standing. Jenner was gripping the wall, but still *standing*. The bleeding slowed. He should have been dead or flat on his back, but he was still hanging on.

No, not just hanging on. He was *recovering*.

Unfortunately, death was not the greatest threat George Jenner faced, nor the only punishment Saimon Hawke had come to deliver. Jenner was a healer; bodily harm was the least of his worries. Hawke opened his aluminum briefcase and drew out a long cylindrical device, glass in the middle, with a metal handle at either end.

"Go on. Heal up," the Hunter said as he prepared the lightkeeper. "We wouldn't want you to die with your debts unsettled, doctor."

Jenner was alive, but too weak to move. Too weak to fight. Too weak to do anything. Magnusson muttered another stream of expletives under his breath as Hawke primed the device. He unscrewed one end and set the cap aside. Then he lifted his badge to it and the lightkeeper began to hum as the two pieces of Solaran tech synchronized. Each recognized the Light signature of a Scion authorized to reap.

Magnusson desperately tried to stand, but fell again. *So much blood*, he thought to himself. He hadn't heard a peep from Gibbs in what felt like ages. One by one, they would all die here. He was sure of it now.

Hawke looked into the doctor's eyes, man to man, Hunter to prey. Jenner raised a feeble hand, but Hawke swatted it away like a bothersome fly. In his present state, one quick jolt of electricity was all it took to incapacitate the doctor. His body went limp while the ruthless Hunter held him pinned against the wall. Hawke tore away the man's shirt. Its buttons tumbled across the blood-stained floor as he pressed the lightkeeper to bare flesh.

"George Albert Jenner, for the crime of abandonment without cause, you are sentenced to donate 1,000 tributes of your Light to the Solaran Registry as atonement. I, Saimon Cornelius Hawke, Hunter Elite and Acolyte of the High Council, have accepted the task of carrying out your sentence, such that your debts be paid in full. May the Light cast no shadows on you, comrade. Let us begin…"

He twisted the handle and the device hummed louder, higher, resonating with an otherworldly droning that vibrated every fiber of Magnusson's being. He could feel it in his teeth, his bones, his skin, and somewhere deep inside which he couldn't explain no matter how hard he might try. His very soul trembled. Until that moment, he had not thought much of souls, not even his own.

Jay was a strong man, who had been many places and seen many things, but this… *this* was difficult to watch. He averted his gaze as the lightkeeper began to glow, extracting a writhing, luminous essence from George Jenner's body. He had never witnessed anything so beautiful and so horrifying all at the same time.

* * *

The mental tug of a Scion's gift flashed through Clyde's mind. Acting on pure instinct, he yanked Desmond back and caught Ell by the wrist, just in time. The car was less than a stone's throw away when it exploded in front of him, so close Clyde felt the heat slap his cheek. The vehicle's insides erupted through its shell, painting the streets with expensive upholstery. Clyde pulled Ell behind him as the pressure wave washed over them and shards of glass and bits of polyurethane peppered his face.

"They planted a bomb in your car!?" Desmond said. He had that jumpy look in his eyes again. If not for Clyde's grip on his forearm, he probably would've bolted already.

"That was no bomb," Clyde said in a low voice.

Until a few days ago, he had no idea what it was like to have something explode in his face. Now he knew it all too well. It warmed his blood and kicked his heart rate up to uncomfortable levels. Even before he turned around to face his attacker, he *knew* who he'd find standing there.

Brock Mason wore a grin far too wide for his face. His thick lips were contorted with amusement.

Clyde would've sworn he was hallucinating were it not for the ten-ringed badge around Mason's muscled neck. He wore the black and silver uniform, prim and tidy, just like the pragmatic hierarchy that had crafted it. But it made him look like a well-dressed ape prowling an urban jungle.

Mason approached slowly, moving with a slight limp. Clyde said nothing, but was already sizing the man up. Other than his gift, Mason appeared to be unarmed. He moved oddly, with a slight hitch in his left leg. They'd rushed him back into service, without even bothering to waste a healer.

If they ran, he was in no condition to give chase…

"What's the matter, Evans? Not glad to see me?" Mason said, spreading his hands in what lesser beings might mistake for a friendly gesture. "The leg's doin' fine, by the way. Thanks for askin.'" He folded his huge arms across his chest and looked from Clyde, to Desmond, to Ell, and back to Clyde again. "Friends of yours?"

"I'm here on business," Clyde said flatly. "Registry business. You can't-"

"I can't *what*?" Mason sneered. "Haven't you heard? I got promoted. I'm a Hunter now, too. Level *ten*. Ain't that great?" He laughed and showed off his shiny badge. "You were right, Evans. They wanted me back. Couldn't have done it without you, *friend*."

"Welcome to the club," Clyde said. "I thought you hated the Registry."

Mason chuckled. "Funny. I thought you did too... or did the lightkeeper malfunction?"

Mason's feigned friendliness was almost as disgusting as the sudden annihilation of their vehicle. The car's emergency protocols kicked in, leaving a cloud of steam hovering over the bombed-out chassis and a lingering odor of fire-suppressing chemicals, laced with burnt plastic and rubber. The acrid smell triggered a sudden realization: neither the police nor the fire department had shown up... and probably never would.

The phones, Clyde thought. The network was down and had been for over an hour. They were completely outclassed. Mason, or someone he worked for, had taken complete control of the situation. Mason had the block to himself. No cameras. No cops. This was his own personal battlefield and slaughterhouse. No witnesses.

"Congratulations on the promotion," Clyde said with a slight smile, still stalling, though he knew there was no cavalry on the way. "Who are you hunting, Brock?"

"Oh, I thought you'd never ask…"

Desmond suddenly snatched Clyde's weapon from his holster and took off running. Clyde had planned to work his way up to that, but now seemed as good a time as any. He immediately took off after the man. Ell was right beside him, her scrawny legs a blur.

"We are so fucked!" she said between breaths. "Can't you *do* anything!?"

"He's… too fast for me," Clyde panted. "Look out!" He shoved her aside as an airburst erupted between them. The force of the blast was enough to send Clyde flying sideways. He tumbled across the sidewalk, but hit the ground running. Ell fared much the same.

He didn't dare look back, but he could hear Mason yelling at them and feel the man's gift activate a millisecond before each blast. "I'm comin' for you, Clyde Evans!" His laughter echoed through the streets. "Run, Registry dog! Run!" He threw back his head and howled at the night sky.

Desmond had a head start. A storefront exploded beside him and he went down hard. The concussive blast shattered the windows of the neighboring shops. Clyde caught Desmond by the arm and snatched him to his feet without missing a step. Ell jumped through a destroyed display window and they both followed her into what seemed to be a clothing and accessory shop. She pounced over the counter, right past a horrified clerk, and they ran toward the store's backrooms and corridors.

Clyde's mind kept telling him how bad an idea this was. Enclosed spaces weren't their friend at the moment. If they hit a dead end, Mason would obliterate them, but running down the open street was equally suicidal. As they wove deeper into the store, a second blast went off somewhere outside. Clyde caught a glimpse of headlights before a compact car crashed through the storefront, upside down and on fire.

Next thing he knew, they were out the back, into a dark alley, and still running. It was like a maze. Ell took a sharp left and then a right. Clyde's lungs were burning. It felt like they'd been running forever and he couldn't keep pace. Ell just kept going and going and going, never slowing, like a perpetual motion machine. She turned a corner, stopped at a grate on the floor, and tugged on it. When it didn't budge, she began running again.

"Where are you taking us?" Clyde finally asked, panting hard.

"Anywhere but here," Desmond wheezed.

"Underground," Ell said, still walking swiftly. "Trick I learned back home. Tunnels. All the Platforms have 'em."

"He probably knows where the ship is," Desmond said. "He'll cut us off there."

"Not if we get there first," Ell said. She found another grate and tugged on it. This one came free, revealing a service hatch into P-222's underworks. Heat washed over their faces from the city's pitch black bowels. Clyde couldn't see how far the drop was, but Ell could. "C'mon. There should be a transit system down here."

She swung her legs over the side, and disappeared into the hole. Clyde heard her land, but saw nothing, only two glowing blue eyes staring up from the gloomy depths. He dropped in next and was immediately attacked.

"Too *fast* for you?" Ell hissed, while pinning him to the wall. "You pulled me outta the way *twice*, but he was 'too fast' for you to block his gift? That's *bullshit*, Clyde. Why the hell are we running from this guy instead of kicking his ass? Because you're too fucking weak to stop him?"

Her blue gaze drilled into him, demanding an answer. In the darkness of the tunnel, those eyes were all he could see. Desmond landed behind him with a soft thump and Clyde could feel the man's mischievous grin mocking them, like a wolf watching through the trees, waiting for an opportunity to pounce.

To his relief, Ell snatched his hand and led him forward. "C'mon," she said, and began to run. "I think I hear a station up ahead."

* * *

The pain subsided into nothingness. Magnusson remained slumped against the wall, numb. In a daze, he stared at the blood on his hands and tried to wipe them clean on his shirt, but they came back redder than before.

"I'm very sorry about this. Truly I am," Hawke said as he returned the glowing lightkeeper to its case. There was another just like it inside, waiting to be filled.

Who else? Clyde? Elli? Gino... Magnusson's thoughts trailed off. It was a wonder his mind could piece together anything at all.

"Liar..." he said, barely above a whisper. He would have screamed it at the top of his lungs if he could. "You're not sorry. Don't apologize, monster. You *enjoyed* it."

Saimon Hawke's eyes briefly shifted to him and there was the ghost of a smile before he looked away. "Liar? No, Mr. Magnusson. Truth is written by the victor." He shut the case. "*You* people are the liars, if only because we make it so." He latched it and stood with the gun in his other hand.

The Hunter knelt before his prey, so they could see eye to eye. "I am only following orders, friend. I do everything I can to do what I must. I do what I must *because* I must. The only men who mustn't do what they must do are dead men." Saimon chuckled. "And they don't do much at all."

In Magnusson's anemia-induced delirium, Hawke's words almost made sense.

Suddenly, the Hunter sprang up. "Someone's here."

Magnusson couldn't hear anyone. Then again, he could barely see straight. "Hold on to this, would you please," Hawke said and shoved the metal case into the dying pilot's lap before departing for the cargo bay in swift, short strides.

Magnusson lost sight of him. His fingers left bloody streaks on the aluminum briefcase. The doctor was sitting on the floor a few feet away, staring vacuously at the opposite wall.

He was still alive, despite being purged of nearly all of his Light. As alive as moss on a rock.

* * *

Gino knew something was very wrong. He'd staked out the *Noble Valiant* for nearly an hour before discovering it was unoccupied. Now he found the *Darkstar* sealed up tight. The control panel for the door was burned as if it'd been struck by lightning. There was no longer any doubt in his mind that the enemy had made its move.

He hated to admit it, but Clyde Evans was right. Some people were worthy of fear, worthy of being thought of as equals. But he was Gino Ainsworth, a champion, immune to things like 'worry' and 'fear.' Something was very wrong, but he would beat and bludgeon it into submission until everything was right.

With that thought firmly in mind, Gino went around back, to the cargo lift's intact control panel. He punched in the keycode and the lift began to open slowly, just as it should. Perhaps things were not as wrong as he thought.

Nevertheless, he was on guard as he entered the ship. A half-inch thick coating of hardened crystal formed around his body, like ice on the glassy surface of a lake. The full suit was over forty pieces, not counting the tiny joints and segments.

Aesthetically, it was vaguely medieval, but that was only a coincidence; Gino couldn't care less what it *looked* like.

It used to take a great deal of concentration to conjure his armor. Now, after years of practice, it was as familiar to him as breathing. Like most Scions, the gift became an extension of self. Within a second, he was protected from the crown of his head to the soles of his feet.

Overkill? Perhaps. But he didn't like being screwed with and someone was definitely screwing with him today. If the Registry had something to say, they should say it to his face, not by toying with the communications, his ship, and his coworkers. Divide and conquer was a coward's tactic and he saw through it as clearly as the crystalline defense covering his body.

Inside the cargo bay, a blonde man in glasses and a long white overcoat waited, with a smile on his face. His hands were empty, but a badge dangled around his neck. His level meant nothing to Gino, who didn't even bother to count the rings. His only thought was how to go about breaking every bone in this man's face.

"You must be Gino Ainsworth," the wiry man said with a smile. "I am Saimon Hawke, Hunter, level-"

"I don't give a damn what level you are. Where is everyone?"

The intruder said nothing. For a moment, he just took in the diamond suit. "You dressed for the occasion. Impressive."

"Are you deaf? Where. Is. Everyone?" Gino demanded again.

"Every*one* is every*where*. You must be more specific."

"Clyde Evans. Elica Niehaus. Isaac Gibbs. Jayce Magnusson. George Jenner..." Gino's eyes narrowed on the man. "Where are they?"

"You're too late."

The answer didn't compute. 'Late' was a measure of time, not place. It was possible to be late for a meeting, late for an appointment, late for a date, late for work, or late for class. But one could not be late for a *location*. 'Where' and 'late' were incompatible.

"I'll show you *late*," Gino snarled and threw himself at the man.

Hawke lifted his hand and white-hot bolts of electricity flashed out, flying every which way like the tentacles of a manic squid. It razed the walls of the cargo bay, leaving blackened scorch marks, and peeled across the surface of Gino's crystal plating, where it had no effect. His fist connected with Hawke's face, with a satisfying thwack that sent the thin man reeling.

Saimon Hawke spiraled into a pile of storage crates in the corner and Gino was instantly on top of him, pummeling him while yelling obscenities. The Hunter vanished in a flash of blue-white light. He disappeared into the metal walls, followed by a shower of sparks as the wiring crackled before he materialized at the far end of the cargo bay, next to a sizzling electrical outlet where he caught his breath and straightened his mangled glasses.

The submachine gun came out from behind his back and he aimed it at the crystal knight, the only thing standing between him and the siege of this castle. "Natural insulator... I never imagined," Hawke said as he shakily held the gun. "What is that, glass? Silicon-based crystalline polymer? I'd love to have a look at a sample under a microscope."

"I'll give you a sample, alright," Gino said, balling a crystal fist.

"Funny thing is, I'm not here for *you*," the Hunter replied. He actually sounded pleased, even as he paused to spit blood from his bruised mouth.

"Get the fuck off my ship," Gino demanded.

"My orders are 'take Evans alive' and 'capture the ship.' Gibbs and Magnusson are disposable and Niehaus and Jenner have debts to be paid," he chuckled. "But *you*... other than siding with the wrong team, you've done nothing wrong, Mr. Ainsworth. You can walk away. I won't stop you." He gestured to the exit, as if it were his to give.

When Gino began to march toward him with balled fists, Hawke vanished back into the walls. Gino followed the sounds of sizzling wiring up the stairs and into the main corridor, where he found Jay slumped against the wall and Doctor Jenner staring blankly into space, with spittle hanging from the corner of his mouth.

"Gino..." Magnusson said, his voice fading.

Gino ran right past them both, past the blood and bullet holes. Another wall panel popped and fizzled. An overhead light exploded in a shower of sparks. *He's headed for the cockpit*, Gino thought, following the trail of electrical carnage. "You're gonna take the ship back to them in pieces, if you keep this up!" he said.

He reached the comm room. Gibbs was lying in the corner, face down in a pool of blood, with his eyes still open, but sightless, the definition of 'too late.'

Hawke materialized again. He flashed out of the overhead lights and reappeared right in front of Gino, aimed the gun at his face, and squeezed the trigger. The shots ricocheted every which way, but the muzzle flash and the battering of bullets staggered the crystal knight just long enough for the Hunter to turn and begin to run... but not fast enough.

In one swift motion, Gino caught him by the neck, jerked him back, and hammered him to the floor, knocking the wind out of him. Hawke, flat on his back, raised the gun, but Gino quickly swatted the weapon away.

"That armor. How fitting," the Hunter wheezed. "Nothing gets through to you, does it? You can't be reasoned with or killed." He coughed out a hoarse chuckle. "It's not even your fight, but here you are, blissfully swinging away. You're the fighter we made you to be, Ainsworth. You'll never change. Look at you... can't even *kill* me. That's right, they didn't teach you *that* in the Arena, did they? Ha, former champion of Class B, the class for *nonlethal* combat."

"Get the fuck outta here," Gino barked.

"I can't. This is what I *must* do," Saimon Hawke said, with a sadistic smile, "and you can't stop me. All you can do is protect *yourself*, White Knight, the way you were taught to. You're a stage actor, not a hitman. And I am lightning, an instrument of the gods. Only my Solaran masters tell *me* where to strike."

"Like hell you are," Gino growled.

"You can't stop me."

We'll see about that, Gino thought. He planted his palm on the man's chest and focused harder than he'd ever focused before. For all his years in the ring, there had to be some part of himself he hadn't tapped into yet, something they hadn't taught him to do.

* * *

"Could someone explain to me what the hell is going on?" Desmond said when they finally caught a breather on the elevator leading up to the landing pad. "I thought you worked for the Registry. Why are they trying to kill us?"

"Stranger betrayed us," Ell muttered.

"No. He told me there'd be rival factions," Clyde said.

"There's no rival factions. The Solarans are all on the same page. They're hive-minded," Ell said.

Clyde shot her a very pointed glance. "What makes you think *that*?" He stood up straight and looked out the elevator's enormous glass panes. "Someone's pitting Hunters against Hunters."

"If only we had some kind of anti-Scion... like, someone who could *disable their powers*," Ell chided. "Wow, wouldn't that be nice?"

"Drop it, Ell."

"I think you've done enough dropping it for the both of us today," she said.

"Either way, the *Darkstar* is ours," Desmond said. "It's *my* ship. I didn't build it for the damn Registry and I ain't lettin' them have it. I don't care how many Hunters they send. I'll send 'em back in body bags."

"Good luck with that," Ell said.

"Drop it," Clyde said again as the elevator slowed to a halt and they stepped out. He briefly turned to Desmond. "Speaking of your ship, you're not off the hook yet. You and I have *a lot* to discuss."

"Yeah, and I ain't forgot what you did," Ell said, glaring at Desmond as she stepped off. "Put a gun to my head, huh? You better sleep with one eye open, asshole."

"I always do," Desmond said as he disembarked. "No apologies, sweetheart. I'd do it all over again."

They found the *Darkstar* with its engines idling. A very angry Gino was sitting by entrance with a shotgun, guarding a man encased in crystal. Clyde picked up the pace. Not until he drew near did he realize the man was still alive. Each breath fogged the crystal, hiding a sly smile.

"What happened?" Clyde asked. "Who's this?" he gestured to Gino's prisoner, but quickly noticed the badge around the man's neck. "Aw, shit..."

"Nobody," Gino snarled as he stood. "We need to go. *Now*. I can only keep this up for so long and I'm sure he has a friend on the way."

"So why is he still alive?" Desmond said. "Blow his head off and dump him over the side."

Gino grabbed him by the shoulder and shoved him into the ship. "That'd only make things worse. We need to get as far from here as possible." He trudged into the cargo bay and Clyde followed, but his eyes lingered on the trapped man for a half second longer.

"We were nearly killed getting this guy," Clyde said with a gesture to their new guest. "Gino, this is Desmond. Where are the others? Are they okay?"

"Find out yourself," Gino said wearily and sat down on a crate as the cargo ramp shut and sealed. He punched the ship's intercom: "Jay, everyone's on board. Take off."

Clyde continued up the stairs with a determined stride, but he and Ell slowed the moment they saw the chaos. The ship looked like a warzone. There were bullet holes in the main corridor and scorch marks along the walls. There was a pool of blood on the floor, with bloody bootprints leading away. Desmond breezed by them both, unfazed, and moved swiftly toward the bow.

"Oh my god…" Ell said, her voice breaking.

Clyde went further. The medical bay was open, with first aid kits strewn across the floor. Doctor Jenner was lying on the bed, heavily sedated. Had it not been for the steady beep of the heart rate monitor, Clyde would've thought the man was dead. Through the windows, he could see the ship was moving. They were flying past the landing pads at an alarming speed.

He continued toward the cockpit. Despite the grim state of affairs, he didn't stop until he reached the comm room, where Gibbs's body lay under a sheet, in a puddle of blood. Too much blood. The moment she saw it, Ell immediately buried her face in her hands and ran the opposite direction. With her artificial eyes, Clyde had no idea if she was capable of tears, but he was sure he heard a sob before she disappeared into her room and locked the door.

"Captain... I think you should get up here," Magnusson's strained voice said via the ship's intercom. "Now, please."

Clyde ran through the hall, seeing nothing, and did not stop until he reached the flight deck. A shirtless and heavily-bandaged Jayce Magnusson was at the controls, with Desmond in the co-pilot's seat... Gibbs's seat.

"Are you fit to fly?" Clyde asked, placing a hand on Magnusson's shoulder. The man looked pale and his hands were shaking. He flinched.

"We ain't flyin' nowhere right now," Desmond said, pointing to the viewscreen. The *Darkstar* was nose-to-wall with P-222's airlock, which was sealed tight.

"They won't... open the doors..." Magnusson said weakly. "Registry... wants... you."

"I get it," Clyde said. "Tell them..." he thought for a moment and could hear his heart pounding in his ears. *Out of options. Out of places to run.* "Tell them we're... umm... tell them I'll give myself up if they-"

"Fuck that," Desmond said and picked up the mic. He transferred control to his side of the cockpit and opened a comm channel. "This is the *ESV Darkstar Abyssal* hailing Platform 222 Docking Authority with an urgent demand. You have fifteen seconds to open this door before we open it ourselves."

"*Noble Valiant*... approaching at... six'o'clock," Magnusson wheezed. "They're... coming for us."

Desmond swung the ship around 180 degrees. The *Darkstar*'s sensors didn't lie. The moment he turned, they found the *Noble Valiant* coming head-on with its missile bays open.

"They won't fire inside the platform," Clyde said, but even he wasn't so sure of that, after everything that had happened. "They want the ship. They won't damage the ship, right?"

"They'll *cripple* the ship to stop us from getting away. You, prep the countermeasures," Desmond said to Jay before putting the mic to his mouth again. "Docking Authority, are you fucking deaf! We are in possession of a class four mass accelerator cannon and *will* fire. One way or another we're *leaving*, through the door or through a hole in the wall. YOU HAVE TEN SECONDS! Nine... eight... seven..."

The *Noble Valiant* was closing fast, but the airlock's inner door began to shut. The interceptor was forced to brake hard to avoid being crushed.

"Took 'em long enough," Desmond muttered as he quickly turned the *Darkstar* around, so they were facing out. The inner doors sealed behind them and the airlock's outer doors opened faster than anyone thought possible.

He punched the throttle forward and the *Darkstar Abyssal* rocketed away through the open airlock, speeding past the line of waiting ships outside, and into deep space, away from the nightmare of Platform 222.

– 10 –

A vast window dominated an entire wall of the *Darkstar*'s port observation deck. Stars zipped by at hyper-relativistic speeds, leaving multicolored lines in their wake, glittering against the black backdrop of deep space.

On the cold floor sat poor George Jenner, devoid of all higher brain functions. His retinas sparkled with a sense of juvenile wonder as he slowly rocked back and forth, unable or unwilling to avert his eyes from the simple marvels of FTL travel.

The door opened and Gino entered. If the doctor noticed, he certainly didn't show it. The fighter crossed his arms and watched silently. It was anyone's guess whether he was observing the vast emptiness of space or the emptiness of this man who'd once been a doctor.

"Clyde told me to keep an eye on him," Jay said, from his seat in the shadows. He'd regained a fraction of his strength in the hours since fleeing Platform 222, but his words were still labored and weary. His muscled arms and chest were covered in bandages and his posture spoke of a man who could barely sit up straight, let alone speak.

Despite being ignored by Gino, he continued: "How long is he gonna be like this?"

For a moment, it seemed that Gino would not reply. Eventually, he took a deep breath, shrugged, and said, "I don't know."

"But you're a-"

"Arena fighter, not a Reaper. I've never..." he gestured to Jenner. "I've never done *that* to anyone, and I never will. It's depraved. I would never."

"And you've never taken a man's life either," Magnusson said, with mild contempt. "You let that son of a bitch go, after what he did." When Gino said nothing, Magnusson released a breath he didn't realize he was holding and cast his eyes to the enormous window. "What if things had been different? What if the Registry had asked you to-"

"I wouldn't. There's only so much they can ask of a man."

Gino balled his fists at his side and Magnusson noticed the fresh bruises on his knuckles, red as wrath itself, and knew exactly where Gino had been the last few hours. He wondered if the punching bag in his room was still standing.

"I'm not accusing you of anything. I just... will he ever get better?" Magnusson asked, with tempered desperation.

"Don't hold your breath. Someday he might remember his own name," Gino said, "or how to tie his shoes, or use the restroom, or button his shirt... but he'll never be the same again."

They should have killed him, Gino thought, but didn't have the heart to say it. He'd never wish for someone to do what he couldn't bring himself to do. But that didn't make the thought any less potent. *Better off dead*, was all he could think every time he looked at George. He hated himself for it, but the thought came all the same, every damn time.

"All I could do is watch," Jay said through clenched teeth. "And look at us now. After what they did to us, we're running away with our tail between our legs."

"It's my fault," Gino said. "Had I arrived sooner-"

"You and I both know that's not true," Jay said, his voice barely a whisper as he watched Jenner's back. The doctor slowly rocked back and forth. "You beat *one* Hunter. One. There are *thousands* more. We're up against the entire Registry, man. We can't run. We can't hide. We can't *win*. Why are we even doing this anymore?"

"This is the last time we'll lose anyone. I swear it."

Magnusson gave him a sideways look from his seat in the corner. "There's not a doubt in my mind that you mean every word of that. But promises you can't keep don't mean a thing. Sorry, man, but you can't guarantee anything right now. No one can. Not you. Not Clyde. Not even The Stranger. We're in too deep."

Gino was red in the face, but truth won in the end. He bit his lip, stiffened his jaw, and watched the stars pass by.

"I can't do this anymore," Jay said and shrank into his chair, as if something inside him had shriveled up. "I already have one friend to bury. Ike's dead. Jenner's a... a vegetable. Ell's probably in her room drinking herself to death or OD'ing on some shit. And Clyde... he's got us flying sine curves in dark space until he can figure out what our next move's gonna be. It's over, man, just no one's ready to admit it yet."

"There's still Williams," Gino said dryly.

"Oh, *him*..." Magnusson threw up his hands. "The guy who threatened to fire a railgun inside a space station, just to save his own ass? Does 450,000 people dying in the vacuum sound like 'winning' to you? I don't care how cornered we were, that was *wrong*. If we're looking to that guy as our saving grace, we've already lost."

"I don't exactly like him either, but he might have important information about what the hell's going on," Gino said, surprisingly calm. "I'll beat it out of him if I have to. He's proving his worth by patching up the damage to the ship, but if he doesn't provide some *real* answers soon, I will *personally* toss him out the airlock."

Bold talk from a man who couldn't bring himself to kill the monster who'd slain one of their own. Magnusson just stared at the floor, too emotionally fractured to carry on this farce any longer. After what seemed like an eternity of silence, he sighed and said:

"It doesn't matter anymore. I'm gonna tell Clyde to drop me off at the next stop. I quit."

* * *

A very fatigued, sleep-deprived Clyde Evans dragged himself into the communications room and sank into the first seat he could reach. He waited, soaking up the relative peace, punctuated by the muted hum of the *Darkstar*'s engines and the occasional click of a wrench or snipping of wires as Desmond worked. After a shuddering breath, Clyde ran a hand through his dark hair and stared up at the skylight with heavy eyelids.

"I think it's time we talked, Mr. Williams."

If the other man noticed Clyde's entrance, he didn't show it. Desmond had burrowed into the navmap's innards. Its panels lay open, revealing a mess of burnt wiring, in which he was buried up to his waist.

"Ya know, my friends just call me 'Des,'" the man said casually, evasively.

"I'm not your friend... not yet," Clyde said with eerie calmness. "You built this ship and there are things I need to know about it. You can start by telling me *why* and what it has to do with a woman named Claire Eisenholm."

"Oh, *her*? So, it wasn't *me* you were after? Look, I'm kinda in the middle of something. Can this wait?"

Clyde released another longsuffering sigh. "This has been a *very* long day for me, *Des*. My first day off-world. My first time on a spaceship. My first time leading a team. My first time losing a teammate. My first time mopping blood off the floors."

"Well, someone's been *very* busy," Desmond mused.

"On my way here, I overheard two members of this crew discussing the best time to toss you out the nearest airlock," Clyde said, his patience thinning. "I've never spaced a man before, but today's a day of firsts. Don't tempt me, Williams."

The sound of turning wrenches and clipping wires ceased, but Desmond did not yet emerge from his claustrophobic retreat.

"Let's see where you stand," Clyde said as he rose. "Of the six people on this ship, one's dead, one's practically dead, and two are plotting against you. That just leaves me and… oh, right, the girl you used as a human shield."

He grabbed Desmond by the ankles and dragged him out from beneath the console in one swift motion. "Look at me, dammit!" Clyde said as he hefted the man up by his shirt collar with strength he didn't know he had. His tired, bloodshot eyes stared directly into Desmond's, but the man stared back, unfazed. "I think you'd better *make time*, Williams. I'm the closest thing you have to an ally. Do not piss me off any more than you already have."

Desmond never let go of the wrench, even while being manhandled by Clyde. Instead, he gripped it all the tighter and smiled all the wider.

"Tough day at the office, captain?"

Despite the overwhelming urge to pound Desmond's face in with the nearest blunt object, Clyde was too tired to carry on playing 'bad cop,' and something about this man suggested violence would only please him. Clyde knew very little about Desmond Williams, but of one thing he was certain: this man knew how to get his hands dirty and delighted in dragging others into the filth with him.

Clyde released him and slumped back into his seat. "Start talking. I'm not gonna play your games."

"Why not? You're already playing someone else's," Desmond replied coolly. He dropped the wrench and it clattered to the floor with a heavy clang. "So, he's after Claire, is he? What is it, revenge? Curiosity? A burning desire to do it all over again? Do you know the definition of lunacy, Mr. Evans?"

"I ask the questions here, not you. What were you doing on Platform 222?"

"Women and drugs, mostly," Desmond said with a casual shrug. "I was celebrating. I was once a wanted man, you see. In exchange for my services, The Stranger purged my record. *All* of it. I was celebrating my newfound freedom when you showed up."

"Yeah, celebrating at the same bar, at the same time, every other night," Clyde said. "Are you always so formulaic in your festivities?"

"You know, you'd make a decent detective if the Registry didn't have you by the balls." Desmond chuckled and spread his hands in mock surrender. "You win this round, Hunter. Shall I begin at the beginning?"

"Begin at the *truth*."

Desmond took a deep breath, but sounded no less amused as he went on: "Truth is, I was trying to get noticed. Claire aborted our mission. She had a... nervous breakdown, panic attack, call it what you want. We were in orbit over a lawless waterworld out in Farside, and about to make a jump to..." He gestured vaguely. "We were never told *where* exactly, though I have my suspicions. Next thing I know, we're all on Numira, without a ship, and Claire's ranting about God-only-knows what. She plucked us outta the mission like rabbits out of a hat."

"I want to know *why*," Clyde said. "She must've said something before-"

"Oh, she said plenty, but the girl was out of her mind and still is. If I could make sense of her tirade, I'd gladly tell you, but I can't. She just dropped us on the planet, said something about destroying the ship, something about The Stranger, Solarans, and beings of Light, and disappeared again. *Poof!* Just like that, she hung me and the rest out to dry... pun unintended."

Desmond paused, significantly. "I eventually found my way off Numira. It was simple, really. Survival's in my blood. I acquired a ship and got off that planet, but the *Darkstar* was gone when I reached orbit. I figured she'd destroyed it, so I made my way back to civilization, alone, to sort out what was left of my life."

"And what about the rest of your crew? Didn't their lives mean anything to you?"

"Numira chews people up and spits them out," Desmond said. "It's a lot like home, only wetter. I put that place in my rearview mirror the first chance I got. I was trying to reach The Stranger and let him know I didn't bail on the mission – it was all Claire's fault. Any platform would do; they're always under surveillance. I knew someone would spot me there. All I had to do was stand out enough. Hell, I didn't mind if the Registry showed up."

"You certainly seemed to mind," Clyde said, remembering their standoff in the street.

Desmond laughed long and hard. "The game changed. Claire dropped by to deliver a message: something about me *dying* on a Registry interceptor three days from now. I'm not a superstitious sort, but when a girl from the future tells you your number's up, you don't wait around to see how things pan out. You just... react."

"Claire intervened on your behalf? She's dying of blacklight and she came back to save your ass?" Clyde said. "What are you to her?"

"A liability. She came back to make sure I wouldn't give information to the Registry. If you're not the Registry, I guess she succeeded." Desmond plopped into a seat opposite Clyde and put his feet up. "She can be kind of smart when she straightens out those loose marbles. Talk to the Registry is *exactly* what I was going to do." He tapped his temple and smiled. "Secrets. Valuable secrets. I have it all up *here*, in my dirty little mind."

"What was she trying to protect?" Clyde asked, but the answer dawned upon him before the words could escape his lips. "The *Darkstar*... You built it and you could-"

"Sell the blueprints to the highest bidder. Claire knows how valuable the *Darkstar* really is," Desmond snickered. "But that stupid look on your face tells me you have no idea how special this ship is, do you?" He sighed as his gaze lingered on the blacked-out touchscreens. "This humble 'research vessel' isn't going to fix itself. You mind if I finish thse repairs while we talk? You know what they say about idle hands."

Naturally, Clyde asked why he was so eager to get the ship patched up, to which Desmond merely replied, "The Stranger will call you. I'm sure of it. The sooner I get the comms working, the sooner you'll know your next move."

"Go ahead. But while you're down there, you tell me everything about this railgun you casually threatened half a million lives with."

"Oh, that? Child's play." With the captain's permission, Desmond disappeared under the console to resume his work. "The railgun is just one part of it, actually. It's the means of delivery for a weapon that's *much* more potent than any ol' mass accelerator." He surfaced long enough to grab his wrench and a datapad before disappearing back under the console.

"I didn't design the *Darkstar* from the ground up. The Stranger came to me with two pieces of Solaran technology and asked me to build a ship around them," Desmond said. "They looked like drive cores – and they sort of *are* – but each has an alternate function.

"One of those warp drives is actually a modified terraformer. It's the primer for the ship's true main weapon," Desmond said proudly. "It alters things on the molecular level, making the atoms go supercritical. The railgun delivers the killing blow, setting off a subatomic chain reaction that can destroy something as large as a planet. It might be The Stranger's tech, but the *theory* behind it is mine. I came up with the idea years ago, but never had the means to build a prototype. Then, one day, the man with no name comes to me, offering unlimited resources… *voila*, a superweapon is born."

"You gave The Stranger a weapon that destroys on the subatomic level?" Clyde said. "Any sane man would've asked what he intended to do with it. No, a sane man wouldn't have designed such a thing in the first place! Solaran technology gave us space travel, climate control, terraforming. It cured world hunger and disease and-"

"Don't lecture me, Scion," Desmond sneered. "I'm well aware of the good, the bad, *and* the ugly. I'm from Mars, you moron. I've seen the seas boil. I've seen gravitational anomalies that turn skyscrapers into whirling storms of steel and concrete. I've seen hail fall like automatic gunfire from clouds of arsenic and chlorine gas. *My world* is not filled with sunshine and rainbows. When Solaran space-magic goes wrong, it goes *very* wrong, so don't you *dare* lecture me about Solaran blessings, Registry dog."

Despite the calmness of his tone, the rage in his eyes was unmistakable. "Mars never forgets," Desmond said. "Solaran technology is *ours* to do with as we please. We've paid and paid and paid a thousandfold for it. Ask your doctor; he paid. Ask your dead engineer; he paid. We've all paid our dues. Solaran technology is *our* technology. Whether I want to make a spaceship, a death ray, or a sex toy with it is no business of theirs. I wipe my ass with your Infinite Charter."

Clyde shut his mouth and waited for the man to relax, not because Desmond was right – whatever that meant – but because he hadn't the strength to argue with a psychopath. Was everyone on Claire's crew nuts?

"Where was I?" Desmond said. "Oh, right... the other warp drive is the one you should be concerned about, not my little pet project. It's the one that gave the *Darkstar Abyssal* its name. It's the one The Stranger kept very tight-lipped about. Even I don't know a damned thing about it... but Claire does. It's coded to only respond to her Light signature. It's some kind of Solaran device, with a human component. He called it an 'amplification chamber.' Beyond that, I don't know what purpose it serves."

"You're telling me this ship has some kind of device capable of interfacing with Claire?" Clyde said. "Some kind of Solaran tech to amplify a Scion's gift?"

He gave Desmond the hardest stare he could muster, but the man wasn't flinching and, honestly, Clyde couldn't muster much.

"This ship had an intended destination," Desmond said, "but we never charted a course. Wherever we were going, I think we were gonna *teleport* there, somewhere far into the Abyss, the dark space between galaxies, forbidden by the Infinite Charter. Conventional space travel can't reach other galaxies in any reasonable timeframe, but if Claire's powers were enhanced, she could teleport the entire ship there instantaneously. There's something out there The Stranger wanted to see. I don't know what it is, but he built this ship to get to it..."

"And armed it with a planet-destroying superweapon," Clyde concluded.

A lengthy silence settled between the two men.

"So this *is* a research vessel," Clyde said at last, just as Desmond returned his attention to repairing the communications console. "It was on an exploratory mission. The Stranger was actually telling the truth?"

"Truth's a very flexible thing," Desmond said. "I was along for the ride, but even I don't know where we were going or what he intended for us to do there. But I went anyway, like a good little errand boy... sort of like what you're doing right now."

Clyde sat back and studied the skylight while he turned over the details in his head. A nameless man commissioned a ship to teleport into dark space, to investigate and possibly destroy something, but refused to explain *anything* to his allies? Why? To what end?

Whatever it was, it frightened Claire Eisenholm out of her mind and she projected that fear onto her employer. She was sent to investigate and possibly destroy something... but came back wanting to destroy The Stranger instead.

It's all come full circle, Clyde thought drowsily.

An ear-splitting shriek from the communications console jerked his head up. Clyde didn't realize he'd nodded off until he wiped away the warm spittle daring to drop from the corner of his mouth.

"Sorry to wake you, *captain*," Desmond said, still under the console, which was now illuminated and in semi-working order. How much time had passed? Desmond's fingers danced across the touchscreens and the incessant ringing stopped. "Looks like an incoming data packet. You've got mail."

"How did anyone find us out here?" Clyde muttered sleepily.

"They didn't. It's an encrypted subspace message, stored on a comm buoy. The digital mailman slung it our way when it picked up our ship's ID as we flew by. This encryption pattern is The Stranger's, dated about an hour ago. Told ya he'd call."

"A pre-recorded message? He couldn't call us himself?" Clyde said as he stood and shuffled toward the hall. "Transfer it to my room. I'll see what he has to say. Gather everyone in the mess hall. We'll have a team meeting as soon as I'm done."

* * *

The room began to tilt at odd angles. Ell shut her eyes and tried to steady herself as she entered the mess hall, clutching a bedsheet to her chest with one hand, while gripping the edge of the table with the other. She quickly dropped into the nearest seat, to avoid stumbling around like a drunken idiot.

Once she had a chair beneath her, Ell looked around to see if anyone had noticed. Gino and Jay were milling around the coffee maker, speaking in low voices. Desmond sat across from her, staring with a twisted grin while his chin rested in his palms.

"Shut up," she said before he could speak. "I don't see why I should get dressed for a stupid meeting."

"I'm not judging you," Desmond teased. "At least it's a clean sheet, right?"

Ell moaned and laid her head on the cold tabletop to soothe the pounding in her temples. "I don't know. My room smells like barf, but I can't figure out where."

"Could you at least *pretend* to have some class?" Gino scolded from across the room. "We lost two people today."

"I think she knows," Jay said as he reasonably sipped from a steaming mug. "We all know. Lay off her, man."

Ell flashed him a weak smile before burying her face again and tuned everything out until she heard steps approaching. Clyde appeared at the doorway with a datapad tucked under his arm, looking very official. Ell stiffened.

"I just received word from our handler," Clyde began. "Most of it confirms what we already know. The Registry wants the

Darkstar. They want me. They want Claire Eisenholm. It's official now: there's a two-man squad dedicated to our capture."

"No way. Seriously? Oh, how dreadful," Desmond gasped, dripping with sarcasm. Clyde shot him a glance and the man promptly shut his mouth.

"The good news: they want the ship intact," Clyde explained, ignoring the interruption. "Hopefully, we can use that to our advantage. The bad news: The Stranger isn't sure if it's just a rival faction or if the entire Registry wants our heads. Until we know for sure, we should assume the worst and avoid Solaran-controlled space as much as possible. We don't want unnecessary confrontation. Our enemy has already shown a willingness to raise hell, with no regard for property damage or casualties."

"That's it?" Gino said. "That's all he can tell us?"

"Let the man finish," Jay said.

"Did you ask him *why* they're after the ship?" Ell said.

"I couldn't *ask* anything," Clyde said. "The message was pre-recorded. But I suspect they're after the same thing Claire wants: a special feature built into this ship. The *Darkstar Abyssal* contains some very valuable and unique Solaran technology, but the ship's documentation is clean. This ship is legally ours. The Registry has no rightful claim to it and can't take it from us."

"That shitstorm on 222 says otherwise," Desmond replied. "He who hits hardest is always right… and they hit us pretty damn hard back there."

"Nevertheless, I still think it's in our best interest to continue the mission," Clyde said. "We don't have a choice. Our goal remains the same: find Claire Eisenholm and protect the *Darkstar*. This isn't as much of a longshot as it might seem. We have things she wants. She'll come to us… we just have to survive until she does."

"Did *he* tell you that?" Gino said, setting down his mug and folding his arms.

"No, that's my opinion. A gut feeling," Clyde said. "I still believe in this mission, not because The Stranger told me to, but because I think we're a part of something big. If any of you have doubts or feel things have gotten out of hand and would rather take your chances elsewhere, I understand, but *I'm* going to stay the course."

As he spoke, his eyes never left Jay. Ell had been shut in her room, romancing a champagne bottle since leaving Platform 222. The subtext went right over her head but, as her mind cleared, his intended meaning dawned on her.

"Whoa, wait... you're *leaving*?" she said, her eyes widening as she looked to the wounded pilot. "You can't leave, Jay... you're... you're, like, the second cutest guy here. Like, seriously, c'mon..."

"Sorry, Ell," Magnusson said with a weak smile. His shoulders sank, illuminating the grief he'd masked so well. "Clyde and I already talked it over. I can't do this anymore. I already have one friend to bury and after what they did to George... I just... I just can't."

"Your best chance of survival is *here*," Gino said sternly. "We're armed. We're capable of flying under the radar, if we must. We still have a chance! We'll hit them back twice as hard as they hit us. Don't listen to this jackass." He gestured to Desmond.

"Jackass or not, he's right," Jay said. "The Registry dealt us one hell of a blow and that was just the opening volley. It doesn't get prettier from here. I've run contraband half my life, but I've never seen anything like this."

"Whatever we're doing has stirred up a hornets' nest," Clyde said to them all. "Someone upstairs is pissed and it's going to get

148   B. Stephens

worse before it gets better, so I understand why Jay doesn't want to stay. The door's open for anyone else who wants out."

"They blindsided us," Gino said. "It was a cheap tactic and it won't work again. I'll be ready for them next time. I was scouting the enemy ship when they struck."

"You weren't at your post," Clyde said coldly.

"You sound like you're looking forward to next time," Ell said eyeing Gino closely. "I'd be happy if we never see another Hunter again."

"Direct confrontation is inevitable," Clyde said. "We're hunting the same target they are. There *will* be a next time. But..." he turned to Gino, "that doesn't mean we should go looking for a fight, especially not in our current condition. You made a mistake, Mr. Ainsworth. We both did. But even on your best day, you're no match for a Hunter Elite."

"Don't tell me what I can and can't do," Gino said through clenched teeth. "You were the one too afraid to let me go check out their ship and see what they were up to. If I can't be allowed to face them, what the hell am I here for? It's my job to-"

"*Defend us*, not seek out confrontation. You're a shield, not a sword," Clyde said. "I'm well aware of what your job is, Ainsworth. You're the one who's forgotten his place on this team. In any case, I didn't call this meeting to hear you beat your chest. I called it to tell you how things are gonna be from now on."

Clyde slapped the datapad down on the tabletop and activated a pre-recorded message, filling the room with the voice of The Stranger's nameless representative.

"I'm sorry about what happened at Platform 222," the recording said. "As your handler, the fault rests with me. We never expected the Registry's response to be so... severe. Now that they've shown their hand, I'll do everything I can to feed you a steady stream of information regarding their movements. In the meantime, you should proceed under the belief that you are now *at war* with the Registry, specifically with Brock Mason and Saimon Hawke, the Hunters assigned to your capture. Along with this message, I've included every piece of intel I have on these two men, but that alone won't be sufficient. In light of their newfound aggression, I recommend making an addition to your team, to provide you with adequate protection while you weather the coming storm..."

"'Protection?' He's *replacing* me?" Gino said. He snatched out a chair and slumped into it. "I'm being replaced?" he said again, but Clyde's silence was an answer unto itself.

The recording went on: "We will fight fire with fire. Against their Hunter Elites, I raise one of my own: Chala'Ran Mahalya al Rao Vashir is one of the most talented Scions on my client's list of contacts. She has been at level ten for longer than some of you have lived and exhibits a degree of control, discipline, and experience you will find beneficial in these difficult times. You are now at war and Chala'Ran is a warrior of the highest caliber.

"However, her involvement is strictly voluntary," the representative said. "When my client informed her of the situation, she leapt at the chance to be a part of what you are doing, but the agreement with her is not yet finalized. She will accept neither payment nor contract of any kind, but has asked to meet with you at a monastery on Adi Zahara before making her final decision. I trust you won't keep her waiting, Mr. Evans."

Clyde stopped the recording there and stuffed the datapad into his coat pocket. "There you have it. I've already plotted the coordinates," he said. "We'll be there in twelve hours."

"You can't be serious!" Gino said, suddenly finding his voice again. "It's an obvious trap. He's planting a Trojan horse in our midst and if she's even half as powerful as he says she is, I don't want her on this ship. As your shield, I can't allow it."

"He's... kinda right," Ell said. "If she's been a level ten for that long, she's gotta be totally indoctrinated. They're all brainwashed. I bet she can't take a piss without getting a Solaran's permission first."

"We'll find out soon enough," Clyde said. "If she proves to be a threat, Gino can deal with her there... can't you, Mr. Ainsworth?"

Gino bit back a curse and grumbled, "I don't trust anyone whose name I can't pronounce. Loyalist or not, she sounds like a religious nutcase... and we're meeting her at a monastery, no less."

"For what it's worth, I support bringing more women on board," Desmond chimed in. "Just saying..."

"She's a moon lady. They're *weird*," Ell remarked.

Clyde sighed. "I don't know what that's supposed to mean, but if you don't have anything nice to say, keep it to yourself. That goes for everyone."

"What she means is Rao Vashir is a lunar colony," Jay explained. "A very old one, full of uppity rich snobs... and, yeah, they tend to be rather weird, from my experience."

"See?" Ell said proudly.

"We'll find out soon enough," Clyde said again, putting the subject to rest. "One more thing: Ike deserves a proper burial and George will need professional care for the rest of his days. When The Stranger told her what happened, that 'moon lady' only asked for one thing in return: that Ike and George be cared for. Thanks to her, a shuttle will meet us on Adi Zahara to take them away to one of the best sancturaries in the galaxy. Wherever they're going, should be relatively safe and peaceful. You're welcome to join them, Jay. Where you go from thee is totally up to you."

"Thank you, captain," Magnusson said.

"Don't. I didn't make that call," Clyde said. "My point is, she's not weird or crazy or brainwashed by Solaran bullshit. She gave a damn about two people she's never even *met*. As bad as things are right now, she sounds like someone I want to work with, or at least someone I want to meet. I'd like to hear what she has to say."

Ell shrugged and Desmond showed no indication either way, but, "I still don't like it," Gino declared after a respectfully long silence.

"You don't have to," Clyde said as he walked out. "Meeting adjourned."

$-11-$

Two suns burned fiercely in the Adrastia System, scorching the lone desert world of Adi Zahara. Nights were short and infrequent, their lengths varying with the cosmic dance. Some days, temperatures would rise well over boiling point as the planet's dunes suffered under the light of Adrastia Alpha, a star not unlike Sol, but much closer. Other days, Adrastia Beta, a much weaker red dwarf, would take its place. The days when the red sun ruled the skies could be bearable and even cool at times, but those cool days produced freezing, moonless nights.

An endless sea of fine silica sand stretched out beneath the *Darkstar*'s belly as she descended into the planet's atmosphere. The air was so dry, clouds were virtually nonexistent. Jay could see for miles as he followed a lonely highway cutting across the featureless desert. With no solid ground, the roadbed perched on high pillars, like an endless bridge, leading to a white tower on the distant horizon: a terraforming spire.

"More sand?" Ell said, frowning as she stood over Desmond's shoulder. He had the co-pilot's seat while Jay gripped the pilot's yoke. The windscreen showed blue skies and ashen dunes as far as the eye could see.

"Next one will be a waterworld, I promise," Clyde said with a smile as he ran a comb through his hair.

Ell turned to him and her eyes traced his body, punctuated by a wink. "Well, look at you, all dolled up," she said coyly. "You clean up nice, captain."

Clyde slipped the comb into his back pocket and adjusted his collar. To him, their visit to Adi Zahara meant first contact with someone The Stranger believed would be a game changer. It was a minor deviation from their mission, but he was determined to put his best foot forward. He even dusted off his favorite polo shirt and some slacks for the occasion.

Meanwhile, Ell wore a black tee three sizes too small and a denim miniskirt with frayed edges, slung low on her bony hips.

Clyde laid a hand on her shoulder and gestured to the viewport and the distant tower. "I have a good feeling about this," he said. "I'm trying to follow my gut. P-222 didn't feel right, and look how *that* turned out."

They were hunting a time traveler. She could be anywhere, at any time, for any reason. Clyde was a man of logic, but logic alone wouldn't bring her to them. At some point he had to start trusting his instincts and now seemed as good a time as any.

But he hadn't entirely given up on logic, yet.

"I have a good feeling about this," Clyde said again as he prodded the bulletproof vest under his polo shirt. "But let's keep the engines running, just in case."

* * *

Adi Zahara's dry but breathable atmosphere was the product of five terraforming spires, dotted across its equatorial line. In the 150 years since the planet's development began, fledgling communities sprang up around each of them. The spires condensed what little water the planet had into drinkable form. It was no surprise they became the pillars of civilization. Wherever there was water, life was sure to follow.

But the planet's population remained just shy of a million, the point at which it would be considered a fully-fledged colony and forced to pay tribute. Thanks to careful population control, no man, woman, or child on Adi Zahara contributed Light.

The Stranger's coordinates guided Clyde and company to Pillar Four. An enormous reservoir, perfectly round and clear as a summer sky, had formed at its base. An arcology tower was built around the spire, concealing the old Solaran tech in manmade stonework. It dwarfed the multitude of smaller buildings dotting the surrounding water, connected by roads and walkways and fields of hydroponic gardens. Sandstone and shimmering steel were the materials of choice. Everything glittered white, spotless and pure.

The rusty *Darkstar Abyssal* circled the tower while Clyde tried to pick up someone, anyone, on the radio, but found only garbled static. The tower's upper floors bristled with landing pads, like tree branches, a quarter mile above ground level. He could already see a sleek late-model shuttle parked on one, with its loading ramp open and waiting, engines idling.

Clyde tried the radio again, while Desmond cycled through every available frequency. They were soon greeted by the voice of a woman, who identified herself as Pernilla, hostess of Endyssia, the local name for the Fourth Pillar. She politely directed them to a landing pad near the tower's precipice, opposite where the shuttle was parked.

Jay guided them down and, within minutes, Clyde and company took their first steps outside. The moment he emerged from the cargo ramp, Adi Zahara's scorching winds hit him, like a blast of dragon's breath. He shielded his eyes from the harsh yellow sun and the fine sand whipping across the landing pad.

Clyde was the first one out. Ell came right behind him and instantly slung a string of colorful expletives when she hit the wall of dry heat. When viewed through thick aerospace-grade glass, with the comfort of air conditioning, Adi Zahara was beautiful. But when experienced directly, it was Hell.

"Is it hot, or is it just me?" Desmond commented wryly as he stepped off.

"Stop complaining," Gino grunted as he boldly stepped out into the burning sun. "Let's meet this woman and go."

Magnusson stood halfway up the ramp, with Doctor Jenner by his side. The doctor was looking all around, with worry in his dull eyes, like a frightened deer.

Clyde momentarily studied his feet, where a thin film of fine white sand flowed between the soles of his shoes. There were strange symbols carved into the landing pad, like ancient hieroglyphics, with images of crude animals, crucifixes, ankhs, pentagrams, ohms, and others he couldn't even begin to decipher.

A woman appeared from a doorless archway, dressed in long robes of heavy, golden-yellow fabric, intricately embroidered. Through the many layers of material and complex seams, it was impossible to determine her figure or proportions, but she had the face of a middle-aged woman and blonde hair pinned into a prim bun. She greeted them with a friendly smile and kind words, but the familiarity of her voice made it clear this was the hostess, Pernilla, not the Scion they sought.

"Welcome to Endyssia," she said as she approached with outstretched hands.

Two men lingered in the doorway from which she'd emerged, loitering in the relative coolness of the shade. They wore the same elaborate robes, only theirs were deep black. The cut and trim of the garments differed slightly, but it was the color that truly stood out.

Between them was a black coffin. Even from a distance, Clyde could see it was surprisingly well-made. He marveled at the craftsmanship and wondered where such a remote place found such finery... or if, perhaps, they'd made it themselves.

His group parted ways with Jay and George at the landing pad. As Clyde and the others followed Pernilla into the tower, the two coffin-bearers disappeared into the *Darkstar* with Jay, presumably to retrieve the body of Isaac Gibbs. They moved with a level of dignity and decorum, as if intimately familiar with death and its associated rituals.

Clyde was sure of it now: they had made the coffin themselves.

As he entered the tower, Pernilla explained that the shuttle had come from Last Light, a nonprofit research institution and sanctuary in the Omicron Ceti system which catered to those who'd been "purged" – drained of their Light. Those people were searching for a cure to one of the worst punishments the Registry could levy against a person.

The study of Light and its effects on the human body was not forbidden by the Infinite Charter. The extraction, storage, and usage of Light was a Solaran invention, but the stuff itself had existed long before First Contact. Humans just didn't know about it until the Solarans dragged it out and showed it to them.

"Chala'Ran has had previous dealings with Last Light, so I know your friends are in good hands," Pernilla explained as she traversed the white stone halls with a complete lack of urgency. "She wishes to meet you in the grand hall and garden on level 49, if you would please follow me to the elevator."

Endyssia's architecture was simple and archaic. Lights were recessed into the ceiling, giving the illusion of natural illumination. Windows were tall, narrow, and glassless, creating warm drafts from all angles. Each doorway was arched and every stone carved with art of some kind, mostly depicting religious motifs. Clyde had never seen anything like it. One brick would have the Virgin Mary and an infant Jesus. Right next to it was Zeus and Athena. Then there was Osiris, Isis, Ra, and obscure deities he'd never seen before. Eventually, he *had* to ask:

"What sort of monastery is this?" he said as Pernilla brought them to an elevator, the first use of metal he'd seen since leaving the landing pad. Everything but the lighting was carved from stone blocks. "I'm not a religious man myself, but I'm interested in knowing who or what is worshipped here."

Their hostess turned to them with a smile. As they awaited the elevator, two robed women passed by, carrying stacks of books. Real books, made of *real* paper. They nodded politely, but did not stray from their task, whatever it might be.

"Endyssia is non-denominational," Pernilla explained. "Everyone here is free to seek their own truths, as they see fit. We are a gathering of various faiths."

"And they haven't killed each other?" Gino muttered, unimpressed. "Fascinating."

Pernilla paid him no mind. "Biblical studies are the most prevalent here, but some study the Talmud, the Quran, the Bhagavad Gita, and even much older texts, from 'lost' civilizations." She smiled. "There's a group on level 33 who worships Poseidon. I can't say I agree but..." she shrugged, "to each their own. Anyway, I would not consider myself 'religious' either, Mr. Evans, but we each search for our own interpretation of God, for our own reasons, in our own ways."

"Interesting," Clyde said. The elevator arrived, preceded by a gentle wind-chimed melody, and the hostess gestured them inside. It was little more than a metal cage, magnetically suspended between rails. "Since First Contact, religious faith has been on the decline," Clyde said conversationally. "Places like this are very important, if only from a cultural or academic standpoint."

"This is more than academic," Pernilla said. "Did you know there are even cults that worship the Solarans as gods? Not *here*, of course, but... elsewhere."

The doors closed with a clang, Pernilla pressed a button, and the elevator began to descend. "Adi Zahara is a refuge for humanity's vanishing culture," she explained. "There is a pillar for the arts, a pillar for craftsmanship, even a pillar for the lost sciences. Endyssia is the pillar of faith and philosophy. All believers are welcome here."

"What about non-believers?" Gino said bluntly. "Or Solaran-worshippers? They're believers, too."

From anyone else, it might have sounded like genuine curiosity. From Gino, it came as a thinly-concealed attack, a passive-aggressive jab at those who did not see things the way he saw them.

"Here, we explore the unseen, the mysteries of this life and the next," Pernilla replied calmly. "Our doors are open to *all* who wish to join us on that journey. If not, such people still have the rest of the galaxy at their disposal."

"It seems like a journey *backwards* to me," Gino grunted.

Clyde cut in, "Maybe you should wait in the ship."

But the hostess merely waved him off. "It's quite alright if he has questions," she said before looking to Gino. "It *is* a step backwards, sir. We believe in going back to a time when man still knew his place in the world and didn't bow to the whims of extraterrestrials as false deities. I cannot speak for everyone here, but Chala'Ran and I are unified in our belief that someday the Solarans will fall — with a little *push* in the right direction — and, once they do, mankind will find his way back to the Lord. Until that day, we shall keep faith alive. She has devoted her life to bringing about the fall... but that is something you must discuss with *her*."

"And here we thought she was a loyalist," Desmond whispered in Clyde's ear. "Instead, we've get a holy crusader. You sure it's not too late to leave?"

* * *

The grand hall occupied an entire level of the tower. The Solaran terraforming spire forming the building's spine ran through the center of the room, but fell short of being its main attraction. That title belonged to the planters, where flowers and fruits of all kinds grew. Grapes, pomegranates, and strawberries shared the space with roses, poppies, lilies, and lotuses, bringing color, life, and fragrance. Instead of walls, there were lattice-like terraces on all sides, allowing natural light to stream in, adding to its earthy appeal.

Three robed women were chatting at a stone table across the room, while enjoying tea and bread. One had her face veiled in a traditional Muslim niqab. After serving tea to her guests, Pernilla joined the ladies. Ell and Desmond declined refreshments and Gino grunted indifferently, but Clyde accepted, which resulted in each of them being served a hot cup. The tea was very fresh and tasted of fruit and honey, likely brewed from the garden itself. After assuring them Chala'Ran would arrive shortly, Pernilla rejoined her social circle.

"I don't like this place or these people," Gino declared the moment she was out of earshot. "How much longer are we going to wait? I suggest we leave if this woman doesn't show up in the next five minutes."

"I wonder what they're wearin' under them robes..." Desmond mused. If the look in his eyes was any indication, it was something he'd been contemplating for a while now.

"It's too hot to wear anything," Ell said as she watched the women. "How do they do it?"

"Oh, but we have *hot tea* to keep us cool," Gino said, gesturing wildly to the steaming cups before them. His eyes locked furiously upon Clyde. "This is ridiculous. You can't tell me you actually trust these space nuns. It's a damned *cult*. They're all out of their minds." He had the decency to keep his voice down, despite his tone.

Clyde merely shrugged. His eyes loitered on Pernilla and her companions, but his thoughts wandered elsewhere. He could feel a presence. He'd felt it from the moment they landed, but it was growing stronger now. No, it was drawing *nearer*. A Scion's gift was approaching, nudging the far corners of his mind, subtle but insistent.

But he said nothing, so as not to alarm the others. He just watched the door and waited, detached from the present conversation. Gino made an off-hand remark about how they were leaving the *Darkstar* unprotected and should go immediately, to which Ell replied it was code-locked and thumb-printed and these 'space nuns' probably couldn't hack an abacus, much less a spaceship. Clyde processed very little of what was being said.

A tall woman emerged from a doorway across the room. Her robes were the dark red of old blood and slit high up the sides, revealing another layer of black beneath, and yet another layer beneath that. She traversed the distance between the entrance and Pernilla's table slowly, but with a confident stride and straight-backed posture that made her seem like a lioness prowling a den of kittens.

That's her, Clyde thought as his eyes followed her across the room.

Her height was made all the more apparent by the sturdy heels she wore, with thick metal anklets. Her skin was the color of burnt caramel and her hair was a thick mane of tight black curls that reached halfway down her back. She knelt slightly as she embraced Pernilla, who wasn't exactly short by female standards. Clyde watched as the two women casually shared a few words before Chala'Ran Mahalya bid the ladies farewell and made her way toward his table.

He knew, from her smile, that coming here was a good idea. Gino ceased his grumblings. Desmond and Ell waited expectantly. Pleased, satisfied, and only marginally wary, Clyde rose and extended his hand.

"You must be Miss Mahalya," he said, and silently hoped he'd nailed the pronunciation.

To his surprise, she gently sandwiched his palm between both of her own and bowed her head, as if in prayer. Her hands were strong, yet cold. For an awkwardly long minute, she neither moved nor spoke. The ritual, whatever it was, soon passed and she released him, lifted her head, and peered at him with big brown eyes that blinked far too rarely.

"Thank you so very much for coming," she said with a small bow. "I am Chala'Ran Mahalya al Rao Vashir. Please forgive me for making you wait. I was deep into my midday meditation when Pern informed me of your arrival."

"Clyde Evans. Thank you for having us," Clyde said, always the diplomat. "The wait wasn't long at all," he added as he pulled out a chair for her, next to his own.

"Can I call you Cha-Cha?" Ell said from beside him. "You seem like a 'Cha-Cha.' I'm Ell, by the way."

"I would be honored, dear," Chala'Ran replied pleasantly. She took her seat, smoothed her robes, and placed her hands in her lap. "You may call me whatever you deem appropriate."

"I will call you a *waste of time*, until you prove otherwise," Gino interjected. "We didn't come all this way for tea and talk and midday meditation. We came expecting a Scion – a *powerful* one at that – and while you may have been a level ten once, why should we believe your skills have not atrophied while cowering in this nunnery?"

Chala observed him from the corners of her eyes. If he had angered her, it certainly didn't show. She remained as placid as ever as she looked to Clyde and said, in a lowered voice, "Is something the matter? If I have offended you in some way…"

"No, you haven't offended us," Clyde replied, casting a cold glance at Gino, across the table. "Chala'Ran, this is Gino Ainsworth. I'm afraid he was offended long before we landed here. It's something of a chronic condition of his. Don't let it get to you."

She looked to Gino and serenely said, "It will not."

"Good. So, answer my question," Gino snapped. "What qualifies you for this job? Give me a reason not to call you a washed-up has-been." He drilled a finger into the tabletop, to drive every syllable home. "You've got *five minutes* to make a case for why we shouldn't take off without you."

He was deadly serious, but Desmond suddenly burst out laughing. Even Clyde was tickled by the thought of Gino having veto privileges, but he contained himself.

"That is a reasonable concern to have," Chala'Ran said with a gentle smile. "However, I fear you are misunderstanding the nature of this meeting, Mr. Ainsworth. The Stranger requested my involvement for a very specific reason: I believe, with all of my heart, that the Solarans are to be opposed in *all* things. They bring strife and chaos wherever they reach. They roam the galaxy, like a lion, seeking whomever they might devour."

Gino rolled his eyes, but Ell joined in on the fun: "Don't forget the part where they steal your soul and put it in a jar," she said, egging the woman on.

Chala'Ran frowned. "That, I do *not* believe. Only the Lord has dominion over a man's immortal soul. I know not what they take, but a soul it is not." She rested her hands on the table, fingers interlocked in a pensive gesture. "The nature of Light intrigues me, but I have resolved that it is almost certainly not one's soul. It is, however, *important*, and that is reason enough to-"

"This isn't about your holy crusade," Gino cut in. "We aren't on a divine mission to drive the Solarans out of the Milky Way and the more you talk about it, the more I'm convinced you don't belong on this team."

"Hey, speak for yourself," Ell chimed in. "I like what she's sayin.' If there's a way to kick a Solaran's ass, I'd love to hear it."

"Do that on your own time," said Desmond. "Some of us are just trying to stay alive, not start a fucking revolution... pardon my French." He winked at Chala'Ran.

"Pardoned, dear. And that is precisely why I requested this meeting," Chala'Ran said graciously. "Let us be clear and speak plainly. Should I join you, I *will* defend you from Solaran interests, for that is my calling. However, you still work for the Registry and, by association, for the Solarans. Surely, you can see why this might cause... friction."

Clyde felt a sinking in the pit of his stomach. As usual, it was Ell who bluntly said what they were all thinking:

"What kind of 'friction' are we talking about? I mean, if it turns out we're doing something that actually helps the Solarans, you'd... hurt us... *kill* us, maybe?"

"I would rather not..." Chala'Ran said sympathetically. It didn't help.

"I knew it," Gino declared, with his fists balled on the tabletop. But they quickly morphed into fingers to point at the woman. "This is punishment for our screw-up on 222. She's a gun to our heads and The Stranger's finger is on the trigger. He doesn't trust us to return the ship or find the Chronomancer, so he sent a failsafe." Vindicated, he laughed. "She's a spy, providing an inside line straight to *him*. It's exactly as I said it'd be."

"You said a lot of things, most of 'em nonsense," Desmond grumbled before looking to Chala. "But maybe he's onto something. The boss doesn't trust us anymore? He sent you to make sure we stick to the plan?" He chuckled. "Strip. I wanna see if you're wearin' a wire under them frocks, dear."

"Both of you cut it out," Clyde said. "This doesn't change a thing."

"Finding out your boss thinks you're trying to double cross him doesn't change a thing?" Ell said. "Dammit, Clyde, you're such a gully sometimes."

"A what?"

"Gullible," she hissed. "Naïve. Idiot. Moron. Sucker. Dumbass." She pointed at Chala'Ran. "She's here to check us if we deviate from the plan. Ain't it obvious?"

"I don't plan on deviating from anything," Clyde retorted. "The Stranger has a vested interest in this. He wouldn't send us to her if he felt we'd set her off."

"Set me off?" Chala inquired, but was ignored.

"He doesn't trust us. This is an insult," Gino raged, gesturing wildly at Chala'Ran, who sat there and took it with grace.

"Trust goes both ways," Clyde rebutted. "No one at this table has trusted The Stranger since day one, myself included. Look, if we just stick to the plan-"

"I've seen plenty of guys 'stick to the plan' and end up dead for it," Desmond said.

Chala'Ran rose from her seat. "This 'gun' has nothing more to say and will now take its leave," she said calmly. "If you knew anything of my past, you would know I am no one's weapon, nor am I easily *set off*."

Clyde opened his mouth to speak, but she raised her hand.

"My allegiance lies with God and I am no one's tool but His," Chala'Ran said. "If you will excuse me, we have nothing more to discuss at this time. I shall return to my chambers to fetch my bags and regroup with you at your ship."

"Wait... you're *coming*?" Clyde said, mouth agape.

"Not if we leave her," Desmond said as he rose. "Let's go. The leash is gettin' a little too short for my liking. I didn't fly all the way out here to pick up our executioner."

Chala'Ran's unblinking gaze slowly turned to him and Clyde felt her gift, which had been little more than background noise for the past few minutes, suddenly quadruple in intensity. "You are welcome to *try*, Mr. Williams," she said coldly. "Should you succeed, I will gladly declare myself a 'washed-up has-been,' as Mr. Ainsworth so eloquently put it. But, should you fail to get your ship off that landing pad without me, let us speak no further of my qualifications or allegiances, please."

She turned to leave, but Clyde quickly got to his feet. "Do you need a hand with your bags?" he said in a vain attempt at salvaging the situation. But Chala'Ran simply turned and strode away, her blood red robes trailing behind her with every measured step.

* * *

They called the woman all manner of things, as they made their way back to the *Darkstar*. But the one word no one could say was 'liar.'

"It's no good," Desmond muttered. The reactor was on the verge of going critical. Both gravity drives were at full output. The engines were belching blue flames and the thermal readings were slipping past the red line.

Still, the ship refused to move. Not one inch. Even with the gravity drives pushed to their brink, the *Darkstar Abyssal* was no lighter than the sum of her parts.

"Shut it down before you break something!" Clyde had to yell over the high-pitched whine of the thrusters. If the thrust could, somehow, get the ship off the landing pad, it wouldn't do them any good. She'd drop like a stone.

Ell suddenly ran onto the flight deck, drenched in sweat and breathing heavily. "I checked *everything*," she said, panting with each word. "There's nothing holding us down. Nothing. I double-checked, triple-checked."

"Check again," Gino barked.

"*You* check! It's hot as balls out there," Ell quipped.

Fed up with it all, Clyde reached over Desmond's shoulder, grabbed the throttle lever, and slammed it down. Slowly, the whine of the thrusters began to subside. Finally seeing the futility of this exercise, Desmond began powering down the other systems, turning all the sliders and dials on their touchscreens down to nil. As the readings on the digital gauges dropped, he slumped back in the pilot's seat, defeated.

"I don't know how, but she's got us," he said. "All that fussing and fighting and nobody bothered to ask the bitch what her gift is? God, I need a fucking cigarette."

"Watch your mouth," Clyde warned. "That woman is your crewmate now. Get used to it."

"Yeah, too bad we don't have someone who could *stop her*," Ell said, glaring at Clyde.

Gino slammed ahis fist on the wall. "I'm gonna go down there and deal with her myself. She will *not* board this ship," he said before storming off, probably headed for the exit, or possibly even the gun rack, but Clyde caught him by the shoulder and hauled him back.

"Sit down before you make a fool of yourself. Has everyone here lost their mind?"

"She basically came right out and *said* she's not on our side!" Ell protested. "Dammit, Clyde, what more do you need? If you love her so much, why don't you just marry her?" In a low murmur she added, "Or fuck her once and get it over with."

Clyde stared until he was sure he hadn't heard what he thought he'd heard. "Chala said she's against the Solarans," he replied patiently. "That means she's against the Registry. Isn't that what we came here for?" He looked around at each and every one of them. "We came to get a level ten Scion who will keep the Registry off our backs and that's exactly what we got. She doesn't work for The Stranger; she has her own agenda and it lines up *perfectly* with ours, so what's the big deal?"

"Everyone on this boat has their own agenda," Desmond muttered. "Difference is, if things go south, I know I could take down any one of you in a fight." He smiled at Gino. "Even you." Desmond stood and faced Clyde. "The balance ain't what it used to be. She's what I call an 'apex predator,' and *that*'s a big deal."

Judging by the looks on their faces, he'd hit the nail on the head. Even Ell, who typically raged against anything Desmond said, nodded in agreement. Clyde couldn't decide whether to laugh or shake his head in pity. They'd come to Adi Zahara looking for a powerful ally. Now they had one and they were afraid she was *too* powerful to be trusted?

He was about to give them a piece of his mind when a blinking light on the console caught his eye. In the chaos, no one had noticed it until now. "Someone's sending us a message," Clyde said, pointing to the flashing beacon. "Transfer it to the comm room. We'll finish this later."

They followed him, of course. Once there, he found Pernilla's face awaiting him on the holo display, distorted with static. Behind her, he could see Chala'Ran pacing, with her arms folded. She looked pissed off... in a very composed, almost elegant, sort of way.

"Clyde Evans? Mr. Evans, are you there?" Pernilla repeated, staring into the monitor.

He mashed the button to speak. "I'm here. What's the matter?"

"We just received a transmission from the shuttle your friend departed on," Pernilla explained. Behind her, Chala'Ran halted and watched the screen expectantly.

"Magnusson? Jayce Magnusson sent you a message?" Clyde said. "Has something happened? Is he okay? Did they make it to-"

"They're fine," Pernilla said reassuringly. "He is safe and well on his journey, but he reported gunships in the desert. The shuttle's sensors caught them approaching at low altitude – pirates, from the looks of it."

"Pirates?" Clyde said incredulously, despite having read a book on the subject less than twenty-four hours ago. He should have finished it. "There's nothing here worth stealing."

Chala'Ran politely brushed Pern aside and took control. The pleasant woman they had met minutes ago was gone. Her features turned hard.

"Your friend was unable to give an exact count, but he reports at least three incoming vessels, dropships and gunships," she explained with unerring diction. "Their trajectory suggests they are headed *here* and their armament is intended for a hardened target. We believe they wish to lay siege to Endyssia. I have never seen such a thing in my ten years here, thus I believe it is safe to assume *your* presence is the catalyst for this act of aggression."

Clyde felt a cold chill at the thought that he'd brought danger to this peaceful place...

But Desmond thought otherwise: "We couldn't have been followed," he said quickly. "We flew a randomized warp pattern through dark space, mathematically impossible to track in such a short time."

"We need to take off *now*," Gino declared, jostling for position with Clyde so he could go another round with Chala'Ran. "Release us, woman! You've made your point, so let us go. They're obviously coming for the *Darkstar*."

"Let them come. It is better to face them *here*. This position is defensible," Chala'Ran said calmly. "Please step aside, Mr. Ainsworth, I wish to speak with your commanding officer." Gino did no such thing, but she continued despite his stubbornness. "Mr. Evans, I humbly request your immediate presence. Please meet me at my residence to discuss tactics – Level 53, Dormitory C. I will release the *Darkstar* upon your arrival. I suggest the ship perform evasive maneuvers while I coordinate a response to the coming threat. Estimated time of arrival: nine minutes and counting. Please move with all due haste. Mahalya, out."

"It's a trap" Gino whispered.

Chala'Ran did not end the transmission, but she turned away from the monitor with such finality, a very shocked Pernilla was left to do it on her behalf. "I... umm... Godspeed to you all," the woman said before the holo projection went dark.

– 12 –

Somewhere on the bleeding edge of an unexplored arm of the Milky Way there exists an unnamed star, known only by its astronomical designation, DST-4856. Only one planet basks in the light of DST-4856: Ossus, a gas giant of the most stunning azure blue.

Three moons orbit Ossus. The largest, Ossus III, was very much like Earth, if Earth were all mud and tropics. Its warm, humid air gave rise to an abundance of plant life. Seen from space, the vast swamps and tropical forests colored the entire planet a beautiful jade green, crisscrossed by thin brown rivers.

The uninitiated might call it a jungle world, but Ossus III was far more dangerous than any mere jungle. Instead of animal tracks, its forests were riddled with deep scars left by tank treads, cratered by mortars, and scorched by napalm and orbital laser strikes. In place of poisonous snakes and carnivorous beasts, there were landmines and IEDs in the underbrush and motion-detecting autoturrets perched in the high branches.

Ossus III was a rare find, a world that didn't need terraforming. No terraforming spires meant no Solaran interference. No policing. No law. No order. Anyone could land there, lay claim to a plot of mud, and do whatever he pleased, ethics laws and tax codes be damned. And that is precisely what

Samonia Pharmaceuticals did when they claimed Ossus III in the late 2140s.

Setting up a secret lab or two in no man's land was pretty much standard practice for companies in that day and age. Unfortunately, there is no such thing as "no man's land." Two centuries of traveling to the stars has taught mankind one thing: wherever you plant your flag, someone will come along to take what is yours. In technical terms, these takers are known as "pirates" – "*space* pirates," to be precise. Most people just call them assholes.

A cost-benefit analysis determined it was better to cut their losses and leave than try to fight off the criminal elements taking over the planet. By 2170, Samonia Pharmaceuticals, the fourth largest drug company in the galaxy, was driven off-world by space pirates, who, unsurprisingly, like places with no laws, no order, no policing, and lots of free stuff. They surrendered Ossus III to the drug dealers and slavers, collected the insurance checks, and never looked back.

But Ossus's story did not end there. The small jungle moon became a warzone as various factions fought for control of its abandoned resources. By 2200, a deadlock was reached, with six regimes each holding a piece of the pie and defending it tooth and nail. Rafiq Seryn, a man who prided himself on his ability to sell premium narcotics to all corners of the galaxy, held 200,000 square miles of slave-tended crop fields, drug labs, and tent cities… but he wanted it *all*. Sharing is not the pirate's way.

Rafiq Seryn, known as "King Ra" by the army of cutthroats backing him, a man wanted dead by nearly every known government agency in the galaxy for crimes against humanity, found an unlikely ally who tipped the odds heavily in his favor. This distant ally gave him all he needed. In two years, he crushed the opposition and took total control of Ossus III and his shadowy helpers asked only one thing in return: On the first day of each solar cycle, his thugs went door to door, tent to tent, hovel to hovel, acting as Reapers, extracting a double portion of Light from every man, woman, and child.

The most disturbing thing about the story of Ossus III, other than how it ended or the fact that the Solaran High Council made a deal with a known mass murderer / drug dealer / human trafficker, is how quietly it all went down. The Solarans didn't send any guns, ammunition, or armor. There was enough of that to go around.

They just sent *one* Scion... and she proved to be a far more effective weapon than they ever imagined.

* * *

Clyde pressed his ear to the warm metal of Chala'Ran's door and listened for any signs of activity. Once he tuned out the muffled sounds of gunfire elsewhere in the tower, he head a soft whisper:

"Thou has given me the shield of thy salvation, and thy gentleness has made me great. Thou has enlarged my steps under me, so that my feet did not slip. I have consumed my enemies and wounded them, that they can rise no more..."

The sharp crack of a distant explosion startled him. Clyde unholstered his sidearm, finding more safety in the contours of its capacitors than in the warmth of the ballistic vest under his polo shirt. He held his breath and waited as he put his ear to the door again.

"Thou has girded me with the strength to battle," she said. "Those who rose up against me, thou has subdued under me. Thou has given me the necks of my enemies, that I might *destroy* them that hate thee. They will look, but there shall be none to save them, not even you, Lord. *None* shall answer their cries..."

"Chala'Ran!" Clyde pleaded, pounding his fist on the hard steel until he feared his wrist might snap. "We don't have time for this! We're under attack!"

A moment of relative silence followed, where the sounds of invasion became like white noise and the door slid aside with such suddenness, Clyde startled.

Chala'Ran stood before him with her bags at her feet: two satchels, a duffel bag, and a large knapsack with everything she owned divided amongst them. She held an assault rifle with a suppressor and extended clip. The chipped, faded paint on its barrel and layers of black tape on its stock gave it veteran status. The gun was probably older than him.

"Before the hour is out, we will kill or be killed, Mr. Evans," Chala'Ran replied as she stepped forward, out of her Spartan chamber. "If now is not the time for prayer, I know not whence. Come, we have much to do."

The bags followed her into the hall, as if drawn by magnets. The door automatically shut behind her and locked. The entire tower was on lockdown. Pernilla had granted them use of the elevator, with instructions to code lock it after they reached their destination.

"I was speaking with Pern some minutes ago," she said, tapping a small communicator pinned to the lapel of her crimson robes. "From a secure location, she will walk us through the operation. But, before we proceed, I am afraid I owe you an apology, dear."

"For making me wait?" Clyde said. "It's fine, Chala, but we really should-"

"No. Not that," she said, piteously shaking her head. "Earlier, you kindly offered to help me with my bags. I ignored you. That was rude of me and I apologize."

"Considering the circumstances, I don't blame you. You were right to walk away from that fiasco. If anything, I should apologize to you for the way Gino and the others behaved." He paused. "And myself as well."

"Thank you, but one cannot apologize for others, only for oneself." Chala'Ran turned and began to walk toward an elevator at the end of the hall. Clyde and the luggage followed. "As for Mr. Ainsworth, I understand his frustration. I know what happened on Platform 222. Each of us handles failure differently. I handled mine by coming here." She gestured to the walls around them.

"What did you do before coming here?"

"Terrible things," she said. For the moment, that seemed like enough of an answer.

Clyde followed in silence, down the hall of locked dormitories with their thick steel-reinforced doors. Fortress or prison, Endyssia would hold. He heard another distant blast, but the tower did not shudder. The Solaran spire that formed its backbone would not allow the foundations to falter, and the mortar and stone surrounding it was just as solid as the woman before him.

Chala'Ran walked on. Neither her feet nor her words hurried. "The Registry exacts a different price from each of us. Light is one thing, but they also take lives and twist ideology. I have seen things you would not believe and done things you would not forgive, all in the service of beings I neither trust nor understand. When I arrived here, ten years ago, I was a broken woman," she explained. "I donated all of my worldly possessions to Last Light. My more intimate belongings I packed into a vehicle and brought here with me."

Clyde unconsciously glanced at the rifle. *Intimate belongings...*

She paused, standing before the elevator. "We are more than the things we carry. We are defined by the things we let go." Chala'Ran turned to punch in a code on the keypad, summoning the carriage. As the doors opened, she turned to Clyde once more and smiled warmly. "I harbor no ill will toward Mr. Ainsworth, but if he hears nothing I say, may he hear this: 'let it go.' Warn him not to cling to that which poisons his soul and weakens his resolve. He can never return to the Registry and his former life; *none* of you can. 'Let it go.' Those words have the power to save him from himself. I speak from personal experience."

Clyde merely nodded as he stepped inside, careful not to trip over her baggage, which entered the elevator as she did. "For now, Gino's his own problem, not ours. What's *our* next move?" he asked as the doors shut.

"Endyssia is a fortress in spirit. She will protect the lives within her walls until reinforcements arrive," Chala said. When Clyde looked at her strangely she added, "You did not think this planet was without defenses, did you? Endyssia is peaceful, but not all of the pillars are so... vulnerable. Khaliya, our neighbor to the west, studies the ancient art of warfare. The entire community there is devoted to the preservation of martial epithets and materiel. They are sending aid as we speak."

For a moment, he wondered why she chose to come to Endyssia, the pillar of theology and philosophy, instead of Khaliya, the pillar of militancy... but Clyde suspected he already knew the answer.

"What about the *Darkstar*?" he asked. "This tower may hold, but the ship can't take much. How are you so casual about this? Why not just pull their ships out of the sky? Ground them, like you did to us."

"No, dear. They are moving too fast, too erratically, and keeping their distance," she said as the elevator began to ascend. "It is as if they know what I am capable of and are deliberately taking advantage of my limitations. I *could* bring them down, with sufficient force and focus... but I refuse. I am not the one who must send a message today, Mr. Evans. You are."

Chala'Ran ejected the magazine from her rifle, gave it a quick inspection and blew in it three times before shoving it back inside with a firm click. She thumbed off the safety, tested the weight of her rifle and eyeballed the iron sights, as if reacquainting herself with the familiar handshake of an old friend.

"Our enemy's knowledge of my abilities will not save them," she said when the ritual was complete. "I have seen more war than peace in my forty-four years in this life, but I have never seen one who knew me better than I know myself now. Let them come. I am ready."

The elevator suddenly lurched to a stop with a metallic clang and a heavy jerk which threw him against the wall. The lights flickered once, twice, and went out, leaving total darkness. Everything beyond the tip of his nose was lost in shadows, though he could still sense the subtle, insistent power of Chala'Ran's gift. Her concentration had not faltered.

"Minor setback," she said pleasantly.

Her metal heels had a distinct ring on the steel floor as she repositioned. Clyde fumbled for his holo communicator, the only light source he had, as they began to ascend, slowly at first, then with almost normal speed.

The elevator was little more than a metal cage, suspended between rails. The electric motors did not activate, nor did the lights, but he could hear the wheels grinding. Shining his light upward, he saw the emergency brakes were still locked. The carriage was not rising under its own power. It was being *dragged* upward. He felt himself being pulled as well, as if he was lighter on his feet.

He cast the light on Chala'Ran. She had the rifle in one hand, while the other was outstretched, like a sorceress casting a spell. Her face was taut with concentration.

"We are wanted on the seventieth floor," she said, still as calm and serene as ever, "and I will not be delayed. Our mission is simple: seek and destroy. We will go floor-by-floor and systematically wipe them out, destroying anyone who stands between us and the ground level. These people struck a blow against you on Platform 222. We will return the favor a hundredfold."

It suddenly occurred to him that going *up* put more obstacles between them and the ground floor. To his horror, he realized *that* was the idea.

* * *

Desmond Williams guided the *Darkstar Abyssal* through a series of acrobatic maneuvers. Her thin, blade-like wings cut sharp contrails through the barely-there condensation of Adi Zahara's searing skies.

Two clumsy hulks masquerading as gunships were hot on his trail. A third vessel, larger than the others, hung back, taking pot shots with a heavy cannon whenever the *Darkstar* passed through its crosshairs.

"Why the hell are they trying to shoot us down?" Ell squawked from her place in the co-pilot's seat. "I thought they wanted the ship in one piece."

"They want what's *inside* the ship," Desmond said. "Even if we crash, the drive cores will survive... and that's all they want, sweetheart."

He'd seen ships hit the ground at Mach 30, leaving nothing but a puddle of molten slag and an intact drive core, as shiny as the day it rolled off The Forge. On a relatively desolate world like Adi Zahara, there would be no one around to ask questions as the Registry sifted through the wreckage to get what they were after.

The thought of them getting *his* ship and *his* designs, free of charge, set Desmond's teeth on edge. The thought of dying in a fiery crash seemed trifling by comparison.

Grimacing, he banked another sharp turn. One of the smaller gunships launched a flurry of missiles, which converged on the *Darkstar*'s heat signature. But the ship's defense lasers cut them down with surgical precision. The *Darkstar* emerged from the smoke and flames relatively unscathed.

"If they kill our engines, we're done," Desmond said. "Gravity drives can keep us airborne, but without engines we're dead in the water."

"Then let's shoot 'em down," Ell said. "Don't we have a huge ass gun for that?"

"A railgun that big can't fire in atmosphere. It'll overheat and cause permanent damage," Desmond said. "Not to mention using the *Darkstar*'s primary weapon to shoot down a gunship is like using a nuke to kill a fly."

Before he was done speaking, Ell had already flipped open her laptop and jacked into the ship's console. "The defense lasers aren't hitting fast enough," she said as her fingers worked across the keys. "I can fix it."

"…Or make it *worse*."

"Trust me," she said.

Desmond's only reply was a string of muttered curses. He doubted she could make anything worse. This game was already like playing tag with an axe murderer in a locked room. Without a suitable weapon, they couldn't fight back. All he could do was endure it and choke back any thoughts of ditching this sandbox and blasting off into space, without Clyde and the gun nun.

Desmond pulled hard on the yoke, reining the *Darkstar* into a rolling negative-g turn. Thanks to the gravity drive, he felt nothing, not even the slightest shudder, but he was acutely aware of the load this was putting on the drives' control systems. Something could overload at any moment.

"How long am I supposed to fly circles around this damn tower?" Desmond said as he pulled out of a complex series of rolls and received a hundred or so rounds in the ass for his trouble. The gunships were faster and more agile than the *Darkstar* and had a big brother waiting on the outskirts. He couldn't win this.

"'Til the Wicked Witch gives Clyde back," Ell said between her teeth. "We could've been halfway across the galaxy by now if it weren't for her." She huffed, snapped her laptop shut and wiped her hands of it. "Done. Those defense lasers should be a li'l quicker now... not that it's gonna make much difference."

"Where'd you learn to calibrate a defense grid that fast?" Desmond asked, seeking a diversion.

"It's all math. Where'd you learn to fly, the circus?"

"Two tours in the Earth Coalition Space Force, engineering corps," Desmond replied as he swooped down low, mere meters from the sand dunes, and swung up again, with the two smaller gunships following. One dropped too low and plowed through the sand, but came up none the worse for it.

"Liar. They don't teach that kind of hotdoggin' in the ECSF. Bet you learned it the same place you learned to take hostages," Ell replied, studying him as he watched the viewport. The flying brick was on their tail again and peppering the *Darkstar* with gunfire.

"I heard you're from Mars," she added, speaking over the sound of shots pinging off the hull.

"Oh, so you were eavesdropping while Clyde 'interrogated' me? Funny, I didn't think you could hear a thing from the bottom of that bottle you crawled into," Desmond said, ignoring the blue-white flash of a laser. "I swear, your Hunter friend's as thick as this windscreen. Does he actually believe half the shit the Registry spoon feeds him?"

"No," Ell said sharply, "so don't lump him in with the rest. He's different."

"A Hunter's still a Hunter. I read his file. If the tables were turned, he'd be huntin' us instead of Claire. Same goes for this woman we're pickin' up. How many more Registry dogs are we gonna haul into this kennel?"

"I expect that from a martian," Ell said. "Fuck Mars. A whole planet of liars, thieves, and inbred shitheads."

"Yeah... and who made it that way?" Desmond said. "Enough about me. You're pretty sharp for some chick from the Plats. Fast runner, too... kind of like you're used to being chased, little girl."

"You don't know me. Stop tryin.'"

"I can read you like a book. You're a frightened little girl who's gotten in over her head. If you're really that scared of the Registry, you should swing by Mars sometime. It's a *lovely* place. The only free place left, really. No Solarans. No gods, no masters."

"No basic human decency."

"It's right up your alley, then. It beats cozying up to that Hunter. Getting in his pants won't earn you a 'get outta jail free' card, you know. He's only a level three. He can't do anything for you, little girl."

"Is that jealousy I hear?"

"Ha! Get over yourself," Desmond scoffed. "Your bra size is 'tea cup' and your ass is nonexistent. Puberty came and went and didn't leave any gifts under the tree for you, little girl. Maybe next year, if you sit on Santa's lap and wish reeeeally hard..."

"I swear, I'm gonna kill this guy," Ell said to herself as she snatched up her computer and stood to leave. "Where's Gino? I need to hurt something."

"Fifty credits says he's sulking in his room."

* * *

Clyde had never been in a full-blown gun battle. He'd been shot at before. He'd shot men before. Both came with the job description. But he'd never encountered a complete, unadulterated exchange of live ammunition.

The seventieth floor was overrun by men with ancient weapons, dressed in a patchwork of stolen body armor, rusting iron plates, and thick overcoats, stitched together with duct tape and shoestring. Never before had he seen such an assortment of ruffians, goons, bruisers, breakers, hoodlums, raiders, wreckers, ragamuffins, scallywags, and ne'er-do-wells.

They were *not* from the Registry. He could have guessed as much from the ramshackle ships they arrived in, the same ships which were now playing a deadly game of cat and mouse with the *Darkstar* in the surrounding airspace.

The men opened fire the moment the elevator arrived. Bullets were whizzing past Clyde's ears a half second before the cage doors opened. Chala'Ran shoved him aside, behind a stone column and went to work. During those moments alone, behind the pillar, he realized how insane – or talented – this woman was. She advanced from cover to cover, trading bullets with the enemy as she went.

When he mustered the courage to peek out, Clyde saw they'd set up some kind of Gatling laser behind a stone desk at the far end of the hall, emitting an electric whir as it threw a steady stream of beams downrange. But, with a wave of her hand, the two men operating the weapon were pulled from their cover and sent sprawling across the floor. Two quick three-round bursts from Chala'Ran's assault rifle ended their day.

A man with a shotgun charged out from behind a pillar. Chala'Ran waved her hand, as if directing an orchestra. The man was jerked aside so quickly, it was as though he'd been struck by an invisible truck. He hit the wall with a sickening 'crack' and slumped to the ground, bleeding from his eyes and ears, but she pumped three shots into his face to be sure.

Another man emerged from cover and made a beeline toward the unmanned laser, but Chala cut him down with three shots to the legs. A final three-round burst left a cloud of red mist where his head had been. He was dead before his body hit the floor.

It was over in a matter of seconds. The apex predator downed her prey and the hall fell eerily silent. Clyde began to step out, but Chala raised a hand, signaling him to wait. She made her way to the far end of the corridor, checking every nook. With Endyssia on lockdown, all of the doors were sealed. Only when she opened her clenched fist and gestured with two fingers for him to approach did Clyde finally emerge.

It was all very precise... and that's what frightened him most. She was a trained killer, the likes of which he'd never seen, in truth or fiction. Even for a level ten Hunter Elite, it was *too much*.

By the time he reached her, Chala was on her comm, listening to instructions: "They're falling back to the east stairwell, moving down to the sixty-ninth floor," Pernilla explained, her voice slightly distorted. "Be careful. They're massing in the atrium on sixty. It looks like they're setting up a blockade there, to cut you off."

"Understood. Mahalya, out," Chala'Ran said and abruptly terminated communications. Her tone was utterly devoid of the warmth she had expressed earlier, as were her mannerisms. She didn't spare Clyde a second glance as she went to inspect a few clips of ammunition from one of the dead men. Their guns were virtually identical to hers.

"Where'd you learn to clear a room like that?" Clyde asked, as an awkward icebreaker. He felt as if they were strangers all over again… not that he had ever known her.

"Not a room. A hall," Chala replied as she stuffed two extra clips and a cluster of grenades into her pockets. "Rooms are more difficult. Nonlinear. Easier to get caught in converging lines of fire, creating complex kill zones. More difficult to establish chokepoints."

Clyde said nothing. He waited until she finished arming herself and rose before he spoke.

"What's our endgame? These aren't Registry men," he said, gesturing to one of the corpses and trying not to look any longer than was necessary. "Why are they even here?"

"Not Registry men?" she queried. "Why do you say that? Because they do not wear the colors? Because they do not carry the badge?" She placed a hand on his shoulder, her touch gentler than a killer's should be. "The Registry can, and *will,* use anyone to serve their needs. They find allies in the darkest of places. *Never* forget that."

Clyde thought for a moment, but Chala'Ran didn't allow for 'moments.' She began to walk. Her luggage followed at her feet as she urged him to stay close and keep his weapon in hand. He did, but the subject still loitered in his mind.

"There's got to be more to it than that," he said as he followed her to a stairwell at the far end of the hall. The Registry couldn't be everywhere, all the time. Ethics aside, calling in help from bandits, mercenaries, and pirates made strategic sense. Clyde didn't doubt the truth of what Chala'Ran said, but one sticking point remained:

How the hell did they get here so fast? He thought. *It's like they knew we were coming.*

Chala'Ran stopped him, with a palm to his chest and quickly pulled him aside. The bottom of the stairwell opened upon a large atrium. The Solaran spire stood at the center, like a massive obelisk. Multiple balconies wrapped around the room. Clyde remembered her words about converging lines of fire and kill zones. A single sniper on one of those balconies could control half the room. Two or three could make the entire area impassable.

He heard men somewhere inside, but the echoing voices made it difficult to pinpoint locations. Chala'Ran lowered her voice to a whisper. "This atrium continues down to the sixtieth floor. That's ten levels. If they're smart – and one should always assume one's enemies are smart – they will have snipers on the balconies and heavy weapons stationed at key vantage points. I will take care of those. Wait for me here. I'll signal you once the room is cleared."

He tried to stop her, but she charged in before he could utter a word, leaving him to wonder who was truly in command.

* * *

Gino's door was locked. Unfortunately for him, there was only one door on the *Darkstar* Ell couldn't hack… and it wasn't his. She had it open in a matter of seconds.

The lights were dimmed. Gino was curled up by the window, completely encased in a thick layer of smooth crystal.

Ell swiftly crossed the room and stood over him. "What the fuck are you doin?' We're gettin' shot full of holes and you're hiding in a glass egg?"

"Crystal," he corrected her, his voice an echo within the protective shell. "Glass is silicon-based. This is a carbon-based, high-density-"

"I don't give a damn what it is!" she screeched as the kicking began. "Get up! I need you to help me with something."

"Evans has condemned us to die," he said coldly. "This mission has taken a turn for the absurd and suicidal. When the ship goes down – and it *will* – you know where to find me. I will avenge the *Darkstar*." He turned his eyes to her, fully serious. "I could make one for you as well… there's no reason for us *all* to die. Not even Desmond."

She just stared at him in furious silence, her luminescent blue gaze burning into him, even as the crystal egg dissolved like evaporating dew at dawn.

"Don't give me that look. I'm not giving up," Gino said as he stood, flexed his wiry muscles, and looked down on her. "I'm only doing this because there's nothing else I *can* do. We have weapons, but they're all anti-personnel and there's no way I could get off a decent shot anyway, with all this dodging and weaving." He groaned. "If I could punch a gunship out of the sky, I would. But I *can't*. A man has to know his limits. So, unless you have a better idea-"

"I do," Ell said as she gripped his shoulders. Big, strong shoulders, she noted. Gino could be somewhat handsome… when he wasn't bitching like a prepubescent pansy. "You gonna cut the nihilistic bullshit and help me out, or not?"

"What do you have in mind?"

"Ammunition. I need you to make something small enough to throw, but dense enough to punch through a ship."

"You can't throw hard enough to penetrate a hip's hull. Unless…" Gino thoughtfully rubbed his chin as his tiny brain began to buzz with activity. "Unless you have some kind of *trick* to make it work."

"Yeah, somethin' like that," Ell teased as gunfire peppered the hull, like miniature feet scurrying along the walls. "Look, you wanna upstage that woman or not? I know you wanna prove you're *better* than her, right? *Stronger* than her…"

"You know I do." The look in his eyes was intense. If Chala'Ran moved a mountain, he'd move a continent. If she parted the sea, he'd part the whole damned ocean and the shoreline with it. Competition was in his blood.

"Good," Ell said. "Come with me."

"Even if you have super strength or something, there's no way you're accurate enough to hit them," Gino said as he followed her. "And they'll gun you down the moment the door opens. This is suicide."

"Damn, you're such a pessimist," she quipped. "Just shut up and help. I'll improvise."

* * *

The massive atrium's waist-high stone walls overlooked a ten-story drop to a lounge at the bottom, where a small pond was built around the Solaran tower which dominated the room. An exposed stairwell zig-zagged down one side of the atrium, but Chala'Ran wouldn't need it.

From the safety of a sealed control room, Pernilla relayed everything she saw on the security cameras. Chala'Ran knew every man's position and armament before she ever set foot in the room. There were eighteen of them. One sniper at the top, with a high-powered rifle. Two more like him waited on opposite sides of the next level beneath that.

Fifteen others congregated in the lounge at the bottom, in case she somehow got through the sniper nest. There was no way into the atrium without being seen and minimal cover once inside. She'd have to strike fast and hard.

Without hesitation, Chala'Ran charged in. She took a few swift steps toward the railing, but swung to the right as the sniper across the way took a shot and missed. Staying fast and low, she floated instead of running, hugging the ground like a shark skimming the ocean floor.

Her eyes were barely a centimeter above the railing, but the sniper still tried in vain to hit her as she closed the distance. He fired a second and a third time, but caught only air. By the fourth shot, Chala'Ran was already within range. The sniper threw aside his rifle and reached for a sidearm, but, with a graceful flick of her wrist, Chala levitated him up and dumped him over the railing.

He hit the bottom level many seconds and ten stories later and all hell broke loose.

There was shouting below and thunderous booms as the other two snipers punched holes in the walls with their high-powered rifles, trying to hit what they could not see. Chala'Ran grabbed the rifle abandoned by the first, relocated, and traced their lines of fire. A minute later, they were dead and she was not.

That just left the men at the bottom. Fifteen thugs, huddled together with enough firepower to easily level her if they weren't scared shitless. She had come out of nowhere and dropped their snipers in under two minutes.

She cast the sniper rifle aside, quickly checked how many rounds remained in her own weapon and charged in. Chala'Ran moved to the railing, hooked one spiked metal heel on its edge and peered down. The firing squad sent up a wall of bullets. Tracer fire buzzed all around her, but the bullets seemed to curve away.

Chala'Ran moved her hand in a sweeping gesture and clenched her fist shut with iron-willed finality. The bandits began to converge, pulled together by an invisible force. Their feet dangled uselessly above the floor. Men, guns, and furniture all found themselves lifted inches off the ground and drawn together. Within seconds, all that remained was a compacted mass, a writing blob of humans and objects hovering near the center of the room.

Chala'Ran stepped over the railing and dropped, descending nine stories before slowing to a graceful landing on the ground level, where her gift-wrapped victims waited. The fifteen-man ball spat impotent curses at her. Many still gripped their weapons, but they were packed so tightly they could barely scratch their asses, let alone shoot. Chala'Ran could have emptied her clip into the lot of them and been done with it, but she had other plans for this captive audience.

With a wave of her hand, she summoned one from the bunch. The blob vomited forth one man, who hit the ground with a shocked and terrified look on his face and a shotgun in his grubby hands. His comrades wasted no time in telling him to "kill the bitch," "blow her fucking head off," "get her!" But he was too slow.

His weight tripled, pinning him to the ground, as Chala stood over him and drew a hand grenade from her pocket.

"I am Chala'Ran Mahalya al Rao Vashir. I have dominion over one of the most fundamental forces in the universe: gravity," she said, looking down on him with unflinching determination. "But I suspect you already knew that, yes?"

He made a vain attempt at spitting up at her, but the wad of phlegm only rose a finger's height before it came back down and slapped him on the cheek with the force of a dropped stone.

"Do not trifle with me. You *will* answer my questions. If you do not, I will pull the pin on this grenade and add it to my collection over there," she said, nodding to his comrades trapped in the gravity well. "First question: who sent you?"

"I ain't got nothin' to say to you. You're gonna kill us all anyway, ya crazy bitch."

She ground her heel into his neck, just above the collar of his makeshift armor. He gagged and wheezed as she went on. "The choice is between a slow death and a swift one." She lifted her foot to allow him to breathe. "There are fifteen here and countless more on other levels. If *you* don't tell me, *someone* will."

"Don't matter who sent us," he struggled to say. "All that matters is that you die. We're here for *you*."

Someone fired off a shot. Soon, there were bullets flying every which way as the ball of men all squeezed the triggers on weapons they could not aim. One got lucky. Chala'Ran staggered back as a volley of automatic gunfire tapdanced across her chest. Her concentration broke and the ball of men tumbled apart, becoming an angry heap.

Her closest prisoner, no longer held down by triple his own weight, raised his weapon and delivered a shotgun blast to her chest at nearly point blank range, knocking Chala'Ran off her feet.

She was on the ground, in pain. The men were getting up. Just as the shotgun-wielding thug rose and prepared to finish what he'd started, a thunderclap snatched him away. His body was thrown aside by what could only have been a sniper's round.

From the corner of her eye, Chala'Ran spotted Clyde on the stairwell a few stories up, with his eye to the scope of a high-powered rifle. He took another shot, and another, attempting to thin or distract the crowd of ruffians. Without hesitation, Chala pulled the pin and tossed her grenade into the mass of men, before they could scatter. As she began to crawl away toward cover, she tossed two more over her shoulder for good measure. She was safely behind a stone bench when the three blasts went off, incinerating them all in a blue-white flash of plasma.

* * *

Gino sat upon a stack of crates, fashioning cannonballs of solid crystal, while Ell added another layer of duct tape to her makeshift slingshot: elastic cargo netting stretched between pipes on opposing sides of the cargo bay. It had a cradle made of duct tape, aimed at the front loading ramp, and was the sketchiest, most untrustworthy contraption he'd ever seen... but Ell assured him it would work.

She would make it work.

"I figured your gift would have something to do with computers or sex," he said.

"I don't need magic tricks to be good at that."

"Whatever you're going to do, I hope you've practiced it as much as you've practiced whoring and hacking. You won't get a second chance at this."

"*I'm* not gonna shoot it. *You* are," Ell said as she tossed aside the duct tape, trudged over to Gino, and picked up one of the cannonballs. "Once I work my magic on your balls, those ships won't stand a chance."

Gino frowned as gunfire clattered along the hull. "Explain," he said

"I can manipulate kinetic energy. Did you pass grade school physics? Remember 'force equals mass times acceleration?'"

"No, but let me guess: force equals something different when you work your *magic*?"

"Yup. It equals 'get the fuck outta the way.'" She cackled her most disturbingly juvenile laugh yet. The cannonball began to hum with pent up energy and became warm to the touch, brimming with stored potential. She gave it back to Gino. "Hang onto that, would ya? And for the love of God, don't drop it!"

"Is it gonna... explode?"

"It could, if I overdo it. I used to have that problem a lot... but I'm gettin' better at this. Right now, that thing has about as much energy as a speeding hovertrain." She smiled gingerly.

"It'll probably punch through the floor if you give it a running start. So, be a good boy and don't drop it, 'kay. F=ma is all about onversation of momentum: 'An objcct in motion, stays in motion…'"

"'Until acted upon by an equal and opposite force,'" Gino concluded. "I get it. I ain't stupid."

"Really? Coulda fooled me," Ell said. She strolled over to the intercom while he carefully positioned the *very* live ammunition in the makeshift sling. If dropping it gave it the force of a speeding train, he didn't want to imagine what launching it from this jury-rigged contraption might do.

"Why didn't you mention this sooner?" he asked.

Ell shrugged. "I don't know. Maybe I like foreplay. I like to keep 'em guessin.' Mystery is sexy, right?" She winked. "I'm susprised Clyde didn't figure it out. I was using my gift right in front of him on 222. It's easy to run fast when your body's charged up with kinetic energy… well, fast in a straight line, anyway."

"Gifts that directly rewrite the laws of physics are considered higher tier," Gino said. "If you were a registered Scion, you'd probably be an eight or higher." He stared blankly at her. "And all you do is use it to run fast?"

Ell just shrugged.

Another volley of gunfire dinged off the hull as she depressed the intercom button next to the cargo ramp. "Hey, jackass, we're ready down here," she said to Desmond on the flight deck. "I'm openin' the doors now."

Desmond's reply was drowned out by roaring wind and the sounds of gunfire and explosions as the ramp began to open. The landscape tilted as the *Darkstar* performed one last sweeping turn before lining up with the enemy flagship, the flying brick bristling with Gatling lasers, missile batteries, and armored plating.

Ell scurried away behind some crates as an impenetrable swarm of tracer rounds poured into the cargo bay, ricocheting off the walls. Even with her hands clamped to her ears, the sound was like flying through a cloud of gravel.

Gino armored himself and manned the catapult. Plates of hardened crystal formed all over his body as he drew back the elastic bands. Bullets buffeted his arms and torso, glancing off every which way. He spotted Ell, huddling behind the steel supply crates, mouthing the words, "*do it*," while tracer rounds buzzed like fireflies through the cargo bay. The enemy gunship was directly in front of them, too large and too confident in its own armor to evade what was coming.

Gino let go. The slingshot tore the crystal ball from his hands and hurled it out of the *Darkstar*'s cargo bay with such force he fell flat on his ass. It appeared to fly slowly through space, but its path was straight and true, as if neither gravity nor wind nor a meter of tack welded steel plating could alter its course or velocity.

* * *

Clyde dropped the rifle and raced down the stairs. He was on the ground floor in seconds, cutting a wide arc around the carnage. The grenades had brought the situation to an abrupt and horrific end. The floor near the pond's edge was littered with charred bodies and shattered weapons. The water was stained red.

An hour ago, Clyde would've been alarmed, but since joining with Chala'Ran he just felt... numb. She showed up and people died, cause and effect.

She was still slumped behind the bench when Clyde reached her, sore, but alive. She looked well for someone who'd just taken a shotgun to the gut. Her crimson robe was riddled with bullet holes and shredded where the pellets had struck, revealing a black layer underneath.

When Clyde arrived and knelt before her, she was already halfway through the process of stripping off her outer robe to inspect the damage. She quietly thanked him as he helped pull her arms free of the heavy fabric. Beneath the intricately stitched red outer robe, she wore an underlay of tightly-woven black fibers: a ballistic trench coat with a twelve-pointed Registry insignia sewn into the left breast.

"Are you okay?" he asked as she discarded the red robe.

For a moment, Chala said nothing. She sucked in a shallow breath as she carefully undid the snaps of her ballistic coat, to see if anything had gotten through. There were bullet fragments lodged in the material. Clyde tried to tell her not to move, but was ignored.

Beneath the ballistic coat was a black bodysuit with neon blue fluid pumping through surgical tubing. The faint hum of electric cooling fans suggested it was some type of cryogenic cooling suit, like those used in spacesuits. She was *wearing* an air conditioner.

Chala'Ran pressed a hand to her abdomen and ribs, checking for injuries, but found her palm drenched in blue chemicals, not blood. Relieved, Clyde helped her to her feet, supporting her while she got her bearings.

"You can't keep going like this," he warned. "You've done enough. It's time to-"

"No... I am fine," she said with a slow shake of her head before taking a step back. The suit fit as if it'd been painted on. Without the multiple layers of fabric, Clyde found she formed an impressive figure, tall and long-legged with powerful thighs, and wide hips. In terms of physical prowess, she trumped most Hunters he knew, but the amount of raw femininity hidden under those robes caught him off guard for a moment and an awkward silence ensued.

Chala'Ran knelt to gather her communicator from the discarded robe and pinned it to the lapel of her overcoat before picking up her rifle and finally facing him.

"I believe you may have saved my life a moment ago. For that, you have my gratitude," she said. "But I still have a task to complete and will not stop on account of one minor misstep."

"*Minor* misstep? Chala, this has gone on long enough. I don't know what it is you're trying to prove, but-" She silenced him with a hard stare and a finger to his lips. Clyde surprised himself with how quickly he shut up.

"With all due respect, Mr. Evans, I have nothing to *prove* to you or anyone else. I have seen the full extent of my capabilities, and, to be quite honest, it frightens me more than anything else in this world, short of God Almighty." She abruptly turned and began to walk away. "You should pray you never see the day I am called upon to 'prove myself,' dear."

Clyde overtook and cut her off. She stopped, but looked down on him with unblinking directness. "It's over," he said, meeting her gaze. "As your captain, I *order* you to stand down. I can't let you do this anymore."

"*Let* me? How *dare* you." The sudden arrogance shocked him, as if the voice wasn't hers. And the look she gave him... if boots had eyes, this was the way they would look on ants before stomping out an entire colony.

"I'm not letting you go a step further. Endyssia doesn't need this," Clyde reasoned, though he saw no reason left in her eyes. "You're not doing it for them. Pernilla and the others are safe. It's just us out here, *slaughtering* people, and for *what!*?"

"Justice. I am protecting these people," she said coldly. "'Bear not the sword in vain.'"

"The sword!? What happened to 'love thy neighbor' and 'thou shalt not kill?'"

"Justice is the truest form of love. I express my love by showing these fools the error of their ways... by force, when necessary. Shall I show you the error of yours?"

"Backup is on the way," Clyde said in a calmer tone. He did not like the direction this conversation was taking. "Everyone's locked up tight and justice is *coming*, but not like this." He gestured to the mangled corpses and scattered gore, but his eyes never left hers.

"Listen to me, Chala. I don't know who you are or where you come from or what *they* did to you. I don't know why you ran away to a convent and buried your head in the sand for ten years. All I know is you need to take your own advice and let it go. I'm trying to *help* you."

The ant said his piece and patiently waited for the boot to drop. By the time he finished, he was sure she would utterly destroy him. Though his hands didn't move, he remained acutely aware of the gun on his hip and the nanoseconds needed to draw it. Clyde could answer her gift with his own, but she was more than parlor tricks. Her training was on another level and he doubted he could survive hand-to-hand combat with this beautiful, deadly creature, even *after* she'd taken a shotgun to the chest.

Thankfully, Chala merely tapped the communicator on her lapel: "Pernilla, are you there? What is the ETA on those reinforcements from Khaliya?" Her voice was neutral as she spoke to Pernilla, but the look she gave Clyde could freeze a desert.

"Chala, is that you? Oh, thank the Lord! I saw what happened," Pernilla said, completely oblivious to her friend's emotional state. "They're ten minutes out and our defenses are holding. I think we're in the clear."

Chala'Ran looked away for a moment, staring thoughtfully off into space.

"Hello?" Pernilla said. "Chala, are you there..."

"I suppose this is goodbye, Pern. Evans and I will take the east elevator to the car park on level one. Thank you for all you've done. God bless." Pernilla began to speak, but Chala'Ran shut off the communicator and tucked it into her side pocket, never to be used again.

"Not one for long goodbyes, are you?" Clyde said, more than a little awkwardly.

"Silence, please. I am still quite cross with you and do not wish to hear your voice at this time," Chala'Ran said, turning her back on him. It was possibly the most polite version of 'shut up' he had ever heard.

"However... there is truth in your words," she confessed after a pause. "I do not know if I am ready to join you, but I am ready to try. This will be a test of restraint. I have much to meditate on when we reach your ship."

* * *

The cannonball punched through the enemy ship as if it were a paper bag. For a moment, it seemed as if it'd done no damage, other than the man-sized hole it left in its wake. A tongue of yellow flames erupted from the breach. A half second later, there was a deafening boom as something within the belly of the beast exploded and the gunship began to tilt at an odd angle, trailing thick black smoke as it sank toward the ground.

"Holy shit..." Ell said, coming out from her hiding place to witness the spectacle. "It's falling... I think we took out a gravity drive."

"Impossible. Must've hit their ammo reserves or reactor," Gino commented as the gunship fell like the brick it was. It crashed into the sand dunes on the outskirts of Endyssia's reservoir and another explosion went off, sending up a fiery mushroom cloud that burned with such intensity it turned the sand to blackened glass.

Ell rocked on her heels. In her wildest dreams she hadn't expected to take the ship down in one shot. Overjoyed, she ran to Gino with outstretched arms and latched onto him, like a squirrel to a tree. "We did it!"

But he shucked her onto the floor. "Lucky shot," Gino grumbled. "Don't start celebrating. There's still two more." But, even as he said this, the sound of gunfire was conspicuously absent, leaving only the roar of wind from the open cargo ramp, the rumble of the *Darkstar*'s thrusters, the rhythmic hum of the drive cores...

And an odd hissing sound, which he hadn't noticed before.

Ell sat on the ground, nursing a sore bum on account of getting body slammed by the brute. Only a few seconds later did she realize she was wet. The entire floor was wet. She sprang up and found herself standing in a slick greenish-blue puddle. Tracing the bullet holes on the walls, she found a ruptured pipe, spraying steam and fluids.

Gino beat her to the intercom. "Williams," he said into the receiver as his crystal armor faded away and the cargo ramp began to close. "We have a problem."

"I thought you just shot down our only problem," Desmond replied, far too casually. "The other two are pulling away. Give Twiggy a pat on the back for me. Whatever she did, it worked."

"This is seious," Ell snapped. "There's some kind of... umm..." She looked at the greenish liquid on her hands, slowly staining her leggings and the frayed hem of her miniskirt. It smelled like antifreeze. "There's some kind of *stuff* leaking down here. I don't know what it is, but there's a lot of it and there's bullet holes all over the place."

"See what happens when you let people shoot *inside* the ship?" Desmond said. "Idiots. I can't leave you people to yourselves for five seconds without somethin' gettin' broken."

* * *

She had a way with elevators. Pernilla cut the power to all of the lifts, to make it more difficult for the intruders to change floors, but that made no difference to Chala'Ran.

The ride from the sixtieth floor to the bottom was quite long, but Chala'Ran didn't say a word most of the way. At first, Clyde thought she was still angry with him but, by the thirtieth floor, he began to suspect the silence was because she required concentration. She was moving an elevator with her *mind*. He could hardly blame her for not wanting to chat while doing so.

But somewhere near the twentieth floor, she surprised him: "Why are you so intent on having me along?" she asked with genuine curiosity. "Your friends doubt me and you fear me, yet you still seek my company? I do not understand."

Clyde just shrugged. "At first I didn't either... but now I think it was meant to happen. There's a theory I've been turning over in my head since P-222: I'm starting to think we've done this before."

The elevator reached the ground floor. Free of the burden, Chala'Ran gave him her undivided attention. She was no longer the wrathful creature he'd dared to oppose on the sixtieth floor. Her eyes had a gentle, inquisitive quality to them. She wasn't perfect, but she was smart − smart enough to see what he saw. From the moment the gunships appeared over Endyssia a half hour ago, they'd both been trying to piece together the same puzzle.

"How did they get here so fast?" Clyde said. "Who called them? What are they here for? I've been asking myself that over and over from the moment we came under attack. It was easy to say they're after the *Darkstar*, but something didn't quite add up... until I found out they were here for *you*."

"The timing? The enemy response is not a response at all," Chala'Ran said. "It is a preemptive strike."

"Exactly," Clyde said. "At warp speed, the *Darkstar*'s faster than those junkers they came in. I think they were on their way *before* we were. Actually, I think they were on their way before we were even *told* to come."

"If you feel there is a leak in your organization, I have my ways of addressing it," Chala'Ran said darkly. "Just say the word and I will weed out the traitor."

"No, I wish it were that simple. This isn't an information leak. This is an enemy who responds to moves *before* we make them." He began prying open the doors of the dead elevator while he spoke: "I'll explain once we're back on the ship and everyone's around to hear. The next planet we travel to will determine whether I'm right or wrong. Until then, it's just a theory."

He shoved the cage doors open. The lights flickered in a narrow concrete hallway, making a play of shadows on the bare walls. Clyde stepped out, pausing to pick up Chala's luggage, despite knowing she could easily move them herself. Perhaps it was old-fashioned chivalry, or perhaps he felt she'd done more than enough for one day.

She took point and led him down the grim corridors. At a wide doorway, she raised her hand, signaling him to stop, and pulled him aside. "Listen," Chala said.

There were sounds inside. An engine. A truck. Something large. She moved to the opposite side of the entryway and signaled him to wait. Clyde peeked inside. They'd arrived at an underground parking deck, where most of the vehicles were open buggies with massive, scooped tires for trekking across the sand dunes. There were even a few hovercrafts.

But what stood out most of all was the large armored personnel carrier patrolling the rows of vehicles, with a single oversized autocannon mounted on top.

Dammit, when did they drop that thing off? Clyde thought as he watched the tank maneuver from aisle to aisle. One shot from that cannon and they'd be done for.

But Chala'Ran had that look in her eyes again. She was spoiling for a fight.

"Chala, don't. Let's find another way around."

"My vehicle is at the far end of the lot, near the exit," she said. "There is no other way out. We are going to go right down the middle. Stay close."

"You don't have to fight everything. Reinforcements are five minutes away."

She smiled, as if amused. "Fight them? Dear, who said anything about *fighting* them?"

He had his arms full with her baggage. She quickly draped her rifle's strap around his neck and stepped out into the parking garage, unarmed. Chala'Ran raised her hands, as if summoning mountains to move. She lifted them, palms up, and everything began to rise. Clyde could feel a shift in the air. Slowly at first, the dune buggies' suspension unweighted, then came unplanted completely. Within seconds, everything not bolted down was levitating. He and Chala'Ran and a lone truck at the far end of the lot were the only things still firmly planted.

"Come," she said as she took him by the wrist and led him through the chaos, toward a battered black pickup truck. Vehicles hovered all around them, turning aimlessly in space. It was like swimming through an aquarium of iron whales. Even the armored personnel carrier was slowly turning, doing a barrel roll in midair with its eight wheels spinning in vain.

Clyde followed her through the maze of levitating obstacles. From behind, he briefly glimpsed a slight smile peeking through her thick mane of black hair. This was the woman he wanted by his side, not the stone-faced killer. She led him to her truck, an extended-cab pickup, caked with old mud that had turned to crust.

Mud? On Adi Zahara?

There was a gun mount in its bed and empty ammunition crates, but no weapons. The cracked solar panels on its roof looked functional, but the thick layer of dust suggested it hadn't been moved or touched in at least a decade, leading Clyde to wonder if it would start or if she intended to fly it out the door like a magic carpet.

He circled around to the passenger side and reached for the handle, but paused to read the words stenciled on its doors, painted over and nearly too faded to decipher: SAMONIA LLC.

"Look at them. Like fishes," Chala'Ran laughed, pointing at the men pouring out of the levitating tank. They struggled in vain to grab hold of something to anchor themselves or their vehicle. Clyde had to admit, there was a certain comedic appeal to watching them struggle in zero-g. Most of all, he was glad she'd spared their lives.

He tossed her baggage into the truck's bed, while Chala'Ran unlocked the doors. The air inside was stale. "We have a clear shot out of here," Chala'Ran explained, still in high spirits as she climbed into the driver's seat. "If we take the west highway onto the... umm..."

Her voice trailed off as she sat bolt upright, both hands gripping the wheel. Her smile vanished, replaced by a look he'd never seen before or since. Everything dropped. The garage was filled with the deafening roar of about thirty vehicles crashing to the ground all at once, some upside down or sideways. The armored personnel carrier landed on its roof, with one poor soul pinned beneath. But the look on Chala'Ran's face, a sudden grief-induced paralysis, prevented her from noticing any of it.

She had completely checked out.

"Chala?" Clyde said, but she continued to stare straight ahead, through the dusty windshield and off into space. "Chala'Ran?" he said again, waving his hand in front of her eyes. She blinked. "Chala, we really need to go..."

The woman snapped to attention with such suddenness he flinched. "I... I am sorry," Chala'Ran said, her voice cracking. "It has just been so long since... since I was *here*, behind the wheel of... ummm..." she trailed off again as she looked around, like a stranger in a strange land.

"If you're having second thoughts about leaving-"

"I am not."

"If you don't remember how to drive, I could-"

"I *do*," she said as she abandoned her seat. "I remember all too well. The last time I was behind this wheel, I was boarding a freighter to leave... that place." The woman dismounted and backed away from the driver's side door as if it were the gate to Hell itself. She locked eyes with Clyde and nodded to the wheel, silently begging him to take over.

Clyde didn't ask. He didn't dare. As he came around the vehicle, Chala pulled herself together enough to swap places with him. She climbed into the passenger seat, shut her eyes, and began whispering quietly to herself. A prayer? A promise? He didn't know.

The truck started on the first go. Much like its owner, it had seen far worse things than ten years in storage, escaped far deadlier places than Endyssia, and carried far more precious cargo than a man, a woman, and some baggage. He put it in gear and took off hard, with all four wheels clawing at the stone.

Minutes later, Endyssia was shrinking in the rearview mirror as he accelerated onto the elevated highway and into the desert, with the *Darkstar Abyssal* flying overhead, trailing thick white smoke silhouetted against Adi Zahara's fierce yellow sun.

– 13 –

A very disgruntled Gino entered the medical bay, where he found Clyde pensively staring out the window, sitting in the doctor's chair with his back to the door.

"Next time you want to have a word with me, I'd appreciate being told *where*," the fighter said as he angrily marched into the room. "I looked everywhere for you."

Clyde did not move from his spot. "This ship's not that big. You could've asked around. I told Chala where I was going and I ran into Desmond on the way here."

"That's beside the point."

"Not really. They're your crewmates. It wouldn't kill you to ask them a simple question," Clyde said as he turned to face the man. "We don't bite."

Gino leaned against the wall and folded his arms across his chest before leveling his gaze with Clyde. "Well what do you want, Evans?"

"I heard through the grapevine you had a little 'moment' while flying over Endyssia. Something about your captain leading you all to your deaths and how you, the lone survivor, would *avenge* us. Is there something we need to talk about, Gino?"

"No."

Gino looked past him, into the darkness of space. The *Darkstar* loitered in Adi Zahara's orbit, where one yellow sun was sinking beyond the curve of the horizon while another lurked as a burning crimson orb on the edge of the atmosphere.

"By 'grapevine' you mean your informant?" Gino added.

"She's not an informant. When Ell has something on her mind, she comes to me. You could learn a lot from her example," Clyde said. "Look, here's the deal: I'm gonna call a team meeting within the hour, after I've tidied up the details and given some things the attention they deserve. I don't want any *surprises* once everyone's gathered, Gino. No repeats of that show you put on when we met Chala. So, I'll ask you again: do we need to talk?"

He waited. Gino said nothing.

"I understand you're out of your element," Clyde said. "We all are. And after what happened on P-222…"

"I am not afraid," Gino said, with fire in his eyes, "and I ain't out of my element. That woman posed a *threat*. I did everything within my power to oppose bringing that threat aboard. That's my job, isn't it?"

"We've all been forced to step outside of our jobs," Clyde said solemnly. "None of this is what we expected."

Gino looked at him strangely. The details of what had taken place within Endyssia's walls remained exclusive to those who'd been there, but he could see something had changed in Clyde. He wasn't the same man.

"Tell me something, Evans. Do you have *any* intention of going back to the Registry?" he asked. "I need to know this now. I need to know where you stand."

"Of course I do. We're with the Registry now, aren't we?"

"Don't lie to me," Gino said, stepping closer, "and don't lie to yourself. This whole thing has gone so far down the rabbit hole we'll be lucky to ever see daylight again. Our mission has *changed*, Evans. Don't tell me you haven't noticed. You may have started as a Hunter, but now you're a survivor... or worse. Where does that leave us?"

"What's worse than a survivor?" Clyde asked at length.

"A revolutionary, the very people you used to hunt." He balled his fists. "We've crossed a line, Evans, and there's no going back. Whose side are we on and who's on *ours*?"

Clyde took a deep breath and leaned back slightly in the doctor's chair, so he could stare into the vacant brightness of the white lights over the examination table. He clasped his hands behind his head, thoughtfully.

"You might not have liked your life much, but I *loved* mine and I want it back," Gino said. "After what happened on 222, and now on Adi Zahara, I'm convinced none of us are ever going back to who we were, Evans. I'll never see the Arena. You'll be lucky to ever set foot on Earth again without showing up on every wanted list this side of the galaxy. We were promised a clean slate and a return to life as we knew it. That won't happen, Evans. Not even The Stranger can clear our names of this."

Clyde's reply caught him off guard: "Yeah. So?"

The simplicity of the statement and casualness with which it was said took Gino back a step, but he was nothing if not persistent.

"Of course *you* don't care," Gino replied. "I've said this before and I'll say it again: I am the only one here with a pedigree. You've never been famous or well paid. You were mired in mediocrity. Niehaus was a nobody who joined this mission so she could remain a nobody. Williams is a scumbag on the run and always will be. Unlike me, you people have *nothing* to return to.

"And then there's that woman..." The disgust in his voice was palpable. "I didn't want her around because I know what she represents. There are people in this world who want to see the

Registry burn and the Solarans unmasked. I know because, unlike you, I was famous once. I got hate mail from those people, people who felt the Arena and everything even remotely associated with the Solarans is an abomination and should be torn down, brick by brick. I've had to listen to that nonsense all my life. I've heard all the arguments."

"I see... now we're getting somewhere," Clyde said with a grin. "You hate Chala'Ran on political grounds and you hate the rest of us because we're not good enough and because you feel the mission is devolving into a campaign to tear down 'the tyrannical Solaran regime.'" He chuckled. "Please, tell me more..."

"Go fuck yourself, Evans. I don't *hate* any of you," Gino said. "I felt she was trying to steer this mission in a direction I don't want it to go."

"This coming from the man who was ousted from the Arena for speaking out *against* the Solarans. I can't keep up with you, Gino. You're all over the place."

"We're not here to make a statement. We're not here to overthrow the goddamn Solarans and I couldn't care less what becomes of *them*," Gino said. "We're here to find the Chronomancer, give her to The Stranger, and get our lives back! That was the mission, right!?"

"It *was*."

"And it's not anymore?"

Here, Clyde sat up a little straighter. "Things change," he said after a long pause.

Gino nodded, resignedly. "At least you finally admitted it, instead of pretending this is all going to end happily. Yes, I had a moment, if that's what you want to call it. My eyes were opened and I realized the chances of any of us *ever* living a normal life again are slim to none... and things are sliding heavily toward 'none.'"

Clyde stood and clapped a hand on his friend's shoulder. "We live in a world of lightkeepers and Reapers and warp drives and people with magic powers... life hasn't been *normal* for 200 years."

"You're insane."

He gripped Gino's shoulders and held him tight. "I'm whatever my crew needs me to be. So, if you have any other complaints, let's hear 'em."

"I'm fine."

"Don't lie to me, Ainsworth, and don't lie to yourself," Clyde said sarcastically, with an obnoxious grin. "But seriously, are we on the same page or not?"

"No," Gino muttered, "but at least I know where you stand."

"Fair enough. Now that that's out of the way, there's something serious I'd like to discuss with you," Clyde said, lowering his voice.

"More serious than our impending demise?"

"Much more. Look, I know you aren't much of a team player, so I have a special assignment, just for you."

"A chance to prove myself?" Gino muttered with a longsuffering roll of his eyes. "Great, just what I've been waiting for."

"I see your sense of humor is intact," Clyde murmured, though there was a hint of genuine eagerness in the fighter's tone. "If you can set aside the cynicism for a minute, I may have something for you... but you're gonna have to trust me on this. Tell no one. It's going to require you to be more than a two-bit bruiser but, if you pull this off, you might even live up to your name. There's a princess in a high tower and I need a knight in shining armor to rescue her."

Gino's eyes narrowed at the analogy, but...

"I'm listening," he said.

* * *

Clyde loitered outside the mess hall, observing his team from the doorway. He was the last to arrive for the meeting he'd called. Even Gino had already entered and taken a seat at the table, with a sour look on his face.

Desmond sat across from him, toying with a datapad, but the two men might as well be on different planets. Chala'Ran stood by the cupboards with Ell, where they seemed to be discussing a box of dried foodstuff.

With the siege of Endyssia still fresh in Clyde's mind, seeing Chala'Ran talking culinary techniques with Ell was strange, to put it lightly. She wore a robe structurally identical to the one she'd worn when they first met, only this one was black with intricate purple stitching, very dark and foreboding.

After tarrying a little longer, Clyde stepped inside. Ell's eyes brightened and she frantically waved, though he was only a few feet away. "Whatcha got for us? Good news? Bad news? Did we get a call from the boss?" she asked excitedly.

"No. He's been strangely silent," Clyde said and Ell flopped into a seat at the table while he continued. "The Stranger will call us when he feels like it and not a moment sooner. That's his prerogative. I don't have news, but I do have a theory and a destination. That's what this meeting's about."

Chala'Ran nodded from where she stood by the counters. He could see understanding in her eyes, but he quickly looked to Desmond instead: "Before we get into anything else, how's the ship holding up?"

"Shot full of holes," Desmond said, surprisingly lighthearted considering the circumstances, "but none big enough to worry 'bout. We're leaking atmosphere at about half a kilo an hour, but I'll patch her up 'fore it becomes an issue."

"A spaceship leaking air isn't an issue?" Gino remarked.

"Ships leak all the time," Desmond replied. "Or are you used to being chauffered around in fancy yachts, mister Arena Champion, sir?"

"And what of the smoke?" Chala'Ran calmly asked, before Gino and Desmond could wander too far off track.

Clyde silently breathed a sigh of relief, glad to have her aboard. While driving away from the tower, they had noticed the ship was leaving a smoke trail and one of its thrusters seemed weaker than the others, as if it were sputtering. He brought this to Desmond's attention the moment they were aboard.

"Vapor trail. It's steam, not smoke," Desmond explained, "and I'm glad you caught it. Saved me a lot of trouble, sweetheart." He gave her his most charming smile before looking to Clyde. "We've got coolant leaking into engine three, so I shut it down. That's where the steam was comin' from. She'll hold fine 'til I can fix the problem... but I can't fix it 'til we land. It's outside and I don't do spacewalks. With that engine off, the leak should ice over in deep space. Gonna have to top off our coolant reserves once we reach our destination, but finding water *there* shouldn't be a problem. It's not ideal, but she'll run with water in the pipes." He gave Clyde a very shrewd glance, an unspoken agreement between them.

"But there's more." Desmond went on: "Shutting down number three means I had to shut down number two to balance out the thrust and keep us flying straight. So, we're gonna hit warp at half strength. You're an Earth-man: ever heard the old saying 'slow boat to China?'"

Warp travel is divided into two phases: acceleration and deceleration. Although ships could achieve hyper-relativistic speeds using altered physics, they didn't reach those speeds instantaneously. To arrive at a destination in the fastest time possible, half of the journey was spent accelerating and half was spent decelerating. Ships with more powerful engines could attain higher speeds before reaching the halfway point and thus get there faster.

But, with two of its engines out of commission…

"So, our ship is crippled?" Gino asked. "We're going to *limp* across the galaxy?"

"Slowed, not crippled. If we stop to land, I can fix it," Desmond said. "We might get there faster if-"

"No, we stay the course," Clyde said sternly. "It's important to stay as faithful to the old timetable as possible. If we're down two engines, I think that's how it's meant to be." He paused to think for a moment and missed the assortment of puzzled glances from everyone.

"What's that supposed to mean? Where are we goin?'" Ell asked, impatiently tapping her fingers on the table. "You said you've got some kinda theory?"

Clyde nodded and dove into his pockets for a few seconds before drawing out a small holographic projector, which he set upon the table. The little orb, dotted with tiny lights, flickered to life, projecting a blank white rectangle, the holographic equivalent of a whiteboard. With his finger, Clyde drew on it. It didn't take long. He drew only one thing: a horizontal line.

"I'll explain *where* we're going once I explain *why*," Clyde said as he added a tick mark near the middle of the line and wrote 'now.' "This is a timeline. My theory relates to Claire's gift. If we want to catch her, we're going to have to start thinking in four dimensions. I don't know her motives or reasoning yet – that's what we were hired to find out, remember – but I'm almost positive she is actively altering events in an attempt to shape the…" He paused for a beat, searching for the right word. "She's attempting to shape the *future*. Or, to be more specific, she's trying to alter a version of the future she has experienced."

He ignored the puzzled looks and went on: "Here's what we know: Claire Eisenholm's first appearance was during my last official assignment, when I was attempting to apprehend Brock Mason. She showed up again at Platform 222, to warn Desmond. That's two appearances. It's no coincidence. Her ability to be in specific places at crucial times suggests she knows what's going to happen and is actively interfering," Clyde said with conviction. "I haven't deciphered her endgame yet, but she's definitely trying to change things by interfering at key moments. The Stranger suspects she aborted his mission to alter its outcome. I think she's trying to abort ours as well, possibly because it doesn't end well for her. We might be able to use this to our advantage."

While Clyde talked, he continued to add to his illustration by drawing a line that branched off from the first: a parallel timeline. To both lines, he added a tick mark entitled 'Mason,' a little past the divergence point. Moving a hand's breadth past that, he added another mark, entitled '222,' to both lines. A little further, he added 'Chala' to both lines. Last of all, was a fourth mark on both lines, with no title at all.

"That's the gist of my theory," Clyde explained. "Something happened — or *will happen* — to Claire a few days from now. Something so *problematic* she went back in time to prevent it from happening again. The Stranger's spokesman told us she's done this before. Claire was born six years ago, to us, but looks like she's in her late twenties because she's gone back and repeated so many years of her life. When life gives her lemons, she travels back in time and tries to get lemonade instead. That's her knee-jerk reaction when things aren't going her way."

"I see, but what happened to make her go back?" Chala'Ran inquired, briefly throwing off his flow, just when he was getting a rhythm going.

"I... umm... well, that's where the guesswork comes in," Clyde said, meeting her gaze. "All we can do is look at what she's done thus far and use that to figure out what she's trying to accomplish." He pointed to the first tick on his timeline: "Brock Mason. For a while, I thought she saved my ass that day... but that's incorrect. Mason wasn't trying to kill me; he was fleeing. The only danger I faced was the danger of him escaping and leading to another demotion. But he ran into Claire first... or she ran into him... either way, they scuffled, he got knifed, and she fled the scene, without really *changing* anything.

"Because it went so haywire, I'm not really sure what she was trying to accomplish there. All I know is it involved me or Brock. She wanted to disrupt what one of us had planned. I had nothing planned, other than carrying on my 'mediocre' existence as a level-three Hunter in District 19. Brock, on the other hand, planned to bomb about a dozen Light collection centers all across the eastern seaboard and was trying to raise an insurgency of rogue Scions." Clyde shrugged. "Which of us was she trying to disrupt? I had no idea... until I remembered Ell put the dossiers together a week *before* the Mason incident. In other words, I was already on The Stranger's radar *before* the Mason encounter. He even said this mission couldn't have happened without me."

"You think Claire was tryin' to kill you to stop this hunt before it began?" Ell said.

Clyde really wished people would stop interrupting, but he nodded in agreement. "Exactly. That was her first attempt, but it failed. Brock raged out on her and things got messy." He pointed to the next tick mark: "Here, she tried again. At Platform 222, Claire warned Desmond he'd die aboard a Registry interceptor in three days, correct?"

Desmond slowly nodded.

"She's been shown to have paranoid, sometimes obsessive tendencies, and blacklight is known to cause neurological damage and mild dementia in some extreme cases," Clyde explained. "But the specificity of her warning suggests it wasn't just deranged ramblings. She gave a specific time, 'three days,' and a specific class of vessel, 'interceptor.' The *Noble Valiant* was docked in plain sight, with Registry badging all over it. But I doubt Claire would know an interceptor from a cruiser unless she had intimate knowledge of the ship. I think Claire was *on* that ship at some point." He looked to Desmond. "I think she witnessed your demise first-hand and felt some way about it. She *watched* you die."

"If only we could all be so fortunate," Ell muttered under her breath.

"Thus far, her attempts at changing the future haven't gone so well," Desmond said as he checked his watch. "But if I'm gonna die in about a day, that leaves just enough time to get laid." He raised his brows at Chala. "Any takers?"

She looked profoundly disappointed in him. "I see your opinion of me has changed since Adi Zahara," Chala'Ran said flatly. "I am both pleased and appalled, Mr. Williams."

Clyde cleared his throat. "If the future were set in stone, Desmond, you wouldn't even *know* Chala'Ran. Take a look at this." He pointed to the third tick mark, the one marked 'Chala.' "Old timeline: Desmond gets captured. Our mission at P-222 ends in failure, so The Stranger sends us to pick up some extra help, in the form of Chala'Ran." He pointed to the same dot on the parallel branch. "Current timeline: we succeed in getting Desmond, but lose Gibbs and Jenner, followed by Jay's resignation. So, The Stranger sends us to pick up some extra help, in the form of Chala'Ran. Different paths, same outcome. I believe *both* scenarios lead to a confrontation with Claire, which doesn't end in her favor." He pointed to the final, untitled tick mark.

"How can you be so sure?" Chala asked.

"I can't. But the resistance we encountered on Adi Zahara proves you've got something to do with the outcome, otherwise she wouldn't be so desperate to block you from joining us, the same way she tried to block Desmond and me. The only way those raiders could've gotten there as fast as they did is if they had advanced warning. Claire could've tipped them off, but Claire doesn't have the clout to make it worth their while."

He paused significantly. "If you were the leader of a gang of space pirates, would you fly out, en masse, to the middle of nowhere, and risk your men and materiel because a half-insane albino girl told you to? Of course not... but you *might* be more inclined to do it if that girl was backed by the Registry."

For the first time, Chala'Ran actually looked somewhat surprised. "You think she has formed an alliance with Hawke and Mason? You think she is on the *Noble Valiant* voluntarily, perhaps even in a position of power?"

"She's absolutely terrified of The Stranger and I'm the only person in the galaxy who can take away her greatest gift," Clyde explained. "Compared to *us,* or going it alone, the Registry is the safer bet for her. She'll get what she wants out of them and slip away. What she wants is the *Darkstar.*" He turned to Desmond. "Mr. Williams, would you say Numira has pirates capable of interstellar travel, like the ones we encountered on Adi Zahara?"

"Thousands," Desmond said quietly. "Numira is crawling with them."

"And, let me guess: you struck a *deal* with them to get off the planet?" Clyde asked. Desmond said nothing, so Clyde drove his point home: "I believe Claire is on or near Numira right now, probably with Hawke and Mason, and she's there because-"

"I did what I had to do," Desmond said quickly, with anger burning just beneath the surface. The jokester was no longer joking. "*Yes*, okay, I *sold* the blueprints to Numiran pirates! I only did it because I knew they couldn't use it. To actually *build* another *Darkstar Abyssal* would require highly-specialized Solaran technology. All I did was sell a pipe dream to a moronic despot. How was I supposed to know the Registry would come behind me and-"

"You couldn't know," Clyde said as he shut off the holographic projector. "No one blames you for the current state of affairs. You did what you had to do to survive."

"I blame him," Ell muttered, but the resident mother hen nudged her and gave a slow, deplorable shake of her head, to which Ell harrumphed and said no more.

"Claire's mission ended on Numira, a waterworld on the edge of Farside. Regardless of whose fault it is," Clyde concluded, "someone on Numira has the knowledge to build an exact replica of this ship... and the Registry has the resources to put that knowledge to use. Claire wants this ship, but wants nothing to do with us or The Stranger. If any of what I've said is true, Claire, the Registry, and those blueprints are going to meet on Numira. I intend to be there when they do."

"If this is all true, what is our plan of action?" Chala'Ran asked. "Let's imagine you *do* find Hawke, Mason, *and* Claire on Numira. What then?"

"We extract her," Clyde said, "by any means necessary."

* * *

The Adi Zahara operation ended in failure. If there was one thing Saimon Hawke hated, it was failure.

He waited until a full minute after the Council adjourned and the video screen went dark before he rose from his seat and left the table, feeling tight as a spring. A wad of anger burned within him, but he looked as calm as an icy draft. He wanted to throw something, but everything in the conference room was bolted down except his mug of coffee, and he wouldn't dare throw good coffee, so Saimon adjusted his glasses, stood, and quietly departed.

Two lefts, a right, and one hundred and thirty-one paces later, he was standing at the airlock which connected the *Noble Valiant* to its mothership, the *Halcyon Infinitum*. He counted every step.

The doors shut behind him and there was a brief hiss as the pressure equalized before the hatch to the *Noble Valiant* allowed him access to his ship. He loved this ship almost as much as he loved his coffee, and found comfort in its white-washed façade and slick stainless steel finish. His ship was the way everything should be: perfect.

Brock Mason leaned against a wall in the main corridor, with his thick gorilla arms folded across his barrel chest. *Why does the High Council insist on shoveling trash aboard my ship?* Hawke thought as he sized up the man.

In a perfect world, he would be able to ignore the ape. Better yet, he'd be able to shove him out the airlock. Sadly, certain beings insisted they work together and Hawke knew better than to cross those beings. As such, he was forced to acknowledge the elephant in the room when it had the audacity to address him as if he were its equal.

"How'd they take the news?" Mason asked, stepping forward in what could only be perceived as an attempt to intimidate Hawke, who was much thinner and far shorter.

"The same way you took it." Hawke calmly drank a sip of his coffee and savored it for a moment, much to Mason's chagrin. He slicked back his long blonde hair and looked to Mason. "The Council is furious, though they handles themselves with markedly more grace than you, Mr. Mason. In the future, please refrain from punching the walls of my ship. Only the *outer* hull is armored. The interior partitions have no such resilience."

Brock Mason turned away for a moment, with his fists clenched, and muttered something under his breath. Hawke could hear quite clearly what was said, but chose to dismiss it from memory, for Mason's sake. *Say what you will, just don't hit anything. Animal.*

He finished his coffee and suddenly found everything significantly less interesting without it, so he moved toward the galley to pour himself another. To his annoyance, Mason followed. Worse, the man insisted on speaking:

"We should have gone in person. They would never have gotten away," the gorilla declared.

Hawke sighed. "How many times must I tell you? We would never have made it in time to stop them. If we had gone, we would have missed them entirely. At least the minions put a dent in them. It is a start."

The *Valiant* wasn't capable of warp, a fact Hawke found quite infuriating the more he thought about it. How *dare* they give him an impotent ship? He had suspicions regarding why this was, but preferred not to dwell upon them. One should never question one's masters. The Light casts no shadows.

But one fact remained: he and Mason couldn't have made it to Adi Zahara in time, despite the invaluable tip they'd been given beforehand. He shared Mason's desire to go in person and see the look on Evans's face when they hammered him and his band of merry men into oblivion, but it was logistically impossible. Phoning those thugs and promising them untold amounts of credits to end the *Darkstar Abyssal* was the best they could do on such short notice.

But their best had failed.

And Saimon Hawke hated failure.

"You overestimate yourself, friend," Hawke said as he poured himself another mug of black gold and, after deliberating for a moment, poured one for Mason as well, thinking he may yet civilize this ape. "Our participation would not have guaranteed victory," he explained as he extended the cup to Mason. "Perhaps it is for the best we couldn't go. We have time to prepare for the *next* engagement. Your performance on P-222 was... lacking."

"Lot of good you did," Mason sneered.

"I faced an empirical dilemma," Hawke reasoned. "For all our data on Ainsworth, no one knew he was shock-proof. Lesson learned." He took a sip of his coffee. "You, however, failed due only to your incompetence. Evans didn't even *use* his gift on you, yet you couldn't seem to hit the broadside of a bus that day. I knew you were stupid, Mr. Mason, but I had no idea you were *blind* as well."

"I held back," the large man said. "I won't next time."

"Please see that you don't. Do that again and I may begin to question your allegiance." With a plastic smile, Hawke offered a steaming mug of black gold. "Have a drink, friend, and put past failures behind you."

Mason scowled at the beverage and lumbered over to the fridge where he grabbed a bottle of some type of hormone-laced muscle juice from the fridge instead.

Disgusting swill, Hawke thought as he watched the man guzzle half of it within seconds. His face twisted indignantly.

"Had I been there, they would never have left Zahara in one piece. I promise you that," Mason declared. "I don't give a damn what the file says. The woman's no match for me. Neither is Evans or Ainsworth. I'd break them like twigs."

Hawke shot him a very shrewd glance, partly because Mason had declined his coffee – his *perfect* coffee – and partly because the man was being a cocky bastard. He hated cockiness, too.

"You hold yourself in very high esteem," he said cheerfully as he turned away and walked down the corridor, carrying a coffee in either hand. "Mind yourself, Mr. Mason. Evans is not to be underestimated and Mahalya is not known as the 'Demon of Ossus' for nothing. I heard she did good work... before she *turned*. Don't be fooled by that badge around your neck. You are a Hunter Elite in name only and have a long way to go before you're on her level or mine. You're only here because someone took a liking to you... and we both know *who* that is."

The last part was spoken in such a low tone, Mason likely wondered if he'd heard correctly. The man grumbled something but, again, Hawke ignored him.

The blonde-haired bespectacled Hunter paused in the war room, to admire the view from the skylight. A blue sun peeked around the edge of Numira's horizon. Another glorious day in the service of his masters. He contemplated the universe and all its splendor before continuing down the hall, leaving Mason behind to brood.

Saimon reached an unmarked door, where an armed guard sat in a chair, perusing the daily news on a datapad, with a sidearm on his hip and a shock baton in his lap. The man quickly rose and stood at attention when Hawke arrived, but the Hunter signaled him to sit.

"This is only a courtesy visit," Saimon Hawke said with a devious smile. "How is she?"

"Quiet, sir. Too quiet."

"There is no such thing. But perhaps I can offer her some stimulation." With the toe of his boot, Hawke tapped lightly on the door. "Miss Eisenholm, would you like some coffee? It is fresh and brewed to perfection."

– 14 –

Points of light streamed by the viewports like neon fireflies against the vastness of space. In under a minute, the *Darkstar Abyssal* would drop out of warp state, after a three day journey. Its remaining engines were in full reverse burn, decelerating toward lightspeed.

On the flight deck, Desmond had the helm and Ell the co-chair. Clyde stood over their shoulders, his eyes glued to the viewscreen. Armed with binoculars, Gino had taken up a post in the port observation room, while Chala did the same on the starboard side.

"Thirty seconds," Desmond declared as time passed like molasses through a straw.

At last, their velocity fell below lightspeed. The distorted physics generated by the ship's gravity drive broke with startling abruptness, replacing the dazzling play of lights with normal space, revealing a single blue-white neutron star shining in the distance. Numira, a murky grayish-brown ball, grew ever larger off the bow.

The crew kept their eyes peeled for any signs of activity. Desmond swept the ship's sensors across Numiran space, hunting for any large debris or suspicious heat signatures, while

Clyde ordered everyone to remain vigilant. Either the *Noble Valiant* was here or he'd completely miscalculated.

"I see something!" Ell said, pointing. "A platform!"

"Can't be. Numira is undeveloped," Clyde said.

"She might be right. Scanners are picking up a lot of metal and habitable heat signatures," Desmond said, briefly glancing at him before returning his eyes to the readouts. "Very big. Could be a ship or a space station, or-"

"One of each," Ell replied and began pecking at the keys of her computer. She'd already uploaded the video feed from her eyes to her laptop and began running an image search to identify the vessels she'd seen.

"I see it too," Gino added, via the ship's intercom. "It's too far to make out, but there's definitely something there, in orbit. It does sort of look like a platform."

"I cannot see anything from this vantage point," Chala'Ran said. "Shall I relocate to another position?"

"Negative. Stay where you are," Clyde said. He couldn't see a damn thing either, but two visual sightings and confirmation from the ship's sensors was more than enough. A ship that large, this far out, had to be the Registry's doing.

"One's definitely the *Valiant*," Ell said, "but it's brought a friend – a *big* friend."

"An armed friend?" Desmond said. "If it's a battleship, we're in trouble."

"I don't care what it is. Slip by and find somewhere to land," Clyde said. "Fly close enough for them to see us, then drop into the atmosphere and lose 'em on the other side of the planet. I want them to know we're here, but we need to lay low while you do repairs. We're small enough that the magnetic interference from that sun should hide us from their sensors. Just break line of sight and find a place to roost planetside."

"Interesting tactic. I see you've been studying ship-to-ship combat," Desmond said before guiding the *Darkstar* in for a close encounter.

Ell spun around in her seat to face Clyde and showed him her computer screen, which was filled with alerts. "That ship's buried in encryption. Whatever it is, it's highly classified and I'm getting firewalled to death. I ran a search on the *Noble Valiant* and faced the usual defenses, but this other ship… everything about it is locked up tighter than a nun's nookie. No offense to Chala, of course."

"Chala's not a nun," Clyde said dryly. "Dig deeper. Hack it. Isn't that your thing?"

"Well, yeah, but *somebody* told me not to play around in the Registry database," she said, giving him a sharp glace. "I'm only doing bot searches in low-tier records. If you want me to bring out the big guns, just say the word."

"That was before they sent hit squads after us. The gloves are off now. I want schematics, layouts, weak points, passenger manifests – *anything* you can find. Claire's in there somewhere and I don't want any surprises when we go to get her out."

Ell flexed her nimble little fingers and returned to her work while Desmond handled the approach. A few minor adjustments to the *Darkstar*'s deceleration vector brought them dangerously close to the two enemy vessels, per Clyde's request.

Although the *Noble Valiant* was his primary reason for coming to Numira, it was dwarfed by the much larger vessel. Clyde had only seen a space carrier once, when the Earth Coalition's *ESV Quester* did a flyover for a Fourth of July celebration. Its shadow turned day to night for twenty blocks of lower Manhattan.

The *Valiant*'s mothership took that scale and amplified it by a magnitude of ten or more. And the shape… it was a symphony of angles, a geometric anomaly, like something perfectly straight attempting to mimic something perfectly round. It molded to its observer's whims, yet defied them at the same time.

At the ship's center was a featureless sphere, which reflected the darkness of space, seeming very much like a black hole with the rest of the ship as its event horizon. Its series of concentric rings – which weren't really rings, but million-sided polygons – were vaguely reminiscent of a Scion's badge, and there was no clear front or back or top or bottom and no two parts shared the same plane. In fact, they seemed to move ever-so-slightly, changing shape just as the human mind began to comprehend its form.

To call it a "ship" would be laughable. To call it a platform would be an insult. It was a work of art, the likes of which Clyde had never seen.

Confusion gave way to creeping fear as he realized he had *no idea* what he was looking at. For a moment, no one uttered a word. Even the tapping of Ell's fingers on her keyboard ceased. The *Darkstar* passed so close he could count the tiny windows on the leviathan's decks and the swarm of spy probes the *Valiant* ejected into orbit. Not a sound was made until they had the strange ship squarely in the wake of their thrusters and rocketed away beyond the horizon to begin final descent.

"You thought *that* was a platform?" Desmond said, glaring at Ell who, for once in her life, had nothing to say. With a slight shrug, she shed the eerie sensation the ship left on them all and returned her attention to the screen of her laptop.

"I still cannot see anything," Chala'Ran said. "Requesting permission to relocate."

"Negative. Sit tight," Clyde said and turned to Ell. "How's it going? Anything yet?"

"No. I need something stronger." She abruptly snapped her computer shut and stood. "There's either nothing to be found or they've got it buried deep. But if there's any info on that... that *thing*, I'll find it. I swear." She darted past him and down the hall, presumably to her room and the more powerful equipment located there.

"Comin' in hot," Desmond said as the *Darkstar* entered Numira's thick atmosphere at over Mach 15, cutting a white-hot streak across the hazy sky.

"Remember the landing site I told you about?" Clyde said, to which Desmond nodded.

Numira had no solid ground. Neither rock nor soil could be found anywhere on the planet's surface and even polar ice was hard to come by. There was only a glassy brownish-blue sea and the rusting hulks of two long lost generation ships, where a tiny population of left-behinds wrung out a meager existence.

The *Darkstar* came in nose-up, burning its way through the thick clouds. She was down to just below Mach 2 when she fell through the last cloud layer with her wings outstretched like switchblades on the attack. Desmond throttled forward ever so slightly, leveling out for the splashdown. The ship's belly slapped the water's surface like a skipping stone, and bounced thrice before settling like a fat duck on the murky waters.

"Well... never thought I'd find myself here again," Desmond said as he began powering down the systems. The rumble of the engines had become a constant over the past few days, but now gradually faded to silence, leaving only the background hum of the drive cores, which waned shortly after.

He said nothing more but, as Desmond rose from his seat to leave the bridge, Clyde noted the jester's grin perpetually plastered on his face was conspicuously absent.

"Desmond?" he called and the man turned, as if startled.

"Yeah?" Desmond said, forcing himself to smile. "Are you about to tell me I'm the best pilot in the galaxy? Well, I'm listening... and money talks."

He had a joke for every occasion and wore his masks well. Clyde studied him for a long moment, before deciding that whatever was on Desmond's mind could wait.

"Nevermind," he said solemnly. "Carry on."

Desmond stuffed his hands in his pockets and trotted away, whistling a tune to himself, while Clyde stood alone, listening to the waves slap the windscreen. With the drive cores offline, he could feel the *Darkstar* rolling beneath his feet, riding the seas.

An alien craft waited in orbit, but a human vessel lurked in the distance: a seed ship, a derelict wreck from one of mankind's first forays into the stars… and one of their first failures. Clyde studied the silhouette of its rusting, pitted remains. The ominous black leviathan loomed on the horizon, never to rise again. Faded white letters stenciled on its hull read '*Liberty N2045.*'

With a sigh, Clyde turned away.

* * *

Half an hour later, he was in Ell's room, with no thoughts of the derelict generation ship. "I'm impressed," Clyde said when they finished reviewing the material she'd gathered.

"You should be." She placed a datapad in his hand containing everything he needed to know about the *Noble Valiant*, inside and out.

"This is starting to look doable," Clyde said as he skimmed the material. "The *Valiant*'s not half as well-protected as I thought. Our defense lasers and flares can suppress her missiles. We might actually pull this off. We've got a level ten Scion, an ace pilot, and the best computer specialist in the galaxy. Hell, even Gino could get behind this."

"Best in the galaxy?" Ell said with a crooked smile as she batted her lashes. "Oh, stop, you'll make me blush."

"I doubt that's possible. What about that other ship?"

Ell avoided his eyes and said, in a small voice, "I'm workin' on it." Although her desk and bed were covered in computers, they were all off with their screens black. The laptop was tucked away in a corner and she didn't seem to be *doing* anything at all. Naturally, Clyde picked up on this instantly and gave her a look that said more than words ever could.

"Hey, I'm a computer hacker. I make programs that do the work for me," she said. "I couldn't find anything, so I sent my best digital minions to comb the Registry's database. Within the hour, they'll report back anything they find on the *Halcyon Infinitum*."

"So our mystery ship has a name?"

"Yeah, it was mentioned in one of Brock Mason's reports to his handler. Ring any bells?"

"No, but I'm sure you'll trace it to the source." Clyde gave her a pat on the shoulder as he stood. "Thanks, Ell. It feels like I'm always asking you to do a million things."

"Because I always deliver."

He gave pause, as he realized how absolutely right she was. Nevertheless, Clyde began to wander toward the door. "Anyway, I should get started on this." He held up her report on the *Noble Valiant*. "There's a lot to take in here. I need to study it. Let me know if-"

"Actually, there's one other thing. While I was in the database, I did some snooping," Ell said. When Clyde did not look surprised, she added, "Okay, *a lot* of snooping. It's mostly nothing, but... well..." Ell approached him and quietly shut the door. "It's about Chala'Ran."

"I thought you two were getting along now. You *still* don't trust her?"

"N-no, it's not like that."

"So you're curious, then? What's new?"

"She's just so... *weird*, ya know. She never talks about herself. And she's always alone, starin' off into space. That thousand-meter stare..."

"She's seen some things, I'm sure. I'd rather not imagine."

"Look, I like her as a person. Seriously, I do. But... I mean... c'mon, don't you just *wonder* sometimes? Where'd she come from?"

"The moon."

"I don't mean *that*."

Clyde sighed and his silence was answer enough. Despite his best efforts, he was still piecing together the puzzle of Chala'Ran. It wasn't that he didn't *trust* her. Something about her inspired trust. It was that he didn't *know* her and she didn't seem interested in being known.

He looked down at Ell, who was practically begging him to stay. "What'd you find?" he asked, unable to resist.

"Not much. I think she's been erased. You know the Registry better than I do. What would cause them to clear a Scion from the database?"

"They don't. Only person I know who offers that is The Stranger," Clyde said. "You think he wiped her ledger?"

"I don't know. Maybe she did a job for him and a clean slate was the payment, like Desmond. Whoever did it was thorough, but they didn't catch everything. Chala's name came up in two places. First, she was on the roster for some place called 'Alpha Point.' What's that?"

She now had his undivided attention. "It's a Registry space station, a training site for high-level Scions. Alpha Point is where the Nemesis Program is based."

Ell gave him a strange look, so he explained:

"Most Scions get basic training. It's like military boot camp, where we're taught to control our gift. Training lasts a year or so, depending on what they're setting you up to do. I was trained for thirteen months, not including field training and my apprenticeship. That's pretty normal for a Hunter. But a Nemesis... they're basically *raised* in combat simulators. We're talking five, six, or more *years* of fighting, fighting, and more *fighting*."

Ell shrugged. "We already knew she's a level ten badass. No surprise there."

"This is different. Nemeses are *above* Hunter Elites. They're... they're basically interstellar super soldiers," Clyde said, searching for the right words. "When one person violates the Charter, you send a Hunter. When a *whole colony* steps out of line, you send a Nemesis. They're the Registry's answer to dissent. Solarans hand pick their Acolytes from Nemesis Program candidates, so it's a pretty big deal." He paused to think for a moment. "So Chala was a Nemesis? I guess that explains a lot... not sure if I should be impressed or terrified, though."

Ell lowered her voice even further: "Her name was linked to something called 'Operation: Warlock' on Ossus III. Everything but the pre-mission brief was wiped, so I don't even know if the op ever took place, but it had something to do with installing a dictator or warlord on behalf of the Registry. Sounds like typical third-world shotgun politics. The Solarans were going to send her to take control of a small *planet*, Clyde. A *planet!*"

He sighed. "I can't say I endorse everything the Registry has its hands in, but I don't think Chala'Ran does either, so let's not jump to conclusions." He drilled his eyes into Ell. "She's on our side now, regardless of what she was asked to do in the past, okay."

"Look... I- I'm terrified, but I'm trying *really* hard not to be. Don't you find it a little funny how everyone else here is on the Registry's shitlist, but she's MVP of their all-star team?"

"Point taken, but Chala's work history is nowhere near the top of my priorities right now," Clyde said, holding up the datapad she'd just given him. "*Halcyon Infinitum, Noble Valiant,* and Claire Eisenholm, in that order. That's what matters to me right now."

Ell frowned. "Your list blows. Her history might not be on *your* mind, but I bet it's on hers. Just *talk* to the woman before we go flyin' into another shitstorm, okay. Can you do that much, at least?"

Talking to Chala'Ran was not an unpleasant request by any means, but talking to her about black ops and third-world dictatorships *was*. Clyde palmed his face for a moment. "You might be right," he said after a long pause.

"Of course I'm right. 'A house divided cannot stand,'" Ell said. "See, I can quote dead guys too. She ain't got a monopoly on all the wisdom in the universe."

"It sounds a lot more sagacious coming from her."

"I don't even know what that means." Ell laughed. "Anyway, I'm takin' the rest of the day off," she said as she shucked off her shirt and tossed it at him. "What's the point of a waterworld if you ain't gonna skinny dip?"

"You realize that water's filthy, right?" Clyde said as he backed away toward the door. He wanted to be gone before she was completely undressed.

"I know. Ain't it great?" Ell said as she kicked off her shoes and began working at the buttons of her jeans.

* * *

The galaxy is filled with tragedies, great and small. Society has chosen to forget the worst of them, greasing the wheels of progress with feigned ignorance. 175 years ago, Numira was the site of one such tragedy. Nearly two centuries later, all that remains are the bones of two derelict ships that share a story no one wishes to hear and none dare to tell.

The weather was balmy with a slight breeze when Desmond climbed out of a service hatch and onto the roof of the *Darkstar Abyssal*. Hazy clouds of hydrocarbons gave Numira's sky its noxious brown tint, the same color as its oily waters. Desmond spared one final glace at the wreck of the *Liberty* adrift in the distance before beginning his work.

He hadn't known the story the first time he found himself stranded on Numira. Well, not the *whole* story. He knew its Revelations, but not its Genesis. Now that he saw it for what it was, this planet and the blackened ship half-submerged in its toxic seas made him ill.

"The sooner I fix this, the sooner we can leave," Desmond muttered under his breath as he hauled up two toolboxes and a tank of argon gas. This was only half of what he needed. The welding torch, electrical cables, and other essentials still waited below.

He was about to begin inspecting the damage when Gino poked his head through the hatch and tossed up a black duffel bag, which landed with a heavy thud. The gruff fighter disappeared for a moment before reappearing with the welder and generator in tow.

Desmond watched with disinterest, refusing to help until Gino had nearly finished dragging the heavy equipment up. He assisted in towing the cumbersome gear the last meter of its journey and stood back, satisfied with his contribution.

"Thanks for nothing," Gino said. "You were just gonna stand there and watch?"

"Yeah. That's what you all do every time I'm fixing this damned ship," Desmond replied as he wheeled the tools aft.

The *Darkstar*'s scorched hull was peppered with bullet holes, revealing the insulation between the bulkheads. In some places, the thick foam was the only thing keeping the interior pressurized. She was no warship, though everyone seemed determined to test that.

"What brings you out here?" Desmond asked. "Clyde put you up to it? Come to make sure ol' Desmond doesn't sell the *Darkstar*'s secrets to the highest bidder again?"

"No. I think you've learned your lesson," Gino said bluntly. He stood straight with his hand shielding his eyes as he gazed out at the *Liberty*, as if gauging the distance.

"Have I?" Desmond sneered. "Nah. I'd do it again, in a heartbeat. I'm a natural salesman." He nodded to the black duffel bag. "Whatcha got there?"

"Nothin.'"

"Well, aren't we fancy? Us normal folk can't afford to carry our nothins around in big black bags," Desmond teased, but ultimately let it go. There was a starship in need of repairs.

Lying flat on his belly, he bent over the edge of the ship's stern with a flashlight to inspect the thrust nozzles and warp rings of engine number three. The ruptured coolant line was plainly visible, thanks to the jagged icicles that had formed on its surface while traveling through deep space. Desmond snapped one off and gave it a lick. He soon grimaced and tossed it in the ocean, deciding that cryogenic coolant smelled better than it tasted.

"We'll be spaceworthy in an hour, maybe two at the most," he declared as he got to his feet. When he began to sort through the tools, he felt Gino's eyes on his back.

"How'd you escape this planet the first time?" the fighter asked.

"I'm pretty sure we covered that already, or did you sleep through the last get-together? What's it to you? Goin' somewhere, with your bag of nothings?"

"I know you sold the plans," Gino said. "What I *don't* know is how that got you off this planet. Are there usable ships here?"

"No, I pulled one outta my ass." Desmond fired up the plasma torch and began melting the ice from the coolant lines, so he could begin the repairs. "I'm kidding. Truth is, I built one outta two balls of string, a cellphone, and a cardboard box... and the phone was just to call your mother and tell her I'm comin' over."

"If you're trying to get a rise out of me, it won't work." With a grunt, Gino emptied his back pocket and tossed a wad of bills at Desmond's feet. "I'll ask again, funny man: how'd you get off Numira? I need specifics."

Cash, the interstellar language. Desmond paused and inspected the warm, crisp, multicolored bills, relishing the way they felt between his fingertips. It was about two grand of legal tender, usable in any Registry-controlled territory.

"I'll tell you one thing," he said with a frown, as he relit the plasma torch and watched the money burn and wither. "This stuff won't do you any good out here."

Desmond laughed madly as the useless paper turned to ash. "There are ships. There are people too, if you can still call 'em that. But if you value your life, don't try on them what you just tried on me. You'll get further with that sack of guns than with a *mountain* of Solaran-printed cash. They don't like Solarans out here. Your money's no good."

Gino's eyes flickered to the duffel bag in his hands.

"You're too obvious. Guys like me spot guys like you ten klicks before you turn the corner," Desmond said, returning to his work. "I'll give you a hint, 'cuz I can see how terrible you are at this game. Once you get inside," he gestured to the wreck floating in the distance, "look for a fella named Stormgren. Victor Stormgren. He's an offworlder. He and his boys run the *Liberty*. He's descended from the raiders who took control of it a generation ago and enslaved the survivors of the crash. Nobody gets on or off that wreck but through him."

Desmond paused a moment before continuing. "I don't know what you're planning to do, but-"

Splash. Desmond sprang up, torch in hand, and found Gino lowering a crystal rowboat into the water.

"Are you seriously this stupid?" Desmond said as he ripped off his welder's mask and set down the torch. "Where do you think you're gonna go?"

"Doesn't concern you. Get back to what you were doing," Gino said as he tossed the black bag into the boat and conjured a crystal oar out of thin air.

"That ship's at least twenty klicks out. You gonna row all the way there, smartass?"

"Yup."

"Even if you *do* get there, slog through Hell, and steal a shuttle –'cuz he ain't gonna *give* you one – where're you gonna go? You think that interceptor is just gonna let you stroll by? You know why it's called an interceptor, right? It intercepts!"

"I have an open invitation."

"From a homicidal maniac!"

"I'm too valuable to kill," Gino said. "You'll see." He was too focused on slipping into the water to see Ell coming up the hatch. She stopped and stared, blankfaced, as she watched him shove off.

"Oooh, a boat," she said... then the situation clicked into place. "Hey, wait... what's goin' on?"

"Mutiny's going on. I didn't think this stupid fucker would actually do it," Desmond said as he drew his sidearm. "Step away from the boat, Ainsworth."

Gino instantly armored up, wrapping himself in crystal from head to toe. The summoned boat dipped under the added weight. "It ain't mutin," he said. "I'm leaving. Alone. Goodbye."

Desmond took a few experimental shots at Gino's armor, only to watch them ricochet off. "Godammit. Ell, get Clyde up here so I can shoot this motherfucker!"

Ell's face went from curious, to confused, to angry in under two seconds as she processed what was happening. She clambered out of the hatch wearing only her bright red panties, stormed up to Desmond, and snatched the gun from him.

"You're wasting your time," the White Knight said as he began to row. "I know which side I'm on. Tell Clyde he's out of his mind. You all are."

"You asshole! We trusted you!" Ell aimed the gun at him. Desmond could feel the air begin to vibrate around the pistol. She fired a shot that sounded like a thunderclap and left a sizable crack in Gino's diamond armor. Startled, he began to paddle away double time.

The next two shots missed completely and the third made a horrible metallic clang, as if something inside the gun had snapped and mangled its innards. Whatever gift she was using to amplify the weapon was too much for it to handle. The trigger seized and it refused to fire again, so Ell threw it, but Gino was already too far out. The gun uselessly plunked into the water.

"Son of a bitch!" She screamed, prepared to swim after him and drag him back if she had to, but Desmond caught her and slammed her to the deck, instantly taking the fight out of her.

"Stop it, Ell! If he wants to leave, that's his business. He's got nowhere to go," he said as they watched Gino shrink away, toward the *Liberty*. "They'll kill him over there. They hate Scions as much as they hate Solarans. If not, Hawke and Mason will. Either way, he's dead to us."

Ell stared back, more dazed than angry. After a long silence, Desmond realized he'd body slammed her pretty hard. He also realized she was naked... not that this was anything new.

"Sorry," he muttered as he climbed off and offered a hand, which she promptly slapped away.

"What if they take him alive? What if he talks?" Ell hissed. "What if he-"

"Let him talk. He's got nothing to say, no secrets to spill." Desmond snatched her hand anyway and hauled her to her feet. "Forget him. I've got a ship to fix. Tell Clyde; he'll figure something out. And put some clothes on."

* * *

Despite surviving a firefight and spending three days hurtling across space in a tin can with her, Clyde still knew next to nothing about Chala'Ran Mahalya. She was forty-four years old and hailed from a lunar colony established by the United Arab Emirates. She was of mixed Persian and Indian ancestry. Her favorite color was royal purple. She left two cats, Nimue and Viola, in Pernilla's care. Beyond that, she remained a mystery.

After some searching, Clyde found Chala'Ran seated on the floor of the cargo bay, with her head bowed, intensely studying a bucket of water.

"Clyde? Is that you?" She did not look up. "Stay, dear. I was just thinking of you."

He slowly descended the stairs. Every cautious step reminded him that 'thinking of you' was not necessarily a good thing. Not all thoughts were pleasant.

"This is my first time at sea," Chala'Ran explained, still staring into the depths of the bucket. "I am afraid the motion does not agree with me, but focusing on this eases my discomfort." She nodded to the water as it rhythmically circled the bucket. "We should all be a little more like water, yes?"

"I never thought you were the type to get seasick," Clyde said as he knelt opposite her, with the bucket between them. He could add this new discovery to the list. "Wouldn't staring at water make it worse? I thought meditation was about shutting things out."

"Yes and no. It is about choosing what to let in. The mind is merely a gate for processing the experiences of the body and soul. I decide what passes through that gate. I decide what takes up residence within."

"And *I've* taken up residence?" Clyde studied her face for a while, but she remained as impassive as ever. "You said you were thinking about me."

"You... the mission... many things. I was thinking of Claire, too." She finally lifted her eyes from the water and met his. "I think of her often. I fear what fate awaits her, should we fail. The number of people who have died at the hands of the Registry pales in comparison to the number who have had their lives taken away. Do you follow my meaning?"

He nodded.

"I have seen what comes of Solaran ambition," Chala'Ran said. "It is an ugly, relentless thing. Now their greed has turned to this girl. They *want* her, Mr. Evans. For them, 'need' and 'want' are one and the same." She resumed staring into the water before adding, in an undeniably firm tone: "They *will not* have her. Not while I still draw breath."

This was not the conversation he'd expected to have, but Chala'Ran had that way about her. There was no telling where her mind was at any given moment. A simple question could lead to a discussion about the meaning of life or a crusade to save a girl she barely knew.

"Aren't you taking this a little too personally?"

"What other way should the plight of a child of God be taken? I joined this mission to keep her from falling into the Solarans' hands. They do not treat people like people. To them, we are meat and Light. Scions are weapons to be used, abused, and cast aside. I should know, since that is precisely what I was to them for so very long."

"You were a Nemesis," Clyde said, swiftly injecting that fact into the conversation like a blowdart. To his surprise, her expression softened.

"Ellica has been busy, I see," Chala'Ran said, amused.

"Don't be cross with her. I put her up to it."

"Charming, but you are as terrible at lying as Ell is at reining in her curiosity. I find your honesty endearing. Do not cast it aside so casually." Chala laughed quietly, a harmonious sort of sound. "The Word says that which is done in the dark shall come to light. I am not *cross* with her. If anything, I blame myself for not being more open. I have been trying to hide that which cannot be hidden."

"No one wants to pry, but I'm sure you can see why the secrecy is making some of us a little… anxious."

"Yes. Perhaps it is time I told you the true reason The Stranger called upon me." She lowered her eyes to the water once more and said at length, "I would love to ease your anxiety – truly, I would – but I think your fear of me is unfounded, considering *your* power. I think you underestimate yourself, Clyde Evans. You have straddled the fence all your life, living under the illusion that your enemy is your friend. You accept them as a norm, an inevitability. If, by the grace of God, I could spur a man like *you* into taking action, we could change the world."

"I don't understand," Clyde said. Something didn't feel right. He couldn't put his finger on it, but something was gnawing at her – something bigger than motion sickness – and he swore he sensed a gift a moment ago, somewhere nearby.

"As you know, the Nemesis Program is intense," Chala'Ran said. "Alpha Point isn't a training facility; it is a weapons factory where little boys and girls go in and stone cold killers come out.

Few are called and even fewer survive. The reason I am here is that I am *strong*. Can you understand that? Do you see the strength you can gain by mastering yourself?"

"No one's denying your strength, Chala."

"You misunderstand." She slowly shook her head. Her mane of dark curls bobbed with every subtle movement. "My strength is not on trial here. *Yours* is."

There was a sensation in the air, which only Clyde could feel. It was neither a sound nor a vibration. It had no association with any of his five senses, but its message was clear: Chala'Ran was using her gift. This wasn't distant. It was right in front of him.

"I was not sent here solely so you could rely on *my* strength," she said as the water began to rise. Within seconds, it was free of the bucket and began forming an amorphous orb, drawn together by gravity, and held in front of him. "I was sent to teach you, Clyde, the only way I know how. Become strong… or die."

He began to back away, scooting on the floor. Chala'Ran wasn't one for fancy displays of power. She was a woman of purpose. If she was levitating water, she intended to *use* it.

"What are you doing?" Clyde asked warily as he got his feet beneath himself and prepared to stand… and *run*, if he had to.

She answered by engulfing him in water from the neck up. The orb of liquid surrounded Clyde's head, and remained locked there, trapped by a gravity well. It flooded his mouth and nostrils. He clawed at it with his hands, splashed at it with his palms, but nothing could remove it.

He fell and it came down with him. His screams vacated what little air remained in his lungs. Soon, he was thrashing on the floor with Chala'Ran kneeling over him. She lifted him up by his shirt collar and forced him to look at her, stop panicking and focus.

"Clyde! Listen to me," she said, her voice distorted by the liquid helmet slowly snuffing out his life. "I am not going to let this go, Clyde. You must do it yourself. Free yourself, or you will die. Do you hear me?"

He heard, but he didn't comprehend. His thoughts became fuzzier by the second.

"Why should you fear *any* Scion? You are stronger than them. Can you not see that? *You* are the answer to the Solaran question. *You* are their downfall." His eyes rolled back. His lips were moving, but there were no more bubbles left to expel. "Clyde? Clyde!? Dear God, don't make me do this…"

He felt his consciousness slipping away. His lungs burned and his veins pumped acid through his starved body. The one constant was Chala'Ran's gift, tapping on the doors of his mind like an invader pounding at the gates. It was right there. All he had to do was decipher it, dismantle it, and force it out of existence. He had the power to do it, but she wasn't making it easy. She wasn't letting up or holding back. She *would* kill him, if he didn't fight back.

So fight back, stupid.

The water suddenly fell away in a puddle on the floor. Chala'Ran held fast to a very blue-faced Clyde. He went limp in her arms as she laid him down and began administering chest compressions, to drive the water from his lungs. When that had no effect, she pressed her lips to his and forced air into his body.

When he finally sputtered to life, she quickly turned him over to expel the water from his system. Clyde coughed and wheezed for nearly a full minute and, by the time he comprehended what was going on, Chala'Ran had wrapped him in her arms and was holding him tightly.

"Thank God," she said softly. "I am sorry I had to do that, dear… but I am not sorry I did. It had to be done. You had to know you are capable of it. I had to *show* you."

Clyde said nothing. He laid his head on her shoulder, not out of tenderness, but out of pure fatigue and confusion. He felt numb, emotionally gutted. On Adi Zahara, he stood up for her when everyone else voted to leave her behind and *this* is what came of it?

She tried to kill me, he thought. *Chala'Ran tried to kill me. I just wanted to talk and she nearly KILLED me.*

When she finally released him and held him at arm's length, he knew he couldn't be more wrong.

She saved me.

From what, he wasn't sure. But he felt... different. Free, as if he'd just stepped out of a cage he hadn't known existed. It was as if he'd just climbed a mountain. Exhausting, yes, but the view from the top...

"Why?" she asked, searching his eyes for any signs of falsehood. "*Why* did you take so long to stop me? Why are you so hesitant to use your gift? Did *they* do this to you?"

Clyde slowly shook his head. "Not everything's their fault, Chala. Stop pinning everything on the Solarans. I just... I just don't like using it. That's *me*, not *them*."

"They taught you to fear your own power, even when your life is in danger," she said. "Even when you are being chased through the streets of P-222 by a madman who easily could have killed you and your companions in the blink of an eye. Gino was right about me, Clyde. I am here to break chains. You cannot show restraint in the face of an enemy who will not. They are without mercy. To face them, you must be without limits."

He didn't expect her to understand. Chala used her gift all the time. It was a part of her, as if levitating battle tanks came as easily as breathing. Her mastery was one of the reasons he regarded her with a sense of awe and wonder. She made everything look *easy*. Too easy.

But his gift worked on living people, not inanimate objects. His power robbed others of theirs. It temporarily stripped them of what makes them special. For some reason, that had always weighed on him... especially when he was doing it for the Registry, an organization that took pride in its ability to take everything special and shove it into a box.

In a way, maybe this *was* their fault.

With her support, Clyde dragged himself to one of the many supply crates in the cargo bay and sat down heavily. "We're different, you and I. I don't like my gift. I don't like what it does to people, or how it makes me feel," he said. "I've *never* liked it. I'd even go so far as to say I hate having this power. I didn't ask for this."

"Is that..." Chala'Ran thought for a moment. "Is that even *possible*? We choose our gifts. No one is quite sure how Scions are created or chosen, but our gifts are a manifestation of our subconscious desires. A Scion's gift is reality, molded by willpower."

"I never *desired* to rob people of their power. It just happened that way."

Chala'Ran sighed as she took a seat beside him and clasped her hands in her lap. "I have never met a man whose gift does not fit his true self. Regardless of what you might think, you have this power for a reason, dear." She took his hand and gave it a gentle squeeze... less than two minutes after nearly drowning him. "You are the right man for this, Clyde Evans, whether you know it or not. The truth is, some people are not worthy of the power they were given. You are *not* such a person. I believe you exist to defend the weak *from* such people."

As noble as that sounded, he didn't want to believe a word of it. "So your desire is to manipulate gravity? Is that what your 'true self' wanted?"

"As a matter of fact, yes," she said with a whimsical smile. "Some of the most beautiful starships in the world call Rao Vashir home. It is a place where wealth is paraded around ad nauseum. When I was a girl, I used to watch the yachts come and go. I was enthralled by the aesthetics of flight. The way they moved, the way they hung in the sky, tethered to nothingness."

"You wanted to fly?" he said, amused.

"Who wouldn't? One day I discovered I had the power to do so – I was *special*. Next thing I knew, I was being taken to Alpha Point at age thirteen. The rest is history." A companionable silence settled between them before she continued:

"Do not pity me. For a long time, I wished I didn't have this power, that way the Registry would not have taken me away from my home, my friends, my dreams. But God always has a plan. My enemy has made me strong, strong enough to *destroy* them. They will not have Claire. Lord willing, they will not have you either, Clyde Evans. Never again. Though your heart is divided and your path uncertain, I can see you do not wish to go back. I will not let them take you back."

She spoke as if they weren't working for the Registry right now, at this very moment. He secretly wished more people would speak to him that way.

Clyde looked to Chala'Ran and forced a slight smile for the woman who had saved him by nearly killing him. "I came down here to comfort you," he sighed, "and then all *this* happened. That's the last time I take advice from Ell." He tried to laugh, but it fell flat. "If I ask about Ossus and the Nemesis Program, will you try to drown me again?"

Chala'Ran smiled apologetically. "No more drowning, I promise. Your training is complete. As for my story, I suppose I owe you that much, dear... though I would prefer we just sit together a while, in silence."

He liked that suggestion, so they did... but not for long.

Ell's shrill voice cut the air like a rusty spoon. "Clyde! Clyyyyyde!" she screeched, piercing the ship's walls. Chala immediately sprang to attention, but Clyde only sighed. A half second later, Ell appeared at the top of the steps, still in her birthday suit. For Clyde, this had become a regular occurrence. Chala'Ran, on the other hand, was shocked... though she didn't seem entirely surprised.

"Clyde, Gino's gone!" Ell said, struggling to catch her breath. Her bony chest heaved with each word. "Gone!"

"Where have you looked?" Chala'Ran asked as she disrobed and draped her garments over Ell's narrow shoulders. As usual, she wore enough layers to dress five people in winter. "Have you tried his room or-"

"No, he's *gone*. Like, *away* gone," Ell said, finally calming, but only a little. "He bailed and ain't comin' back. Desmond and I tried to talk him outta it, but he wouldn't stop. It's a mutiny."

"Takes more than one guy to make it a mutiny," Clyde said, surprisingly calm.

"One is more than enough. This matter should be dealt with swiftly. He cannot have gotten far," Chala'Ran declared. She began to march off, but Clyde caught her by the wrist before she could take two long steps.

"Let him go," he said. "If Gino doesn't want to be a part of this, so be it. He's his own problem now."

Ell's jaw dropped. "You can't be serious! That flipass didn't even have the guts to tell you to your face. He snuck out, like a coward. You ought to stomp a hole in him just for that! Wait... why are you guys wet?" She looked from Clyde to Chala, and back to Clyde, as a seedy little grin began to invade her face.

"I agree," Chala'Ran said, ignoring the latter bit. "Mr. Ainsworth's insurrectionist behavior cannot be tolerated. This is mutiny, captain, an offense worthy of death or, at the least, physical retaliation."

"And what would that accomplish?" Clyde said, looking at them both, but especially Ell. "If he doesn't want to be here, he's useless to us. Time spent chasing him would be better spent focusing on Claire. Speaking of whom, where's my report on that other ship, Ell?"

"Still workin' on it… *sir*," she mumbled.

"Good. Get dressed, get back to work, and leave Gino to whatever it is he's doing."

− 15 −

Clarice Elizabeth Eisenholm was born July 3, 2216, in room 223 of the maternity ward of Yulia Tymoshenko Memorial Hospital in Odessa, Ukraine. At precisely 4:53PM, a 3.28 kilogram healthy baby girl became the first and only child of Gemma and Sergei Eisenholm.

Her mother was a literature teacher at an inner city public school and Claire later became one of her favorite students. She was smart, obedient, and studious. Gemma even made preparations to transfer schools to follow Claire's development. This would later prove impossible.

Her father was a scoundrel in a decent man's clothing, a wolf in wool. Thankfully, he was not around often. As a Hunter with a broad jurisdiction, Sergei was frequently away, but his irregular visits involved varying degrees of drinking and violence. The absence of one was filled by the other, such that Claire became accustomed to seeing her father piss drunk or her mother beaten senseless. On rare occasions, she would witness both.

Claire slowly began to see her father for what he truly was, a man of shifting passions, like a human flame to match his fiery gift. Every bruise, welt, and burn he left on her mother was like a blow to her. Claire was only eleven when his attention began to shift to his daughter, too young to understand what his wandering hands or the hungry look in his eyes meant. He tested the boundaries for two years, gradually opening her eyes to things her doting mother had sheltered her from.

But in 2229, he did the unspeakable. She was thirteen. In one cruel act, Claire's eyes became as open as any young girl's could ever be. All she wanted was to be anywhere but there, anyplace but home. With every ounce of her being, Claire wished to disappear... and she did... eventually.

She never understood *why* her gift didn't save her that day. Where was her incredible power at the moment she felt the most powerless? That question would haunt her for the rest of her life.

Despite its brevity, the incident – and her inability to escape it – shook young Clarice Eisenholm to her very core. Not until her father crawled off of her and passed out, with alcohol on his breath, did Claire finally vanish. She left home. She left Odessa. She left 2229 and embarked on a journey which she knew could only end as violently as it had begun... *if* such a journey could end at all.

* * *

Gino paddled until his arms ached, and then paddled some more. By the time he reached the outer hull of the *Liberty*, his limbs burned as fiercely as the dying sun in the Numiran sky. Worst of all, he knew this was only the start of his journey.

The *Liberty* was massive, its hull a sheer wall of rusting steel plates, and the *smell* was a wall of a different kind. The acrid aroma of decay stopped him dead in his tracks. Man and machine were slowly rotting away, giving off the oppressive odor of old iron, sweat, and festering wounds. In his tiny boat, Gino drifted in the shadow of the derelict generation ship, while he gathered his strength and tried to become accustomed to the foulness of it all.

The sun lay low on the horizon, under a sickly sky the color of raw sewage and orange juice. Shadowy figures moved high atop the walls, like archers on the ramparts of a medieval fortress. The way they watched was too direct for mere curiosity. They pointed and shouted messages back and forth amongst themselves. Gino couldn't make out what was said, but he knew they were raising an alarm. He'd lost the element of surprise hours ago.

None of them were armed, as far as he could see, but after the initial excitement ran its course, two men with rifles arrived and took matters into their hands.

Gino quickly sized them up and concluded they couldn't pierce his armor if they tried. Regardless, they kept him in their sights, while others waved him toward what appeared to be an entrance. Gino obeyed and began to paddle. The gunmen followed, walking along the high wall, ensuring they had a clear line of fire at all times.

He soon reached what used to be an airlock, the same way the *Liberty* used to be a spacecraft. It was open and perched far above the water's surface. The rust caked on its hinges suggested it had been that way for a century or more. An untrustworthy chain ladder dangled from the opening. Gino shouldered his duffel bag and began to climb, still fully armored. His crystal rowboat and oars vanished shortly after.

He was halfway up when a greeting party arrived in the open airlock with shotguns.

* * *

Claire awoke in 2224, in Izmail, a Ukrainian town she'd only seen once before. She was the color of fresh snow, as thin as a rail, and shivering in the summer heat. Her erratic heartbeat pumped black sludge through her veins and her lungs burned with every labored breath. She promptly passed out.

Blacklight is not a widely understood phenomenon outside of the Registry. To the medical community, Claire was nothing more than a very sickly albino girl suckling on the country's socialized healthcare system. They nearly gave up on her, but she began to show signs of a slow recovery. By the end of her second week, the constant blood transfusions stopped turning black in her veins and she was off the respirator. However, her heart never resumed its natural rhythm and required surgical implants. She was thirteen, with a pacemaker.

Throughout her life, this became the norm. Every case of blacklight left her with a new scar, a few more pieces of medical tech in her body, and a little older and frailer than before. But her mind was the greatest casualty of her travels.

Claire spent a month in a coma, where she concluded time was a figment of her imagination. In the span of that month, she dreamt for years and wrestled with vivid nightmares of beings of light consuming the Earth and cleansing the galaxy in cosmic fire. This was her new Hell. This is what awaited her if she closed her eyes – sleep was death. Claire awoke screaming. She'd traveled hundreds of miles and five years into the past in the blink of an eye and it all made *perfect* sense to her... in a nonsensical way.

The nurses flooded into her room. "Who are you?" "Where are your parents?" "Who did this to you?" They asked.

"None of your business." "They're dead." "Fuck you."

White-haired and wild-eyed, Claire ditched the clinic within 24 hours of awakening. Bare-footed, she ran off into the night. If her thirteen-year old self was lying in a hospital bed in 2224, where was the *real* Claire? Was there an eight-year old girl in

Odessa still dealing with a demon for a father and a well-meaning fool for a mother? Could she be in two places at once?

Impossible? She had to find out.

As her strength and color slowly returned, she stumbled upon her ability to teleport and realized she could go places *without* going back in time. That's when the world really opened up to her.

In 2225, now fourteen and drowning in undiagnosed psychoses, Claire stalked the neighborhood around her mother's apartment, searching for her paradoxical nine-year old self. But she found only a grieving literature teacher who cried herself to sleep at night over a missing daughter... except for the nights Sergei came home. On those nights, Gemma Eisenholm did not sleep at all, but still cried a lot.

Claire was eventually dragged into foster care, and adopted by a family who were, to her, little more than bodies in a house-shaped box. Their presence didn't stop her from regularly wandering back to her home turf, where she would loiter with binoculars and a datapad for hours, dictating meticulous notes of everything that took place inside and outside the apartment of Subject Mother. Her final entry translates as follows:

"December 24, 2228. 2200 hours. Negative three degrees Celsius. Heavy snow. Can't feel my fingers. No one is home. I go inside. Warm. Living room shows no signs of occupation. Kitchen shows signs of recent meal preparation. Pasta for one. Two wine bottles on countertop. One empty, one three-quarters full. Proceeding to sleeping quarters. My room is as it was on December 23, 22, 21, etcetera. Unchanged. Proceeding to mother's room. Opening door..."

On Christmas Eve of 2228, Claire Eisenholm, 17, caught Gemma Eisenholm standing on a chair, preparing a noose. A mother at her wits' end locked eyes with a too-old version of the missing daughter she hadn't seen in four years. Claire's heart would've stopped had her pacemaker allowed it.

Say something. Say something. Say anything...

The room was so silent, they could hear their hearts breaking. It was like staring into a mirror. They cried the same tears, only Claire's were black as fresh tar. She dropped the recorder and vanished before it hit the floor.

* * *

"I like dat armor," one of the three gunmen said, speaking through the bandana that concealed all but his beady eyes. He smelled of old urine and wore a tattered ballistic vest. A machete was sheathed on one thigh, with some kind of energy pistol holstered on the other. His two companions were just as smelly and just as armed.

Gino stood with the duffel bag over his shoulder and looked each of them squarely in the eyes. There were others standing on the outskirts, wearing tattered clothing, but no weapons. Some had only loincloths or the shredded remains of what used to be pants. Shirts seemed to be in short supply. Ribs poked through their bare chests, but their arms were tightly knotted with sinewy worker's muscles.

Slaves, Gino realized.

"You's gonna give us dat fancy armah an' whateva's in da bag," the leader of the welcoming party demanded. "An' where'd ya boat go? We cud use a boat roun' here."

"It disappeared," someone in the crowd of skin and bones added. "Seen it with my own eyes, I did." There was a murmur of agreement from those who had also witnessed this minor miracle.

"Bullshit," one of the gunmen said and waved his shotgun at the crowd, as if the firearm proved he was right and they were wrong. "Off with it," he said, with a nod to Gino's crystal attire. "I dunno what tha' is, but it belong ta me now. Take it off, 'fore I blast it off."

Gino merely shook his head, slowly. "Not gonna happen... But I need a shuttle and I'm willing to trade weapons." He nodded to the bag at his hip. "Take me to your leader."

To his surprise, there was no posturing or senseless verbal bravado. These gentlemen − for lack of a better word − didn't horse around the way low-level goons often do. The moment he denied their demands, they opened fire.

The crowd scattered like cockroaches in light. The first few shots staggered Gino, but he quickly recovered, snatched the shotgun from the nearest thug and turned it on him, blasting the man across the hall and leaving him slumped on a gutted computer console.

They hadn't expected him to be *completely* impervious to damage. Few wearable materials could take a shotgun blast at point blank without at least making the wearer give pause. They were facing a problem that couldn't be solved with the proper application of ammunition. They were facing *the* White Knight.

The moment the thugs realized their error, they turned and ran. Gino threw the shotgun aside, and charged after the nearest man. One escaped and scurried off down a dark corridor, where wires and cables hung like jungle vines, but Gino swiftly caught the other and tackled him from behind.

"Where's Stormgren!?" Gino growled as he flipped the man onto his back and pinned him there. The scent of stale urine wafted up from his prey. He snatched the bandana from the thug's face, revealing a sniveling coward. Tears and spittle ran down the man's grimy cheeks. Gino easily lifted him up and slammed him against the wall as he repeated the question.

Tall and lanky, Gino wasn't exactly a large or intimidating man, but the emaciated denizens of the *Liberty* were little more than the walking dead. Even Stormgren's minions weren't well-fed or solidly built. Gino didn't have to be a giant among men. He was a branch, beating up twigs.

"I'll take you! I'll take you 'dere," the thug whimpered. "Jus' don' kill me, brud!"

With a timetable to keep, Gino promptly released the man. He even shoved the shotgun back into the thug's hands as a show of good faith – faith in the protection of his armor. Gino's faith in everything else was severely lacking.

He picked up his duffle bag and gestured for the man to start walking. "Lead the way. The sooner I get my hands on a ship, the sooner I can leave this hellhole."

* * *

2226 was one of the hottest summers in Odessa's history. Claire knew because she'd been there before. This time, she arrived in a full winter coat, thermal underwear, snow boots, and two layers of sweaters. Her Christmas cap and fluffy mittens were still sitting on mom's kitchen counter in 2228.

Or were they?

What became of the future when she returned to the past? The look on her mother's face was seared into Claire's addled brain, but did the *pain* linger? Did the incident even happen or was it all in her head? Stuck in the past, she had no way of finding out. Her gift could not take her forward, back to the future she'd fled. There is no future, only the past and the now.

She ditched her winter gear in a trash can and looked at her reflection in a shop window. Long dark hair. Smoky gray eyes. No hideous black lines crisscrossing her body like an infernal circuit board. She could feel the summer sun on her fair skin. Fair, but not deathly pale.

No blacklight.

She had to test this. She had to find her limits. She needed to understand what she was doing to herself as well as to the world at large. Fate. Continuity. Destiny. She had to experiment. The space-time continuum was not to be taken lightly. Every Scion wrestled with the repercussions of their gift, but Claire could literally erase people and events from existence. The realization of this hit her *hard*.

Lost and confused, a very disillusioned Claire disappeared into Odessa's back alleys and catacombs to brood and plot and put the pieces of her newly nonlinear life back together. The future she had come from only existed in her head. She carried memories of things that hadn't really happened. Not yet, anyhow.

But she *knew* things. She knew how things *could* happen... if she *made* them happen. For the first time in her life, Claire realized she had power. Not just the power to run away, but the power to come back and − if she could muster the courage to do so − *change* the future.

She fell in with a group of teenage nihilists, while, on paper, she wasn't old enough to ride in the front seat. By the time 2228 rolled around again, nineteen year old Claire was smoking blunts on park benches covered in faded two year old flyers with pictures of her ten-year old self. She was a lost child, in more ways than one.

Her so-called friends didn't exist to her. Nothing truly did. In her mind, everything was one screw-up away from having never happened. Life was meaningless. She would've slit her wrists a long time ago if it weren't for the nightmares. If she died now, who would stop those beings of light? Someone had to, right?

She regularly stayed awake for weeks or more, walking around in a chemically-induced daze. In late 2228, Claire was burnt-out on life but too afraid to die. She stuffed her pockets with stolen cash and shot back to 2224 to test a theory. Her first intentional trip through time ended with her on her knees, naked, broke, and struggling to breathe. She was well enough to get by without a hospital this time, but the lesson was clear: four years was too far.

She spent a night in jail for her nakedness and lack of ID, where she saw a news story about 53,000 credit chips mysteriously disappearing from a Ukrainian bank. She escaped once she got her strength up. It was all becoming very formulaic for her. Very scientific.

But none of her old connections were around in 2224. Her friends weren't old enough to drive yet. Damned kids. Claire ditched Odessa and slummed around Europe for a year. Kiev. Moscow. St. Petersburg. She got sick of the Slavic nations and started moving west. She even turned her eyes to space, but decided against it. She became a solitary ship, tossing from one stormy sea to another, and quickly realized she didn't want to cast her anchor anywhere. People were trouble. People didn't understand her. They didn't go through what she went through.

She found herself shacking with a Parisian lover in 2225. While staring at the Eiffel Tower, she had an epiphany: things were too perfect now. Claire feared stability and happiness almost as much as she feared chaos and pain. It was all temporary. It could all vanish in the blink of an eye. Why wait for that to happen?

She packed a suitcase and went hurtling three years into the past to get away from it all.

* * *

The odor intensified as Gino ventured deeper into the belly of the beast. His reluctant guide, Raif, led him through the derelict generation ship with promises of a confrontation with the almighty Stormgren.

Oil. Crude oil. There were bubbling, steaming, festering vats of black sludge in the bowels of the ship. Men with pipes, sticks, and anything they could find or hack together were slowly stirring the slop. It was noisy. It was hot. It was brutal on the senses and disgusting to behold. The emaciated bodies of the outcasts wore more sweat and grime than clothing.

"What is this?" Gino asked as he followed Raif through this gallery of human suffering, safe behind his crystal shell. The eyes of the laborers tracked him like cave-dwellers' fixated on a point of light. But none put down their sticks. Their work was the foundation of their existence and nothing short of death would drive them away from it.

"Da pits," Raif said. "We skim d'oil off de watah, filtah it, an' ship it offworld. Big money. Big money fah Starmgren an' his boys."

"How big?"

"Big. Ask tha man. I dunno tha numbahs," Raif said as he strolled along the edges of the massive room, which was dominated by the vats and the slaves who tended them.

"What's your cut?" Gino asked.

"Cut?" Raif shook his head. "I still alive. Dat be da on'y cut I git, brud. Bettah a gun-man 'dan a pit-man. I used ta stir dah pits. Now, I make sure *they* stir." He abruptly changed his tone and gestured for Gino to walk a little faster. "Follow me. Almos' there."

"I'm looking for a ship," Gino said as he followed his guide through the underworld. "A very specific ship. A freighter. Four engines. Skinny wings. Dual drive cores."

"I dunno. Starmgren an' his boys bring ships all de time," Raif said. "Has de pit-men tear 'em apaht and sends 'em off in pieces. Sells 'em, methinks."

"So that's his angle?" Gino said. This was all one big chop shop, with an army of slaves to scuttle stolen ships and sell the drive cores elsewhere. With crude oil sales on the side, this place could turn a tidy profit.

The fact that the *Valiant* hadn't swooped down and leveled it all proved some sort of agreement was in place. The Registry was turning a blind eye to what was happening on the *Liberty*. Clyde's theory that this place launched the attack on Adi Zahara was beginning to hold water. His theory that this might be the construction site for a new *Darkstar Abyssal* was also edging dangerously close to truth.

But Raif wasn't done yet: "'Bout a week ago, folks stahted sayin' he buildin' sumtin. Folks say lotta tings, can't always believe 'em, but 'dis a big ship, wit' lotta places nobody go an' nobody know. Maybe he *is* buildin' sumtin," he said with a shrug. "Starmgren can do what he want and we be none da wisah. But we *talk*. Sumtin' look funny, people talk. Talk's about all we got left, bruddah."

"Well keep talking," Gino said.

* * *

Claire woke up in 2222 and spent a sleepless year in solitude, wandering Europe. Her mind was slipping. She could feel it every time she used her power and every time it used her.

Focus. I have to focus. I have this ability for a reason, but it's getting away from me. I exist for a reason. Beings of light... devouring the Earth... fire... death...

In 2223, on her 20th birthday, when she should only be seven years old, Claire safely jumped three years backwards on a whim, and arrived in 2220.

I exist for a reason.

She made her way back to Ukraine under a false identity and did what she told herself she'd never do again: stalk her mother. Claire sat outside the Eisenholm apartment in a stolen van for hours, filming. Sometimes she would teleport inside to use the restroom. Other times, she would relieve herself in jars and bottles. She survived off food pilfered from various residences and frequently stayed awake for 72 hours or more.

This went on for a month before she was picked up by Odessa police following an altercation with a local resident. Claire was tranquilized after a psychotic tirade in the back of a police cruiser, where she kicked out a window and ranted about beings of light and fire and the end of days. She awoke in Registry custody with no memory of how she got there and two Hunters standing over her.

One was her father.

She instantly jumped to 2217, suffering the worst case of blacklight since her first. She spent the next two months in Izmail, at the same clinic, only this time she was tied to the bed by leather straps while a pump replaced her black blood with red. Her heart wanted to leap from her chest, but the trusty old pacemaker ensured she ticked like a Swiss timepiece. Claire thrashed and cursed until the nurses didn't dare approach, but she listened to their murmurs when they thought she was asleep.

"Neural decay," they called it. When Claire was drugged enough to calmly look the nurse in the eye and form a coherent question, the woman's only reply was, "I don't know what's causing it, ma'am, but you should get some rest."

The woman's smile made Claire burn inside, but she channeled the hatred into something *real*. At 21, she checked herself out of the same clinic that had saved her life when she was thirteen, seven years later. Claire returned to the life of a vagrant, with no goal or purpose and only one rule: stay away from mama and papa. Dad was scary. Mom was fragile.

The year was still 2217. She should only be a year old. She spent months by the sea, staring at the water, shaking cans for loose change. Claire could easily teleport into a bank vault and become an overnight millionaire, but money never interested her, only survival.

Besides, she'd discovered that taking only loose change –a little here, a little there– lessened her temporal footprint if she tried to take it with her into the past. She was learning.

But Claire's interests came and went like the wind. Survival? She tried to drown herself twice and ended up in a psych ward. The words 'asocial' and 'psychosis' came up a lot. Once the orderlies let her have needles and yarn, she began knitting sweaters all summer. She was only buying time, letting her body and mind heal for one last push.

On July 3, 2218, Claire left. With her meager savings, she bought herself a birthday present: a nine inch hunting knife, the sort of thing that really makes a statement when you bury it in someone. To celebrate, she blew out a single candle on a single chocolate cupcake before leaving on a 'business trip' two years into the past.

* * *

Gino dismissed his guide with an apathetic wave and headed up the corridor the man had indicated. *Could be a trap,* he thought. If the roof wasn't coming down on top of him, the floor was threatening to give out beneath him. The whole ship was an accident waiting to happen. Parts scavenged from one place were bolted on elsewhere. One room's hole was another's floorboards. There were jagged corners and places where rust compromised integrity.

'Integrity' was in short supply on the *Liberty*. Its structure was just as untrustworthy as its residents. Raif had coughed up a wealth of information, but that didn't change the fact that he was a slave who kept his fellow slaves in check at gunpoint. No one was innocent.

Gino soon reached a set of double doors on a landing at the top of a stairwell, guarded by two gentlemen with assault rifles. He thought of them as 'gentlemen' because they wore suits – dirty, ill-fitting suits, but suits nonetheless. They were junkyard chic, like bouncers at a landfill.

"I need a ship. Which of you is the man to talk to?" Gino said, assuming one of these dapper lads might be Stormgren. They weren't.

The two men opened fire. Bullets must be the traditional greeting aboard the *Liberty*. Gino's fist cratered one man's face and he collapsed with blood gushing from a broken nose as the fighter's knee buried itself in the groin of the other guard. Anything resembling a lock had rusted solid ages ago, so Gino easily snatched the double doors open, revealing a hallway with only one entry ahead, marked 'bridge,' and about a dozen men standing between him and it. Gino charged forward, but was immediately met with the hiss of a fast-approaching projectile.

The average rocket-propelled grenade travels at three hundred meters per second. Gino had less than a tenth of that to sidestep the shoulder-launched missile. It struck the wall beside him and detonated, hurling him *through* the opposite wall, like a crystal wrecking ball.

As his vision refocused, Gino found himself lying on the floor of what could best be described as the devil's throne room. The bridge of the *Liberty* was probably once an impressive sight. One wall was all glass, allowing the ship's captain to peer out at the infinite vastness of the cosmos and plot a course for this once-great ship, which was designed to give half a million brave souls a fresh start on a new world.

Unfortunately, the greatness died 150 years ago, along with a third of its human cargo, when the *Liberty* and her sister ship missed their mark. Both ships splashed down on a waterworld beyond Farside, where no one dared defy the Solarans by coming to their rescue. The windows, or what remained of them, now overlooked a scarred, pitted, blackened deck where survivors slowly wasted away, toiling beneath a sickly brown sky.

The helm was gone and the captain's chair had been replaced with a rusty throne made of turbine blades scavenged from the ship's unused nuclear reactors. The metal was bent, twisted, and welded into a grotesque piece of furniture, bristling with spikes and dangerous angles.

Gino couldn't see who sat in the chair – its back was to him – but all along the perimeter of the room were cages filled with women and young girls, locked up like animals. Their cramped living quarters contained bowls of what was either food or feces. Most sprang to attention when Gino was blasted into the room. The ones who didn't were either dead or drugged.

As Gino got to his feet and his mind processed everything before him, he began to make his way toward the throne, ignoring the pulse in his ears and the cries of the female captives. As he circled around, he found the devil himself perched in the infernal chair.

Stormgren wasn't a large man, but he certainly had more meat on his bones than the rest. His boots were clean and his cargo pants bulged with extra ammunition for the gold-plated rifle resting beside his throne. He wore a thick ballistic vest, with no shirt beneath, and a heavy black overcoat lined with matted fur. Its collar bristled with metal spines, like the quills of a porcupine, matching his bladed throne.

Their eyes locked just as Stormgren's men poured through the door, weapons ready.

"How the hell did you-?"

Stormgren never finished. Gino began pounding the man's face in. He'd come to bargain. He'd come to negotiate. All he wanted was a shuttle and whatever plans Desmond had sold. But something in him snapped the moment the man opened his mouth. The oil pits. The women in cages. The smell of human suffering. The rotting corpse of a shattered dream. How the hell had a journey to the stars ended like *this*? It assaulted his senses, lit a fire in the depths of his soul, and his fists just... *reacted*. He couldn't stop himself if he tried.

By the time he came to and took a step back, Stormgren's face was a bloody pulp and Gino's crystal armor was stained crimson. The bludgeoned man was still gurgling up bubbles of gore and phlegm, hanging on to his worthless life with the same tenacity that had allowed him to enslave a quarter million stranded refugees. Gino lifted him up by the metal collar of his coat and dumped him on the floor like the worthless sack of shit he was. The armed men at the door stood wide-eyed and shocked to see their leader and oppressor brutalized beyond recognition.

"Here's what's gonna happen..." Gino began as he picked up the golden rifle and thumbed off the safety. The time for negotiations had passed.

* * *

Claire arrived in late 2015, exactly nine months before her birth, and went straight to the train station. She journeyed west, with no intended destination, just an iron-clad determination not to interfere until the right moment. Making ripples in the timeline was unavoidable, but she could avoid making waves.

The thought of her father siring another daughter turned Claire's stomach nearly as much as what he'd done to her. But her mother... Claire's love for her mother never faltered. Gemma Eisenholm *deserved* a daughter. Claire would move heaven and earth to see that she got one. A *good* daughter, not one who was half-insane.

Through the window of a bullet train, Claire watched the Swiss countryside go by at 800 KPH, and smiled at the thought of rewriting history.

On July 3, 2216, at precisely 4:00 PM, after nine months in exile, Claire Eisenholm returned to Yulia Tymoshenko Memorial Hospital in Odessa, Ukraine. She sat in the lobby and watched as Gemma Eisenholm was wheeled in at 4:07, with Sergei following close behind.

Claire took an issue of *Ukraine Today* from the waiting room, teleported up to the second floor, and waited in a chair outside room 223 of the maternity ward. She read some articles on parenting as her mother was wheeled into labor, followed by Sergei, who was doing his best impersonation of an anxious father-to-be.

The general commotion of bringing new life into the world followed soon after. *Much ado about nothing*, Claire thought as she thumbed through the digital pages of her magazine.

Finally, at 4:53: "Congratulations, Mrs. Eisenholm, you've given birth to a healthy baby girl," the doctor said from inside the room. "What will you name her?"

"Clarice," Sergei said. "Clarice Elizabeth Eisenholm." There was joyous laughter.

The doctor left the room a minute later. Claire stood up and let herself in. Her parents were too busy cuddling Other Claire to pay her any mind. Her father didn't even notice her until the lock clicked. He turned to face her as she drew the knife. Happy Birthday, Claire.

Claire buried the blade up to its handle in his genitals again and again and again. When he hit the floor, she stabbed him repeatedly in the chest and did not stop until long after the fountain of blood was reduced to a mild gurgle and hospital staff were pounding at the door. Her mother's screams didn't faze her any more than the child's.

When Claire was satisfied her father was very dead, she left the knife in him, stood up, and fixated on the window for a long, long time. Now what? After what seemed like an eternity, she looked her mother and newborn twin sister square in the eyes and said, "You're welcome," before unlocking the door. Security staff poured in.

Five minutes later, Claire was in the back of a police car, on her way to spending the remainder of her life in a padded cell. At least that's what she let them believe.

* * *

With his chin resting on his fist, Saimon Hawke sat contemplating the implications of what he was observing. A dozen probes dumped into orbit fed high-resolution images of the *Darkstar* to monitors in his room on the *Valiant,* where he stalked his prey.

He watched Ainsworth's defection with mounting amusement, knowing he'd be the first to fold. He'd planted a seed on P-222 and now watched it blossom beautifully. The fighter paddled away in a crystal rowboat, while Niehaus and Williams raged. When the girl disappeared below decks and returned with Evans and Mahalya minutes later, Saimon was beside himself. There was no audio, but he took great pleasure in watching the four of them stand around like lost sheep. It was destined to be.

Evans was a lifelong loser, with glaring performance issues, liable to get him canned any day now. The only reason he was still employed – and thus, *alive* – was because this 'Stranger' had taken pity on him. Neihaus was a drug addled slut and good-for-nothing gutter rat who wouldn't last two days without someone to latch onto. She was as much a parasite as the computer viruses she wrote. Williams was a slick-talking coward wearing a hustler's clothes. He'd do anything to save his own ass and, if he could pull a boat out of it, he'd be the one paddling away, not Ainsworth.

And then there was Mahalya... a wild card, that one. *How long before she flips out and slaughters them all in the name of a god who doesn't even exist?* Saimon thought as he adjusted his glasses and stared through the monitor. *Given enough time, they'll kill one another and spare me the trouble.*

But Ainsworth... that's the one he had high hopes for. The one with something to lose. The one he knew would come crawling back, as long as the door was left open for him. The White Knight's popularity soared after he was ousted from the ring. Saimon couldn't help but wonder if that was the Solarans' plan all along. Take a fighter who is already a fan favorite, toss him out to whip the fanbase into a frenzy, and then bring him back and watch the Light come pouring in. A Gino Ainsworth comeback fight would make a killing.

But they never expected Ainsworth to go rogue. He didn't take the ban lying down. Saimon admired the man's tenacity, to some extent, but loathed his willingness to defy the Solarans. To think, they actually *wanted* him back, even after all he'd done! Disgraceful.

He hated Mason for many of the same reasons. Someone high up was making a fool of him. Someone was being too damn lenient with these traitors. That and the smoke trails rising from the *Liberty* made him seethe. He'd seen Ainsworth disappear into the ship nearly an hour ago. Minutes later, all hell broke loose. Gunfire. Flames. Explosions. People were being thrown overboard. Filthy hooligans in loincloths were running around, waving weapons and firing into the air. Whatever passed for social order down there had been turned on its head in under an hour. Soon, they would reach the shuttles.

The proverbial cat was out of the bag.

268   B. Stephens

Saimon Hawke looked forward to the forthcoming shooting gallery. A menagerie of jury-rigged starships fleeing Numira would make a fine test for the *Valiant*'s missiles.

He watched as the first taker emerged from the columns of smoke. A small shuttle sped into the upper atmosphere, accelerating toward the fringes of space. Hawke couldn't see who was aboard, nor did he know its intended destination or purpose, but he felt it in his bones.

"Ainsworth… you son of a bitch," he hissed between his teeth.

Sensing a presence in the room, Saimon turned, but found no one was there. The door was shut. The lights were dimmed, but it was nowhere near dark enough for someone to hide. The one thing he hated more than chaos was someone in *his* room, on *his* ship, without *his* permission. He was the watcher, not the watched.

Annoyed, he adjusted his glasses once more and slicked back his hair before switching the video feed to the ship's security cameras. Eisenholm was still in her room, huddled in the corner, exactly as she'd been for days. She only moved when she needed to take a piss. As far as he could tell, she didn't even sleep, despite the plush bed and comfortable furnishings he had given her. That girl was wiping her ass with his hospitality.

Saimon took a deep breath before hailing her on the ship's intercom. "Miss Eisenholm, I'd like to have a word with you in my quarters," he said pleasantly. She didn't budge. Her face was buried between her knees. The cup of coffee he'd given her days ago was on the floor, untouched, and that was nearly as maddening as being ignored.

Annoyed, he tapped the intercom once more. "Miss Eisenholm, meet me in my room in-"

"Already been there," she said, her voice nearly too low to hear.

"I suspected as much. We need to have a talk about your behavior. Article four, section three, of the Registry guidelines dictates-"

"Fuck your guidelines," she murmured under her breath. A faint Russian accent played at the edges of her words. Claire lifted her head and peered up at the camera from beneath her unkempt fringe of snowy white hair. "I've got a guideline for *you*, birdman."

"Hawke," he corrected.

"Whatever." Claire stood and approached the hidden camera. How did she know? The lenses were so small and well-hidden, there was no way she could've known where it was. "Listen to me," she said, peering straight into the monitor. Her eyes were completely colorless, the pupils pinpoints of black on pearly white orbs, behind thick glasses.

Saimon was listening. He had no choice. This girl constantly teetered on the razor edge of crazy and he didn't want to set her off. If he gave her even the *slightest* reason to flee, his head would roll. Not the pilot's head, or the janitor's, or Brock Mason's. It would be *his* head, because he was the ranking captain of this assignment. That is why, when Claire Eisenholm told Saimon Hawke to listen, he *Listened*.

Worst of all, she *knew* the power she had over him.

"I want to see Gino Ainsworth," she said sternly. Saimon was already shaking his head, but he snapped to attention when she screamed into the camera: "He's coming here and I *want him*! Bring him to *me*. Not you. Not Mason. Not your damned Solarans. *Me!*"

"You weren't entirely honest with us, Claire," Saimon said calmly. "You were right about 222. You were right about Adi Zahara. You were even right about the *Darkstar* coming here. But you said *nothing* about Ainsworth's defection and the destabilization of Numira. We can't build you a ship if the builders are *rioting*. Did you know this would happen?"

"What does it matter to you?" she said. Her gaze was unsteady. "I need to know what the hell he did down there and what it *means*."

"It means we're deviating from the timeline you laid out," Hawke warned, "and it's screwing with our plans. I don't like my plans screwed with, Miss Eisenholm."

But Claire had turned away. Her hand was trembling at her side as she put her back to the camera. Slowly, her white fingers curled into a fist. When she spoke, her voice had that low, whispering quality to it once more. The fire within had died, but something still smoldered, like the embers of a coming inferno.

"Hail. His. Shuttle. Now," she said. "Bring him to *me*, or I will go to *him*, and show you what it means to have your plans screwed with. I *will see* that man."

– 16 –

Gino hadn't flinched as he traversed the chaotic decks of the *Liberty*, nor did he shy away when Stormgren's men attacked him. But he nearly leapt out of his seat when the shuttle's radio chirped. He was fast approaching the *Noble Valiant*, without a clue what to say or do once he got there, and now the enemy was hailing him.

The sudden urge to wrap his hands around Clyde's neck and squeeze bubbled up in Gino's guts, but he was forced to face the truth that he was just one man, alone in a shuttle, with no one to blame but himself.

Screw that, he thought. *I can blame Clyde. This was all his stupid idea anyway.*

With a determined grunt and a white-knuckle grip on the flight stick, he tapped the ship's communicator and an instantly recognizable voice pierced the silence:

"Incoming shuttle, identify yourself," Saimon Hawke demanded. Now *here* was a man Gino would truly like to strangle the life out of.

"This is Gino Ainsworth. I'm approaching in a stolen shuttle," he said through clenched teeth, biting back his thinly-veiled contempt. "I've parted ways with the *Darkstar Abyssal* and its crew and I am seeking asylum. Does your offer still stand?"

"Perhaps," Hawke mused. "One moment please."

Nerve-shattering silence followed, but a request for video communication eventually flashed on the console. Stormgren's shuttle was an old model, with none of the fancy holographic displays. The grimy, oil-smudged screen flickered to life as soon as Gino accepted the vid request. He wiped it with his coatsleeve, revealing the hazy image of a white-haired, snowy-eyed girl, who could be none other than Claire Eisenholm, in the flesh.

Well, that was easier than expected, Gino thought.

"Ainsworth," she hissed.

Gino frowned.

"From here on, you talk to *me* and me only," Eisenholm declared. "I want to deal with you *myself* and I don't want anyone else interfering. I need to know what's going through that tiny brain of yours, Ainsworth."

On that, they could agree. Gino also wondered what the hell he was thinking. The contempt in her voice made him question Clyde's claims that this girl was his 'biggest fan.' She sounded like she'd rather have his head, not his autograph.

"We need to talk about *this*," Eisenholm demanded. The viewscreen switched to a satellite image of smoke clouds billowing off the decks of the *Liberty*, thick and black. The contrast jarred him when the image reverted to Claire's pale, scowling face.

"I had friends down there," she hissed, putting her bleached eyes uncomfortably close to the camera. Her unsteady gaze reminded him of all the things he'd heard about this 'Chronomancer.' Insane. Imbalanced. Unpredictable. This psychotic albino had the twitchiness of a coiled spring.

"What the *hell* did you do down there?" Claire demanded. But, when Gino opened his mouth to reply: "No, no, no, shhhhh shhhhush," she said, putting a finger to her lips as her eyes darted from left to right. "Beware of wolves," said the pale-faced sheep. "Not here. Too many listening. Soon, my knight. Soon..."

She began pacing. At least that's what he assumed she was doing. Her face left the screen, but she continued to pass by the camera every few seconds, going one direction, then the other, then the other, again and again and...

Gino, thoroughly confused, was slowly drawing nearer to the *Valiant* and wondering when someone would get this nutcase off the line and walk him through the docking procedure. He could barely fly a shuttle, let alone dock one. That was the autopilot's job, but it needed docking codes to proceed.

"Claire?" he said. "Claire...?" Just as he began to fear the white windshield wiper would continue indefinitely, the screen went blank and Saimon's scowling mug reappeared.

"I'll transmit the docking codes shortly," he whispered quickly. "Enjoy your stay, Ainsworth. I'll have a word with you after Claire's had her fun. We need to talk about your-"

Claire reappeared as a picture-within-a-picture. "Hawke!? Son of a bitch, what did I tell you!?" She was red in the face, a feat Gino didn't know was possible for someone in her condition. "Get off the line *now* or I'm *gone*! I'll count to five... four... three..."

"The-coordinates-are-sent-goodbye," Saimon blurted out and was gone instantly.

Confused, yet oddly satisfied, Gino breathed a sigh of relief and sank deep into the pilot's seat. *It's a madhouse in there*, he thought. Her control of Hawke was pleasing... but, he wondered, did she have any control of herself? Should he be relieved or terrified?

* * *

"Hey! Clyde," Ell yelped the moment he entered the communications room, with Desmond by his side. She tugged at the collar of her spacesuit. "What's with this thing? How long we gotta wear this shit?"

"Ah, we've finally found something she can't strip off in ten seconds flat," Desmond quipped. "Amazing."

"Wanna bet?"

"Both of you knock it off. We've got business to attend to," Clyde said as he took a seat at the central console. "The spacesuits are just a precaution, Ell. I admit they're a little... tight, but you'll appreciate them if there's a hull breach. We're going up soon and I don't expect the *Valiant* or her mothership to take kindly to that. Okay?"

"Fine," Ell sighed. "I can deal with the suit. It's the waitin' that's killin' me. When are we gonna get this show on the road? Every sec we wait, Gino's getting away."

Desmond snickered.

"If I may speak freely, captain," Chala'Ran said, "I agree with Miss Neihaus's assessment. Would I be wrong in assuming you called this meeting to discuss our next course of action and thus *end* the waiting? The ship's repairs have been complete for over an hour."

"The ship's at a hundred percent," Desmond reported. "We can fly circles around 'em if we have to, or hit 'em hard. I even ran some diagnostics on the main gun. If a direct assault is what you want, we're as ready as we'll ever be. Our secret weapon's ready to go... and I'm dying to see it in action."

"The goal is to extract Claire Eisenholm, is it not?" Chala said. "Neither a direct assault nor 'flying circles' will accomplish that without further action, and your 'secret weapon' sounds like it would do more harm than good, Mr. Williams. A functioning ship is for naught if we lack a sound strategy." Her gaze turned to Clyde. "We have not confirmed Eisenholm's location and

Miss Neihaus's attempts at gathering intelligence on the enemy ship have failed. We are at a severe logistical disadvantage, captain, and lack direction... unless the waiting entails a purpose we are not yet aware of. Does it, Mr. Evans?"

She stared through him in her eerily perceptive way and he was struck speechless, despite having called this meeting to answer precisely that question.

Again, Desmond snickered, and Clyde shot him a sharp glance. "It does," he said after far too long. "We're waiting for a call."

"A call? From who? Not The Stranger again," Ell groaned. "I thought we were done waiting on him."

"No, not him," Clyde said. "I've a feeling we won't be hearing from him much anymore. We're on our own."

"So why bother?" Desmond said. "Forget Claire."

"She's one of us. Stranger or no Stranger, leaving her isn't an option," Clyde said and his eyes momentarily wandered to Chala'Ran, who nodded approvingly. "We're going to get her out of there... just not *now*."

"So we're seriously just gonna sit here and do *nothing*?" Ell said, fidgeting uneasily. "Ugh, you know I *hate* that."

"Seventy-three minutes," Clyde said. "That's the deadline. If we don't get a call by then, we fly up there and do this the hard way."

"You mean the 'shoot first and ask questions later' way?" Desmond mused.

"They shot first. We are merely returning the favor," Chala'Ran said.

"I know Eisenholm's up there," Clyde added. "I know she'll run to us if she has no place else to go. Numira's done for and smoking her out of the *Valiant* or *Infinitum* isn't impossible." He looked to Chala'Ran: "When the dust settles, she'll be on *this* ship, even if you and I have to storm the castle and get her ourselves."

"Ready when you are, captain."

"Well, that's just dandy," Desmond said and rubbed his mitts together before digging into the pockets of his tight black spacesuit. He fished out a full deck of well-worn playing cards and began to shuffle them, making quite a show of it. "I know what you're up to, Evans. I'll play along with this ruse, but I won't sit here and do *nothing* while we wait for Gino to phone home."

Desmond snickered yet again. "Only reason I told that meathead where to find a shuttle is because I knew you put him up to it. I'm not sure if those Hunters can actually see us from orbit, but I think I put on a convincing show and made the 'betrayal' look real." He flicked the first card across the table and flashed a smile at Clyde as he began to deal. "Sorry, boss, but your poker face needs some work. C'mon, how about a little practice while we wait? How much money you got?"

With a sigh, Clyde took a seat at the table as the cards began to pile up. "Was it really that obvious?"

* * *

Docking terrified him. Despite the shuttle's simplistic controls, Gino was forced to sit back and let the autopilot take over, while hoping Hawke didn't retract his offer and open fire. By the time the clamps secured the shuttle and the hiss of pressurization sounded, Gino's face was drenched in a cold sweat.

The stolen shuttle was the size of a box van, old and unreliable. While it was nowhere near as decrepit as the *Liberty*, it was bad enough that Gino wanted to be off of it and onto a secure craft as soon as possible. As much as he feared what awaited him on the other side of the airlock, he wasted no time in boarding the *Noble Valiant*.

Surely, it was the dangers of space travel that set his innards aflutter, and not the prospect of having an audience with the psychotic, time-traveling enigma who'd singled him out for inspection. Surely, it wasn't *that*.

Gino quickly undid his safety straps the moment the autopilot light dimmed and stood from his seat, awaiting further instructions. But none came.

He called into the silence, but only silence replied.

After a moment of hesitation, he opened the hatch, but summoned no armor, despite feeling he should. *Claire seems to have a handle on them*, he reasoned. *They need her. I need her. And, for some reason, she needs me.*

What a twisted web they'd woven. There was an uneasy peace and she was the nucleus of it all. He remembered Clyde's words to him, en route to Numira: "I'm going to need you to be more than a two bit bruiser."

"Diplomacy? Not my strong suit," Gino murmured to himself.

The shuttle's hatch closed behind him. A half second later, the *Noble Valiant*'s opened upon a bright, but empty, corridor. Right in front of him was another airlock, this one leading to the *Halcyon Infinitum*, which was mated to the *Valiant*'s opposite side.

He was in the thick of it now. Despite the ship's pristine white interior and its polished stainless steel floors, he felt more at risk here than in the confines of the derelict *Liberty*, where he couldn't tell which stains were rust and which were blood.

Gino hugged the spiky collar of Stormgren's coat a little closer to his shoulders. He liked it too much to leave it on the dead man, and it'd come away with minimal blood splatter. A fighter needed trophies, so he took it as a final posthumous insult to the crushed despot.

To his right was a closed hatch, marked 'Flight Deck,' but a small red light indicated it was locked. The hall had many more doors, also locked. The layout wasn't much different from the *Darkstar*, though everything was sleeker, cleaner, and uncluttered by industrial epithets.

Only one door lay open, at the far end of the hall. As Gino drew nearer, he could hear pounding, screeching; the destructive sounds of metal on metal and maddened thrashing. The racket rose in volume as the active party became increasingly frustrated with whatever he or she was attempting to destroy.

"Hello?" Gino said again, cautiously. He reached the room in short order and found a medium-sized residence, oddly similar to the *Darkstar*'s observation rooms, but with an untouched bed, a small table, and chairs set upon their heads. Three cups of black coffee and untouched meals remained on the floor while Claire attempted to tear a computer console from its wall mounting beside the door.

"Don't just stand there!" she said, while trying to sever a mess of wires from the clunky box attached to them. "Do this, dammit. I'm sick of it." She dropped the offending item and stomped away, defeated. It dangled by its assorted cables.

Swallowing his mild confusion, Gino decided he might as well help. A small crystal blade formed in his hand and he snipped the wires, tossed the electronic box on the ground and looked to Claire with an expression that said, 'okay, now what?'

"Smash it." She sat on the floor and curled up with her knees to her chest and her back to the expansive window, which revealed a breathtaking view of the *Halcyon Infinitum*. It was so close he could see tiny people in tiny windows on the rings of the massive ship, watching them.

"Smash it!" Claire repeated, snapping him out of his reverie. "And shut the door."

With a crystal boot, Gino came down hard on the box and it shattered into a mess of circuit boards and silicon chips. A tiny camera and microphones lay amongst the rubble. Hawke and Mason were spying on her. He stomped it until the bits were ground into dust.

Gino had no idea what this girl was all about, but anyone who began a conversation by giving him things to smash was okay by him. He headed over to the thick door and shut it. At her request, he locked it and drew the shutters on the expansive window as well, isolating them from the outside world.

"Sit," she said. Gino moved toward the table and reached for an upturned chair. "No! Floor! Sit on the floor!" Claire screamed, pointing at the *exact* spot she wanted him to plant his ass.

With an annoyed grunt, he seated himself opposite her, on the cold floor. Just as her demands were beginning to annoy him, Claire suddenly became docile. The minor acts of compliance brought her fleeting peace. She could barely control herself, but controlling others steadied her mind and took the crazy out of her eyes. As they sat, she studied his face, but he looked through her as if she weren't there. An intimate silence formed between them.

Gino, the enemy of all things intimate, spoke: "Anything else, Your Highness? Shine your shoes? Fluff your pillows? Rearrange your-"

Claire put a finger to her pale lips. "Shhhhhhh. Not yet. Just listen."

He was amazed how colorless she was, ghost-like, as if she'd been doused with a sack of flour. Due to the rumors about blacklight, Gino expected her to be frailer, thinner, wasted. But, excluding her lack of color, Claire was fairly average-looking. She wasn't thin or emaciated by any means. In fact, she had a round baby face, complete with pinchable cheeks and cute little dimples under the square frames of her glasses.

Little by little, Gino realized he was admiring her. The thought greatly upset him.

She looked to the left, then the right, searching for apparitions lurking in the shadows. But this room had no shadows. Satisfied, she turned to Gino once more and whispered, "I think it's safe now. They're gone."

Okay, so why are you whispering? He thought, but voted against voicing his concerns. He'd rather not risk a psychotic outburst.

"They can't hear us now. Can't spy on us," Claire said with a self-approving nod. "We have the ship all to ourselves. I sent Hawke and Mason and the crew away. Over there." She pointed to the closed shutters, indicating the *Halcyon Infinitum*. "But the ship's on lockdown. Hawke told me to tell you your shuttle's not going anywhere. He slipped some kind of virus in with the docking codes."

Gino scowled. "You mean you *let him* slip a virus in with the docking codes?"

She shrugged indifferently. He sighed. Despite everything, Gino was forced to acknowledge that Claire had eased his passage. She didn't do *everything*, but she'd done plenty. For all her volatility, she'd gotten him here in one piece. Now he just had to figure out how to get back.

"You've come to rescue me?" she said, but the question was no question at all. "Of course you did. That's why you came last time. Lone wolf thinks he can do *everything* himself." She rolled her eyes. "Gimme a break."

"'Last time,' huh? I was here before?"

"Obviously… but you didn't set fire to the *Liberty* last time." Her tone suddenly became darker, almost frightening. Had she not remained stark still during the outburst, he would've sworn she was going to take a swing at him. "What the *hell* did you do down there? Explain!"

"I went there to get a shuttle, so I could get here. But I didn't like what I saw, so I..." he hesitated, searching for the right words, "I *liberated* them, dethroned their leader."

Claire's face wrinkled with anger.

"If you had seen that place, you'd know why I had to do it," Gino said. "Those people were slaves. There were enough ships for them to escape; they just needed someone to come along and shift the balance of power. I did. Now they're in a position to fight for their freedom... or murder one another like animals. Either way, the choice is theirs."

"Animals are the freest of all... especially the dead ones," Claire murmured.

"Well, aren't you a ray of sunshine."

She buried her face in her knees until only her expansive white eyes peered out at him, beneath a fringe of snowy hair and the black plastic frames of her glasses. "I was gonna ask if you saw any of my old crewmates down there, but what's the point? I don't care anymore. I'm sick of feeling responsible for every goddamned thing that happens."

"Desmond said they were as good as dead."

"Desmond's a dirty liar! You should've *looked* for them!" she hissed. "You were *there*!"

"You can *teleport*," Gino said sharply. "If you actually gave a damn about them, you would've gone down there and looked for them yourself! Better yet, you wouldn't have dropped them into that meat grinder in the first place, you nutjob. You have all this power and you use it to help the fucking Registry! They only want to bottle you up and use you for-"

"Oh, and The Stranger is *so* different? You have no fucking clue!" Claire huddled up even tighter and buried her face between her knees. She began rambling in Russian and her voice cracked with distress or the onset of tears when she finally returned to English. "You're one to talk. You didn't do a damn thing last time. You got your shuttle and left them to rot, you self-righteous prick. Now look at you, with your chest puffed out like you're some kind of *hero*. There's so many versions of everything, so many alternatives. This time, you're the hero. Last time, you couldn't be bothered. Next time, what, the villain? Ha!"

Gino didn't consider himself a hero at all, but his attempts at denying the allegation only led to more spats of Russian. She clearly had a lot to get off her chest. He quieted himself and waited out the storm, partly out of futility and partly out of... sympathy?

How had they ended up yelling at one another in the first place? She was the endgame, the goal, the holy grail. And here he was, fussing at her like a bitter old nag, when he should be trying to get her out of this place. That's what a 'hero' would do.

But he wasn't one of those. He just wished she'd shut the hell up and return to the *Darkstar* with him.

"I hate you," Claire muttered. "I used to think you were something special when I saw you in vids. But now I hate you. I *hate* you." She lapsed into her native tongue again and showed no signs of stopping.

Black teardrops rolled down her white cheeks. The disease was worse than he imagined. Perhaps she really *couldn't* teleport down there. And even if she could, where would she take them? There was only one planet in this system. Even she couldn't travel that far and ships weren't easy to come by in this system. She didn't have Desmond's guile or Gino's brute force.

Claire Eisenholm, the Chronomancer, wasn't all-powerful or all-knowing. She couldn't solve every problem with a wave of her hand. She was used-up, burnt-out, and tired... but people *still* wanted things from her.

Gino finally surrendered and wrapped his arms around her. It was a stupid thing to do, hugging someone who said she hated him. She could've vanished in the blink of an eye and this would all be for naught. But he moved without thinking. She needn't go far to escape him, but she didn't even try. Instead, Claire seemed to melt in his arms.

Her trembling hand tentatively clawed his back, like a baby cub trying to find purchase on mama bear's furry pelt. She hesitantly accepted the embrace for what it was: a fumbling man's weak attempt at building trust in a woman who trusted no one. She was lonely. She hated him, but he was all she had right now. The ability to disappear is overrated.

Despite himself, Gino felt for Claire. She was odd, of course, but endearing in a way. She was immensely powerful, but fragile. She was incredibly simple, but grasped everything going on around her with unblinking surety. She was damaged goods, but still valuable beyond measure, teetering between the competing realities of what once was and what could be.

"Damn you, Evans, for sending me here," Gino muttered under his breath while he gave this pathetic creature a soft pat on the back. He broke the embrace and held her at arm's length as he fished a handkerchief from his pocket.

"No, no, stay," Claire whimpered as she tried to cling to him. Thin rivulets of black tears streamed from her eyes. This is why you don't touch groupies, his agent once said. Once they latch on, they'll never let you go.

"There's no time for this. I didn't come here for cuddles," Gino grunted. He took her hand and slapped the handkerchief into her palm. "Take this. Fix your face. I'm sorry about your friends down there, but we have a lot to discuss."

"We can discuss later." She wiped her eyes, leaving messy black streaks like mascara, then stared into him with such directness Gino felt something grip his heart. Something he didn't like. "You're different. You've changed."

"No, I haven't. And if I did, you wouldn't know. This is the first time we've met," he said sternly. "Don't compare me to some past-Gino who did something shitty. That wasn't *me*." He gripped her shoulders and tried to force her to focus. "Clyde sent me here to figure out where you stand. Don't you get it? The Stranger doesn't want to hold you down. He just wants to know what made you run. We're here to *help you*, Claire, but you have to-"

She pressed her lips to his and Gino nearly gagged, startled by the suddenness of it. She drew back after many long seconds and licked her lips, with only the slightest trace of embarrassment. Her tongue was pale pink.

"No!" Gino said firmly, as if talking to a dog who'd wet the carpet. "*NO*, Claire." But she would hear none of that. There was mischief in her eyes, so he attempted to appeal to reason. "Listen to me. I have a communicator. I'm going to call Clyde. He'll come with the *Darkstar* and-"

"And we'll steal it and run away together!" Claire said, enthusiastically. "Just the two of us. No Registry. No Stranger. No Hunters. Once I get my ship back, and the blacklight goes away, I'll finish what I started. You'll help me, right?"

"I'm trying to help you now, if you'd *listen*." She kept trying to move in closer, but Gino held her at arm's length, his face scrunched with disgust. "About this *other* Gino... did you and he... umm... did anything happen between-"

"No, but there's a first time for everything." Claire pounced and toppled him over. Her fingers worked quickly and she had him halfway out of his coat before he could get a hold of her hands and wrestle her off.

"You're not in your right mind," Gino said, pinning her. Her wild eyes seemed to steady for a brief time, like a night creature catching its first glimpse of sun, indirectly. "Do you have *any* idea where you are or what's going on? This is neither the place nor the time."

"First it was 'no,' now it's 'later?' Make up your mind," she said and Gino instantly realized he'd misspoken.

In a moment of fleeting clarity, Claire looked into him and spoke, calm and level, as if reciting scripture from the pages of her manic subconscious: "The human mind is a rowboat tethered to a lonely dock. We bounce with every ebb and flow of the still waters, until a big wave comes, and you gotta decide: cut the rope or get dragged under?" She laughed openly, shattering any lingering illusions that she wasn't nuts. "I'm not *crazy*," she lied. "I am, but I'm *not*. I cut my rope, so I can ride the waves. Enjoy your pond, little man, but I'm unsinkable. *Unsinkable*!"

"You're insane."

Claire writhed beneath him, struggling to free herself, and laughing all the while. "Not if I admit it! Crazy people don't *know* they're crazy!"

She suddenly vanished and Gino fell flat on his face. He thumped his chin on the cold floor and bit his tongue. Panic instantly washed over him. He'd lost her.

"Let's play a game," Claire said from the bed. Gino instantly sprang to his feet, with a cold sweat on his brow. She was already under the covers. "I have a question for you: which parts of my body aren't white?" she said with a devilish smirk as she began tossing articles of clothing out from beneath the sheets.

Gino continued to shake his head. Denial, denial to the bitter end.

"Come here. Let's study the answer sheet together," she said with a wink.

"That is not going to happen! My role here is strictly diplomatic." Gino was adamant. He stomped and deepened his voice. If she wanted to make this a battle of wills, he was game.

He collected the discarded clothing and threw it back at her. "Put this shit back on and stop being ridiculous."

But the fussing and posturing only enticed her more. "See, that's why you're my favorite Arena fighter." Claire smiled all the wider. "This *is* diplomacy. You answer my question and I'll answer yours."

* * *

The card game lapsed into a discussion of strategy and hypothetical scenarios. Desmond was giving a dissertation on the mythical properties of explosive decompression, the limitations of thrust vectoring, and their odds of successfully surviving a direct engagement with a Registry interceptor. The others were pretending to listen while wondering how he continued to win, despite running his damned mouth the entire game.

Suddenly, like a light at the end of a dreary tunnel, Clyde noticed the green beacon blinking on the communications console: the call.

Ell spotted it the same time he did and squealed like a giddy schoolgirl as she mashed the answering button. Even Desmond stopped yapping long enough to hear the tinny distortion and background noise emanating from the speakers. Everyone listened intently to the soft whooshing, like driving wind or sheets of rain.

"Hello?" Chala ventured, when no one else took the initiative.

"Hello?" a gravelly voice said from the other side. "Chala'Ran, is that you? Dammit, of all people..."

"It is such a pleasure to hear your voice, Mr. Ainsworth," Chala'Ran said with warm laughter.

"Wish I could say the same," he grumbled. "Go away. Put Clyde on."

"Everyone's here but, before we begin, I'm afraid I owe you an apology," Chala'Ran added. "I misjudged your character, dear. When Clyde confessed you'd volunteered to do this, I thought-"

"Apologies can wait. Gino, this is Clyde. Where are you?" Despite the question, Clyde's fingers were already working across the keys of the console. The holo display flickered to life, revealing markers representing the *Halcyon Infinitum* and *Noble Valiant* adrift on the fringe of space. "Is your tracking beacon on yet? I'm trying to pinpoint your... nevermind, there it is. I've got you."

A red blip on the display signified Gino's tracker, aboard the latter vessel. He'd successfully infiltrated the *Valiant* and everyone in the comm room breathed a collective sigh of relief to see he was unharmed and in position. A dangerous position, but better than dead.

"Whoa... he actually made it," Ell said.

"Was there any doubt I would?" Gino boasted.

"Ell owes me twenty credits now," Desmond said. "I'll put it on her poker tab. Anyway, what's it like up there?"

"Everything's clean and shiny," Gino said. "I *hate* it."

"Well, you won't be there for long," Clyde replied.

"I know. I'm transmitting something to you now," Gino said. "Claire had blueprints for the *Infinitum* waiting. She stole them *days* ago, 'cuz knew we'd need them, and she says she knows what happens next"

"Well, tell Little Miss Know-it-All, I said 'thanks,'" Ell commented as she pulled up to a console to decrypt the massive amounts of incoming data.

Clyde whispered to Desmond to get the pre-flight checks underway, a task which could be accomplished from right there in the comm room. "What I have in mind doesn't involve the

Infinitum," he said to Gino. "Can you reach your shuttle? Is Claire with you now?"

Gino grunted indifferently.

"Put her on," Clyde said. "I'd like to speak with her."

"She's… in the shower." Gino's pace quickened: "Look, there are *complications*. The girl has demands. Worse, my shuttle's locked down by some kind of virus in the avionics. Hawke pulled a fast one. We're safe for now, but we aren't *going* anywhere."

"Can she not teleport you out?" Chala replied. "We can move into position and-"

"It doesn't work like that!" Gino spat. "Without the *Darkstar*, she can only teleport herself; that ship boosts her power. But that's all beside the point. She's in no condition to teleport *anywhere*, even alone."

"Gino, I can deal with the virus. You know that," Ell said as she extracted the rather large series of files he was transmitting. "Once your shuttle's free, getting you guys outta there'll be cake."

"You're not *listening*. There's more to it than that," Gino said breathlessly. He grunted an airy sigh. "She has demands. Claire is being treated for blacklight. She mentioned some kind of… *machine*, on the other ship. They take her there for a few hours each day and it helps speed her recovery. It's some kind of cure for blacklight."

"Don't believe it," Clyde said, shaking his head. He'd never heard of such a thing. Used-up Scions were tossed out like last week's garbage. Severe blacklight was a career-ender, even for the best of them. If the Solarans had a means of easily reversing its effects, why hadn't he heard of it before? It *had* to be a lie, a ploy to keep Claire under their control.

"I also find that highly questionable," Chala'Ran added. "There is no *cure* for blacklight. How does Miss Eisenholm look, healthwise?"

"Lies or not, she ain't going anywhere without that machine. I can't talk her down," Gino said. "I keep trying to tell her it's bullshit, but-"

"Gino?" a female voice cooed somewhere in the distance. It had to be Claire. "Gino, who ya talkin' to?" There was a rustling sound, as if a hand covered the receiver. Gino and Claire spoke in muffled voices for a moment.

Clyde and the others could only hear broken sentences: "Something, something... Clyde... something, something... Darkstar... something, something... my friends..."

"Aw, cute, he thinks we're his friends," Ell snickered.

A half second later, Claire's voice filled the speakers, loud and clear. "Hey," she said and tapped the communicator. "Ay, you people still there? Helloooo..."

"Yes, we're here. This is Clyde Evans of the *Darkstar Abyssal.* I'd like to ask you a few questions, if you don't mind, Miss Eisenholm."

"Miss Eisenholm's my mum and you're on my ship. I hope you like it, Hunter. It won't be yours for long."

"We're just keeping it warm for you," he said, trying to avoid sounding half as nervous as he was. "We need to talk, but not like this. This line isn't secure. Are you willing to come aboard, so we can speak directly?"

"You mean come to *you,* so you can lock me down with that freaky power of yours? I know your tricks, Hunter," Claire said. "You'll do things my way. I need my blacklight treatments; it's the only thing keeping me here. The machine's not that big. Desmond can install it in the cargo bay. Chala can move it. She's good at that sort of thing. I know her tricks too."

"Umm... pardon my asking, dear, but have we met?" A very puzzled Chala'Ran asked. "This is Chala'Ran Mahalya. I don't recall ever-"

"You wouldn't. Here's a hint: you put a gun in my face when Clyde's shit plan went to shit last time," Claire said. Chala recoiled. There was no contempt in the girl's voice, merely a statement of 'this is how it happened' and an iron-willed refusal to *ever* let it happen again.

"It wasn't just you," Claire said. "Every one of you people dropped the ball. You were just the curtain-closer. Despite what my shrink says, I'm not out of my fucking mind. I've seen how this ends. Only an idiot does the same thing twice and expects a different outcome, so listen up. Here's how it's gonna go down. I've got five rules. You stick to 'em or this whole thing is off. Got it, Evans?"

"I'm listening," he said, subdued.

Her speech quickened: "First rule: Charlie doesn't get a gun. Period. I see her with a gun, this thing is *off*."

"Charlie?" Chala'Ran said. "Well, that is a first..."

"Second rule: Gino stays with me *at all times*. I like him. He's mine. Period," Claire said. A background groan could be heard from Gino, like the wail of a dying animal. But Claire wasn't finished: "Third rule: Desmond stays on the *Darkstar*. Fourth rule: I *will* get that rehab machine. It's on the *Infinitum*, third deck, sector G, room 379. Write it down if you have to. I'm not going *anywhere* without it. Fifth rule: nobody –*NOBODY* – goes near S-deck, the core of the *Infinitum*. Do you understand me? Don't even *think* about it. Don't even ask."

Clyde silently nodded as he mulled over these new developments. "Claire, can I speak? About the machine-"

"I don't wanna hear it," she said dismissively. "Whether it works or not is irrelevant. Right now, it's a hoop you gotta jump through to earn my trust. So jump, doggy. Woof, woof!"

Clyde was momentarily taken aback. Ell mouthed an obscenity.

"Claire, this is Desmond. Long time no see," her old crewmate said, cheerfully. "Just between you and me, what's on S-deck?" he asked, immediately defying her demands. Clyde quickly shot him a sharp glance, which the man ignored.

Ell did them one better and brought up the *Halcyon Infinitum*'s blueprints on the holo display, to conduct her own investigations. Silently, of course.

"Are you deaf, stupid, or both?" Claire said. "Don't mess with me, Desmond. I know your tricks, too. Do it and I'm gone."

"Where?" Ell said. "Where you gonna go, smartass? You've got nothin' left."

"Where you can't," Claire said with chilling finality. "Evans, keep your people in line and I'll cooperate. Break the rules and you'll never see me again. It's as simple as that. Gino, turn this thing off. I'm done talking to them."

"Claire, wait," Clyde said. "Can't you tell us anything? How can you expect us to-"

"What's with you people, always wanting to know everything!?" she said. "It's always, 'tell me this, tell me that.' I wish I didn't now half the things I know." Claire made a low humming noise, which was likely the sound of her trying to bottle up the crazy and save some for later. "No more questions, Evans. Do as you're told. That's what you're good at. I have nothing more to say to you."

There was a loud thump, followed by a crunch before the line went dead.

"Good ol' Claire... Still as fun as fuckin' a sack of tacks," Desmond said before looking to Clyde. "Why not go straight for her? She can't do anything with you around, right?"

"I think we should at least *try* to play by her rules," Chala'Ran said, "if only to establish trust."

"I agree," Clyde said, though he was admittedly disappointed with how poorly this first encounter had gone. Desmond's line of thinking definitely had a certain appeal, now that he'd witnessed just how cracked Eisenholm was. "We need to get moving. Williams, get us airborne. Looks like Chala and I *are* going in. Ell, what do the blueprints say about-"

"I'm already on it," she said, studying the holo display. With a few strokes of her hands, she enlarged the *Halcyon Infinitum*, zeroing in on the spherical core of the ringed starship. Some portions of the ship were still incomplete as the *Darkstar*'s computer extracted the enormously detailed blueprints, but one part was clear. "This is S-Deck, the heart of the *Halcyon Infinitum*. It's about a kilometer across," Ell explained. "I don't know what to make of it, but I've got some good news: we won't have any trouble stayin' outta that part of the ship."

"Why? Is it out of the way?" Chala'Ran asked, squinting at the fine details.

"Well, that's the funny part," Ell said, activating a cutaway view and zooming in further. "None of the rooms on S-Deck have doors. There's no way in or out. The elevator doesn't even stop there. It's… weird."

"If no one can get in, what's it for?" Clyde asked.

The room fell silent, except for one person:

"It is for Solarans," Chala'Ran said with far more confidence than should ever be used when referring to Solarans. Her gaze trembled as she stared intensely into the holo image. The colors danced on her pupils, like Light in a keeper. "There is no question. The *Halcyon Infinitum* is a Solaran capital ship."

− 17 −

Impossible, he thought.

There couldn't possibly be Solarans on that ship. Clyde knew they'd taken an interest, but the thought of them showing up in person was unfathomable. This was so far above his pay grade he'd dismissed it from reality and shoved it into a secluded corner of his subconscious.

With their arrival two hundred years ago, the Solarans delivered the keys to unlocking casual interstellar travel, environmental alchemy, and energy sources which defied conventional physics. Every modern civilization relied on some form of Solaran technology for survival. Forcibly boarding or − God forbid − *firing upon* a vessel transporting a Solaran was high treason in nearly every corner of the galaxy. Despite The Stranger's claims that this mission placed Clyde above the law, he was not above Solarans. No one was.

"How do you know?" Desmond asked, watching Chala'Ran the way one watches a bull through the walls of a glass house.

"I *know*," she said firmly before shifting to Clyde. "I wish I had seen these blueprints sooner. This is my first glimpse of the ship, but I've seen such architecture before. You are looking at a Solaran capital ship, a symbol of power and authority. There may be humans aboard, but it is not a human vessel. It is *for*

Solarans. You are about to attack a Solaran ship and you will be the first human ever to do so."

"But how do you *know*?" Desmond said again. "Have you been near one, inside of one?"

Her gaze didn't break from Clyde, who was beginning to feel she was trying to drill a hole through him. "No," Chala'Ran replied icily, "but my experience qualifies me for the task we are about to undertake."

"You think it's wise to infiltrate a Solaran ship?" Clyde said warily. "That would be-"

"An act of *war*? Yes," she said, suddenly standing. "The Solarans have waged war on us for two hundred years. It is high time we returned the favor. We wrestle not against flesh and blood, but against principalities and powers..."

"Chala, slow down and think about this for a moment."

She moved toward Ell, who quickly abandoned the computer console. The prospect of laying siege to a Solaran ship lit a fire that had been smoldering in her for far too long, and everyone in the room saw it, especially Clyde. She had ten years to think about it. This was the conversation they should have had, but didn't.

"First, we cripple their engines," Chala'Ran explained, as she commandeered the computer and highlighted sectors of the *Halcyon Infinitum*'s blueprints. "Go for the reactors next, *here* and *here*. Plunge them into darkness. These vessels carry a minimal human crew. They will move toward the escape pods to avoid the radiation from the breached reactors. It should take no more than two shots to force an evacuation and put them on the defensive."

"It'll only take *one* if Ell uses her gift," Desmond said. "She can charge the shells with kinetic energy and we fire them at half strength."

"Don't encourage her," Ell said.

"Chala, this is insane," Clyde said. He thought he'd gotten through to her when she backed away from the console, but he was mistaken.

"We should take off immediately," she declared, completely usurping the mantle of leadership. She stepped toward the door with one final gesture to the holographic display. "If *that* ship is here, there are Solarans on it, and that is all the more reason to strike immediately. We take the machine, get the girl, and leave nothing standing. I give you my word, they are *there*, and deserve whatever they get. Now, if you'll excuse me, time is short and there are preparations to be made. I wish to have a moment of meditation before we take up arms against this vessel and the demons it shelters."

Clyde moved to stop her, but, with a long, determined stride, she departed without awaiting reply or reprimand, leaving them all in a stunned silence.

Only Desmond remained seated, with his chin resting in his hands and an uncharacteristically contemplative look on his face. "Capital ship?" he muttered. "Same kind of ship that dropped the terraformers on Mars..."

"This isn't Mars," Clyde said and Desmond flinched, as if he'd been slapped out of a nightmare. "Williams, get us airborne. Ell, load the railgun, just as she said."

"What!?" she squealed. "You can't be serious-"

"I *am*. We need to be ready for anything... including a full-blown assault. We'll try diplomacy, but I don't think Hawke will give up Eisenholm peacefully, not with his Solaran 'gods' watching over him. He's a loyalist. It would be the ultimate disgrace for him."

"We've got a world-destroyer and all they've got is an interceptor and an unarmed capital ship with some goddamned aliens on it," Desmond said. "It would be *suicide* for them to resist. There's no way-"

"If they wanna take this to the tenth degree, we'll go there with them," Clyde said. "If not, we won't. It's as simple as that. I'll deal with Chala'Ran. You both have your orders and I expect you to follow them."

* * *

"Order makes the world go round," Saimon said, standing on the bridge of the *Halcyon Infinitum* and taking in the view while he sipped a tall glass of iced coffee. Gazing out at the ship's monolithic rings, stretching for miles beneath him, made him feel as if anything was possible.

This could all be mine, he thought. On a long enough timeline, everything *would* be his. The Solarans would give it all to him someday, he needed only wait and do their bidding. It was theirs to give and his to receive.

"We're nothing without order," he added, enjoying the taste of his own words. "Don't you agree, captain?"

Captain Gavin Ridgemond had a ship to command and was hardly paying the man any mind. Hawke was only a visitor, a temporary nuisance. But, as a level ten Hunter Elite *and* Acolyte, this 'temporary nuisance' out-ranked any mere captain, even the captain of a ship as illustrious as the *Halcyon Infinitum*. Neither Ridgemond nor his crew cared much for Acolytes, but they were accustomed to having them aboard this ship and respected the chain of command just enough to get by.

He muttered a noncommittal reply, to which Hawke smiled and continued his soliloquy:

"I may be displaced for the moment, but there is an order to these things. There is a *plan*. From the stars to the planets to their moons, every*thing* has a natural order," said Saimon. "Except humans… there's something *unnatural* about humans. That's why this state of affairs exists, this imposed order, this hierarchy.

We are now exactly where we were meant to be and we have the Solarans to thank for that. Forget the technology. Their greatest gift to us is *order*. The Infinite Charter is a plan built to last an eternity."

He paused significantly, took another sip of his beverage. The bridge was alive all around him, though he stood apart, like an iceberg among rapids. The captain was called away to check on some readouts at a nearby console. Crewmen leaned over glowing displays, observing sensor arrays, power levels, and fluctuations in the ship's physics envelope.

Hawke was inhumanly casual as he glanced at the antique platinum timepiece dangling from his coat pocket by a silver chain. His badge hung around his neck. "Claire's hour is nearly up," he said as he returned the chronometer to its resting place. "Frankly, I'm disappointed with her the most. For a time traveler, her grasp of history is severely lacking. Two hundred years ago, when twelve glorious Solarans made first contact with humankind and the Original Six boarded the legendary ark and emerged as the first Scions, *everything* changed," he said proudly. "It was mankind's finest hour. Humans are an expansionist species; we weren't meant to be confined to one town, one continent, one planet. The Solarans gave us the galaxy and everything in it.

"But this... this *Darkstar Abyssal*... the very name turns my stomach. They are an abomination against the natural order. Solarans turning against Solarans. Scions turning against Scions. It's chaos incarnate. Our masters gave them a gift and they threw it back and called called *us* the oppressors?" he scoffed. "To think, there are corners of the galaxy where our masters are regarded as tyrants. The blasphemy, the sheer *ignorance* of it is awe-inspiring. This cannot go unpunished."

Saimon stroked his blonde hair until it lay slick against his skull. He calmed himself by petting, the way one might appease an angry dog. He took another sip of his drink but now it tasted like bile. His appetite turned with the suddenness of a twisting serpent and he felt the urge to shatter the glass against the nearest object – preferably a *living* object – if only to have someone share his agony.

But violent outbursts were for plebes and apes. He was too refined for that, too trained, too disciplined. The source of his righteous indignation was also the source of his calm. Instead, Saimon seethed beneath the surface, red-faced but sober. A thin crackle of electricity flickered between his fingertips and danced along the condensation-coated surface of his glass.

"What *is* a monster?" he asked himself. "I think a monster is a creature whose individual needs conflict with the needs of society at large." He smiled. "It's simple, really. The *Darkstar* and its supporters, *they're* the monsters. It is my righteous duty, my anointed purpose, to give no quarter to such crimes against the natural order. I have an obligation to-"

"Sir," the captain tapped him on the shoulder. Hawke wheeled around with such suddenness, the man flinched.

"What is it, boy?" the Hunter replied, forgetting himself for a moment. Saimon was in his mid-thirties, while Ridgemond was well into his gray years. The older man frowned slightly, but professionally held his composure as he offered a datapad.

"The *Darkstar Abyssal* just lifted off from Numira," Ridgemond said. "Their trajectory suggests they'll be here in-"

The glass in Saimon's hand exploded with a sharp snap and a flicker of arcing discharge. Miraculously, his white attire took very little of the splatter, most of which ended up on the captain's pressed uniform.

Saimon took a deep breath… held it… and exhaled. "Where. Is. Mister. Mason?" he said through clenched teeth.

"Meeting with his handler, I believe." The captain dabbed at his face with a handkerchief as he found a slew of new reasons to hate working with Acolytes. The normal Scions, he could tolerate, but the Acolytes... damn them all. Something about working directly under Solarans made them think they were the center of the universe.

"His handler?" Saimon sneered.

"I can hail him on the PA and have him report here," the captain added.

"Never mind that. Have him report to my ship," Hawke said as he wheeled around and marched from the room, dropping the shattered remnants of his glass. "And have someone clean this up. It's unbecoming. There are Solarans on this ship. Act like it."

Brimming with defiance, he marched away through the glossy, sterile corridors of the *Halcyon Infinitum,* headed for the equally glossy, equally sterile halls of his own ship. In his mind's eye, he could already see the burning *Darkstar Abyssal* ensnared in the *Infinitum*'s pull while the *Valiant*'s full arsenal was unleashed upon it. He could taste victory on his tongue. It had the savory metallic taste of blood.

Brock Mason rounded a corner and fell in step, lumbering to keep up with the proud acolyte's much longer stride. Blinded by delusions of victory, Hawke didn't even notice him.

"What's goin' on?" Mason said. "Are they comin' or we gonna chase 'em down?"

"Chasing is what we do. We are monster hunters," Hawke said as they entered an elevator, which swiftly took them to A-Deck, where the *Valiant* was docked. "A lion in the wild fits into the natural order of things; it is no monster. But let one venture into the village, unfettered, and feast upon children and babies – a monster is born. A monster is a creature whose individual needs conflict with the needs of society at large. Society *needs* babies and children, so eating them is unacceptable. Society *needs* Solarans; lifting a hand against them is *unacceptable*."

The elevator dinged. Its doors opened.

"I don't know *what* you're talkin' about. Are they comin' or not?" Mason demanded. "Are we gonna shoot 'em down? I hope not. I wanna git 'em myself, with my own hands." He ground a meaty fist into his leathery palm.

"Of course they're coming. We have a defenseless ship filled with babies, ready to eat. Monsters *will come*," Hawke said with a sadist's grin as he rounded a bend and arrived at airlock nine. He punched in his passcode and the doors slid open with an airy swish. "What did you discuss with your handler?" He asked as the pressure equalized.

Mason smiled. "That's classified."

Hawke glowered at him. "I am an Acolyte; the Council is my handler. We invented 'classified.'" He straightened and spoke in an even tone: "From here on, listen to *me*, not that soft-headed handler whispering nonsense into your ears. I outrank you. I outrank *him*. Remember that! Now, follow me and you'll get your chance, Mr. Mason. Clyde Evans and the rest will be made an example of today, before they face utter annihilation."

The interior door opened and both men stepped aboard the *Noble Valiant* and moved toward Eisenholm's quarters. "First thing's first," Hawke added. "We get the girl and-"

The door opened a fraction of a second before he could lay a finger on the keypad. Saimon Hawke only caught a glimpse of something glassy and smooth before the crystal bat connected with his head. His world turned to stars and the floor rushed up to meet him. Through unfocused eyes, he saw Gino Ainsworth step over him while Mason staggered aside, clutching his groin. Eisenholm emerged with a sinister smirk on her pale face.

"Monsters..." Was all Saimon could mutter as he watched them scamper away through the airlock to the *Halcyon Infinitum* and struggled to stay conscious. "Stop them, dammit."

* * *

Clyde firmly knocked on Chala'Ran's door with his stance squared, shoulders tensed. Memories of their first outing flitted through his mind, only this time he heard no prayers on the other side of the door. It opened without a word from either party and Clyde flinched, half expecting to find her blocking the threshold. But she was seated at the far end of the room, where she'd pulled up a chair before her large window to watch the clouds race by.

When she spoke, her words were bereft of the force she'd shown earlier: "I have nothing to say. I wish only to pray and focus my mind on the coming battle."

"So why let me in at all?"

"I have nothing to say, but I am willing to listen," said the woman who didn't turn to face him. The irony wasn't lost. Did she expect him to speak to the back of her head, a wall of tight black curls? "I walked out on you and that was rude of me," Chala confessed. "The least I can do is allow you to finish. But our time is short and I wish to meditate while I still can, so I ask that you please be brief, dear."

Dear. The word stung in a way it hadn't before.

"No, I won't be brief. This will take as long as it takes," Clyde said, now standing behind her. "I asked Desmond to fly around the dark side of the planet, the long way. We've got twenty minutes, instead of five. I can make it thirty, forty. Gino and Claire can't afford to wait, but it's all for naught if we fly in there and your head isn't screwed on straight. Since I'm going in *with you*, the least you can do is look me in the eyes and tell me what's wrong, Chala. You can't fly off the handle like that and expect me to pretend everything's okay."

The *Darkstar* broke cloud cover and grazed the pillowy tops of Numira's stratosphere, tracing white lines across the window panes as they raced toward the fringe of space.

When the woman said nothing, Clyde took a seat on the edge of her bed. "Chala, look at me. We're going to settle this *now*."

She half-turned in her chair, crossed one leg over the other, and laced her hands in her lap. Now that they were truly face to face, the sharp lines at the corners of her eyes were clearly visible, as well as the tight set of her jaw.

She was *angry*.

But not at him. He could see that. She bottled it up for his benefit, and her features seemed to soften slightly when she looked upon him, as if she was ashamed of her rage.

"I suppose you are here to punish me. I commandeered your briefing, disrespected the chain of command, and put forth my own agenda in a most disgraceful manner. I accept whatever rebukes you see fit," Chala'Ran said. "But I take back *none* of what I said. I *hate* the Solarans, Clyde. Now you know. I despise them with a passion that is unbecoming of a child of God and, if I had my way, they would burn in an especially hot corner of Hell."

He attempted to speak, but she raised her hand.

"No, let me finish," Chala'Ran said before continuing in a slow, even tone. "If this alarms you, I am sorry, dear. Rest assured, the depths of my hatred trouble me as much as anyone. No one should feel what I feel at this moment. It is a part of myself I have gone to great lengths to refine. *Ten years*, Mr. Evans. I spent ten years teaching myself to relinquish the desire to murder everything that moves. That's how bad this is. Now we have a chance to strike at them and you expect me to show *restraint*? I... I just don't know if I can do that."

"Why?" Clyde asked. "What happened on Ossus to-"

She shot him an icy glare and he abruptly stopped. His fear of her had changed. He knew Chala'Ran would never intentionally harm him, but he began to understand that he could potentially harm her if they continued on like this. There were things he *needed* to know, but at what cost?

The sky outside was already turning from the deep blues and purples of twilight to the inky black of space, speckled with stars. Numira's night side stretched out beneath them as an oily shadow. Chala'Ran transitioned to the bed and seated herself beside him where she could witness the spectacle without putting her back to him.

With a wave of her hand, the chair neatly returned itself to the bedside desk, a drawer opened, and a piece of black cloth floated out. She plucked it from the air and began to tie back her hair, finding solace in such a mundane task.

"I wish I had recognized the ship sooner," she said. "I couldn't tell from the outside, but the internal layout is definitely Solaran. They have technology that allows them to phase through walls. That portion of the ship is reserved for them. An inner sanctum, if you will."

"So that's what S-Deck is?"

She nodded. "The Solarans come from very, very far away. They have no homeworld we know of. Their only 'home' is aboard those ships and they tend to travel together."

"You think the entire Council is here? All twelve?"

Again, she nodded. "They used to come to Alpha Point in such ships. They would take some of us aboard, where some would be *chosen*... but only the most gifted and loyal. Each Solaran has an Acolyte hand-picked from the best the Nemesis Program has to offer. It is the highest 'honor' a Scion can receive."

"Were you chosen?"

Chala'Ran wrung her gloved hands in her lap and studied the ceiling panels and LED lighting. "No. Thank God, Nemesis is as high as I went. I trained at Alpha Point for ten years. It is not like an academy, where you graduate and move on. The best are kept there the longest, to be hardened and honed to perfection. Brainwashed. Indoctrinated. They held on to me until they found the perfect assignment: Ossus III."

"So, you were... twenty-three when you arrived on Ossus?" Clyde said. With brows raised, Chala turned to him and they both couldn't help but smile. "Last time we talked, you said you were thirteen when they took you to Alpha Point. I figured thirteen, plus ten..."

"So, you've taken a vested interest in committing my life story to memory?" she said warmly. "Should I be flattered or wary of your attention, Mr. Evans?"

He merely shrugged. "What happened next? When did you start to hate them?"

The warmth vanished as quickly as it'd come. "You say that as if you want to learn to hate them, too." She took a deep breath. "All the evil happened. I was sent to Ossus III to install a dictator, a man by the name of Rafiq Seryn. The... umm... *colony* there had reached threshold ages ago, but hadn't been brought into the fold. It was too wild, too untamed. They needed a Nemesis to quell the warring factions, so they could begin the reapings.

"It was far too easy. The competition didn't have an answer to me. Battles become very one-sided when you can turn back an armored platoon with a wave of your hand. What you saw on Adi Zahara was nothing compared to the old me," she said with a ghost of pride. "I had no control back then, no restraint. I enjoyed it. I was *trained* to enjoy it. I was a force of nature."

But pride abruptly met hubris. Her pace quickened, only to reach a sudden stop, a wall. It wasn't so much a pause as a collision.

"Don't mistake me," Chala said coldly. "Ossus was a dungeon. The people there were something *less* than human. I know it's wrong of me to say this, but I felt nothing for them and still don't. I killed thousands, but no one was innocent there.

Even after the Reapers arrived and the taxation began, I felt *nothing* when they were lined up like cattle and harvested for Light, sometimes to the point of death. I sometimes held them down as the lightkeepers extracted payment. It was such an ugly place, even the sight of their glittering essence bottled in the keepers was devoid of any sense of beauty."

"You don't sound like you felt nothing."

"Oh, the feelings came later... but not for them," she said, a little too matter-of-factly. "Everyone there feared me, except Rafiq. I was young and impressionable. Twenty-seven is hardly *young*, but when you've been taking orders all your life... I was... I just..." She sighed. "He would tell me where to go, who to kill, how to do it. He was my god."

Chala's gloved fists clenched in her lap, clutching at the surface of her spacesuit, but the tight material yielded nothing she could hold. Clyde offered his hand, but she either didn't notice or didn't accept.

"He was your *handler*," he said. "They played on your emotions to keep you in check."

"I know that *now*," Chala'Ran said quickly, "but at the time I would have moved heaven and earth for that man. I... I thought that was my place. I thought that was *normal*. I fought his war, gave him an empire, gave him my body. Never mind the Registry, the Light tax, and the Solarans secretly pulling our strings. That was *nothing* to me. There was only Rafiq and I. Master and servant. King and queen."

"What happened?"

"My daughter happened," she concluded. "Ossus was a human tragedy. We are such weak creatures. The Solarans didn't make us this way, but... God, did they know how to capitalize on it. Patience. Insistence. Persistence. That is all it takes to turn a mind into a machine, to turn a person into a slave. They make us think what they want us to think because we are too foolish to resist. And when we do, they hurt us and the ones we love in the worst ways imaginable. The Light casts shadows, Clyde. Dark, dark shadows."

She locked eyes with him. The intensity was gone, but the vulnerability he saw there was intense in its own way.

"The only one I ever truly loved was my Roschanna. I rebelled and she paid the price. What he did to her − what I *allowed* him to do to her − is what snapped me out of it and broke their hold over me. I pray you do not have to lose as much before you and the rest of the human race wake up and realize the yoke we have shackled ourselves with.

"They thought they could control me through a man. When I began to see that for what it was, they tried to control me through my daughter's suffering. I unmade everything we did together, every evil. I tore his empire down, brick by brick, and refused to stop, even as his threats against her became reality. My child bore the weight of Ossus's liberation, but *I* will bear the weight of the galaxy's. *No one* can control me."

"You can control you," Clyde said, but she did not seem to hear.

"I wasn't hiding when I went to Adi Zahara. I was reprogramming myself to serve a God of my own choosing. I had to clear the rules, the doctrine, the dogma from my mind, and replace it with something solid, dependable. Something *human*. If you want to go to war with the Solarans − and I *know* you do, Clyde − I strongly advise you to do the same. Clad your convictions in iron because they will make you doubt yourself at every turn.

"First Contact wasn't an alien encounter. It was an *invasion*," she said sternly. "The Infinite Charter is a *lie*. We signed our surrender that day and have been under the gun for two hundred years, too blinded by false progress to see what they are doing to us. Open your eyes, Clyde Evans. Your life is not your own and never will be, as long as *they* are in charge.

"I know this isn't what you wanted to hear. I know you came here expecting me to soften my stance. You came to ask what I will do when we get up there," Chala'Ran said as she took his hand and squeezed it between her own. "You already know the answer to that, Clyde. The real question is, what are *you* going to do? The time for straddling the fence is long gone, dear. If you stand with me, I promise not to allow my passion to cloud *our* purpose."

* * *

Claire took the lead, pulling Gino along by the wrist while he urged her to slow down. The alarms hadn't even sounded yet. They barreled through the halls of the *Halcyon Infinitum* unimpeded. The massive ship may as well be theirs and theirs alone. At this rate, they would defeat themselves, lost in the maze of undifferentiated corridors.

Gino finally had enough and jerked her to a halt so suddenly Claire was nearly yanked off her feet. "What are you running from?" he declared as he yoked her into a small nook, concealing them from unseen adversaries.

Her eyes darted left to right and back again, searching the white-washed corridors for threats. The walls were seamless, with no rivets, panels, or welds, as if the ship were carved from a single block of alien metal. It was definitely Solaran. Gino only noticed it now that they were stopped, but he marveled and, somewhere deep down inside, fear slithered down his spine. Never mind S-Deck, they shouldn't be on *any* deck of this ship.

Claire attempted to capitalize on his momentary lack of focus, but he tugged her back the moment she tried to pull away.

She whimpered about her arm and complained he was being rough, but Gino caught her eyes and urged her to calm down.

"We can't stay on the *Valiant*. Why are you so afraid of this ship?" he demanded hypocritically, but her only reply was a slow sliding gaze to the left, as if nodding off to sleep. "Focus. Clyde and Chala'Ran are coming *here* to grab that machine. We need to get in touch with them and get in position."

She pouted like a child and Gino shook her until her glasses were skewed.

"Dammit, Claire, what's going on? Talk! You've been through this before, right? We can change the outcome if you just tell me what to do differently."

"It's already different. You weren't with me last time, we didn't try to get the machine, and..." She began to smile, "I didn't get to kick Mason in the balls last time. That was fun. I guess things are a *little* better this time."

With a small sigh of relief, Gino released her. "See, things are looking up. Silver linings."

"Doesn't mean anything. Time travel is a crapshoot and I can't afford to try again. Look at me − I'm dying. If your friend puts a gun in my face again, maybe I should just stand there and take it this time. What's the point?"

"Don't say that." As much as he wished he could assure her that wasn't going to happen again, Gino knew enough about Chala'Ran to know she wouldn't hesitate to pull the trigger if she felt it was necessary. The best he could offer was his protection, whatever that was worth. "Hawke and Mason are probably on their way now. We gotta keep moving."

Begrudgingly, she stepped out, made sure the coast was clear, and began to walk, slower now, but more focused. An elevator waited at the far end of the hall.

"She only did it because there was no other option," Claire explained. "You were dead. Clyde, too. The *Darkstar* got blown up. Everything fell apart and we were the last ones left. She *tried*. She even crashed the *Valiant* into the *Infinitum* and took out half a deck, but Hawke survived and there wasn't much she could do to stop a guy made of lightning, even if she can control gravity." Claire shrugged. "So, Charlie said 'sorry' and put a gun to my temple, but I checked out before she could finish. I've never seen anybody fight that hard for me. I've never seen people willing to *die* for me. I don't wanna see that again."

"By 'checked out' you mean you went back in time?"

"Two weeks," she said. "If I could've gone further I would have, but my blacklight was bad... and still is. I figured I'd start where it all went wrong. I tried to take Evans out of the picture. That didn't work. I tried to keep Desmond alive, but that stupid fucker *still* tagged along. I did *everything* I could to change this... but we're right back here *again*." She muttered a string of Russian curses under her breath. "What's the point of time travel if people are too stupid to know what's good for them?"

They reached the elevator and she vanished. There was no fanfare or hocus pocus or puff of smoke. She was there one moment and gone the next. Gino's heart missed a beat.

"Claire!" he called out in a panic. "Claire!"

Seconds later, the elevator doors opened and there she was, grinning. "Did I scare you?"

"Dammit, don't do that! If you're gonna disappear, say something first."

"Awww, you really do care," she teased. "The lift was code-locked. I had to open it from the inside or the alarm would've gone off. I think we should disable this one and use it as a safe room while we wait for the cavalry. It's got a communicator, but I think it can only make calls inside the *Infinitum*."

"For someone so pessimistic about our chances of survival, you're really trying to make this work," Gino said as he stepped inside and the doors shut.

Occupying enclosed spaces with her made him uneasy, but they functioned on the same wavelength. Without being asked, he conjured a screwdriver and they pried open the elevator's control panel together. The ship was a blend of human and Solaran architecture and the elevator had some very human weaknesses. After crossing a few wires, it began to descend.

"How do you do it?" Gino asked. "How do you keep going when you know how it ends?"

"I don't know everything. I told you it's a crapshoot," Claire replied. She crossed some wires and the carriage stopped between levels. "Every once in a while, I get something right and it feels good. I put my head down and say, 'you can do this, Claire, you can *do this*,' even when I don't have a clue what 'this' is… and then I go out and make it happen."

She smiled slightly. "I have a twin sister out there, 'cuz I didn't give up. She turns six soon. She's gonna live a happy life with my – I mean *her* – mom, and nobody's gonna take that away from me," Claire said, but her tone turned frighteningly dark as she added: "*Nobody.*"

"So there are some things you wouldn't change?" Gino said.

"Yeah." Claire shoved the control panel back into the wall. "July 2216 is off limits. For Little Claire's sake, I'll never touch that day or any day before it. And then there's March 2222. That's the day I saved the galaxy from *him*."

"March?" Gino eyed her very closely. "That's when you ditched your crew, took the *Darkstar,* and sent it through a sun. Who did you 'save' the galaxy from? The Stranger?"

"Not yet, but I'm getting there." She gripped the screwdriver tightly. "Once I get back to normal, I'll finish it. I'm gonna take my ship and deal with him, once and for all. Him and the rest of them. You'll see."

* * *

As Ell loaded the *Darkstar*'s main gun, her mind cycled through the thousands of ways she could die just by being near it. The wires stored enough amperage to instantly vaporize her if one shorted out. If it were activated without the shielding, its magnetic field would be powerful enough to rip the iron from her bloodstream, like grains of sand through wet tissue paper.

When fired, capacitors in the *Darkstar*'s belly would dump 15 million amps through the rails and punch a 20 kilogram ferrous slug into space at over 40 times the speed of sound. The gravity drive had to work overtime to keep the weapon from tearing itself apart in the process.

Simply put, it was nothing to toy with. Lines of video distortion danced across her camera lens eyes as Ell opened the access panel and inspected the coils of wires encircling the railgun's barrel, which ran the length of the ship. She didn't have to know what every part did to know it was fast, loud and dangerous − her three favorite things.

Slowly, carefully, she loaded a dozen football-sized rounds into the gun's reserves, handling each like a newborn baby. She'd already worked her gift on them, imbuing them with absurd amounts of kinetic energy. Visions of flaming wreckage half-buried in the Adi Zaharan sand lingered in her mind, memories of her first kill.

With the last slug loaded, Ell lowered the mechanism into the floor, via a hand-cranked lift, and locked it in place with the turn of a large handle. A green light and buzzer indicated the weapon was loaded. Finally, she exhaled.

"Done?" Clyde asked and she sprang up like a cat caught in a sudden downpour. He leaned casually on a doorjamb with his arms folded and a sly look on his face.

"Don't do that!" Ell screeched at him. "You scared the shit outta me. I almost pissed in this fucking spacesuit."

"It probably has a filter for that."

She scowled at him, but found it impossible to stay angry. "How long have you been standing there?"

"Long enough to see you trembling over a gun," he said. "It *is* just a gun, you know, no matter how big it is."

"Hate to break it to ya, but size matters."

"Anyway, are you okay?" he asked as he stepped forward and placed his hands on her shoulders. "You seem jumpy. Chala'Ran is wound a little tighter than usual, but she's fine. Don't *you* start falling apart on me now, Ell."

"Who? Me? Never."

He looked deep into her eyes and asked, "Is there anything you need before we do this?"

"I haven't gotten laid in, like, a month."

"Other than that."

"Nope," Ell said as she knelt and shut the access panel, sealing the beast beneath the leaden floorboards. "One of these days, Clyde…" She wagged a finger at him. "One of these days, you're gonna forget to say 'no,' and I'm gonna blow your mind."

"We're ten minutes away from committing high treason, and that's all you can think about?" Despite his attempt at sounding very serious, his face lost the battle and a slight smile crept in. "Never change, Ell. Never change."

"I won't. Someone's gotta keep you loose. Don't start falling apart on me, Clyde."

"If you two are done," Desmond said via loudspeaker, "we're in communications range and I'm receiving a hailing frequency from the *Halcyon Infinitum*. I suppose you'll wanna answer that, right, *captain*?"

"Patch it through to the ship's intercom. I'll take it in the cargo bay," Clyde said and quickly turned to Ell. "Cover us from the communications room. It's showtime." He placed a hand on her shoulder before he departed for the stairs, but was gone too soon.

* * *

Saimon Hawke paced the *Halcyon Infinitum*'s bridge with an ice pack pressed to his temple, which had already begun to turn a fierce shade of purple. His head throbbed but his mind was as sharp as a razor blade. Behind him, Brock Mason slowly rocked on his heels.

The *Infinitum*'s crew flowed around them, preparing their ship for the fast-approaching blip on their radar. The grim-faced captain stood nearby, eyeing the two Hunters with a mixture of contempt and resignation. In the expansive viewscreen, the *Noble Valiant* drifted across the *Infinitum*'s deck, slowly turning toward the incoming vessel. The *Darkstar* was little more than a rising speck approaching from the planet below, but Hawke watched it with hunger in his steely blue eyes, behind the cracked lenses of his glasses.

The holo display flickered to life with Clyde's face, and Hawke brightened, as if the fires within him had received a splash of new fuel. Ainsworth had struck him with a diamond bat and Eisenholm had buried her foot in Mason's gonads, but the blame rested solely on Clyde Evans's shoulders. *He* was the ringleader of this iconoclastic circus.

"Is this thing on? Do I have audio?" Saimon demanded, glaring at the cluster of technicians hovering around the communications consoles. They nodded and he directed his rage to the digital representation of his archenemy. "Let's cut to the chase, Evans. Can you hear me? I don't know what you're trying to pull here, but we both know how this ends. I have Claire Eisenholm in custody. If you come for them, you're a dead man." He snapped his fingers and turned to the technicians. "Show him."

His wounded pride swelled as the surveillance video of Gino and Claire trapped in an elevator was broadcast to the *Darkstar*. The Chronomancer paced like a caged animal, while her White Knight milled around with his arms crossed and a scowl on his face. They looked more bored than endangered, but it was all the same to Saimon.

Clyde Evans, however, did not seem fazed. He stared blankly, leading Hawke to wonder if the man had heard a word he'd said.

"I'm not playing around," Hawke added. "Ainsworth is trapped and I won't hesitate to kill him. His gift won't save him this time. As for you, my crew aboard the *Noble Valiant* is already obtaining a missile lock on your vessel. I *know* you're coming. Did you think you'd just fly up here and do as you please?

"I'm through playing games. This is checkmate, Evans. Everything you try will come to naught. All offers of amnesty are hereby revoked. By the powers vested in me, in accordance with Article 16, Section 4, of the Registry's Rules and Guidelines, I strip you of rank and privilege and sentence you *all* to death. Come peacefully and I will consider a lesser punishment, but do *not* test my magnanimity, boy. Do you agree to these terms, or do you choose death?"

"Request denied," Evans said dispassionately. "By the power vested in *me*, I render the same terms unto you. I'm on official Registry business, so if you have the right to attack us on public streets and send death squads after us on peaceful planets, I have the right to board your vessel and take Eisenholm by *any* means I see fit."

"You hear, but you do not comprehend," Hawke said between clenched teeth. "Let me explain this in tiny words you can understand: I will permit you access to hangar three on the *Halcyon Infinitum*'s starboard side. I will have the *Noble Valiant* escort you inside. You and your crewmates will be taken into custody and-"

"Let me say it slowly, so *you* can comprehend," Clyde replied. "Request. Denied."

"I don't think you understand the seriousness of your situation, Evans."

"I don't think you understand we're done listening to you!" a screechy female voice added. "Clyde, why are you talking to this jackass?"

"I say we blast this guy away," someone else said off-camera, a man. "Just gimme the word and I'll drop the hammer on this guy."

"No. Let him take the first shot," Clyde said as he bowed his head to don a space helmet.

"You think this is funny?" Saimon said, red in the face. "I am not amused. This is your last warning, Evans. Let's settle this like adults. I want that ship and I'd rather not have to fish the wreckage out of orbit. Why do you think I gave you time to repair it and fly it to me?"

Clyde said nothing for a moment as he secured his helmet and snapped the clasps on its collar into place. "I'm on my way," he said, his voice distorted by the suit's built-in communicator. "The terms are simple: hand over Claire Eisenholm and Gino Ainsworth, alive. If you don't, we will take them by force. You know what this ship is capable of, Hawke. I won't use its full capabilities, but I *will* use just enough to cripple your ship and get what I've asked for. Like you said, let's settle this like adults."

Saimon Hawke's anger bubbled to the point that he was physically shaking. Despite the ice pack gripped in his hand, he looked like a teapot about to boil over. "Your negotiation skills are abysmal. No wonder Mason tried to blow your fucking head off that day!"

Clyde slowly shook his head. "He tried to kill me because of who I worked for. All he saw was a Solaran slave ordering him about… and that's exactly what I see when I look at you, Saimon. You have five minutes to get Claire and Gino in a shuttle. If you don't intend to comply, I suggest you spend that time prepping the escape pods and calling a tow truck."

Saimon threw down the ice pack. "You wouldn't *dare* fire on this ship! To even insinuate such a thing is treason of the highest order! Go on, take the shot, Evans. I dare you! The moment you do, I will have the *Noble Valiant* annihilate you. There won't be enough of you left to serve as kindling in Hell. We will build our own *Darkstar*, just as we planned to do on Numira before your brutish knight came along and ruined it."

"Is that so?" Evans said, uninterested. "Rather than rescue those stranded people, you were going to use them as slave labor? Thank you, Saimon. I see I've chosen correctly."

"Of course you did," Chala'Ran said, joining the debate. "I told you there is no reasoning with these people, Clyde."

"Mahalya!" Saimon spat with contempt. "Speak of treason and here we have the devil herself on the line, you masterless cur. You bit the hand that raised you. Redeem yourself and talk some sense into your 'captain'… if he can even be called such a thing."

"I call him far better things than I would ever call you, dear," Chala'Ran replied serenely.

"If mutual destruction is what you want, so be it. I may not be aboard the *Valiant*, but with one word I can order my crew to open fire on you," Hawke warned. "This is your last warning. One word and we'll shove a dozen missiles up your ass, Evans."

"And I will shove that shiny interceptor up yours without uttering a single word," Chala replied. "Do not tempt me, Mr.

Hawke. You are already on your *second* last warning and I have run out of patience. Clyde, I will be down shortly, so we can get this operation underway. We both know this man has no intention of complying. Mahalya, out."

"See you soon, Chala. As for you, Saimon Hawke... I'll see you too," Clyde said and looked squarely into the view screen, more serious than death itself. Saimon could've sworn the man was peering into his soul, tiny and shriveled as it was. "By the way," he said, "it's not treason. The Solarans aren't a governing body, so attacking them isn't treason. Maybe you should reread that Charter you hold so dearly. I think you've got your facts twisted. The Charter never gave them the right to *rule* over us, only to *trade* with us. Light for technology. Where did it all go so wrong?"

"Is this how you repay them, after all they've done for us?" Saimon said. "Two hundred years of human progress and you bite the hand that feeds you?"

"No," Clyde said. "This is how I repay them for what they've done *to* us."

"You'll burn for this," Hawke said. "We will hunt you to the ends of the universe."

"You've made your choice and I've made mine. A Hunter is all you'll ever be," Clyde said. "See you soon."

– 18 –

Undaunted, the *Darkstar Abyssal* raced upward, banking toward the *Halcyon Infinitum*, dumping scorching flares into the cold vacuum of space as she twisted toward her hallowed target. The defending *Noble Valiant* tried to make good on Hawke's promise and unleashed a barrage of missiles. One hit would be enough to rip her target to shreds, but a spiraling starburst of flares sent the heat-seeking projectiles every which way but home. Slicing through the double-helixed trails of missile smoke, the *Darkstar* swept past the *Valiant* as a rust-colored blur and cut a wide arc through black space, never slowing as she swung around for a second pass.

Desmond worked the pedals and yoke in unison, commanding the ship's vectoring nozzles to pull harder than ever before. After slingshotting around the planet, he had a significant speed advantage and refused to let any of it go to waste. The *Darkstar*'s more powerful engines could accelerate faster than the *Valiant* could react, but the interceptor had a sharper turning radius and could fire again at a moment's notice.

In space, mundane objects became deadly projectiles. Anything, be it a grain of sand or a railgun round, could kill if it carried enough speed. In the vacuum, a loosed shell could travel lightyears and come crashing down on a distant world or obliterate a space station on the other side of the galaxy, decades after being fired.

No one doubted that the *Darkstar*'s main gun could rip right through the *Infinitum*. That was the idea: maximum penetration, with minimal collateral damage. Desmond was given very clear instructions on where to aim this glorified hole puncher: only fire while facing Numira. For all its power, there was no way the railgun could punch through a planet, and a waterworld would absorb the impact with far less trauma than a terrestrial world.

Desmond completed the turn with an ear-to-ear grin and all the world seemed to slow before his eyes. Off the *Darkstar*'s bow, the *Noble Valiant* turned aside, attempting to build speed for evasive maneuvers, but could not move fast enough. The turn only succeeded in making her a wider target. The *Halcyon Infinitum* lay behind her, impossible to miss, and behind them both was Numira, big, and bright, and ready to devour the carcass of the losing vessel.

Flipping open a glass cover on the center console, Desmond depressed a red button and the groan of metal and electric motors signaled the railgun's barrel emerging from the nose of the ship and telescoping out to its full length. Ell finalized the targeting solution with equal parts joy and stoicism, and informed him they were ready to fire just as the *Valiant* unleashed another volley of missiles in a vain attempt at fighting off the inevitable. The *Darkstar*'s defense lasers denied them with surgical precision.

Without hesitation, Desmond squeezed the trigger and returned fire.

* * *

From the bridge of the *Halcyon Infinitum*, Saimon watched the two ships dance around one another. With folded arms, he studied the way the *Darkstar* rolled through the twisting smoke trails of the *Valiant*'s missiles. The crisis was blunted by his inability to accept what was happening right before his eyes. Even as he watched the railgun barrel emerge from beneath the *Darkstar*'s chin, he couldn't accept what was about to happen.

Evans wouldn't do it. Despite what the man had said, he couldn't *possibly* fire on a Solaran capital ship. It was preposterous.

Captain Ridgemond tugged at his arm, barking orders into the Hunter's ear, but Saimon could hear only a dull ringing and the thud of blood pulsing behind his glassy eyes as he stared into the maw of impending doom and all the world fell silent around him.

It took only a millisecond for the *Darkstar* to loose its payload. The projectile erupted forth with a flash of ionized gases and electrical arcs. Almost instantly, the *Noble Valiant*'s port side lit up in a shower of sparks as the shot grazed her titanium skin, slicing a gash along her fuselage before tearing through one of her engine nacelles and continuing on.

After scarring his precious interceptor, the iron round whizzed by the *Infinitum*'s bridge and Saimon lost sight of it as it headed aft. A second later, there was a tremendous crash and the horrific gnashing of metal. Every man and woman on the bridge was thrown to the floor, with the exception of Saimon, who barely kept his footing by maintaining a white-knuckle grip on the nearest computer console.

He still didn't fully process what had happened, even as the alarms blared and an automated voice declared hull breaches in the engineering sector. Crewmen were on their feet immediately and back at their consoles, assessing the damage as they shouted words like "engine four," "reactor breach," and "decompression." Far beyond the window panes, the *Darkstar* sped away and turned for another pass, while the *Valiant* drifted aimlessly, trailing smoke from an obliterated engine.

Someone's hand tugged Saimon's shoulder, trying to get his attention, but he felt nothing. He stared blankly into space, absurdly numb as he observed the graceful movements of the offending vessel. The *Darkstar*'s cargo bay ramp began to open, like the jaws of a demon preparing to spread its venom across the cosmos. This was the monster he was sworn to slay.

Fed up with being ignored, Brock Mason buried his fist in Hawke's gut so hard it brought the Acolyte to his knees. Through the cracked lenses of his glasses, Saimon stared up at his partner as if they were complete strangers.

"Wake up!" Brock demanded and only then did Saimon notice the captain standing beside the big man, red-faced and exasperated. "They've come to us lookin' for a fight and I'm gonna give 'em one, with or without you," Brock said as he hoisted Saimon up by the collar of his white coat. "Get up and let's finish this."

Saimon swayed uneasily, still in a trancelike state. "Yes... let's," he said in a shuddering tone. He'd lost his voice along with his grip on reality.

"You've got one chance to get this right," the *Infinitum*'s captain said. "This isn't a warship and I won't give the lives of my men for you, that girl, or the damn aliens! The entire Council is here and they've only got *one* Acolyte to defend us? This is ridiculous."

This all went in one ear and out the other for Hawke, whose mind was busily ticking down a list of who to kill first. He'd start by dealing with Ainsworth and secure the girl once and for all. Subdue her, sedate her, and lock her in the deepest, darkest hole imaginable.

"I'm going after Eisenholm," he said in an icy tone.

Brock Mason was about to say something, but the topic wasn't up for discussion. Hawke vanished in a flash of lightning. He zapped into the nearest console, causing a flicker of sparks and a flash fire that sent two crewmen scrambling for the nearest extinguisher, and left Mason and the captain staring at the singed patch of flooring where Hawke had stood a moment ago.

"Son of a bitch," the captain muttered under his breath and turned to Mason. "We can survive, but only if you squash this *now*," he said, pointing at the *Darkstar*. "They can't get off another shot from that main gun anytime soon. A ship that small can't crank out enough juice to charge up a railgun in under thirty minutes. Stop 'em before they fire again."

"That's no normal ship," Mason said. He'd seen the same thing Hawke had but, unlike the other man, Mason wasn't blinded by delusions of shattered invincibility. The Solarans weren't gods and their ship wasn't untouchable. To Hawke, what had just happened was a horror story. To Mason, it was beautiful.

Although the shell traveled slowly, it hit as hard as if it'd been fired at full power. It was a magic bullet and Mason knew only one member of Evans's crew was capable of that. "They're firing at half-strength, possibly less," he said as he turned to leave. "Now that they've breached the hull, they're gonna board this ship through the hole they've made… and I'll be waiting for them. I suggest you evacuate your people. Keep 'em outta my way."

Captain Ridgemond's face became hard. "Evacuate? Have you lost your mind!? I can't go down in history as the man who surrendered the Council's flagship to-"

"You'll go down in history as a man who put humans *first*. Fuck the Council," Mason said with a smile that was the stuff of nightmares. "You'll be remembered as a *hero*. We will *both* be remembered as heroes… if we're remembered at all."

Brock Mason laughed a sinister sort of laugh as he turned and departed the bridge.

* * *

The sound of the main gun firing was like steel nails dragging across rusty iron. The cacophony ceased in less than a second, but rang in Clyde's ears for far longer. Even muffled as it was by his spacesuit, it still seemed as if the gun fired freight trains rather than shells. He would gladly go a lifetime without ever hearing such a thing again.

The gravity drive's best attempts at dampening its effects still left enough recoil to jolt the *Darkstar* so sharply Clyde was thrown against the fender of Chala's truck, which is precisely where she found him when she entered the cargo bay a few seconds later.

Still gripping the truck's peeling chrome grille, Clyde looked up in time to see Chala'Ran appear at the top of the stairs. She stepped over the railing and drifted down, like a descending angel. The ballistic overcoat worn over her form-fitting black spacesuit billowed out like wings as she gracefully landed before him. Chala'Ran donned her helmet and approached with neither smile nor flourish, fastening its clasps with every step.

"Can you read me?" she asked, testing the suit's internal communicator.

Clyde replied with a brisk thumbs up.

"Miss Neihaus asked me to give you this." She handed him a small electronic device — a black box of some sort — and he briefly turned it over in his hands.

"Thanks. We can use this," Clyde said before tucking it into a pocket of his suit for safekeeping. "Are you ready? I'm surprised you didn't try to bring your rifle. You seemed rather... *fond* of it."

"Indeed, that is a habit I am trying to break," she said with a slight smile and a fleeting glance at the sidearm holstered on his hip. "Lord willing, we will be in and out without the need for violence. Miss Eisenholm will have nothing to fear from me. Anyway, Mr. Williams says we should leave immediately, while the enemy is in disarray."

"I agree," Clyde said as they moved toward the bay door together, where he pressed a button to open the ramp. "Did we hit our mark? There're no windows down here." A shallow wind tugged at his extremities as the ship's gravity drive clung to a thin atmosphere in the now-exposed cargo bay.

"Roger that. We struck two birds with one stone," Desmond confirmed, reminding them that their communicators shared a single channel and he'd been listening all along. "If you two are done chatting, there's a battle going on."

The vastness of space lay beyond the ramp's edge. The *Darkstar* was in the midst of executing another sharp turn, a maneuver that should be bombarding the hull with half a dozen g's of force. If not for the physics envelope, Clyde and Chala'Ran would be flattened against the walls, not standing on the razor edge of infinity, staring at the silhouette of the crippled *Noble Valiant* slowly turning to launch another swarm of missiles. Behind it, the *Halcyon Infinitum* was trailing thick plumes of smoke from her aft section, where a clean puncture could be seen.

"We should go," Chala said as her fingers intertwined with his and she took the first step toward the void. But Clyde wouldn't be budged. The brick in his stomach migrated to his feet and fastened him to the floor.

"Hold on," he said, his voice trembling. "L-let's wait 'til Desmond gets off the next shot." From the corner of her eyes, Chala gave him a pitying glance, but relented.

"Hang tight, I'm almost there," Desmond replied as the *Darkstar* closed in. "Still waiting for Ell to come up with a targeting solution."

"I'm workin' on it. I've almost got a lock on Gino's tracker, if you'll stop zigzagging like a leaf in the wind. Stay on course and you'll have a targeting solution in eight seconds."

"You're not eyeballin' it are you?" Desmond said. "This is a bad time to start guessing where to shoot."

"That ship is almost two kilometers long, with a crew of less than two hundred," Ell said. "I don't see why we're bothering to aim for the reactors when we could just Swiss cheese the whole damn ship and probably not hit anybody."

"Because we're trying to cripple it, not destroy it," Clyde said. "Pick your shots, Ell. This isn't a video game. '*Probably* not hit anybody' isn't good enough."

The words were meant as much for himself as they were for Ell. Clyde balled his left hand into a fist, to stop it from shaking. His right hand was trapped in Chala's firm grip and he knew she wouldn't let him hesitate a second time. This was happening. No turning back.

Without warning, a blinding flash of blue-white plasma sparked just beyond the edge of the cargo bay and the *Darkstar* jolted under the strain. The railgun had fired and Desmond didn't bother to warn them first. The floor beneath his soles lurched so hard, Clyde was knocked off his feet. He was knocked off his *everything*. The ship jerked one way while he and Chala'Ran went the other, out the open ramp. His free hand reached for anything, but found only air. Soon, he couldn't even find that.

Her hand was the only thing he could trust as they drifted weightlessly into the void. Even as the *Darkstar*'s rusty nose fell away behind him, Clyde didn't fully accept that he was no longer aboard the ship. He remained firmly in denial of the fact that was free floating in the vacuum of space, with only a few layers of synthetic fibers and a polycarbonate helmet standing between his flesh and a grisly death. Chala'Ran gripped his hand all the tighter, giving it a reassuring sqeeze, but he never felt so alone in all his life. This was outer space.

* * *

The violent impact slammed Gino against the wall of the elevator. His head bounced off the aluminum siding, made all the worse when Claire piled into him like a plump ragdoll, sending them both to the floor. The carriage lost its footing and dropped a meter or so, threatening to plummet the full ten stories before its brakes regained a solid purchase on the magnetic rails.

Another shot like that and they would go down. The elevator had seemed like a good idea at first, but this 'panic room' caused more panic than it cured.

"We need to get out of here," Gino said, his voice a hardened growl as he hauled himself out from beneath the pasty girl and offered a hand. Claire seemed too dazed to accept, so he took her by the elbow and hefted her up, leaving faint bruises on her delicate skin.

Her eyes searched his face as he brushed the back of his hand across her forehead to check her temperature. There was another new bruise on her temple, under the fringe of white hair, but her vision was steady and she wasn't running a fever. Claire may be fragile, but they hadn't broken her yet. *Not on my watch,* Gino thought.

"Can you get the elevator moving again? Do that thing you did with the wires," he said. "We need to get to the machine. Evans and that woman are counting on us bein' there and I wanna be gone before this place is crawling with Acolytes. One Hawke is enough."

"There aren't any others," Claire said.

"Are you telling me the Council came out here, to the lawless edge of the galaxy, without their personal guard?"

She nodded.

"...On a defenseless ship, with only *one* interceptor to watch over them?" Gino added.

Claire nodded again.

"Doesn't that seem strange to you? They've left themselves wide open to an attack."

"My head hurts," Claire whimpered as she set about ripping off the control panel again to start the elevator.

"You'll have worse than a headache if this thing drops," Gino said, keeping close in case she needed him to conjure any tools. He felt caged here. Between the lights, he could see a seam in the roof panels; a possible escape route.

Claire fished out a pink wire and a blue one, touched the hot leads together and... nothing happened. She looked around expectantly, tapped them together again. Nothing. "They cut the power," she said, repeatedly joining the leads, but finding no spark. "This should work. Why isn't it working!? They cut the power! They trapped us!"

Gino swatted the wires from her hands. "Stop freaking out. Relax, we'll think of something else. I'm right here, Claire. Look at me."

She rolled her eyes in indifference, which momentarily seemed like a loss, but an apathetic Claire was better than a ranting psycho-Claire. He was learning to work through her mood swings.

"How far can you teleport from here?"

"Do I *look* like I'm in any condition to start teleporting all over the ship?" Claire said and folded her arms across her chest. "You're not getting rid of me that easily."

"Alright, we'll find another way." Gino conjured a simple block of crystal to use as a footstool, so he could reach the ceiling panels. With a few turns of a crystal screwdriver, he had access to the carriage's roof and the dark elevator shaft, where he could hear the buzz of electricity from the magnetic rails lining either side.

Claire was only half-correct. The power hadn't been *cut*. Someone deliberately shut down this elevator and that was all the more reason to get as far away from it as possible.

They know where we are, Gino thought as he knelt and braced his hands. "C'mon, I'll give you a boost up."

"This is so stupid," Claire muttered, but the prospect of trampling all over her gallant manservant was too good to ignore. She gripped his shoulders and, using his linked hands as a rung, climbed up and through the opening. When Gino adjusted his hold to lift her higher, she gazed down at him and winked. "I knew it. You just wanted an excuse to grab my ass again."

Gino grunted with disgust... or perhaps it was a grunt of exertion. She was no featherweight. "I didn't want your ass the first time you threw it at me, why the hell would I want it now?" he said as he shoved her topside. "Get off."

"It was a joke, stupid. I don't even like you, like, at all, seriously," Claire said... whatever that was supposed to mean. "But you're better than nothing, I guess."

She hauled herself out of the elevator and turned to offer a hand, just as the buzzing of electricity intensified, rising to a dizzying crescendo. Claire clapped her hands over her ears, but the noise was deafening. She couldn't hear herself scream over the sound of the red bulbs in the elevator shaft shattering in unison. The lights inside the carriage ebbed with the electrical tide.

This was too much to be a mere power surge. Something was *very* wrong.

That realization saved Gino's life.

The control panel exploded with a blinding flash and a bolt of bluish-white lightning erupted forth. It hit with physical force, knocking Gino against the carriage wall. His crystal armor, conjured an instant before the flash, saved him from instant electrocution.

Saimon Hawke materialized from the forking bolts of lightning and leveled a handgun with the fighter's face. He empted a full clip into Gino's armored helm, pouring all his rage into each impotent bullet.

"Do you have any idea how many kilometers of wiring this ship has?" The mad Acolyte hissed. His finger continued mashing the trigger of the empty weapon, making an obnoxious click. "Do you have any idea how many of them I went through to get to you, Ainsworth? It's a goddamned maze in there, but watching you die will make it all worthwhile."

At last, he flipped the depleted weapon around and proceeded to pistol whip Gino, who finally decided he'd had enough. The fighter stood and tried to tackle Saimon against the wall, but the man vanished in another flash of white electrons. He disappeared into the metal walls of the carriage, which danced with forks of lightning before he materialized behind Gino once more.

"Your Chronomancer's not the only one who can teleport," Hawke sneered. "P-222 was a warning. Now it's serious. I am Saimon Hawke, direct descendent of one of the Original Six. The blood of Elena Halliwell courses through my veins!" he declared, as if this should mean something. "I *will* find a way through that armor, boy, and when I do you will rue the day you crossed-"

Gino swung, but his crystalline fist struck only the wall where Saimon's face had been, leaving a crater in the brushed aluminum panels. Inside his hardened gauntlet, his knuckles were bloodied, while Saimon gloated behind him.

"Trapped in a metal box with the god of lightning. What are you going to do, little man? What *are* you going to do?"

Another shot from the *Darkstar*'s gun rocked the carriage, which dropped another meter, before jolting to a stop as the magnetic brakes regained their grip. Gino lost his balance and was thrown to the floor as Hawke vanished again. The lights went wild, frenzied by a million volts.

"Claire, get out of here!" Gino said as he struggled to his feet. But the girl was long gone by the time the walls came alive. The last of the bulbs exploded as bolts of arcing discharge danced along them, crisscrossing the elevator like the webs of a spider. Hawke had made a thunderstorm in a box, with Gino trapped inside.

He didn't dare move, lest the joints of his armor allow the deadly current inside. He couldn't trap Hawke; the man was *everywhere* at once. There was no evading him, so Gino curled up and sealed every seam of his armor. It grounded the electrical onslaught, but even the greatest resistors had a limit. He could already feel his shell beginning to heat up as the elevator became an electric oven.

Hawke was going to cook him alive.

* * *

Clyde watched as the *Darkstar*'s shot struck the *Halcyon Infinitum* in poetic silence, adding another hole through which they could board. The shot punched clean through and sailed out the other side, where it became a white-hot flash in Numira's atmosphere and continued on, to either burn up or splash down.

"We're going too fast," Clyde said, surprised by the panic in his own voice, suddenly a few octaves too high. He kicked his legs, swimming against nothingness. "We're coming in at the wrong angle. We're gonna overshoot."

"Stay calm," Chala said placidly. Her fingers gave his hand another reassuring squeeze. "I will get us there. Trust me."

They passed under the *Noble Valiant*, far enough away that the enemy interceptor probably didn't notice them. Two humans adrift in space were merely ants in an ocean, dust in the void. But they passed so close Clyde could make out the valley of impacted metal along the ship's port side where the *Darkstar*'s first shot had grazed her, and the thin stream of grayish-green antiproton fuel vapor spurting from her damaged engine, leaving a sparkling cloud of ice crystals. She would be a dead stick within the hour, completely out of fuel and unable to maneuver into anything remotely resembling an attack position.

"Gravity can pull, but it cannot push," Chala said, presumably still trying to calm him, though Clyde's mind had wandered to greener pastures. "I will use Hawke's ship as an anchor to slow us down. Brace yourself."

The gentle tug of an invisible force pulled in the direction of the vessel they'd just drifted past. There were no pressure points, just an all-encompassing embrace, like floating against the tide. Chala's gift touched nothing, but enveloped everything. They were still coming upon the *Infinitum* at a high rate of speed, but Clyde felt himself decelerating rapidly.

The moment he landed, the force suddenly switched vectors. Instead of pulling up, it pulled *down*, fastening him to the *Halcyon Infinitum*'s hull. Although they carried the same velocity, Chala'Ran touched down elegantly, while he crumpled to the deck.

"So that's what flying feels like?" Clyde grumbled as she helped him up. "Seems too much like falling, to me."

Above their heads, the *Noble Valiant* slowly turned, looming like a storm cloud, guided by spurts from its reaction jets. Far away, the *Darkstar* cut a wide turn, its engines twinkling like distant stars as the enemy interceptor unleashed what was probably the last of its dwindling missile reserves. A burst of bright red defense lasers cut down the missiles in flight and a swarm of flares sent the remainder spiraling off course.

"I don't like it out here," Clyde said as he watched the dueling ships. "We need to get inside."

"Agreed. We are too exposed."

Ell joined them, via communicator: "You guys alive down there? I have a read on your trackers. You're about half a klick from Gino's location. Can you see the breach?"

"It's not far," Clyde replied. On a ship the size of a small city, that was saying something. "Give us a few minutes and hold your fire, if possible. I'd rather not have any surprises."

"Got it," Desmond replied. "I'll stick to evasive maneuvers 'til you're in, but I don't think there's much left to evade. Looks like the *Valiant*'s almost outta steam."

"How's the view out there?" Ell asked.

"Beautiful," Chala said pleasantly. Her personal gravitas anchored them to the Solaran ship, negating the need for magnetic boots. Aside from being surrounded by the vacuum of space, the brief trek felt no different from taking a stroll through the park on a summer day.

But, no matter how normal it might feel, 'beautiful' was not the word Clyde would use to describe a spacewalk in the middle of a warzone.

They reached the hole soon enough. The *Infinitum*'s surface sloped toward the breach and the violence of impact left the metal increasingly agitated as they descended the ever-steepening gradient. The bulkheads had bubbled in some places, boiled by the heat. Bent, twisted pieces of steel and plastic, scorched and mangled beyond recognition, jutted out at grotesque angles, putting the ship's architecture on display.

The floors and ceilings of every level were laid bare, like rock layers on a canyon wall. Severed plumbing spewed vapor into space, where the vacuum boiled water instantly, before freezing it. Wires dangled precariously, and girders pointed every which way, like the branches of an angry metal forest.

Debris drifted in the weightless void around the hole, where it'd been driven out by the forces of decompression. Here, a desk. There, a lamp. The floaters abruptly dropped as Chala'Ran drew near, captured by her gravity field. She stood over Clyde's shoulder as he knelt at the ragged edge and peered down into the breach they'd created. He could see clear through to Numira on the other side.

"I found the hole," he relayed to Ell. "It's, umm... big enough to crawl through."

"I can lower us in," Chala offered.

"You're gonna need to go down three levels," Ell explained. "Gino's somewhere 'tween the third and fourth decks, near sector J. He doesn't seem to be moving. Meet up with him and Claire, then head to the machine, which is on third in G. If you plug in the black box, I'll be able to hijack their security systems, open doors for you guys, and throw off their surveillance. Hull breaches probably got the whole ship on lockdown. I'll need to override that to get you guys in."

* * *

Blaring alarms announced a second hull breach mere minutes after the first. When would it stop? The captain's voice spilled from the garbled intercom, ordering crewmen here and there and everywhere, summoning emergency responders to the latest breach and engineers to the aft section in a failing attempt at holding together his tortured ship.

They had no idea what hit them. They had no idea the enemy ship was armed with an even more powerful weapon than what was already hammering them. The *Halcyon Infinitum* could not win. This entire encounter was engineered to assure that outcome.

I tried to tell you, you old fool, Brock thought.

He waded through the steady stream of feckless humanoids fleeing ground zero. Trained Registry officers, their faces contorted in terror and confusion, scrambled through the halls like rats. Brock was unfazed. This was *his* battle and would be *his* victory. The battle over Numira and the death of the *Halcyon Infinitum* would be his masterpiece. Giving that victory to Clyde Evans was a mistake.

He shouldered his way through the opposing tide, splitting them like an icebreaker. "You can't go that way! Stop!" a technician in a bright orange vest warned at a juncture. Brock muscled through the man and continued on. His surroundings became increasingly depopulated until he was alone in a corridor strewn with debris, and tuned his ears to the silence.

"Where are you?" Brock muttered under his breath as he unclipped his sidearm, a nickel plated submachine gun, and slowly made his way down the rows of abandoned offices, with their empty desks and conference tables. "I know you're here, Evans. I know you're coming."

The air had the stale smell of a used vacuum cleaner bag. The far end of the hall was blocked by a sealed bulkhead. Beyond it was the airless void created by decompression.

Perhaps he'd misjudged. He thought Evans would surely be here, at the latest hull breach. Brock Mason lowered his weapon and, with it, his pulse dropped and his shoulders slumped. *Damn it all.* He would try again elsewhere. They would be at the next hull breach, he was sure. If not there, the next. He would find them. He would find Evans, dammit.

An office desk flipped up so suddenly he barely had time to react. The heavy chunk of black oak furniture came sailing at him, computer and all. Anyone with good sense would've ducked it. Instead, Brock planted his feet and plowed the object aside, barreling through it with his burly shoulder leading the way. He caught a glimpse of someone moving from one cubicle to another, and raised his weapon, but a trio of office chairs came flying at him from another angle.

Smarter now, he caught the first chair, used it to swat the second and third, and then hurled it back at his attacker, whose identity he'd already guessed. The thrown chair halted mid-flight, frozen in place, and Brock Mason retaliated by detonating her cover. The desk under which Chala'Ran Mahalya was hiding exploded in a shower of splinters and she spilled out onto the floor. The chair abruptly dropped.

The game was on. A very pleased Brock Mason raised his weapon. Dumping a thousand rounds per minute into her fine ass seemed more satisfying than simply blasting her to pieces. She would make a pretty corpse. But a sudden pressure on his temple changed his mind.

"I wouldn't do that if I were you," Clyde said, pressing the cold muzzle of a handgun to the man's head. "Let's slow things down, big guy. No need for anyone to get hurt."

"She threw a desk at me," the big man muttered.

"Because we knew you could take it," Clyde said. "She could've done a lot worse." The woman was already getting to her feet and, unless looks could kill, appeared to be unarmed.

"How did you find us so soon?" she asked. "Who else knows we've boarded?"

"You knocked. I answered," Brock Mason replied, quite amused with himself. He pointed up. "Everyone will know soon enough. The security cameras…"

"We have someone on top of that," Evans replied. "Your surveillance system belongs to us now, which means no one will know if you just walk away and pretend you never saw us here.

This isn't your fight, Mason. You don't even *like* the Registry or the Solarans."

"They ain't so bad." Mason laughed. Every hearty chuckle posed the risk of setting off Evans's trigger finger, but the man didn't care in the slightest. "*She* can walk," he nodded to Chala'Ran, "but you and I have unfinished business, Evans."

Mason moved surprisingly fast for his size. He buried a fist in Clyde's gut and the Hunter lost his weapon as Mason's knuckles twisted into his spleen and rocked him from his ribs to his spine. Mason could've gunned Evans down right there, while he was dazed and wheezing for air. But he hadn't chased him halfway across the galaxy to let bullets do his dirty work. Instead, he tossed aside his weapon as well, and laid a three-punch combo into his stunned adversary.

"I can't believe he chose *you*. You don't deserve to be the one who starts this war," Mason said as he easily lifted the man up and slammed him atop the nearest desk. "You never had the courage to stand up, until we *forced* you to. That's not courage!" He raised his fist, poised to drive the next blow right through Clyde's chest and rip his heart out with his bare hands. "You wanna start a revolution? Okay. I'll make a martyr of you, right here."

Chala'Ran caught him by the forearm and pulled him away. "You will do no such thing," she firmly declared as Mason whirled around.

His wild fist caught only air as she bobbed away from his blows. In the heat of the moment, he didn't calculate *why* she was there. He didn't ask *why* she'd chosen hand-to-hand combat over tossing another desk at him or using her gift to immobilize him. They traded a dozen swings before backing off. Panting, they stood apart, stances squared. Only then did he figure out what her presence meant, as Clyde Evans got to his feet, clutching his bruised midsection.

Brock Mason tried to use his gift. He focused on the woman in front of him, and imagined her molecules igniting and detonating with the force of her weight in dynamite... but nothing happened.

"Ohhh, I get it." Mason roared with laughter. "You can't block *me* without blocking *her* too. Is that what this is, Evans? Are you really that weak? Fucking amateur! Why'd he choose *you*, of all people?"

"Eyes on me," the woman said and came in with a straight jab. Brock caught her arm and went for a takedown, but she somehow got her feet under herself and countered him, sending him staggering through a glass partition. He took it the way a bull takes a China shop.

"Not bad for an old dame," he said, brushing shattered bits of glass from his uniform. "Hawke talks about you like you're the shit and the flies with it. Some kind of history between you two?"

"I've never seen him before in my life," Chala'Ran said as she circled around, keeping her distance. "Perhaps the reason he speaks so lowly of me is because he worships the ground the Solarans walk on, the same ground I *spit* on. He is a willing slave and I am his liberator. The thought of freedom physically sickens him."

"Heh, that sounds about right," Mason replied with a smile. His eyes flicked to the other man. "See, Evans, *that*'s what a revolutionary sounds like. Not you, Registry dog."

"Chala, get out of here. I'll deal with Mason," Clyde said, finally finding his second wind.

She sharply turned. "I will not leave you with this-"

"Check your comm. Gino's in trouble and Claire took off. Ell is tracking a major power surge in his vicinity. It's gotta be hawke. You need to go *now*," he said desperately, before turning his attention to Brock Mason. "I'm the one he wants. Isn't that right, Brock? You don't care if we get Claire or not, do you? It's *me* you're after."

Brock Mason snickered as he shed his slick uniform jacket with its Registry badging. He tossed it aside and rolled his thick neck muscles as he cracked his knuckles.

"We don't have time for chauvinistic grudge matches," the woman said to Evans.

"It's all an act," Clyde said. "Mason's not stupid. On his last assessment he had an IQ of 139. All the steroids and gene therapy in the world won't change that. He's a fucking mastermind, pretending to be a meathead. I'm not walking away 'til I figure out what the hell he's up to. *You*, on the other hand, need to go."

"Better listen to your boy," Mason chuckled. "Get lost, lady. You ain't his mama."

With a sigh and a piercing glance, Chala relaxed her stance. "So help me God, if anything happens to him, Mason, I will *find* you and-"

"I'll have him home by midnight, promise."

"Nothing's going to happen," Clyde added, sizing up his opponent. "He just wants to have a few words with me. Isn't that right, Brock?"

After a moment of hesitation, Chala'Ran began to back away, toward the hall. "Such a shame," she said. "You dishonor your wife's memory, Mr. Mason."

"You don't know shit about her!" the big man barked, as he snatched up the nearest object he could grab and hurled it at the empty spot where she'd been. But Chala'Ran was long gone. By the time he turned again, Clyde Evans was in his face. The first blow struck the side of Mason's head with more force than expected. His vision doubled as he staggered back, clutching at the edge of a desk to keep from falling.

"I don't know her either," Clyde Evans admitted, dropping the keyboard he'd just brained the man with. "But I know letting that lightkeeper go was the best thing I could do for you." He grabbed Mason by the collar and delivered a solid right hook that rocked the big man backwards. "Anyone else would've blown your fucking head off and turned her Light in, but I *didn't*. It felt wrong, so I didn't do it! Call me a 'Registry dog' one more fucking time! Do you have any idea how many rogue Scions I've let slip away, how many orders I've disobeyed? If I had a credit for every time I turned a blind eye to a runaway, I'd be able to buy your freedom, mine, *and* hers."

"Why buy it? I was going to *fight* for it!" Mason barked as he staggered away, trying to grab anything he could find to fight back or steady himself with. "Now look at me, working for the same bastard who signed *you*."

He turned to the side and spat blood before lunging at Clyde again, but the Hunter sidestepped him and drove Mason's head into a desk. Or a table. It was hard to tell. Next thing Brock knew, he was on the floor, seeing double again and fighting to remain conscious.

"I didn't come after you because someone *told* me to," Clyde said over his downed opponent. "You were plotting to bomb half a dozen Light collection centers all over the east coast. You got a problem with the Solarans? *Fine*, get in line with the rest of us. But when you wanna kill *innocent* people to get your point across, you're going to have to get through *me* to do it." He pointed to himself. "If murdering people is your idea of a 'revolution' you've got a problem with *me*, Brock. Now get up and solve it."

Mason was slow in recovering from the beating. Clyde waited, pacing a small patch of linoleum, his spaceboots crunching on the debris-strewn floor, while the man sluggishly rose first to his knees and then to his feet.

"What I can't seem to understand is *why* they would take you back," Clyde said, though the words seemed distant and hollow to the toppled giant. "You're insane. You're a damn time bomb. What could they possibly expect to get from you other than *more* destruction?"

Brock Mason grinned, his teeth stained red with blood as a thick knot swelled on the side of his head. "Stop saying 'they.' Only *one* Solaran wanted me back, you idiot. The rest of them hate me as much as they hate you. We work for the same person, you moron. You thought The Stranger was *human*? Hahahahaha!"

Brock kept talking, knowing his words bought time while his eyes searched for his discarded weapon.

"Claire's not the first Scion he asked you to capture. You were doin' The Stranger's dirty work before you even knew he existed. He needed an inside man and you *delivered* me to him," the big man said.

There it was, his gun, half-buried in plaster and rubble, almost within reach. Brock inched toward it... "Wake up. He's playing both sides, Hunter."

"You're lying," Clyde said, though the tremor in his voice betrayed him.

Brock dove for the submachine gun and gleefully wrapped his fingers around the prize. But, as he turned to take aim, Clyde Evans reached behind himself and produced *his* gun. He must've picked it up amidst the chaos. In one swift motion, Evans shoved the barrel into Mason's eye socket.

"Explain!" he said, with a stern finger on the trigger.

To Brock, Clyde Evans had always seemed like a boy in men's pants. All talk, no action. The type of 'man' who doesn't know how to squeeze a trigger unless there's nothing but clear air and smooth sailing in front of the muzzle. But, as he looked into those cold brown eyes, he realized he couldn't be more wrong.

"You like to know how the world works," Mason said. "Finding out the gears don't turn the way you thought they do scares you, doesn't it?" He grinned. "I'm the machine, Evans. *You're* the wrench in the works. But we're the same, you and I."

"I'm only going to ask this once," Clyde said, with the gun still poised to paint the walls with Mason's brain if the man so much as flinched the wrong way. "Why are we here? A defenseless capital ship, in the middle of nowhere, with the entire Council aboard it, comes face-to-face with the only ship in the galaxy that can utterly obliterate it in one shot? Why!? It's too convenient, too easy. I know a set-up when I see one, Mason. We were lured out here and forced into a confrontation we can't lose. What the hell has The Stranger gotten us into? What the hell were we put here to do!?"

"Just like a dog," Mason sneered. "You can't even lift your leg without your master's permission. A Hunter is all *you*'ll ever be." He laughed. "You're here to murder the Council, stupid… but I'm gonna kill you and do it myself."

– 19 –

No matter which way she turned, it was all the same, each angle a mirror image of the last. Floor, ceiling, walls – if there were any – were all the same pure shade of white, without so much as a shadow or hard line for reference. No dust, no dirt, no earthy, human presence, but her own. Claire staggered back, disoriented by the blankness of it all, unsure if she was standing, falling, or floating. She reached out, groping in the blinding light, but found nothing.

Her legs trembled. The solid ground beneath her was all she could trust, but Claire didn't dare plant her feet here. This was *their* territory. To loiter here was to die.

In an instant, she'd broken two rules. First, she'd left Gino behind. Second, she went where she said no one should go: S-Deck. She'd lost control and everything was falling apart again.

Claire swayed unsteadily. The tremors began at her fingertips and worked up her arms until her entire body shivered, and only then did she realize how labored her breathing had become. Her lungs burned. Though the ticker in her chest kept a steady beat, she could feel the frailty of the life pumping through her veins and knew how easily it could be snuffed out by the heartless creatures who called this place home.

If she hadn't shut her eyes, she would've seen the colors forming, a transcendent glow of mingled blues and reds. Purples and oranges coalesced around her. Distant at first, the luminous crowd converged, like a gathering of St. Elmo's fire or spectral wisps coming to inspect the weak flesh in their midst.

Voices, more emotion than sound, tore at the corners of her mind, nipping at her subconscious. A swirling red cloud hung over her, hurling insults she couldn't hear, but could *feel* like physical blows trying to dismantle the legitimacy of her existence. A shade of orange joined the attack, brimming with hate, until the thoughts became actual pain. Claire felt warmth on her upper lip and found black blood dripping from her nostrils.

She cupped her hands to her ears, but it did no good. She could still feel them in her mind, planting barbs of spite and wishing suffering on her. A pale purple shadow lingered on the outskirts, watching as if overcome with shy curiosity, unable to turn away, but too introverted to join in. A deep blue fog loitered at her feet, lazily observing the onslaught. Claire could feel its lethargy creeping into her, urging her to relinquish her hold on her mind and life itself. She began to notice more colors surrounding her, overwhelming her with feelings that weren't hers. Giving up would be so easy…

But just as she reached her limit and began to sink down to her knees in pain and exhaustion, a burst of yellow revitalized her, like a golden lightning bolt splitting the multicolored clouds. Claire staggered back as it encircled her, driving back Red and Orange, the two most vicious assailants. Blue and Purple slowly departed, leaving only the three fiery hues. Orange was the first to fall. It slunk away, defeated, but still flinging barbs of hate at Claire's mind as it retreated. Red and Yellow continued circling one another in a visceral embrace.

By the time the red phantom was finally driven away, Claire had sunk to the floor, with her knees to her chest and her eyes shut tightly, no longer caring what the outcome might be. She saw nothing, but could feel a weight lifting as the savage presence of the Red Solaran faded away. Only then did she dare peek out and find the yellow specter still lingering above her, like a halo of color. It spoke without words, requesting she follow it.

Now it was her turn to project hatred. Claire didn't have to *say* anything. She knew he could hear her and she him. These beings had evolved past the need for spoken words.

I hate you, she said to the creature that had caused her so much grief and suffering, the one who had brought her out of Odessa and to the edge of the universe on a journey she never wished to take and who now *dared* to ask her to go a few steps further.

But she followed anyway as The Stranger quickly led her through the hollows of S-deck. He urged her to hurry and transmitted thoughts of impending confinement. If they didn't move quickly, they would be sealed inside. The walk was short, but every step of the way she kept a wary eye out for the other Solarans, the ones who wanted her dead.

In the blinding whiteness, Claire almost didn't notice the partition. She would have walked into it, like a bird flying into a glass door, had The Stranger not warned her. Claire teleported to the other side while her ethereal guide fazed through the wall. Once they crossed, a barrier activated, preventing passage. He sealed the others in.

I can take care of myself, Claire projected angrily, despite the throbbing in her skull and the tremors in her fingertips. Each use of her gift drove her closer to death. Even trivial acts were becoming detrimental to her health.

She found herself in a simple lounge, with two white couches and a low table between them. On one side was a desk with an office chair, where an empty Solaran suit lay, like a deflated skin. On the other side was a bay of large windows.

Outside, the *Durkstar Abyssal* circled a heavily damaged *Noble Valiant*. An open panel on the side of the wounded interceptor revealed an escape pod. Hawke's crew was abandoning ship, but this was nothing new to Claire. She'd seen it before, only not from this vantage point, not from S-Deck.

Large portions of the *Infinitum* were completely dark, or flickering with rolling power outages. As she watched, a massive explosion ejected fragments of glass and metal into space. The debris lit up like candles as it fell away into Numira's atmosphere and burned. The explosion was too messy to be the result of the railgun strikes. It was like a bomb went off inside the ship. *This* was new.

Mason, she thought. He was tearing the *Infinitum* apart from the inside.

Behind her, The Stranger's spectral form fazed into his empty suit, animating it with the Solaran equivalent of life. He stood from the chair, with the suit's electric motors whirring as he rose to its full seven foot height, slender and long, like a snake with limbs. Claire watched without watching, observing his reflection in the glass, while refusing to look at him directly.

"This ship will fall," The Stranger said, his voice a deep, synthesized monotone, echoing from somewhere within the humanoid suit, a black and blue affair, faceless and mechanical. At least in this form they could communicate as equals, without him worming his way into her mind. "Mr. Mason is attacking the gravity drives, just as I ordered him to. There is much I would like to say, Miss Eisenholm, but you should not have come here. This is a dangerous place and our time is short."

"You think I came here on purpose!?" Claire retorted. "Why would I ever want to see *you*? I don't trust you! I don't like you!

I don't want anything from you and don't you *dare* ask anything of me!"

Yet here she was. Somewhere in her subconscious, she wanted this meeting, otherwise she would not have instinctively teleported to his location. Claire rested her head on the glass and watched the destruction unfold in a longing, almost dream-like state.

For a while, The Stranger said nothing. He lowered his lanky body into the office chair, folding the way a giraffe bows to a watering hole, but slow and mechanical. There he sat, thinking. But Solarans had no need for deep thought; they were creatures of impulse and singularity.

Thought was merely the time it took to rearrange the synapses and neurons within the human brain to dredge up an idea buried in the folds of gray matter. Solarans had evolved past such organic inefficiency.

"This is stupid," Claire said, dabbing at her eyes and bloodied nose. "Talk, Solaran. You chased me all across the galaxy for this, so *talk!* But I want you to know I'm not doing this for you. It's for *them*," she pointed to the glass. "They've come too far not to get an explanation. Start talking, dammit."

"That is all I ever wanted," he replied. "All I ever wanted was to speak with you."

"Liar!" she wheeled around to face him, her eyes pink with tears that refused to form. "I did as you asked and it nearly killed me! Was that your plan? To send us to the edge of the universe, so your friends back home can see what human Light tastes like?"

She swore she saw him flinch at the accusation, but Claire cruelly went on, without missing a beat: "You thought we'd 'talk' to them? You thought they'd be friendly? What the hell did you expect us to find there, if not a world of Light-hungry savages? Your people are monsters, Solaran! Your planet is Hell itself.

And *you...*" Claire's body trembled as her anger overcame her and she turned to face the glass once more, unable and unwilling to look at him – *it* – any longer.

The Solaran stood. From the corner of her eyes, Claire watched the lanky figure approach. She felt compelled to order it not to come any closer, but by the time she summoned words to her lips, it had already ceased its advance. The Stranger had no intention of drawing nearer than was comfortable for her and it seemed to know exactly where that boundary was. It waited with its long, thin metal fingers intertwined, watching as they always do.

"This suit gives me a voice," The Stranger said, "so we can speak with words. But words have limits. Words stand in place of ideas. I would rather speak mind-to-mind, but I know how that makes you feel, Claire, so words must suffice." It paused, as if hunting for proper phrasing. Perhaps it *did* have thoughts after all, like a human. "No words can express the look I saw on your face the day we parted. My only desire is to know what happened. What did you see? Why did you try to destroy me? And where do we go from here?"

Claire scoffed, struggling to keep her eyes on the window, while still watching him –no, *it*– in her peripheral vision.

The Stranger continued: "The truth is, I am young by Solaran standards. We do not reproduce the way humans do. We are creatures of Light, like you, but without flesh. We do not require a vessel, the way human Light does. This mechanical suit is only a shell, for your benefit," it explained, gesturing to itself.

"When a Solaran grows too powerful, it divides, and the thoughts, memories, and experiences of one are split amongst two or more. When we pass on, all that we were is divided amongst our kind. I suppose... *cannibalism* is in our nature. That is the Solaran life cycle. Fragmentation and redistribution. Nothing lost, nothing gained."

Claire impatiently tapped her foot as he continued:

"I am the child of a child of a child, a fragment of a fragment of a fragment. Pieces of those who created the Infinite Charter reside within me, but I am *not* them," The Stranger said. "I beg you to understand that."

Claire turned up her nose.

"The knowledge of *how* and *why* we arrived on Earth is as much a mystery to me as it is to you and your kind," The Stranger explained. "Whatever we once knew has been divided again and again. I do not know the *full* story of First Contact and I doubt any amongst us does. Lately, they have lost the inclination to share knowledge with me... so I took it upon myself to *find* our homeworld and reach out to it, the only way I knew how."

Claire watched the window, forcing herself to show no sympathy or emotion. She silently reassured herself she was only biding her time, resting until she was stable enough to teleport out of here and back to Gino. Time was running out... but time was a luxury she would always have, right?

"Get to the point, Solaran," she said.

"I am. If you do not wish to speak to me, please allow me to explain myself to you, at length," The Stranger requested. "We both know you can undo this conversation if you feel it has dragged on too long, Miss Eisenholm. Nothing is holding you here. Even in your current state, you are capable of traveling back ten or fifteen minutes, yes, to a time *before* you came to S-Deck?"

Claire muttered a Russian swear under her breath and kept her eyes on the window. She hated the way he seemed to know her so well. They had almost been friends once, but that was before she knew what he is.

"You want an explanation for my actions. I am giving you one," The Stranger said. "I have seen the horrors that emerge from this mad exchange of Light and technology, this biased symbiosis between humans and Solarans. We are bleeding your people dry, little by little. I refuse to believe this is what we were sent here to do... *if* we were sent at all. I refuse to believe this was our destiny. Therefore, I did what anyone would do when he begins to question the path he is on: I traced it back to the source.

"Our homeworld's exact location is unknown to me, but vague images of it exist in my mind. For decades, I struggled with what to do with this knowledge... until I heard of a young lady who could teleport anywhere she wished. All she needed was an image, a means of visualizing her destination, and she could take me there. I earned her trust and built a ship to magnify her power, in the hopes that we could reach my homeworld and learn the true nature of my people."

Claire laughed, loudly. She doubled over, clutching her sides. The Stranger abruptly stopped and waited, shifting uneasily on its metal feet, as if unsure if she was okay and unsure if it should inquire about her wellbeing. But, just as abruptly as it had began, her laughter ceased. Claire sobered with crushing suddenness and whipped around to face him. She bravely marched up to the Solaran and stared into the blank metal plate which served as its face:

"Oh, I saw your *true nature* alright," Claire said, nose to nose with the creature that had sent her to the edge of the universe. "The moment the *Darkstar* appeared, your people descended on the ship like piranhas in a feeding frenzy. They wanted our Light. They fazed right through the walls, the floors, the ceiling... they started tearing into my crew, sucking the life out of them!" With a sharp finger, she prodded his synthetic mesh chest piece. "Your 'exploratory mission' got them all killed! I couldn't let that happen."

"So you traveled back in time to abort the mission? You traveled back to when the *Darkstar* was still loitering over

Numira, in the final phase of its testing? Now I see why you looked upon me with such contempt that day..." The Stranger hung his head in shame, a very human gesture. "Claire, I am sorry."

"Wanna know what the worst part was?" she said, panting and wheezing between sobs, while he just stood there, like a lanky extraterrestrial sculpture. "You were *there*, you son of a bitch. You were hiding on the *Darkstar* the whole fucking time. It was bad enough seeing those monsters closing on all sides, but when I saw you were *one of them*-"

"How else was I to reach the homeworld? I had to be on the ship, Claire. But if I had told you what I was, you would never have journeyed with me aboard. No one trusts a Solaran. Stowing away on my own ship was the only way I could accompany you."

"Well, you chose a hell of a time to reveal yourself," Claire muttered and turned away from him again. She folded her arms and tried to look like the bigger person, which was hard to do with every inch of her body trembling. Just thinking about that day gave her chills. "If you people would stop trying to be so goddamned mysterious all the time, maybe we'd trust you once in a while. How was I supposed to react?"

"We are a mystery even unto ourselves," The Stranger said. "My attempt at unraveling that mystery has caused you pain and suffering. I cannot apologize enough."

A distant explosion rocked the room and a white flash illuminated the window, showcasing a blast which tore away nearly a fifth of the *Halcyon Infinitum*. Claire lost her footing as the floor shifted beneath her. It wasn't just the blast that had thrown her off her feet. The ship was literally dropping out from beneath them. She could feel a slow, subtle shift, like a rollercoaster at its precipice. The *Halcyon Infinitum* was falling.

"Our time is up," The Stranger said as he set her back on her feet. Wait, when had he caught her? Claire looked at the talon-like bruises his metal grip had left on her pallid skin. He had not handled her roughly, yet she felt violated by his touch... but relieved all the same.

"This ship is going down and it will take the Council with it," The Stranger said, gesturing to the window. "My Acolyte and I lured the *Darkstar* here, cornered them, provoked them, and now I have sealed the Council in the central chamber. That is what I meant when I said you should not have come here, Claire. You were supposed to depart with Evans and make sure he uses Desmond's superweapon. All of the pieces are in place. This plan hinges on the absolute destruction of the *Halcyon Infinitum* at the hands of the *Darkstar Abyssal* – a human vessel must destroy an icon of Solaran power."

"Damn Solarans and their plans," Claire muttered.

"Yes, I know," the alien said, "but change will not come from the far end of the universe. I was mistaken in thinking I could change this world by traveling home. It starts *here*. I saw this in your eyes the day you tried to kill me by flying the *Darkstar* through a sun. Light cannot be destroyed by mortal means but, after studying human history, I have concluded violence is the best catalyst."

"You can't pin this on us," she exclaimed.

The Stranger gestured to the window as the *Darkstar Abyssal* emerged from a small hangar, presumably with Evans, Mahalya and –she hoped– Gino safely on board. But, rather than flee, the ship hovered close to the dying *Infinitum*, clinging to a desperate hope that they might find her inside and make a last-minute save. They'd crossed the galaxy to find the Chronomancer and would not give up, no matter how dark.

"There are other ways, but this is the path I have chosen," The Stranger said as he unclipped something from his suit and placed it in the palm of her hand. It appeared to be a data storage device of some kind, a smooth mirrored sphere.

"I know you told me not to ask anything more of you, but please hear me out. You have two options," he said. "Option number one: teleport onto the *Darkstar Abyssal*, leaving me and the rest of the Council to our fate. You escape and we all go down with the *Infinitum*. Or option number two..." he pointed to the window and the searching starship, "travel back to *before* this conversation, when we *both* had time to escape."

"What does it matter? Either way, the Council goes down," Claire said, but as she looked at the energy barrier between them and the rest of S-Deck, something dawned upon her: "You'd be the only Solaran left in the galaxy. This is a coup? You son of a bitch..."

The Stranger's shoulders slumped. "If that is how you see me, perhaps we have not reached an understanding after all." He closed her fingers around the data sphere, which was like none she'd ever seen before, black as the depths of space. "Solarans cannot die. This ship will be destroyed all around them, but in a few weeks or months, the Council will be recovered and return to power. The question is, do you want months with *no* Solarans or months with *one* Solaran you can trust? In their absence, *I* can make a difference."

A heavy silence fell before he added, "I am *trying*, Claire. *This* Solaran is trying to make things right. Whether you believe me or not, you have a choice to make..." The room shuddered as the *Infinitum* began to enter Numira's atmosphere. "...And very little time to make it."

* * *

Claire gasped. When her eyes snapped open, she was lying in an empty hall, under flickering lights. Her stomach wrenched as a bout of nausea tore at her insides and for a moment she feared she might vomit. She lifted a hand to her mouth in anticipation and it came back dabbed in black blood. That and the Solaran data sphere clenched tightly in her fist proved that the encounter had not been a figment of her imagination.

Her hearing soon caught up with the rest of her senses. The distant sounds of gunfire drew nearer. She wasn't safe here. Claire stuffed the sphere into her pocket and her trembling hands stretched out, searching for the nearest wall to steady herself. She found the smooth metal of an elevator door and could hear Gino's muffled groans somewhere inside, punctuated by the crackling hiss of arcing electricity. He was still fighting Hawke.

A sudden blast tore her attention from the elevator. A cracked riot shield sailed across the hall from an adjourning corridor, followed by the body of a guard dressed in ballistic gear. The unfortunate man struck the wall hard and slumped down, just as three more like him came flying after, with their weapons and equipment.

"You were warned," Chala'Ran said as she stepped out, planted the muzzle of a 'borrowed' rifle in a man's face and dumped three rounds into him. She ejected her spent magazine, flipped the gun around, and reloaded with machine-like precision. Déjà vu...

What little color Claire had promptly drained from her face as she scrambled to her feet and flattened herself against the wall, trying to escape this nightmare.

When 'Charlie' spotted her, the woman's eyes widened. "I... I... umm..." She dropped the rifle as if it were made of hot coals and raised her empty hands in a gesture of peace. "Claire... I... I am sorry you had to see that," the woman said, nodding to the dead men as she slowly approached. "I understand you and Mr. Ainsworth ran into some difficulties. I am here to... umm... smooth them over. I will not harm you, Claire."

Claire's head was swimming. She felt ill and barely comprehended the woman's words, but nodded anyway. Once Chala'Ran was close enough to hear the sounds coming from the elevator shaft, she slowly moved past Claire, while trying to be as non-threatening as possible, and put her ear to the door.

"Gino's still alive." Chala'Ran drew a combat knife and Claire flinched. "Stand back, dear, I'm going in."

"Aren't you going to ask where I've been?" Claire said hoarsely. "Or why I left him?"

Chala turned to her, curiosity etched on her elegant features. "Ell had you on the security cameras almost the entire time," she said and began prying open the elevator doors with her blade. "You never left this spot for more than a fraction of a second."

"Oh... that's good..." Claire said and lifted a hand to her head, suddenly feeling very dizzy. A moment later, her knees buckled beneath her. She fell into Chala'Ran's arms and everything went black.

− 20 −

"How much more can you take?" Saimon Hawke said as he stood over his downed adversary. The lights continued to fluctuate, holding a residual charge long after the power was cut. Smoke seeped through the seams of the red-hot elevator walls, wafting from charred wiring and annihilated fuses.

Gino's armor had thickened threefold since the assault began. Every crack was sealed airtight, to the point that he couldn't move and could barely breathe. The air inside grew thick and hot as he sat slumped against the wall, drenched in sweat, with eyes half-shut and ears half-hearing the arrogant man's gloating.

"It's only a matter of time," Saimon chuckled as he shrugged off his white coat. He lifted his feet and found the soles of his shoes left gummy black residue on the glowing floor. "You're going to die here, Ainsworth. You should've paid attention in science class. Resistors heat up as a current runs through them. It's how ovens work. This is *elementary*, boy."

He laughed as he patiently reloaded his sidearm with a sick grin. "You can block the lightning all day, but the heat will get you," he said as the magazine clicked into place. "You're going to boil in that egg, Ainsworth. I admit, you're making me *work* for this, but it's only a matter of time. Once you pass out of heat stroke and your gift fails, I'm going to put a bullet through your head and lay your steaming corpse at Eisenholm's feet. I'm looking forward to it."

Gino knew the man was right. His mind could no longer form clear pictures. His armor had become a shapeless, inelegant blob, not the finely-crafted medieval suit he was accustomed to. Soon, he'd lose focus entirely and his defenses would vanish. He should be pounding Hawke's face in. Instead, he could barely lift his arms, barely think, barely muster the energy to hate the man standing in front of him. The critical stages of heat exhaustion were coming fast.

"Wakey, wakey," Hawke teased, tapping his gun on the crystal shell to see if anyone was home. "You don't have the right to pass out yet. That was a clever trick you used last time, caging me like that. Won't work again, boy. Go on... give it a try... I'll wait."

Gino *had* tried, minutes ago. The man was too fast then and was definitely too fast now. He was slowly coming to the grim realization that Hawke had let him win on P-222 and was in complete control of the situation. So why stop? Why did he keep returning to human form to gloat and prance like a sadistic fairy?

"You're trying to figure me out, aren't you?" Hawke said. He leaned in, lowering himself to Gino's level, a once-great prize fighter reduced to a sweat-soaked sack of meat, slowly cooking in a crystal coffin.

Let him talk, Gino thought. The one clear idea he could wrap his head around told him to delay the man by any means necessary. Every minute Hawke stood there, running his mouth, was a minute he wasn't sizzling through the walls as a human lightning bolt, slowly driving the temperature up.

Then it dawned upon him:

"You can't see me," Gino muttered through parched lips. Hawke grimaced and Gino realized he'd struck gold. "You can't see me," he said again and laughed, despite everything.

Saimon Hawke vanished again in a flicker of lightning so bright Gino had to shield his eyes. The mad Hunter disappeared into the walls, arcing back and forth through the metal until it began to glow and the temperature began to climb again.

So close to the end, Gino should be afraid. But he'd been here before. He savored the thrill of finding a weak spot in his enemy's technique, a glass jaw left unprotected, a misstep that led right into a haymaker. He wasn't sure *how* to capitalize on Hawke's weakness, but at least he'd *found* one.

Lightning is blind. The reason Hawke stopped every minute or so was to check if his prey was still there. He couldn't see a damned thing in his lightning form. No wonder he'd blazed through hundreds of kilometers of wiring to get here. The idiot couldn't tell where he was going.

Focus, Gino thought. If he could get out of this elevator and to a place where evasion was actually possible, he could fight back. Here, there was no way to dodge the arcing bolts and any gaps in his armor would let the deadly voltage in. Somehow, he had to maneuver himself out of the elevator while maintaining a solid, impenetrable shell... or he would die.

While he pondered this conundrum, Gino began to rise. For a moment, his heat-stricken mind thought this was his own doing, as if he'd somehow tapped into an unknown power through sheer will and determination. Or perhaps he'd died and was floating away to a heaven he didn't believe existed.

In any case, he rose up and out of the open panel in the elevator's roof, shell and all. Looking down, he could see Saimon darting back and forth, completely oblivious to the fact that his target had escaped the hotbox.

After wiping the sweat from his eyes, Gino spotted Chala'Ran kneeling in the open doorway two stories above. A mixture of grief and shame washed over him, but quickly devolved to anger as she levitated him out and set him on the cool ground. He didn't *need* her help. How *dare* she rescue him!

His protective shell vanished and the pool of sweat trapped inside hit the floor with a sickening splash. The chill of fresh air instantly cleared his heat-addled mind and Gino shivered as he took a deep breath, letting it fill his lungs and revitalize him from the inside out. Chala backed away a step as a pungent wave of body odor unfurled from his reddened skin. Her placid features held a look of disdain for a moment too long, before she composed herself.

Then he noticed Claire slumped against the wall, and immediately went to her side. "Claire!" he exclaimed, giving her a shake. When Chala'Ran placed a hand on his shoulder, he swatted her away. "What did you do to her!"

"Nothing. She fainted," Chala said. "Her pulse is steady. I checked. Please, calm yourself, Mr. Ainsworth. She will be okay."

"So you're a fucking doctor now?" he snapped, but checked himself when he saw the concern in Chala's eyes. An apology nearly came to his lips, but Gino suppressed it and lifted Claire's limp body onto his shoulder. "What's next?"

The woman ignored him for a moment as she looked back down the elevator shaft. The carriage still flickered with canned lightning as Saimon Hawke continued his assault on an enemy who was no longer present. "He does not seem to realize you are gone. If you wish to terminate him…"

"I'd love to," Gino muttered. "But he said something about how many kilometers of wiring are in this ship. Let's go before he knows up from down. The *Infinitum* is dying anyway. Let him go down with the Solarans he loves so damn much."

"Seems a sound strategy," Chala replied, still kneeling at the edge of the drop. With a downward flick of her wrist, she overpowered the brakes and the elevator plummeted ten stories.

Gino grimaced at the distant sounds of wrenching metal when it hit the bottom.

Chala'Ran stood and tapped her communicator. "I will have Ell direct us to the machine-"

"Don't bother," Gino said, with a stern look in his eyes. In the past few hours, he'd seen more sides of Claire than he could stomach. "I know her better than any of you. She doesn't need that damn machine. Forget about it and get us back to the *Darkstar*."

"Are you sure? What if she awakes and finds we have not done as promised? She may leave us, *permanently*."

"Only thing I promised to do is look after her," Gino said, adjusting his hold, so he was cradling her, rather than toting her over his shoulder like a sack of manure. "The machine's bullshit. She knows it. We know it. And even if it isn't..." he looked down on her sleeping face. "Claire's stronger than she thinks. She can survive without it."

Even as he said this, his eyes lingered on an oddly-shaped bruise on her wrist, which hadn't been there before. It looked as if she'd been nabbed by a clawed creature...

"Chala'Ran, get us the hell out of here."

"As you wish." To his dismay, she smiled. "You two have certainly grown close, Mr. Ainsworth. I did not think it possible," she said as she tapped the communicator on her lapel. "Fear not. This nightmare is nearing its end."

* * *

Ell sat in the comm room, where a dozen displays illuminated her face, each monitoring a different symptom of the *Halcyon Infinitum*'s slow death. Entire decks had gone dark, but her trackers showed Clyde and Chala moving farther apart with every passing second. The latter had regrouped with Gino, but

Clyde remained a lonely blip, isolated somewhere on a deck where she couldn't see a damned thing.

The *Halcyon Infinitum* had five gravity drives, each the size of a small house, but they were dying, one after another. When only two remained, and the ship was visibly losing altitude, Ell reached the grim conclusion that it wasn't going to stop. The *Infinitum* was already hemorrhaging escape pods. They flashed in the atmosphere, headed for splashdown on Numira.

The *Darkstar* hadn't fired in over half an hour, so why was everything still going to shit in there? There was no way three or four shots from the railgun could've caused all of this destruction.

"Desmond," she said, contacting him through her suit's communicator. "Unless something else blows up, I think I've got an extraction point. It's a hangar. I'm sending the coordinates to you. Get us there quick, 'kay."

"Can't. I'm in the middle of something," he replied, far too casually.

"Like hell you are! What the fuck are you doing up there!?"

"Collecting the spoils of war," he snickered. "I've managed to tow the *Valiant* into our gravity wake. I wonder what a slightly-used interceptor goes for on the black market."

Although she knew he was only kidding – sort of – Ell's temper flared. "Stop playing around and get this fucking heap to the location I sent you! They could *die* in there, you ass!"

"Relax, I'm on it," Desmond said as the *Darkstar* swung around and accelerated toward the *Infinitum*, dragging the crippled *Noble Valiant* with it. "No need to be testy. We won. Getting them out of there will be *easy*."

"No one 'won,'" Ell murmured as she returned her attention to the projections. Another sector went dark. Another gravity drive dropped off the grid. Her displays were inundated with fire suppression protocols, anti-decompression fail safes, and endless waves of error codes as the *Infinitum*'s systems responded to whatever was slowly killing it.

Amidst all the clutter, was also an incoming call.

"For fuck's sake," Ell muttered as she answered the hail. "I told you not to call me on the main frequency. As if I don't have enough shit going on-"

She abruptly stopped, mid-thought, as the video feed revealed the caller. It wasn't Clyde. It wasn't Chala'Ran. It wasn't anyone she'd ever seen before. A man in a white longcoat stared back, with a grave look on his face and a ten-ringed badge dangling from his neck.

But she detected no decryption attempts. Whoever it was, he knew the *Darkstar*'s encoded frequency and contacted her as easily as one might order a pizza.

"Who the hell are you and how'd you get this number?" Ell said as she held him in her unflinching gaze, like blue lasers scanning his face for any signs of deception.

"Who am I? Oh, if I had a credit for every time I've heard that one," the man said with a scowl. "I'm your handler, stupid. The one you were rather fond of calling 'Flipass.' Remember me?"

"You don't look like him."

"I don't?" He shrugged. "Well, what did he look like?"

"He was... umm..." She tried to remember, but her brain did a backflip and landed on its head. "Where are you?" Ell asked instead, closely scrutinizing the holo-image, which only captured him from the chest up. She saw he was seated in a pilot's chair. His hands worked a flight yoke too large to be an escape pod's. "You're on a shuttle? All this time, you've been right under our noses? What the fuck!?"

"I was aboard the *Infinitum*, but that's not important," the man said, his patience thinning. "Is Evans with you? Has he extracted Eisenholm yet?"

"What's it to you?"

"Answer the question, Neihaus. This is no time for games."

"Claire's still in there, along with Clyde, Chala, and Gino. Maybe you shoulda nabbed the damn Psychomancer yourself, since you've been here all along. Fucking flipass, where were you when we *needed* you?"

"Same place I've always been: right behind you and two steps ahead," he said smugly. "Listen, Neihaus, today's encounter has been a *very* long time in the making. Don't screw this up. Events were set in motion with the expectation that extracting Claire wouldn't take this long. I *need* Evans and Eisenholm aboard the *Darkstar* immediately."

Ell nervously chewed her lip. When she realized he could see this, she quickly steeled herself and covertly patched into an open frequency, so everyone could hear. *Play it smart*, she warned herself. *Don't face him alone.*

"I need you to get them out *now*," the man said again. "An associate of mine is sabotaging the ship from within. In less than ten minutes, the *Halcyon Infinitum* is going down, taking eleven of the twelve members of the Solaran Council with it. They are to be the *only* casualty. I need your people out of there."

"Oh, now it's '*my* people?' A min ago, you only wanted Evans and Eisenholm. Are Chala and Gino expendable?"

"Just do as I've asked. Do your job."

"You didn't *ask*. You demanded." Ell dialed the volume up a notch, to ensure no one missed a word. "Desmond, stop the ship. We ain't extracting anybody 'til this asshole gives me a straight answer." She leaned into the camera and spoke in a level tone: "*Why* do you need Clyde and Claire on the *Darkstar*? If you can't answer that, rescue 'em yourself, but good luck getting inside. I'm in control."

"You're bluffing. You wouldn't leave Evans to die."

"Watch me," she said as the *Darkstar* slowed to a halt.

"Desmond, ignore that order," Clyde said, suddenly joining the conversation. "Ell, you're wasting your breath. He knows you're bluffing. This guy's been playing us right from the start. Mason told me everything."

"You broadcast this conversation!?" the handler said, his eyes zeroing in on Ell. "You little bitch."

"Just doing my *job*," Ell said with a wink and a smile. "Clyde, how are you holding up?"

"One more gravity drive and this ship falls. We need a way out," Clyde said. "It's over, Ell. He's won."

"Won?" Desmond said. "He's framing us for killing the Council… well, eleven of them anyway. And once that ship hits Numira, we'll also be blamed for killing the thousands of people stranded down there, too."

"That's not going to happen," Clyde said. "I'll explain later. For now, just do as he says."

Ell sighed. "Chala, are you listening, too?"

"Yes, dear," the woman said. "I have been listening. Gino and Miss Eisenholm are with me. If you direct us to an extraction point, I will comply."

"Yeah, we'll all 'comply' and dance like good little puppets," Ell muttered. "I'm losing surveillance with the power outages, but there's a hangar less than fifty meters from your current location. We'll meet you there."

"Good girl," the handler said coolly.

"I'm not done with you yet," Ell said before switching to a private channel. "Desmond, I have a lock on his shuttle. Can you capture him, like you did the *Valiant*?"

As she spoke, the man's fingers were quickly keying something into his shuttle's computer. "Changing frequencies doesn't stop me from reading your lips, Neihaus," the handler said as his shuttle's drive core powered on. "You have a job to do and I have somewhere to be. Finish your mission. I'll be waiting for you on Earth after the dust settles. You know the place."

"Desmond, he's getting away!"

By the time the *Darkstar* swung around, the tiny shuttle with its oversized warp core had already plotted a course and boosted away at lightspeed.

* * *

Under the flashing red strobes and wailing sirens, Saimon Hawke found a side of himself he did not know existed. A feral, brutal side. A man could learn a lot about himself when pushed to the edge –no, when pushed *beyond* it. There was a reason the Solarans gave gifts to select humans. There was a reason his ancestors received these gifts and passed them down through the generations. For all their might and majesty, there were things only he, a lowly human, could do that his masters could not.

It's up to me, Saimon thought as he roamed the halls of the dying ship. His hair was strewn about his head in disheveled strands, whiter than it had been before. It fell away in clumps when he stroked it. The black webs had already blossomed on his chest and were creeping up his neck, but the look in his silvery blue eyes was as focused as ever. Despite the encroaching blacklight, he still had his honor and his orders.

Nothing else mattered to him. Nothing ever had.

He paused at a window to catch his breath. The damage to the *Halcyon Infinitum* had sealed the steel shutters but Saimon commanded them to open with a wave of his hand and a spark of electricity from his fingertips.

The debris field outside was larger than he remembered and the planet much, much closer. Too close. While he stood there wheezing, a dark, rusty ship moved purposefully through the detritus. The *Darkstar Abyssal* was coming to collect its human cargo. Saimon knew the *Infinitum* well enough to know exactly where the *Darkstar* was headed just by watching its trajectory. He couldn't save this ship, nor his own life, but his masters would live on and they would know their loyal servant had fought to his last breath.

He began to walk, slowly at first, and then faster, until he broke into a full sprint. His soft-soled shoes covered huge swaths of the whitewashed floors with each stride. Saimon turned onto a darkened hall littered with broken glass, struck an overturned custodian's cart and nearly fell on his face. With a hop, a skip, and a smattering of colorful language, he regained his footing and carried on, undeterred.

Another blast rocked the *Halcyon Infinitum*. With four of its five gravity drives out of commission, he felt this one. There was no physics envelope left to dampen the blow. Saimon's body struck the wall, and then the ceiling, before he slammed to the floor again, and lay shuddering in a corner, with black blood dripping from his nostrils.

No. Not like this. Get up, you fool. GET UP!

The hatred pulled him to his feet and drove him on, even as the floor began to slant. The artificial gravity was gone. Only the pull of the planet 3,200 kilometers below grounded him. The same pull which was now shearing the ship apart. The last gravity drive desperately tried to keep one fifth of her aloft while the other four-fifths were dragged down.

Saimon Hawke trudged on, groping the walls as his vision blurred. Never in his life had he felt death so close, so *real*. He didn't feel it in the simulators at Alpha Point. He didn't feel it the day he scored his first kill or reaped his first tribute of Light. He hadn't even felt it when Ainsworth overpowered him on P-222 or when that elevator plummeted with him inside.

What Saimon Hawke *felt* when he charged into hangar nine and saw the *Darkstar Abyssal* backing out, with its reverse thrusters flaring, was not a fear of 'death.' Acolytes weren't allowed to die. As long as he took his final breath in the service of his masters, he would live on forever, as all loyal soldiers do. Saimon Hawke's greatest fear was that he would 'die' in that hangar, while this monster slipped quietly into the night, and only his failure would live on.

There was a mighty wind as the last gravity drive detonated, allowing the vacuum of space to suck the air from the hangar. Saimon squeezed through the emergency hatch a moment before it shut. Once inside the hangar, he half-ran, half-swam through the clutter of starship parts, fallen scaffolding, and cargo containers. He bounded over a writhing fuel hose and sprinted the last ten meters, with burning lungs.

He didn't know if they saw him. He would like to believe they did, in his final glorious moments, as he lit up like a bolt of lightning. The world became a blur to him as he crackled through the airless void, bridged the gap between the hangar and the retreating *Darkstar Abyssal*, and struck the nose of the craft. Sparks rippled down the ship's rusty fuselage and dispersed, forming a web of arcing electrical discharge.

Saimon felt himself infiltrate every circuit he could find and envisioned himself tearing the ship's electronics apart. In his mind, he was a mighty warrior, storming across a battlefield of wires, ripping through hordes of enemy fuses and conduits.

But that was only in his mind. In reality, the *Darkstar*, like any decent starship, was built to withstand lightning strikes. A charged rod embedded in the hull plucked him out, ejected him from the wiring harnesses, and flung him back into the vacuum of space.

The first thing Saimon Hawke felt as he rematerialized was that he was very cold and could not breathe. The last thing he saw before the void snatched away his last gasp of air was the

Darkstar Abyssal's lights flicker once before going out. A second later, the ship's circuit breaker reset and all was well.

* * *

"We have a problem," Desmond said, bursting into the medical bay, where everyone was hovering over the unconscious Chronomancer. His gaze momentarily fell upon Claire's peaceful face, but gave no pause. "Clyde, we have a problem," he repeated.

"I know," Clyde said, moving through the small crowd gathered at Claire's bedside. He met Desmond in the hall, but whispered something to Chala'Ran, his de facto second-in-command, as he exited the room. She followed.

From the corners of her eyes, Ell watched them depart, fidgeting uneasily. A few seconds later, she slipped away as well, leaving Gino and his sleeping companion alone. The fighter didn't even look up from where he sat, clutching Claire's pale hand.

"It's the *Halcyon Infinitum*," Desmond explained as he led Clyde and Chala to the flight deck. "That ship is the size of a small city and it's made of Solaran metal. It won't break up on re-entry. When it hits the planet, everything down there's as good as dead. I mean, I don't exactly have a soft spot for anyone down there, but... we're talking about planetary-scale destruction here."

"I told you that's not going to happen," Clyde said.

They soon reached the flight deck, where they found the viewscreen filled with fireflies. Pieces of the dying capitol ship were reentering the atmosphere. Some were as large as houses, while others were mere specks, blazing like fireworks. The *Darkstar* hovered at a safe distance, but a swarm of escape pods and shuttles lay in the path of the debris and countless more had already splashed down on the planet.

"The reason he wanted Claire or me on board was because there's only one weapon that can avert this," Clyde explained, "and it's coded to our Light signature."

"Of course," Chala'Ran said as the re-entry fires glinted in her eyes. "Miss Eisenholm was the original owner of this vessel. Now it belongs to you."

Clyde nodded. "Mason told me it'd come to this. He was ordered to destroy the gravity drives. That was the plan all along: force us into a confrontation with the High Council, destroy their ship, and frame us for it. The blame for *this*," he gestured to the wreckage, "is already on our heads. The Council is sealed inside S-deck and they're going down with the ship. But it doesn't have to take Numira with it; we have the power to stop that."

"No, *you* have the power to stop it. The only other person who can activate the weapon is currently comatose," Desmond said as he pressed a series of buttons on the overhead console. A tall, narrow pedestal rose up between the pilot and co-pilot's chairs. It stopped at waist height and a cylindrical compartment extended from the top, with a keypad. Desmond quickly punched in a ten-digit code.

Outside, a large chunk of the *Infinitum* met the stratosphere and began streaming rays of plasma as it entered. It was S-Deck, Clyde realized, the heart of the ship and its largest fragment. He wondered if the eleven Solarans inside could feel the heat? Could they *feel* anything at all, or would they just quietly ride their piece of the wreckage down and wait for a Registry search team to come scoop them up? How long would that take?

Not long at all, Clyde thought. *If S-Deck makes it to the surface in one piece...*

No weapon could kill a Solaran, but if he destroyed that part of the ship, he could make them *very* hard to find.

"It's kind of ironic," Desmond said. "When I designed this thing, it was only a theory. Mars was my inspiration. The Solarans showed us what a weaponized terraformer could do. When The Stranger's rep asked me to install my theoretical superweapon on an experimental starship, I never bothered to ask what it would be used for. Now here we are, about to use it against Solarans. It's all come full circle."

"What does it do?" Ell asked, lurking in the doorway.

"It... unmakes things," Desmond explained as the keypad folded away, revealing a silver handle. "But it's much tidier than what they did to Mars."

"Mason told me the *Darkstar*'s original destination was the Solaran homeworld," Clyde said, looking to Chala'Ran. "He wanted to reconnect with his people and built this ship to do it. But he was also afraid of what he might find there. He saw them as a threat and armed this ship with a weapon that could potentially wipe out his own homeworld."

"He does not trust his own kind, but trusted you and Claire enough to encode such a weapon to your Light signatures?" Chala asked. "What manner of Solaran is this Stranger, that he would give humans access to such a thing?"

Desmond turned the handle ninety degrees clockwise, 270 degrees counter-clockwise, and pulled up. There was a pneumatic hiss and every light on the flight deck turned red. Every screen on the center console read 'QDC SYSTEM ARMED' in enormous letters. A dull groan emanated from the aft section of the ship as the *Darkstar*'s wings shifted forward and fanned out. The railgun, which was still deployed under the bow, began to buzz with energy.

Clyde didn't like the look of it. Although Mason told him the *Darkstar* would have to be the one to finish off the *Halcyon Infinitum* and ensure the Council stayed gone for a good, long while, he didn't explain how. The way all the avionics and flight data vanished from the screens made it very clear his starship was no longer a starship: it was now a weapon.

It even made Chala'Ran uneasy. She took a half-step back, away from the trigger mechanism. Clyde felt alone before the pedestal. Even the hum of the drive cores changed frequency. The ship's soul was being reformatted toward a new purpose. He felt a tingling in the marrow of his bones, as if the *Darkstar* itself had a gift, a new power awakening.

Desmond gestured to the burning debris and bluish-brown curve of the planet's horizon. "The Quantum Dissonance Cannon is a very simple concept. A terraformer is supposed to transmute molecules of one element into another, but I took that idea and twisted it. This ship will project a field that destabilizes matter on the quantum level. After that, one good hit is all it takes to set off a nuclear chain reaction. There'll be nothing left of the *Infinitum*. It's like a nuclear blast, like splitting the atom, but without all the nasty bits."

Desmond stepped back and gestured to the illuminated red handle, with a dramatic flourish. "She's all yours, captain. Push down, half turn clockwise, and don't look into the flash."

Clyde took a deep breath and reached for the handle. He looked to Chala'Ran, but she averted her gaze. He looked back and saw Ell peeking around the doorframe, but she slowly shook her head. He was on his own now.

"We're playing right into his hands," Clyde said, to no one in particular. "Eleven of the twelve members of the Solaran High Council are aboard that ship... and we all know who the twelfth is. The Stranger sealed them on S-Deck, his Acolyte had Mason detonate the drive cores so the ship would fall, and now the ball's in our court. We're playing right into his hands."

"There is no choice," Chala'Ran said.

"There's always a choice. This won't change anything. Mason told me Solarans are beings of Light," Clyde said, looking to her. "We can't *kill* them anymore than Claire could kill The Stranger. She sent this ship through a *sun* to destroy him. It didn't work. At best, we'll buy the galaxy a few months without a Council, a few months of... 'freedom,' for lack of a better word, while Registry officials scour Numira and track down the eleven. Eventually they'll find them, probably floating in orbit somewhere, and the full Council will return to power.

"And they'll be angry. Very angry. If you think the Solarans are cold now, just wait 'til they come back from this. I don't know if we can trust The Stranger. I don't know if he's doing this with the hopes of making a difference or if it's just a shameless power grab. But, even if his intentions are good, his reign will be brief. The other eleven will be back with a vengeance and they'll hunt us from one end of the galaxy to the other for this. That's the one thing Hawke was right about. For as long as we live, we'll never sleep with both eyes shut."

"We already don't," Ell said.

"I know. Brock Mason was ready to throw his life away today because he knew, after this, it was all over for him," Clyde said, unwavering. "Numira, the *Darkstar Abyssal*, and the *Halcyon Infinitum* will go down in history whether I turn this handle or not. To some people, this will make all the difference − the *appearance* of a group of people successfully rebelling against the High Council − but I honestly don't know what the galaxy will make of it all."

With a strong hand, Clyde pushed down and turned the handle 180 degrees clockwise until it firmly clicked into position. A green light signaled that his Light signature was approved and the weapon activated. Although he would've loved to watch, he put his back to the viewscreen as the *Infinitum*'s remains began to glow white. The escape pods did not appear to be affected. A moment later, the railgun fired a single round.

Chala'Ran bowed her head and Desmond shielded his eyes with his sleeve. Only Ell stared into the blast as the *Infinitum*'s atoms went supercritical. Her eyes recorded the birth and death of a new star as a blinding flash flooded the room with white light, which cast no shadows. When the glow faded, nothing remained of the *Halcyon Infinitum*, not even stardust.

– 21 –

Nothing worked. The paint had faded decades ago. The wallpaper was peeling away, curling down to the baseboards in tattered sheets. Ceiling tiles littered the floor, leaving a scaffolding of bare metal frames and naked light fixtures overhead. The wires were live, courtesy of an aging solar array on the rooftop, but no one dared flip a switch, lest the entire facility go up in flames.

The one redeeming feature of Serenity Acres' air traffic control tower was that it had windows on all sides, a full 360 degree panoramic view.... or it *used to* have windows. Decades of bird strikes and sandstorms had turned the tower into something akin to an open air gazebo. Somehow, this only added to its quaint charm.

"If you do not stop pacing, dear, I fear you will wear a hole in the floor and fall through," Chala'Ran said, "And I cannot guarantee I will catch you."

She sat cross-legged at a table for two, scribbling lines of scripture in an ancient leather-bound notebook. The room was silent, save the scratching of her pen on the yellowed pages and the staccato pang of Desmond driving rivets into the *Noble Valiant*'s hull outside.

Clyde stopped. She was right. Looking down, he noticed a distinct wear pattern at his feet. Hanging out in the same place for days could do that.

After filling another page, Chala'Ran paused, took a sip of her tea and flipped to the next. The steam rising off the aromatic beverage brought back fond memories of their first encounter in Endyssia's tower garden, a prelude to war. The memory was scarcely a week old, but he felt as if it'd been forged ages ago, in another world, another reality.

Everything was different now, yet nothing had changed.

"He's not coming," Clyde said, burrowing his hands deep in his pants pockets. His fingers lightly brushed the metal sphere hidden inside. It was cold to the touch.

Chala'Ran lifted her eyes. "Who?"

"Andrew Leitner. His name is Andrew Leitner."

Clyde turned to face her, but Chala'Ran resumed writing. "Oh... him," she said dismissively. "I hope you did not actually think he would meet us here. That man is a professional liar. In all likelihood, we will not hear from him again until he requires something more of us."

Clyde slowly nodded. "Yeah, I know. But at least I have his name now, something to pin him down. Last night, I spent six hours listening to the transmission he sent us after leaving P-222. I just put it on a loop and let my brain marinate in it. That's how long it took me to crack his gift and break through the mental block he created. That man's an illusionist – a very powerful one at that."

"Unsurprising. He is an Acolyte after all." Chala'Ran shut her book and gave Clyde her undivided attention, staring into his eyes in the eerily piercing manner he'd come to expect from her. Sometimes he needed someone to look at him that way, as if his soul was under the microscope.

"Most illusionists put things *into* your head. They insert a reality of their own creation to make you see things that aren't real," Clyde explained. "In Leitner's case, he takes things *out*, like editing himself out of a picture." He paused. "I'm amazed I was able to break his gift at all. He's The Stranger's Acolyte; if I can find *him*, I can find his boss."

"I told you, you are more powerful than you know, dear. Now what? Do you intend to track him down?"

"No. I intend to keep an eye out for him. I might be the only one who can."

"A man like that will not show his face here," Chala'Ran said. "He would not risk his anonymity."

"Of course not. The Stranger's probably at The Forge by now, taking his rightful place as the only Solaran left in the galaxy, and Leitner will be right there with him. If anything Mason said is true, I bet they're speaking with galactic leaders right now, preparing to release a statement dictating the 'new rules.' He thinks he can create a world where Light is volunteered, where it'll be a tribute, rather than a tax or a penance, and people won't be punished for refusing to surrender it to them."

"Whatever he does, The High Council will revoke it the moment they return," Chala'Ran said. "This state of affairs cannot last and the transition will get messy. I would prepare for civil war, if I were you."

"True... but after 200 years of ruling as a single unit, I'm glad to have *one* Solaran on our side... even if he did dupe us into doing his dirty work," Clyde said. "The other eleven are going to raise hell when they get back and realize what he's done, but, in the time between now and then, The Stranger could redraft the Infinite Charter... which isn't looking so *infinite* anymore. Even though we were forced into this, I think it was all for the best."

Chala'Ran frowned slightly. "Yet here you are, pacing a hole in the floor. What's *really* on your mind, dear?"

"'Beings of Light will cleanse the Earth in fire.'"

"Oh... that." Chala stood and lifted a second cup of tea from the table. She had poured it for him over an hour ago, yet it remained untouched until now. "I would not place too much stock in anything Miss Eisenholm says," she replied softly as she offered it to him. "She is... unwell."

"You of all people should know prophets are never perfect," Clyde said. "We're not talking about divine inspiration here. She's interdimensional. Claire has seen alternate realities – *dangerous* realities – and any of them could prove true. I don't think even she understands what's going on in her head or the full extent of her gift. Chala, we have a tiger by its tail. She's seen a future where the Solarans 'cleanse the Earth in fire.' I can't shake the thought that it could be because of what we did. You said yourself, this could lead to *war*."

"You are confusing fact with delusion," Chala'Ran said, meeting his gaze once more. "I know the Solarans are capable of great evil but even *I* do not think they would ravage an entire planet for what the six of us have done."

"Mars," he said.

Chala sighed and momentarily bowed her head. "Clyde, you have never seen Mars," she said in a small voice. "No one who has would dare lay that atrocity at anyone's feet. To see the desolation there is to see God's wrath made manifest. It is an act too great for mortal hands."

"Mars wasn't an act of god. Solaran tech did that and they can do it again if-"

"Your work is *done*, Clyde," Chala'Ran said forcibly before extending the teacup to him. "We are free. Stop torturing yourself with what could've been or could be. Do you honestly think the blacklight is what drove Miss Eisenholm mad? These thoughts will break you too, if you let them."

A heavy silence descended before Clyde took the peace offering. "Two hundred years ago, six humans, just like us, stumbled across an alien ship," he said, staring into the steaming drink. "Those six drafted the Infinite Charter and became the first Scions. They were arrogant enough to think they could build a perfect world by writing an accord that would last forever... and it nearly did. All I'm saying is six people *can* make a difference, Chala. What if we chose wrong? What if *I* chose wrong?"

With a sigh, Chala'Ran placed her hands on either side of his head and cradled his face until he looked up and met her eyes. "As iron sharpens iron, so too does a man sharpen the countenance of a friend," she said, whispering softly as she held him close, until their foreheads touched. "Clyde, you are *afraid*. Your heart has told me so. Do not allow this fear to cloud your judgment the way I allowed anger to cloud mine. We will sharpen one another, dear. I am with you, as you are with me. If *we* have chosen wrong, *we* will make it right."

"And what if you can't?" Claire said.

At the sound of her voice, Clyde whipped around to see the Chronomancer sitting in Chala'Ran's seat, slowly running her pale finger around the rim of the porcelain teacup the woman had abandoned there.

"Oh, I'm sorry. Did I interrupt?" Claire said, her clear white eyes cutting deep into them both. After a pause, she zeroed in on Chala'Ran. "Why does it seem like every time I see him, *you're* there too?"

Chala'Ran smiled, albeit nervously. "You could say we are kindred spirits, dear."

"I *could* say you're spying on him... which means you're spying on me too."

"And I could say you're a paranoid schizophrenic and occasional megalomaniac with obsessive, often homicidal, tendencies... but I won't," Chala'Ran said, "because *that* would be rude. Shall I fetch Mr. Ainsworth for you?"

"Not if you don't want me to vomit all over this table," Claire murmured. "Get lost. I wanna talk to the Hunter, *alone*."

"Claire, you shouldn't be teleporting around in your condition," Clyde said.

"Beats the stairs. Speaking of which, the skinny little slut's on her way up here – the long way – to tell you I'm back."

"That 'skinny little slut' has a name," Chala said, "And you would do well to remember it, Miss Eisenholm. I know you are confused and not feeling well, but that does not give you the right to lash out at the people who are trying to help you."

Her words went entirely unheard. Claire's attention had already shifted to Clyde, as if the other woman wasn't even there anymore. "Who told you about the beings of Light and the end of the world?" she asked.

"You did. You've been in and out of consciousness for the last three days, Claire, and completely comatose for two days prior to that," Clyde explained. "We've been taking turns watching over you. Sometimes, you're willing to talk. Other times... well..." He lifted his shirt, revealing a bandage on his side, where he'd been dealt a glancing blow by a sharp blade.

Claire's brows rose. "Oh, so *you* have my knife. Where is it? Give it back."

"I have a few things I need to give to you, but first-"

Ell decided this would be the perfect moment to burst through the door, panting like a desert dog... or like a girl who'd just done twenty flights of stairs at full sprint. She sagged in the doorway, with her eyes lazily going from Claire to Clyde and back again, with utter disbelief etched on her face, as if she were watching a flock of pigs fly by.

After a lengthy silence, she murmured a string of obscenities under her breath before turning to leave.

Chala'Ran sighed and followed her out. "Call me if you need anything," she said to Clyde before departing.

"I'm sure his *heart* will tell you," Claire sneered, but the woman was already gone. Claire grinned as she leaned back, put her bare feet up on the table, and gave the Hunter her undivided attention. "Well, here we are," she said, spreading her hands, "Claire Eisenholm and Clyde Evans... the mighty Chronomancer and the unflushable shit who chased me halfway across the known universe. Well, here I am. What do you want?"

"You've already told me just about everything I'd like to know. The Stranger, your mission, the *Darkstar*'s intended purpose... *all* of it. You even leaked a few personal details about yourself. For example..." he walked over to a nearby file cabinet and opened the top drawer, with his back to her. "You told me where you first developed your love of sharp, pointy things."

He presented Claire's favorite knife, a smoky black blade with a serrated backside and a handle that fit her hand far too well. She loved that knife; lots of fond memories attached to this one. It took every ounce of restraint not to leap up and snatch it from him, like a pet snapping up a tasty treat.

Her patience was soon rewarded. Clyde gently set it on the table in front of her and took a step back, not out of fear, but out of respect. Claire studied it for a moment, as if trying to determine if it was real or if he'd somehow swapped it with an imitation. One look at her was enough to see she felt that way about nearly everything around her – every person, every object, every event. What does 'real' even mean, when you can rewrite history in the blink of an eye?

"I have something else for you, too," Clyde said, reaching deep into his pocket.

Claire instantly snatched up the weapon and recoiled from him, but her face flushed with embarrassment when she realized his only armament was an irregularly-shaped metal key, at the end of a thin chain. It was studded with microchips and conductive prongs made of the same silvery-blue metal used in drive cores, terraformers, and Scion badges. Clyde carefully extended it to her, holding it at arm's length.

"This is the key to your ship," he said.

"Liar. The *Darkstar* doesn't need a key. It's coded to my Light signature," Claire said.

"This key is for the *Noble Valiant*. Under interstellar salvage code, article five, section 37, we have the right to legally claim and reregister any vessel abandoned for more than 48 earth-hours. The repairs should be complete by the end of the week. The *Valiant* is yours and you're free to take it anywhere you please… but the *Darkstar* stays with me.

"I'm also taking this," Clyde added as he held up the smooth metal orb. "It's a Solaran data sphere, an information storage device capable of containing billions of libraries worth of information on a sphere the size of a tennis ball. Just like the *Darkstar*, it was coded to *both* of our Light signatures. I already had Ell take a peek inside, while you were sleeping."

Her eyes darted from him, to the knife, to the key, to the orb, and back to the knife. "So, you're taking my stuff now?" she said. "is that what this is?"

"It's an address book," Clyde said, ignoring her as he slipped the data sphere back into his pocket, "a list of every contact The Stranger has ever made. There are dossiers on *thousands* of people he's gathered over the years to fight this 'war.' I think he gave you the sphere so you could find them and bring them together. They might rally together behind the 'mighty' Chronomancer. But, unless you're going to do that, unless you're going to bear the *full* weight of this so-called 'revolution,' you don't need the list or the *Darkstar*. I'm taking both. I'm taking the responsibility off your shoulders so you can enjoy the freedom you seem to want so badly, Claire."

"No, you're taking my stuff," Claire said. "That's *my stuff*. It belongs to me."

"About as much as a leash belongs to a dog."

Claire sighed and her pale face turned a shade of pink in the silence that followed. He could not tell if she was flustered or furious or just plain confused, but she was *quiet,* and that said far more than words could.

She sat still for a moment, slowly chewing her lip as she mulled over everything he'd said. They had had this conversation before − twice, actually − and he suspected she knew that, but, for some absurd reason, she seemed to think the conclusion would be different this time, that he might crack under the pressure and dump it all on her shoulders. She was a time traveler, after all. Someone with that kind of power could be trusted with this. Why should he take up the torch and let her slip quietly into the dark?

"Fine," Claire said as she wrapped her fingers around the *Noble Valiant*'s ignition key for the third and final time. If she blacked out again, he'd take it, put it back in the drawer, along with the knife, and they would do this all over again when –if– she woke up.

But she wasn't passing out this time. She stared back at him with an intensity she hadn't shown before and spoke clearly. "Take it. It's yours… but there's something you ought to know about that ship, where it's been, and what I saw. I've seen things, things I haven't told *anyone*, not even The Stranger. Nothing is what you think it is."

Her eyes slowly panned to the left and then to the right, hunting for eavesdroppers in the wings as the paranoia seeped under her skin like a parasite. These momentary psychotic breaks were the reason she couldn't be trusted with more than a knife and an interceptor saved from the junkheap. Nevertheless, Clyde calmly took a seat opposite her and settled in for storytime.

"I was scared shitless when the Solarans attacked the ship," she said as she tucked the knife into her waistband and scanned the room one last time, to make sure they were alone. Once she was certain no invisible spooks and specters were peeping, she lowered her voice to a whisper and leaned in so close, Clyde could feel her cold breath on his ear. "Wanna know why I didn't kill 'em all?" she said. "The QDC is coded to my Light signature, same as it's coded to yours. I could've wiped out the Solaran homeworld, easy." She snapped her fingers. "So, why not?"

"You panicked. That's a normal response. It all happened so fast," he said, but Claire slowly shook her head.

"Nope. I knew the QDC was there. That big knife in the *Darkstar*'s back pocket was always with me. Never leave home without it, I say." She smiled. "The reason I didn't turn 'their' planet to stardust is because I *saw* something... something that shouldn't be there... something a little too close to home."

Claire leaned back with a devilish grin and a look of absolute vindication. "I'm not gonna spell it all out for you. You're the detective, not me, so I'll leave you with a question: Who do you trust, a psychopath armed with a planet-destroying superweapon... or the monster who pointed her at Earth?"

She began to laugh hysterically, while Clyde slowly shook his head. "Get help, Claire," he said as he pushed back his chair and stood. "I mean it. You need professional psychiatric help..."

"Even a broken clock is right twice a day," she said, wagging a disapproving finger at him. "Can *you* afford to be wrong?"

And then she was gone and the truth went with her.

About the Author

Brandon M. Stephens (b. 1988) is a graduate of the Georgia Institute of Technology and has been writing since he was old enough to hold a thought and a pen. This New Orleans-born independent novelist and poet currently resides in Stone Mountain, Georgia, where he dreams up new ways to blow minds. When he is not in his lair, huddled over a smoking keyboard, he can be found perusing the pages of a book.

His debut novel, *The Light at the End of the Wormhole*, is the first installment of his *Infinite Charter* series, a fantasy epic masquerading as a science fiction mystery/thriller.

35475788R00236

Made in the USA
Charleston, SC
11 November 2014